A CHANGE OF FLAG

Hong Kong in 1983, a city extraordinarily diverse and vital, yet taut with underlying anxiety and suspense as London negotiates with Beijing about the future of this final jewel in Britain's Imperial Crown.

Eurasian Michael Denton had always hoped his wealth would protect his family in times like these, but when he receives a message from his sister in Shanghai, he feels the ground move under his feet. Once a devoted communist, Lily has now lost her faith and wants him to help her escape from China. Michael cannot refuse, but the risks are high — if he fails he will be ruined.

As Hong Kong's fate hovers in the balance, so too does Michael's. Haunted by the past, he faces agonising choices, which will affect many other lives besides his own.

Books by Christopher New

GOODBYE CHAIRMAN MAO

The China Coast Trilogy

SHANGHAI
THE CHINESE BOX
A CHANGE OF FLAG

PHILOSOPHY OF LITERATURE: AN INTRODUCTION

A CHANGE OF FLAG

Christopher New

Asia 2000 Limited
Hong Kong

ISBN   962–7160–95–4

Published by Asia 2000 Ltd
Fifth Floor, 31A Wyndham Street
Central, Hong Kong

http://www.asia2000.com.hk

Typeset in Adobe Garamond by Asia 2000 Ltd
Printed in Hong Kong by Editions Quaille

First Printing 2000

PRINTING HISTORY
Bantam edition 1990

For C.M.

We are come to the end appointed
With sands not many to run;
Divinities disanointed
And kings whose kingdom is done.

A.E. Housman

1

Flinching in the sun

When the engines faltered and the plane canted definitely downwards, Rachel's stomach performed its usual panicky turnover. She glanced tensely out of the window, but no, she couldn't see anything wrong — the wing wasn't streaming flames or juddering or slowly breaking off. And a bland voice reassured her over the speakers that they were only commencing their descent to Hong Kong. Her fingers slowly unclawed from the armrest, and she leant back, taking out the little white immigration card the stewardess had given her.

She knew what people meant about the miracle of flight. Only a sheet of metal between the soles of your feet and the ridged blue-grey sea thirty thousand dizzying feet below, and full of sharks at that. Her toes curled in her sneakers. The miracle of flight, the thing just staying up against the laws of gravity, it was a miracle all right.

A Chinese in the aisle-seat across the gangway was smoking. Rachel sent him a signalling look, but his blank eyes bounced it straight back. She didn't want to complain; it might look racist. Maybe a stewardess would come by and remind him he was in the non-smokers'.

She filled in the form and slipped it into her passport, pausing briefly at the photo-page to examine her plain neuter face. Then she searched her shoulder bag for her address-book. *Michael and Grace Denton, Mount Kellett Road, The Peak, Hong Kong.* And a phone number. She'd clipped Michael's letter to the page, together with the old photo he'd sent her. *'If by any chance we aren't there to meet you, please telephone this number,'* the PS said in black precise ink. *Telephone.* Who said telephone now? Call, phone, ring, buzz (if you were British, she guessed) . . . but *telephone*? She imagined

Michael as a very stately Britisher who talked like the royal family. Except that he was half-Chinese. 'Stodgy', Jenny had called him in LA. 'Even though he is my half-brother.' But, then, what Jenny called stodgy, normal people might call normal.

Rachel read the letter through once more.

Dear Rachel,

We were most interested to hear you are coming to study in Hong Kong, particularly as we have not met you yet. Of course you can stay with us until you find your feet — or longer if you wish. Incidentally, we know both the supervisors you propose for your thesis; not only Patrick Denton — who is, as you know, my nephew — but also Dimitri Johnston, who is an old friend.

When your travel arrangements are settled, let us know which flight you are arriving on, and we will meet you at the airport.

You might like to show the enclosed photograph to your stepmother. She will be able to tell you who everyone is. It is the last photograph taken of my family before the Japanese occupied Shanghai in the Second World War. As it is one of the only two copies I have (there is no negative), I'd be glad if you could return it eventually.

We look forward to meeting you soon.

With best wishes,
Michael Denton

Rachel gazed at the forty-two-year-old photo (Photograph — who said that any more? He probably called a radio a wireless, too), neatly inscribed in the same precise hand *Shanghai 1941 (November?)*. A double row of assorted Western and Chinese Dentons stood rigid and square to the lens, their smileless faces flinching in the sun. Light must have been a problem for the photographer — the Chinese faces had come out very dark, the Western white as chalk. Only the two Eurasians had a living colour to them. There was Western Jenny, now Rachel's stepmother, young and fair then, and not yet fat. Michael was the young Eurasian with the brooding eyes, Jenny's half-brother. Next to him stood the other Eurasian, Michael's sister Lily, cradling her baby son.

'God knows what became of Lily,' Jenny had said with a shrug. 'Ran off to join the commies. I never got on very well with her. Or Michael. In fact, to tell the truth, I think we hated each other. Hardly surprising, considering my father divorced my mother to marry theirs. It was a hell of a thing in those days in Shanghai, divorcing a white woman to marry a Chinese — we were all treated like pariahs.'

The baby son Lily was cradling was Patrick Denton, who might now become Rachel's thesis adviser in Hong Kong. Or supervisor, as they apparently called them there — was that significant?

And all the others were dead, long dead, Jenny had added with a shrug and a yawn.

Looking inward

On the Peak in Hong Kong, Jenny's Eurasian half-brother, Michael Denton, leant back from his severe blackwood Chinese desk and gazed through the french window at Grace, his Chinese wife. He still had the brooding look in his eyes that Rachel had noticed in the old photo, though *pensive* might perhaps have been a better word, and he was only slightly heavier now than then, his hair only just beginning to thin and grey. It was the deepening lines in his sallow cheeks and forehead, the mauvish pouches under his eyes that showed his age.

He was gazing at Grace, and Grace was gazing down the garden, out over the sea, a cutting of purple bougainvillaea hanging forgotten — he could tell that — from her hand. Her back was towards him, but he knew, too, that she wouldn't be looking at anything in particular — not at the lawn or the flowers and shrubs, nor at the sea six hundred feet below, nor even at the huge glowing disc of the sun that was perceptibly sinking minute by minute, behind the dark lumpy hills of Lantau Island. No, she'd scarcely be aware of any of that; her eyes would be still and hazy, looking inward.

She was wearing a pale lilac cheong-sam. Not many Chinese women wore a cheong-sam these days, Michael reflected. And most of them — of her age and class at least — would have dyed their hair to keep it black and glossy. But Grace had never bothered with appearances. Especially not since the thing with Paul. Her hair was greyer than his own was now. It seemed to enhance her air of detachment — the fact that she hadn't bothered to dye it, he meant.

Over the quiet whirr and intermittent humming of the air-conditioner he could hear his daughter San San practising, always stopping at the same phrase, playing it over and over again. Listening to the violin's tones plunging from light to dark, he noticed he was massaging the stump of his little finger, stroking and squeezing the mutilated joint. How smooth and clear the skin looked, almost as though the finger had simply grown like that — but for the deformed blunt shape. It ached more as he got older, especially in that hot sticky weather. Well, it would get better soon, when the air dried and cooled as if at the touch of a switch, and it became almost like a perfect English summer. Four or five weeks at most.

He stirred on the thick cushion, which raised him just high enough on his chair to enable his increasingly long-sighted eyes to read without glasses. Holding his head back and looking down his nose, he considered the notes he'd just written.

San San appeared round the door — she'd always had a way of opening doors noiselessly — violin and bow in hand. 'What time does this American girl arrive? I don't have to go to the airport, do I?'

She was like her mother to look at, but with a difference: there was no trace in her of her mother's remoteness, nor of that fragile snap-in-your-hand delicacy that had captivated him in Shanghai forty years ago. They were both serene, though — he couldn't recall San San ever losing her temper, even as a child, and the idea of Grace losing hers was somehow absurd — but Grace's serenity came from never fighting, San San's from never needing to. Everything San San had wanted she'd got, and without a struggle. So far. Of course having money helped. She wasn't spoiled exactly, but —

'What time . . . ?' she began again, coming further into the room.

'Seven-forty.'

'From America?'

'Bangkok. She's been travelling in Thailand for a few weeks apparently. No, there's no need for you to come. Why don't you stay and practise?'

No, not spoiled, he decided. Just young and unscarred. Nothing had ever hurt her yet. Which was how he'd wanted it. For twenty-two years, nothing had hurt her. But it couldn't be long now, he supposed, before something did.

'What was that on the news?' San San was asking. 'I only got the tail end of it. Something about the talks on Hong Kong not making any progress.'

'China is accusing Britain of being obstructive. Which probably means the British haven't given the Chinese everything they want.' *Yet*, he added mentally.

'So they can talk some more?'

'But in the mean time people are scrambling to get their money out. Next it'll be themselves. The Hong Kong dollar's falling like a stone.'

She lowered her violin and looked out of the window again. 'It'd be awful if the whole place just disappeared,' she said slowly. She'd never seriously thought their money would; her father was nothing if not safe.

'It wouldn't be the place,' he said exactly. 'It would be the people. As many as could.' He thought of the end of Shanghai, the end of Saigon, the end of Phnom Penh. Last planes leaving, frantic faces, clutching hands, riots in the streets, gunfire, looters . . . . *The end of Hong Kong?*

He thought of his communist sister Lily, and of her letter in his pocket, the first for thirteen years.

'Well, I suppose it'll be all right in the end?' San San said, not wanting to believe it might not be.

He didn't answer.

While they were talking, the sun had edged below the highest hills, and the sky above them was a dying fire.

They both watched Grace turn and walk across the lawn like someone who'd just awoken, the bougainvillaea still trailing in her hand.

'I'll stay and practise, then,' San San said after a moment. 'I have a lesson the day after I get back to the States. Maybe I'll talk to Paul a bit, too.'

'Yes, he misses you when you're away.'

They both felt his voice dragging.

'I should hate to be met by the whole pack of us anyway,' San San went on quickly. 'If I were her. What's her name? Rachel?'

'Rachel, yes.'

Grace passed across the window without noticing them, walking towards the kitchen. Michael switched on the lamp.

He was writing again, head held stiffly back, when Grace came in. She'd put the bougainvillaea in a vase, which she placed carefully on the corner of the desk.

'Ah Choi wants to know when to bring the car round,' she said absently. 'He's cleaning it now.'

'He's always cleaning it. Twenty past seven should be all right, shouldn't it? He doesn't *clean* it really; he grooms it, like a horse.'

Grace's hand withdrew from the vase, as if stroking it goodbye. It was a way she often handled inanimate things, as though they were alive. She never wore any rings, except her wedding ring. It was still, at sixty, a fine hand, not mottled or corrugated with veins. Thinking forebodingly of his sister Lily's letter in his pocket, he said Grace's name in Shanghainese, which was also Grace, and she paused.

You were well named, he'd meant to say, and perhaps more, but when it came to the point the impulse failed him. He'd feel a fool, as if he'd gone down on one knee. He shook his head, pretending he'd forgotten, and she smiled, turning away.

'Oh, yes,' he said. 'Hadn't we better phone Patrick, to remind him he's coming tonight? To meet Rachel.'

'Wasn't he going to Macao for the day, though? He may not be back yet.'

Even the way she spoke seemed disengaged, as if already, while she was uttering the words, her mind had drifted away to something far off, more absorbing. Half the time, when he talked with her, she seemed to be simultaneously listening to someone or something else. And yet she always heard him. And what she answered made perfect sense. Or as much as what anyone said did.

'Well, I'll try before we leave, then.' Slipping his pen into his pocket, he felt Lily's letter again. Lily, Patrick's mother.

She wants to come out

They left at twenty past seven. The city's lights appeared intermittently through the trees below them as the car looped its leisurely way down the Peak. Every corner presented a different view, a different lower slant, like a shaken kaleidoscope, until gradually they themselves merged into the pattern they'd been watching. Michael waited until Ah Choi was driving along the waterfront before he took the envelope out of his pocket. 'It's from Lily apparently,' he said, handing it to Grace.

'Lily?'

'Apparently. It came yesterday.'

She turned it over, fingering the torn flap. 'Where from? Where is she?'

'That's the funny thing. It was posted in Kowloon.'

'Lily over there?' She glanced incredulously across the harbour at the slabs and slabs of honeycombed lights, the giant neon-lit hoardings of Kowloon.

'No, it was *posted* there. Someone must have smuggled it out of China. If it really is from her.'

Grace gazed at the oblong envelope in the dimness of the car. The street-lamps splashed regular pools of lifeless light over the large clumsy Chinese characters, obviously not Lily's educated hand. She drew the single coarse sheet of paper out with a feeling of reluctance, as though she knew already it could only mean trouble, and unfolded it slowly. It was in English, tightly written. She couldn't read it in that uncertain light, but she shook her head when Michael offered to switch on the reading-lamp. As she always had, she preferred to put the moment off. 'It came yesterday?' she asked, slipping the letter back.

He nodded. 'I've been thinking about it.'

She wasn't surprised. It was like him to have kept it to himself till then. Especially if it was trouble.

'She says she wants to come out, she wants us to help,' Michael said when she didn't ask. 'If it's genuine, that is. I suppose it is. It looks like her writing. And the style is certainly hers.'

'Severe,' Grace suggested, as they entered the harbour tunnel.

'Peremptory, almost. She's back in Shanghai now apparently. A room in our old house, believe it or not. I never really expected to hear from her again.'

'What will Patrick think, I wonder. He can hardly want his mother back now, after all his life without her.'

Hell's Angels

That man was still smoking. The *No Smoking* sign had been on for at least five minutes, but he hadn't taken a blind bit of notice. Rachel saw tomorrow's headline printed behind her eyes: *Single Cigarette Causes Fire on Landing Plane*. Fear got the better of her weakening reserve at last, and she leant towards him.

'The not smoke advertisement is published,' she said in the tense Mandarin she'd been rehearsing in her mind, and smiled pleadingly, making stubbing motions on her ashtray.

The man's face was a plank. He stared flatly through her, past her, without a flicker, then turned away. He couldn't have looked at a bare wall with less interest.

A moment later they were over the crowded city, a million lights on either side floating up towards them. She thought they'd hit something when the wheels clunked down beneath her, and her stomach did another frantic turnover, but no, it wasn't yet. Her fists clenched as buildings surged up relentlessly to meet them. She could see buses, cars, people in the lighted streets, and she caught her breath as they skimmed a rooftop. Then suddenly the runway appeared a few feet below her, black, straight and secure. She hardly felt the bounce.

While she checked her bag for her passport and traveller's cheques, peered under her seat, and rummaged through the seat-pocket for anything she might have left behind, the Chinese man got up and walked past the protesting stewardesses to the rear of the plane. He sat in an empty seat two rows behind a red-haired sunburnt young tourist who was nursing his backpack on his knees. When the tourist got up, the Chinese followed him.

The young tourist wore the conventional thongs with bare feet, frayed blue jeans and a check shirt. The Chinese, who wore a light grey suit and polished black shoes, glanced at him from time to time with wooden contempt. The tourist seemed unaware of that, or of him. In the immigration-hall, the Chinese queued at the Hong Kong Residents counter while the tourist languished in the Other Nationalities line.

The Chinese placed his passport on the smooth white plastic ledge. A plump young woman official glanced at the name — Yau Yin Hong — leafed through the pages, then consulted the black ring-file that was fitted upright at the corner of her desk. The passport lay open at the photograph-page, and Yin Hong regarded his upside-down face dourly. The photo was five years old now, but it showed a man already ageing. Drumming his fingers on the ledge, he leant over to watch the tip of the woman's biro travel down the printed list of names, hesitate, then travel on.

'Stand further back, please,' she said in Cantonese, without looking up.

Yin Hong moved a fraction. 'Afraid I'll see down your blouse?' he muttered into the space above her head. He had a scraping voice, like sand off a shovel.

Her nostrils flared faintly, and she flushed under her olive skin as she silently passed his passport across and nodded to the next passenger.

In the Customs-hall, Yin Hong pretended to be using one of the free phones in the far wall while he watched the red-haired foreign-devil place his pack on the counter. The Customs officer delved thoughtfully inside, testing and weighing, his head half-turned away with the assessing eyes of a connoisseur, while the foreign-devil stood advertising unconcern, gazing innocently round; then the officer waved him through.

Yin Hong followed. He had only a smart cheap nylon travel-bag.

The foreign-devil swung his pack on to one shoulder and walked, hesitantly at first, then, following the arrows, directly towards the airport coach-stand. A young Chinese with bulging, freshly tattooed biceps, wearing a white T-shirt emblazoned with *Hell's Angels*, lounged by the sliding doors. His eyes met Yin Hong's, and Yin Hong nodded minimally. The young man joined the queue just behind the foreign-devil.

Yin Hong watched until they boarded the coach.

From a long time back

Michael and Grace waited by a round pillar, apart from the expectant patient crowd that pressed against the barriers. Michael watched the passengers as they emerged through the sliding doors as if on to an unanticipated stage. Bemused, anxious, hopeful, weary, they paused to scan the blur of faces beneath them like amateur actors dazzled by the footlights, then wheeled their trolleys down the ramp, evincing every emotion from delight to dejection. It reminded him of returning prisoners of war, of refugees, exiles, orphans. It reminded him of his sister Lily, who wanted to come out of China.

'That must be her,' Grace said, and for a moment he thought she meant Lily. Then he saw a slight straw-haired young woman approaching them with an enquiring grin that crinkled her eyes.

'Rachel?'

'Yes,' she said in a low voice. Then: 'Hi'.

About twenty-six, he thought as he shook her hand. And a spinster.

'I thought it was you from the photo,' Rachel said.

He smiled silent incredulity. 'This is my wife, Grace.'

Grace placed her limp delicate hand into Rachel's firm American grip and met her frank smile with a vague one.

'Hi,' Rachel said again in her low voice. 'Very kind of you to meet me.'

They all looked down at the luggage-trolley she'd been pushing, on which a rucksack sprawled precariously over two or three canvas bags and a suitcase.

'The car's over here.' Michael laid a guiding hand on the trolley, and they started pushing it along together, awkwardly. 'Did you have a good flight?'

'I guess it was OK. Flying's like being seasick for me. I'm just glad when it's over and I'm still alive.'

'Oh, do you get air-sick?' Grace asked with polite solicitude.

'Er, not exactly, no. In fact not at all.'

They paused expectantly, but luckily she didn't have to explain, because just then someone touched Michael familiarly on the shoulder. It was the unrepentant smoker from the plane. And smoking again. Michael turned.

The man grinned, a mouthful of crooked yellowing teeth, muttered something in a grating voice, then went on with a kind of seedy jauntiness. Like an ageing hustler, Rachel thought. Though what would she know about that?

Michael and Grace exchanged speaking looks.

'Was that a friend of yours?' Rachel asked, sure he wasn't. 'He was sitting near me in the plane.'

'We know each other,' Michael conceded. 'From a long time back.'

It hadn't sounded like Mandarin the man was speaking. 'I hope I'll be able to learn some Cantonese here,' Rachel offered gamely in the preoccupied silence that had settled over her hosts like a sudden frost.

'That was Shanghainese,' Michael said abstractedly. 'Not Cantonese.'

Grace had heard it, too. 'Did you get Lily's letter all right?' Yin Hong had asked.

They went out into the heat of the night, moist as a warm flannel perfumed with the scent of petrol fumes.

'We've asked a few people to dinner, by the way,' Michael said, halting at the kerb. 'I hope you're not too tired.'

'Oh, no, I'm not *tired*,' Rachel said, as if there might be some other objection. She was thinking apprehensively of her rumpled clothes — she'd been travelling for six weeks now.

'Just Patrick and Dimitri Johnston, apart from ourselves.'

'Dimitri . . . ?'

'Dimitri Johnston. The other one of your prospective supervisors. And Dimitri's family. They're old friends.'

A lustrously black, but ancient, limousine drew up beside them, square, upright and sedate. The Chinese driver, in dark trousers and immaculate cool white shirt, got out to take her bags. He was short, shorter than she was, but compact, with a trim way of moving on slightly bandy legs.

Rachel thought she'd better warn them. 'I'm afraid I don't have any formal clothes.'

'Oh, we're never formal,' Michael said as the driver opened the door for them.

Rachel wondered what he understood by *formal*.

The driver closed the door with a solid rich-sounding clunk.

'This isn't a Rolls-Royce, is it?' Rachel asked. 'I've never been in one before.'

'I got it second-hand,' Michael said.

The wrong kind

Yin Hong found a phone in the arrival-hall and dialled a Wanchai number. Lai Ying's voice answered almost at once. He visualized her jewel-encrusted glasses and ringed fingers.

'He's on his way,' Yin Hong said, drawing deep on his cigarette. 'Ah Keung's just taken him over.'

'OK' she said crisply. 'See you tomorrow, Yin Hong.'

'He was just the type the Customs muscle like to pick up,' he added quickly, before she could hang up. 'You should tell them to be more careful over there. They're getting the wrong kind of foreign-devils. I don't know how he got through.'

There was a moment's silence, as though that had set her back a bit, but then she answered as sharp and cocky as ever: 'There're lots of things you don't know, Ah Hong. And you don't need to know them either.'

He heard her chuckling to someone, repeating what he'd said, then the phone clicked in his ear. His cheeks stiffened as he placed the receiver slowly down on its cradle. So it was *Ah* Hong now, and cut him off, was it? *Ah* Hong! As if he was some kid just hanging up the blue lantern, just taking his triad oath, instead of. . .. And sniggering about him with her cronies, too! He felt his eyes smarting and growing hot. Was that it, then, after all these years? He rasped some phlegm up from the back of his throat but, as he never spat indoors, restrained himself till he was outside. Then he spat violently into an orange litter-bin with *No Spitting* stencilled on it in English and Chinese, imagining the bin was Lai Ying's face.

Distant connection

Rachel sat uneasily in the cool silent car with her cool silent hosts and the remote yet listening driver, whose neat round head scarcely rose above the steering wheel. The Rolls sailed regally along overpasses thrown like rigid arms across the amazed faces of scarred tenement-blocks, through the bright aseptic tube of a tunnel — 'We're crossing the harbour now,' Michael remarked — and into a network of freeways on Hong Kong island that reminded Rachel of a miniature New York. It wasn't until they'd filtered on to a highway, which seemed to lead steeply up into the blank mass of a mountain that Michael asked about Jenny. 'How is your . . . your stepmother, I suppose I should call her?'

'She's fine.' Rachel superimposed Jenny's short blue-rinsed hair and de-wrinkled face on to the dense formations and scattered galaxies of lights that glittered on the lower slopes of the mountain. 'I call her Jenny actually.'

Michael nodded, as if that was to be expected, if not approved. 'It must be thirteen years since we saw her. Just before she married your father.'

'Fourteen, in that case,' Rachel said authoritatively. Jenny used to dye her hair brown then. And she hadn't had her face-lift yet. Rachel hoped Michael wouldn't want to go on about her, even though she was his half-sister.

Apparently he didn't. After giving Rachel a slow enquiring look, he nodded fractionally to his right. 'Government House back there.'

'Oh.' Craning her neck, she saw a large white floodlit building with an odd disproportionate square tower rising from it, turreted like a fairy castle.

'It's the governor's official residence,' Michael added — redundantly, Rachel thought.

She imagined a testy old man inside, wearing a quaint ostrich-plumed hat and a white uniform, performing effete colonial rituals with a toy ceremonial sword. Well, that shouldn't last much longer. 'I guess his days are numbered,' she suggested.

'Numbered?'

'Now that they're talking about handing Hong Kong back to China, I mean.'

Michael gazed ruminatively ahead for a few seconds. 'I suppose everyone's days are numbered,' he delivered deliberately at last.

The car glided up a long snaky road overhung with trees. Every fifty yards or so old lantern-shaped street-lamps appeared amongst the branches, sending a dim greenish light through the leaves. It was how Rachel imagined an English country lane would look, but this was cut into the rocky side of a subtropical mountain, from which she caught sudden vertiginous glimpses of lights and sea and ships beneath her.

She inspected Michael's face surreptitiously. How Chinese he looked, almost as Chinese as his pure Chinese wife. Maybe his eyes were a little rounder, maybe his nose was longer, the bridge a little more prominent, but all the same it was hard to credit that Jenny and he had had the same English father in Shanghai.

She wondered sometimes whether that distant connection through Jenny had nudged her towards Chinese studies when she went to college. Hardly likely, she thought now, as, glancing at Michael — and at Grace — she realized how distant the connection really was.

The car swung sedately off the road on to a long, steep, shrub-lined drive and drew up in front of a large house that seemed to perch on a ledge of the mountain — beyond the dark outlines of the shrubs was nothing but the empty sky and the sea glimmering below. A couple of black Chow dogs raced round the car barking excitedly.

'I really appreciate you letting me stay a while,' she said as the driver opened the door. 'Especially as I'm not even a relative really.'

'Stay as long as you like.' Grace smiled, more past than at her. 'It's no trouble at all.'

'And you are almost a relative, in a way.' Michael added dubiously, as if he'd been searching for something in her favour.

They stood watching the driver take her bags out of the car, his movements mirrored shadowily in the glistening paintwork. The dogs sniffed her, then the bags, then sat back on their haunches, watching with cocked heads and lolling blue tongues.

Scouring her mind for something to say, Rachel turned back to the Rolls.

'It's an unusual car, isn't it?' she produced discreetly, thinking really that it looked like a hearse. 'Have you had it long?'

'I bought it eighteen years ago,' Michael said, 'in the hope it would last me the rest of my life. It looks as though it will, too. It was a hotel car before. My father had one for thirty years in Shanghai. He thought they were works of art. I expect Jenny told you.'

'Er, no, she didn't.' Jenny hardly ever told her anything unless it was about herself.

'Could we eat in about an hour?' Michael added quickly, as though he thought the small talk had gone on quite long enough or, perhaps, was getting too personal. 'If that's not rushing you.'

'Your room's this way,' Grace said. 'I thought you'd like to look over the sea. Ah Yee will take your things.'

A small, plump, white-jacketed amah who called her 'missy' was, despite her size and Rachel's egalitarian misgivings, already lugging the heaviest bags with apparent ease.

Rachel followed Grace up flights of stairs and across landings decked with scrolls and pictures. She had no time to examine them, but 'It is an exceedingly beautiful mansion' she said to the amah in slow and careful Mandarin.

The amah giggled with polite incomprehension; and Grace, too, half-turning, seemed nonplussed at first. Then she answered in English: 'I'm afraid Ah Yee only speaks Cantonese. And my Mandarin's rather bad, like Michael's. Of course Patrick and Dimitri Johnston speak it well. Have you been learning long?'

'Four years, on and off.'

Grace's gaze was floating away already. 'On and off?' she repeated as if she'd forgotten what they were talking about.

She opened a door and pressed the light-switch, revealing a spacious room with heavy blue velvet curtains and warm rugs on the floor.

'Oh,' Rachel said, going in, 'this is wonderful.'

The amah dumped the bags and opened a smaller door, gesturing and smiling an expansive gold-toothed smile.

'Yes, that's the bathroom,' Grace said vaguely.

Settled already?

'Who else will be at the Dentons'?' Elena Johnston asked her father, plaiting her long fair hair in front of the hall mirror.

'Just Patrick, as far as I know,' Dimitri said. 'One of us is going to supervise this American girl's thesis. Or both of us.'

'Poor girl. What a choice: someone old enough to be her father, or a raging poofter.'

The Johnstons lived on the southern coast of Hong Kong, in an old house between a Chinese Christian cemetery and a fish-market. The house overlooked the sea and was surrounded by neglected bamboo and bauhinia, the branches of which brushed against the windows or nudged their way between the stonework of both the upstairs and the downstairs verandas.

'I wouldn't have thought it would matter much who her supervisor was,' Dimitri said. 'Unless she's a nymphomaniac. Actually I'd prefer Patrick to supervise her. I'd rather not supervise anyone any more.'

Elena, turning her face from side to side in the mirror, suddenly reminded him with a faint numb shock of her dead mother, Helen, when she was young. How young? He couldn't remember, but he knew the gesture was Helen's as well. Was it before he married her? Could Helen once have been as carefree as her daughter Elena was now?

'Are you going in that shirt?' Dimitri's second wife, Mila, asked, coming down the stairs.

'I was,' Dimitri said. 'Is your back hurting?'

'Why?'

'The way you're walking.'

'A bit stiff, that is all. You are not really going in that shirt, are you?' She still spoke English, after all these years, in that clearly separated way, without elision or slur, that made him think of pebbles being dropped one by one into a pool. And that level Chinese inflection made it hard to tell whether she was reproaching him or only asking.

'Not good enough for the Dentons?'

'Not good enough for me.'

He glanced ironically at Mila's dress, one of those sacks that dancers liked to wear merely because other people looked even worse in them — although she'd stopped dancing now. She'd cut her hair short as well, saying she was too old to wear it long any more — she was thirty-six. Yet with her still-slender body and poised head, her high Chinese cheekbones holding the skin taut, she scarcely looked more than five or six years older than Elena, whose dancing career had only just begun.

'I put the blue one out for you,' she said. 'It matches your socks. Is Alex making his own way there?'

'Bet he's there already,' Elena said. 'Mooning round San San. What a wimp my brother is. Why on earth doesn't he just get down to it and *have* her? It's what she wants after all, and she's absolutely loaded as well. Sometimes I feel ashamed of him.'

Mila silently raised her eyebrows, then silently lowered her lids.

Elena's ginger cat flowed up the steps from the kitchen and leapt with a single mew on to the telephone table, where it sat watching her, one white paw elegantly raised.

Elena gathered the animal in her arms, pressing her face in the long fluffy fur of its belly. 'Hope the food's good. I'm starving.'

'It usually is,' Dimitri said, going up the stairs. 'It's the conversation I'm worried about.'

'I thought Michael Denton was one of your best friends?'

'I didn't pick him for his dinner conversation, though. I didn't pick him at all, as a matter of fact.'

It was Michael who'd picked *him*, if anything. At that extramural course he gave at the university, soon after Helen's death. He still remembered the dismal lecture-room — it was a bit smarter now — with its square brown desks and square brown chairs, sprinkled with middle-aged expatriate housewives and shy young Chinese schoolteachers. Michael had arrived late, he remembered, and asked some question that threw him (he'd no idea what it was, now), then introduced himself apologetically afterwards, mentioning that his daughter went to the same ballet class as Elena. The class Mila had taught.

He looked out over the veranda. An oil tanker was making for the western anchorage. The air was so quiet and still, he could hear the deep throbbing of the tanker's engines. The glistening reflection of its lights swam beside it like tranquil ghosts. If only all his ghosts were tranquil.

He put on the blue shirt.

When he came down, his loyal, perverse and tyrannical amah, Ah Wong, was loudly deploring the fall of the Hong Kong dollar to Mila and Elena, her eyes wide and indignant. Her radio was announcing the news on the table beside her, adding to the noise. 'Rich people take their money out, poor people pay,' she kept repeating in Cantonese. 'Soon our money will be worthless; we won't even be able to buy a bag of rice with it!'

Dimitri watched her milky-green jade bracelet quivering as she gesticulated. She turned and appealed to him, shaking her head with its glossy black coil of hair. 'Rich people take their money out, poor people pay — right?'

He shrugged as if he didn't know, but simultaneously said: 'Yes, right.' Hedging his bets, as usual.

They walked through the sultry air towards the garage, accompanied by the shrill chirpings of the cicadas.

'I thought it was the commies she blamed for everything that went wrong,' Elena asked, 'not the capitalists?'

'She subscribes to both theories,' Dimitri said, swinging the meshed-wire gates open. Though not simultaneously. Each view has some plausibility of course.'

'And which one's right?'

He felt Mila watching him attentively. 'Wait and see,' he said, hedging again. I suppose we'll know the verdict in a few months, when the talks are over.'

'I would have thought the talks were only a formality,' Mila said with composed resignation as she got into their rusting unpolished Japanese car. 'As far as China is concerned, surely the verdict is settled already, and all we have to wait for is the sentence.'

Greedily at the violin

San San stopped playing. Paul's face had closed again; he wasn't listening any more.

'Someone's come to stay with us, Paul,' she said slowly, resting her violin on her knees. 'A sort of relative from America.'

It was her tone of voice he'd comprehend, if anything, not the words of course. If he was in the mood, he'd listen alertly, his eyes on her face like a dog's or a small child's, fathoming, wondering. Only Paul wasn't a small child; he was twenty-seven. This time his shoulders stayed drooped, though, his eyes still and dead. He just sat there hunched like a sack, a well-dressed, well-cared-for sack, with a vacant moonish face.

'No, don't go off again,' she pleaded. 'Draw a picture. Draw this.' She held the violin up in front of him and made wide drawing motions with the bow, gesturing encouragingly at all his sketches and paintings hanging round the walls.

Not a glimmer. He just stared past her, mouth slackly open, a flat changeless gleam in his eyes.

'Oh, come *on*, Paul.' She opened his drawing-book on the table and coaxed him to hold a green crayon, closing his fingers round it.

Then, slowly, at last he stirred, something flickered behind the smooth blank panes of his eyes. He sat forward. His mouth closed, and he smiled, an anticipating smile. He rolled the crayon between his fingers and thumb, as San San sometimes rolled her bow before she began playing.

'Go on,' she encouraged him, holding the violin upright on her knee. 'Go on, draw it.'

His gaze grew gradually more alive, more intent. With one hand he stroked the paper on the table, caressing it lovingly, while with the other he fingered the crayon. For several seconds he was still, staring greedily at the violin, as though trying to absorb it through his eyes. Then at last he began to draw, unhesitatingly, with firm generous lines, frowning in concentration. Occasionally he made little grunts like 'No' or 'Mm', and when her arm tired so that the violin shifted slightly he shook his head impatiently. 'No, no, no!' He never said more than that, never.

San San heard the dogs barking, then Alex Johnston asking for her, then his step outside the half-open door.

'Come in, Alex,' she said, without turning her head. 'I knew it was you.'

Alex stood silently behind her, watching Paul, but chiefly watching her.

'I wonder why he only draws *things?*' San San asked. 'Never people?'

'I hadn't noticed.' Alex glanced round the walls. It was true. Every drawing was of some object, solid, strong and full of life but there were no people.

'I suppose he knows where he is with things,' San San suggested, trying to stay as still as a thing herself. 'He must find people rather weird and unpredictable.'

'Well, who doesn't?' Alex said.

2

Always have candles

After she'd showered the Bangkok dirt and sweat off her, Rachel changed into her least-rumpled dress and glanced round the room while she tugged her brush through her rebellious fair hair. There were pale-tinted prints on the walls and a tall statue of the goddess Kuan Yin curving in her usual pose on a Chinese black-wood table. It was carved from an elephant's tusk, she realized, and turned away.

The prints seemed to be of early Hong Kong; it must be a hundred years ago at least. Sailing ships with enormous British flags, junks, redcoat soldiers, cramped villages, imposing colonial buildings and unpaved narrow streets. English ladies holding delicate parasols sauntered along them in hooped skirts while pigtailed Chinese coolies trudged barefoot under the massive loads swinging from their bamboo shoulder-poles. Bourgeois, she thought they looked. Complacent arrogant colonials. Well, what would you expect?

The polished teak floor shone with a waxed honey-gleam. The rugs were soft and deep-piled, with rich tones; Persian or Afghan, she guessed. From the window she could see a dim black shadow, the grounds of the house; then, on the shore far below, a wavy string of glittering bluish lights, like a sapphire necklace dropped negligently on a soft black cloth.

She smoothed her dress and went down apprehensively to meet the rest of them. At least it couldn't be worse than flying.

But when Grace led her in she thought maybe it could be after all. A whole roomful that had been loud with chattering voices suddenly hushed, and she felt a dozen pair of eyes coolly appraising every inch of her as she was taken round to be introduced to each person in turn — Chinese, English, Eurasian. She knew she'd been thoroughly valued, labelled and docketed by the time all the handshakes (slack Chinese or tight English) and cool pleased-to-meet-yous were over, while she herself could hardly even remember a single name.

'Patrick isn't here yet,' Grace said when she'd presented Rachel to everyone. 'He isn't very dependable, I'm afraid.'

Vaguely visualizing an absent-minded professor with a bald head and a puzzled frown, Rachel noticed Grace hadn't mentioned Paul yet, who she knew was mentally handicapped. 'Some kind of zombie,' Jenny had told her. 'They don't talk about him.'

The Dentons' conception of a casual meal seemed to be two or three amahs in black trousers and white tunics laying dish after dish of Chinese food and bottles of French wine on a spotless table decked with flowers and candles.

'My, candles!' Rachel said incautiously when they sat down. 'Is it someone's birthday?'

Grace looked at her perplexedly. 'We always have candles,' she said, in a tone that asked, *Doesn't everyone?*

At least nobody was wearing evening dress. Just summery dresses and open-necked shirts, though all very expensive except the Johnstons', Rachel observed, which did help her to tell them apart from the elegant Denton clan by the end of the meal. It wouldn't always have been easy otherwise: one of Michael's sons was married to a blonde English girl, but another blonde English girl was Dimitri Johnston's daughter, and Rachel wasn't sure which was which. On the other hand, Dimitri Johnston's wife was Chinese, but so was the wife of Michael's other son, and again Rachel wasn't sure which was which. And if Dimitri's wife was Chinese why were his son and daughter pure English? And why did everyone speak with such flawless British accents that if she'd closed her eyes she could never have told whether the speaker was English, Chinese or Eurasian? Had they all been to Oxford or Cambridge?

She gave it up, and concentrated on avoiding the morsels of meat in her bowl. She didn't want to tell them she was a vegetarian — it might sound like a complaint. Her fingers began to ache as she manipulated her chopsticks. How hard it was to pick up slippery mushrooms with them and not to scatter the rice! She said little, preferring to watch and listen; it would all go in her diary later. If only she could fix the right names to their faces, though.

Then Patrick Denton arrived at last.

'Hallo, everybody. Sorry I'm late,' a voice sang out from the doorway behind Rachel. 'The simply most appalling queue for taxis; one positively couldn't get one for love nor money.'

She knew he must be about forty, but except for the lines round his eyes, and the faint bruised shadows beneath them, Patrick scarcely looked thirty. He had a lean, rather angular, Chinese-looking face, was very slim, and wore a navy blue blazer with an ascot and matching handkerchief in his breast pocket. He was jaunty, dapper, debonair, and spoke with the most pronounced British accent of them all, loud, ringing and mannered. Rachel tried to match his face to the scholarly articles that bore his name, and failed. He looked more interesting than the absentminded professor she'd visualized; but much more bizarre. When he moved, it was with a flourish, like Fred Astaire impersonating Oscar Wilde.

'So I went to a flower-stall and got a rose for you.' He handed the pink unopened bud to Grace with an elaborate gesture. 'Alas, the taxi queue was absolutely twice as long when I got back.' He slipped into the empty chair between Mila and Dimitri, opposite Rachel. 'Mila, dear girl, you're looking inscrutably divine as always. Dimitri, how's the lightness of being today, dear boy?' (The lightness of *what*? Rachel wondered — or was he alluding to that novel by the Hungarian with the unpronounceable name that she'd found a bit too clever when she'd read it a year or two ago?) 'No, nothing fattening, just a little of that delectable fish if I may. Would you believe it? I won six thousand dollars at fantan in Macao. I shall simply be barred from the casinos if this goes on. I say, this wine is most refreshing.' Then, with everyone watching, he appeared to notice Rachel for the first time — in fact their eyes had met almost as soon as he'd come in. 'And you must be Rachel Martin, whose thesis either Dimitri or I is to have the honour of supervising. Delighted to meet you.' He rose and bowed with exaggerated courtesy.

The amahs seemed to like him, smiling and nodding as they placed the food nearer his bowl. He said something to one in Cantonese, which made her laugh, and the other amahs, too, when she repeated it to them. Then he turned back to Rachel, brushing a lock of his longish black hair away from his temple with a delicate little flick of his middle finger.

She noticed how flushed his cheeks were beneath the smooth clear skin. And she noticed, or thought she noticed, an anxious elusive little glimmer in his dark shining eyes, before he started speaking again.

Nearly forgot your lines then, didn't you? she thought.

Old man with knobbly shoulders

Yin Hong ate his evening rice in one of the teahouses the triad brothers looked after. He would have paid the bill — he knew *they* were always on time with their payments, and he liked to give favours to people like that — but Lam, the owner, wanted to show him some respect, and kept bowing and waving the money away.

'All right, then,' Yin Hong said in the end. 'How are the kids?' Lam's wife smiled and nodded gratefully from the cash-desk. It made him feel better after that phone call with that bitch Lai Ying. At least some people still gave him face.

He sauntered through Temple Street market, belching comfortably and picking his teeth. The stalls, close-packed beneath their incandescent glaring lamps, were still crowded, the hawkers sweating in their singlets as they bargained, wrapped and gave change. Their older children helped; the younger ones, squatting on wooden stools, did their homework on their laps, or else simply slept on folded arms, their schoolbooks open beneath them. Yin Hong liked kids. He sometimes wished he knew what had become of his. But he'd left them years ago; it was too late now.

He liked it in Temple Street, too. He liked the noise, the closeness of the people, the steamy smells from the cooked-food stalls, the songs of the kerbside opera-singers and the blind musicians, even the dead smiles of the old tarts loitering by the park. It was where he belonged, where he was somebody and people knew it. He'd always liked it in the streets, and there above all, because it reminded him of the old days in Shanghai, when he was young and still had it all before him. Things were better then. They'd never been the same since he'd come to Hong Kong — not for a long time anyway. He felt a sudden gush of bitterness and self-pity, thinking of those times. It was all so long ago, and he was getting old. And working for a woman, too, of all things. He hated that, especially Lai Ying. Thought she had all the answers and called him Ah Hong now. *Ah* Hong! Like a kid, a servant! Talk about having a big nose, she wasn't in it. A woman half his age, and she didn't give him any face!

A coach-load of foreign-devil tourists with red peeling skin and bellies sagging over their jazzy shorts, men and women alike, waddled into the market. They all had round plastic name-labels on their multi-coloured shirts, like kids going to nursery school, and Japanese cameras slung round their jowly pink necks. The tour guide, a young girl, leant against the coach, chatting with the driver. Their eyes met Yin Hong's and for a second all three of them shared their contempt for the clumsy clucking foreign-devil suckers who were paying small fortunes for trash and enjoying it, too.

Passing by the fortune-tellers, he thought of stopping to have his palm read by the old man with all the charts spread out on the pavement beside him, but he was getting tired and, besides, there were things to do in the walled city. Michael Denton, for instance, he'd give him a ring. That one needed warming up a bit. Stroke of luck that, about Lily. Lily Denton after all these years. To think he grew up in the same house as them, even if it was the servants' quarters. Narrow world. He'd make something out of that; at his age he needed it, too. Sometimes when he thought of the future, even just six months away, never mind a year, it looked like a black hole, he just couldn't see anything there at all, and he felt he was sliding slowly into it. Old age, he was getting on. He needed some security, he wasn't making enough any more. That black hole almost made him shudder sometimes, waking up at night thinking about it.

He flicked his toothpick into the gutter and walked on into Kansu Street, waving to a taxi.

At the steps down into the narrow greasy alleys of the walled city, a bunch of middle-aged Japanese businessmen were hanging round Limpy Ng, getting his sales pitch for the sex show he was touting for. They looked pretty doubtful, and Limpy was trying to persuade them they'd be as safe with him as with a police patrol. 'Isn't that right?' he called out. 'You tell 'em, Yin Hong.'

'Sure, safer than the police,' Yin Hong muttered brusquely. He didn't mind giving Limpy a hand, but he didn't like the oily way he tried to make himself out to be his friend and equal. What was he but a grubby crippled little pimp after all, nothing but a hanger-on?

The Japs' goggly glasses shifted from Limpy's face to his and back again. They still didn't look too sure, but Limpy was pleased.

'Thanks, brother,' Limpy called after him. 'I've got a tip for the races, if you could use it.'

Yin Hong ignored him. *Brother!* It felt like the lame little runt was laying his arm round his shoulder. He shrugged it off as he started into the dark burrow of dank yard-wide alleys. Past the heroin-dens where skeletal men lay dazed on planks, past the coolies' brothels with sacking curtains between their plywood cubicles, past the piece-workers sewing shirts beside the rancid open drains, past the plastic-flower makers and the sandal-sole cutters, past the blind lanes rotting with refuse where squeaking rats foraged like cats or dogs. He walked past them all obliviously, on to the cramped entrance of his own apartment-block.

Ah Keung was there already, lolling in the doorway, fingering the new still-burning tattoo on his biceps, the fine orange and blue dragon Yin Hong had noticed at the airport.

'Go all right, did it?'

Ah Keung nodded. 'The stuff's on its way now.'

'Nice dragon, that.'

Ah Keung looked down at his arm. 'Got one on my chest, too.'

'Have you? She'll like that.'

'Who will?'

'Who d'you think? The one it gets on top of. What's her name? Good-looker, isn't she?'

'Ling Kwan.'

'Ling Kwan, that's right.' He started climbing the bare cement stairs. 'Everything all right, here, ah?'

Ah Keung nodded again.

Yin Hong thumbed a ten-dollar bill off his roll and handed it to Ah Keung. 'Get a beer, will you?' He started trudging up the stairs. 'Tsing Tao, in the bottle. That tinned stuff tastes like gassy horse-piss. And ask Limpy Ng what his tip is for the races. Told me he had a tip just now.'

Seven flights, steep and long. They didn't get any easier as you got older, either. On each dingy landing the metal gates were locked, and plastic bags leant against the corners, full of garbage.

He unlocked his own iron grille, breathing heavily, then the door, and put on the light. The room smelt mouldy with trapped stale heat. He opened the narrow window, reaching between the rusty bars. If he stretched his arm out, he could touch the slimy grey wall opposite. Outside it was like a sweating tunnel, but with all its smells it was cooler and fresher than the air inside. Yin Hong noticed that his spare shoes, neatly placed beneath the window, had grown a greyish fur of mildew on them again, after only half a week.

The boom of televisions and radios, the clack of mah-jong tiles, the occasional shouting or crying voice floated in with the night air — every sound was magnified and blurred in the clammy narrow cavity between the buildings. Yin Hong switched the green pedestal fan on and methodically took off his jacket, tie and shirt, hanging the jacket and shirt carefully over the back of the folding chair, then laying the tie, neatly rolled, on the yellow plastic table.

The room was bare except for the table and three chairs, a portable television and a little crude red wooden altar in the corner. Even the light bulb had no shade. Half-burnt joss sticks stood in front of the altar like the stems of withered flowers. Grey powdery ash lay on the floor around them, like the dust of desiccated blossoms.

Dressed only in his singlet and trousers, he seemed to have suddenly changed, to have become what he really was: an old man with knobbly shoulders, narrow chest and pale flabby flesh hanging from his arms. There were whitish slash scars on both forearms and on his right side along the prominent ribs. His right forearm had a dragon tattooed on it, like Ah Keung's, only smaller and faded — a feeble ancestor of the young one.

He felt through his jacket pockets for his lighter, then lit the joss sticks. The heavy bluish smoke, smelling of sandalwood, drifted in a flat lazy layer across the room until, snatched by the whirling currents from the fan, it scattered and dissipated.

The chair squeaked as he sat down in front of the fan's cool stream.

Ah Keung came in with the beer, slamming the grille shut behind him. In the tiny kitchen, scarcely bigger than a cupboard, he found two glasses, standing on the shelf beside Yin Hong's black hair-dye. When he picked them up, an inch-long metallic-brown cockroach scuttled away with a frantic little rustle. He set the glasses down on the table and poured the beer.

'See Limpy?' Yin Hong asked after he'd drunk half a glass.

Ah Keung nodded. 'First meeting, last race. It's been fixed, he said.'

'Better had be.'

Ah Keung was wearing the latest-style jeans, his red Hell's Angels singlet pulled down tight inside the waistband. Yin Hong eyed him up and down. In Shanghai in the old days, he himself had worn foreign clothes, but they were decent — what they called the Chicago style. Loose trousers, double-breasted jacket and a wide-brimmed trilby. At least you could tell the men from the women then. He still thought that was the proper way to dress, and his jacket was still a double-breasted one. That modern foreign-devil get-up made them all look like fairies, men and women alike.

'See what's on the box?' Ah Keung suggested, reaching forward for the knob already.

'Wait a minute!' Yin Hong said sharply. 'I've got to make a call, ah. Hand me the phone-book, will you?'

He wiped his lips on the back of his hand, narrowing his eyes to focus on the blurry rows of characters.

' "Denton, Michael," ' he read out slowly, frowning at the closely printed number. 'That's our man.'

Political reasons

The candles were burning low. The wine, or Patrick Denton's extravagantly extroverted personality, had gradually warmed them all, and Rachel no longer felt so much like a specimen being passed round for inspection.

'Yes, I want to visit China while I'm here,' she told Dimitri Johnston. 'That's partly why I came, to get the chance of seeing Beijing, the Forbidden City, the Temple of Heaven . . . all those places.'

'And the temple of Mao, I trust?' Patrick asked, laying down his chopsticks. 'No visit to the centre of the world is complete without a pilgrimage to the Mao-soleum. It will tell you more about China nowadays than the Temple of Heaven ever will, I'm afraid.'

'You've seen it?'

'A couple of years ago, yes. I joined the reverent files of docile school children and gawping peasants up from the farm for the day. We had about twenty seconds to stop and bow to the Great Helmsman in his glass canoe before we were ushered on by the officious functionaries. When my turn came I thought: My god, dear boy, the moths are getting at you. Positively patchy, I thought. Emblematic, wouldn't you say? The Great Helmsman's deteriorating condition is the simply perfect symbol of the state of communism in China today.'

'It makes me shudder to think of those people taking over Hong Kong,' one of the blonde women said. Rachel could place her now as Alison, the wife of Michael's second son, Peter, who she thought was a doctor. Her smoothly handsome husband never looked at her when she spoke; but he paused in whatever he was doing and listened intently, as if holding his breath. 'By what right I don't know,' Alison added truculently. 'They can't even run their own country properly.'

Rachel protested mildly. She'd joined the movement against the Vietnam War in her first year at college, and some vestiges of what she now thought of as her naive radicalism remained. 'But Hong Kong does historically belong to China, doesn't it?'

'As North America historically belongs to the Red Indians, dear girl,' Patrick said languidly. 'But one doesn't see many wigwams round the White House — not that they'd necessarily do a better job if there were of course.'

Alison seemed to take this as a vindication, and jutted her chin triumphantly. She had a large discontented mouth, which had left a wide lipstick-stain on her glass.

'Well, anyway, that's past now,' Michael's other daughter-in-law, Stella, said briskly. 'What matters now is what people being here want in This Day and Age.' Her smooth Chinese face was level and disc-like — forehead, cheekbones and chin all in the same plane, all part of the same flat oval surface. Just like the smooth discs of her glasses, Rachel thought.

'Most of them just want to be left alone,' Mila Johnston said coolly.

To Rachel her voice sounded quite cutting, but Stella only nodded. 'That's why it's so important to get an Understanding with Beijing,' she said, setting her glasses a little more firmly in place. She spoke quickly and fluently, with heavy stress on what Rachel guessed she considered were the Key Words. Her husband John, who looked very much like Michael, nodded agreement with everything she said, sometimes before she said it. Rachel had gathered they were both lawyers.

'After all, it shouldn't be impossible, as we're All Chinese.'

'Or half-Chinese, or three-quarters,' Dimitri said, glancing pointedly round the table. 'Or Portuguese or Indian or Pakistani for that matter. Or even British.'

'Well, thanks!' Alison said, dabbing her lips with her napkin.

'Ninety per cent Chinese,' Stella said. 'Ninety-five.'

'Most of whom came here because they didn't want to be ruled by the comrades,' Patrick said, fitting a cigarette into an ebony holder. 'For which they have quite exemplary reasons, as I'm sure Mila can testify, if testimony is really needed.'

Mila's eyelids fluttered, but she didn't speak. Patrick lit his cigarette at the candle and leant back. 'And in the meantime, because of all this beastly brouhaha about the negotiations, the money I extracted from the Macao gambling-halls is simply wasting away in my pocket. *Wasting* away! It's too depressing for words. Twenty-five per cent down in a few months — and ten per cent since Friday, I hear. I suppose I shall simply have to rush madly to the bank tomorrow to change what's left of it into US dollars. Imagine the crowds! Too, too depressing!'

Alex Johnston, who taught English in a local school, said there was a rumour on Friday that government department-heads had been told to prepare plans for a handover in six months.

'Pearls before swine,' Alison sniffed into the silence this produced.

The phone rang. Grace went to answer it. She seemed not to have been listening anyway, gazing abstractedly down at a pattern she was tracing with her finger on the cloth.

'Did . . . Dr. Denton say you came from China?' Rachel asked Mila.

'Patrick,' Patrick said. 'Patrick, dear girl.'

'Yes,' said Mila, neither offering nor refusing more.

'When was that?'

'Nine, ten years ago.'

'Did you leave for political reasons?' Rachel asked tentatively, while Grace returned to whisper in Michael's ear and Michael went to the phone himself. 'Or . . . ?'

'Political reasons,' Mila shrugged. 'I had been in a labour reform camp for three years. I felt it was time for a change.' She said that almost without irony, as if it really had been just a matter of switching jobs.

'That must have been tough,' Rachel murmured uncertainly.

'Not as tough as what happened before, dear girl,' Patrick declared in his ringing voice. 'She was a dancer, you know, and some Red Guards threw her off the stage. Literally *threw* her bodily off the stage. She was lucky not to break her back. I must say one doesn't have the positively *deepest* respect for the Great Helmsman when one recalls episodes like that.'

'I went into the camp on my back and came out on my feet,' Mila said neutrally. 'Better than the other way round.'

'But why did they do it?' Rachel exclaimed more than asked. Violence, the sudden snap and rush of blood, had always been incomprehensible to her. It was like the molten core of the earth; she knew it was there, but she couldn't feel it.

'Do they have to have a reason?' There *was* a faint glint of irony in Mila's voice now. 'In my case, they said it was my foreign connections — my father sent me to school in Hong Kong when the communists came to Shanghai, and . . . . ' She paused as if checking herself, then went on, nodding at Dimitri: 'And I was mixed up with this foreign-devil, so they had plenty of excuses. But the real reason was probably that it made them feel important. It was my fault; I should not have gone back.'

'Half the people in Hong Kong know someone with a story like that,' Stella said, fixing Rachel through her lenses with severe magnified eyes, like an attorney ramming her point home to the jury. 'That's why we must Work Things Out with Beijing before 1997. Otherwise it could be Disastrous.'

'Catastrophic,' her husband, John Denton, said.

'We won't care by 1997,' Dimitri shrugged, finishing his wine. 'We'll all be old. Even you, Stella. Comparatively.'

'Old or dead,' Michael said, returning to his seat. He shook some tiny white pills from a silver case into his hand and swallowed them with a little gulp of the green tea, which the amahs had left when they cleared the food away.

'Elena wants to go swimming,' San San called out. 'Anyone else for a dip?'

'Love to,' Rachel said.

Everyone left the table, except the older people, John and Stella. Alison would have stayed, too, if she hadn't noticed Peter leaving with the others.

'You're not going, are you?' she called after him petulantly.

'What does it look like?' Peter asked softly, smiling with his lips.

Her face reddened, but she only shrugged and blinked. 'Might as well go myself then,' she muttered, her voice abruptly plaintive and uncertain. 'Keep an eye on him.'

'Could you show me the way?' Rachel asked her quietly.

The rest of them, sitting round the table, silently avoided each other's eyes, as if Alison had gone out in tears.

'Let's go into the garden,' Michael said at last. He didn't want the servants to overhear what he had to tell Patrick.

Safe shadowed lawn

The water smacked and scattered, then hissed down like rain behind the thick screen of bamboo. Lamplight filtered palely through the rustling green leaves. The swimmers' voices carried across, remote and disembodied, to where the others sat. A mosquito-coil smouldered by their feet, its heavy acrid smoke wafting past them. Cicadas shrilled their wavering chorus. The two Chows lay head-on-paws, dozing and twitching.

'I must say this news makes me feel rather dismal,' Patrick said, looking up from Lily's letter. 'I'm not at all sure I want a mother back in my life, having managed so long without one. Especially a mother who still apparently regards me only as an afterthought. I don't wish to sound callous, but. . . .' He returned the letter to Michael, who silently gave it to John.

Stella read it over John's shoulder, frowning through her glasses in the poor light. 'If she really wants to come out,' she looked up, 'why can't she just apply for an exit permit?'

'Why couldn't I?' Mila said, lowering her lids.

'But it's different now.'

Mila looked away over the garden. 'They will not let her out if she has beans to spread,' she said with cool certainty.

'Spill,' Dimitri corrected her. 'Manure is what you spread — she might have that, too, of course.' Now that he was forty-six and generally considered a failure — not that he usually respected the general opinion, but in this case it was his own as well — an intermittent flippancy was his way of whistling in the dark.

'What do you think of the letter?' Michael asked Mila. 'You knew her in that labour-camp after all.'

John passed it across. She held it up to the light, and Dimitri read it with her.

Dear Michael,

After all these years you will be surprised to learn that for various reasons I have decided to leave China and settle abroad. If you can help at all, please do. You will know from the messenger who brings you this that it is genuine. For obvious reasons I am not using the ordinary mail.

I also hope I will be able to see Patrick again and get to know him. Please help if you can.

Please send your reply by the same messenger, again for obvious reasons.

Lily

PS. You will be interested to know that I'm now living in our old house in Shanghai — or, rather, a partitioned part of the main bedroom.

'What's this bit about the messenger?' Dimitri asked.

'The man who got the letter to me. Yau Yin Hong. He's the son of one of my father's amahs in Shanghai, so he knows Lily and me very well.' Michael thought of their meeting at the airport and Yin Hong's phone call during the meal. 'Let's meet and talk about it,' he'd said in that sandpaper voice that Michael remembered instantly. 'When you've had a chance to think it over. I'll give you a ring in a couple of days, all right?' It was years since Michael had heard his voice, but there was that same brusque familiarity in it that he'd known in his early childhood, before Yin Hong joined the triads, when he was like an older brother to Michael, amah's son or not. Through all the vicissitudes of a lifetime, that older-brother tone, established before Michael was even conscious of it, had persisted. He could see Yin Hong now in the kitchen in Shanghai, showing him his pet cricket, warning him in that same gritty presuming voice not to stick his chopstick through the cage. But he must be an old man now, nearly as old as Lily.

'The paper is certainly genuine,' Mila was saying.

'I think the writing is, too,' Michael said.

Mila felt the paper's scabrous texture between her finger and thumb. Even in that light she could see the little chips of wood in it. It was like a rough hand on her arm, shaking her awake with memories of feeble yellow light-bulbs in shabby rooms, of barred windows and thin tasteless soup with puddles of cold grease floating on it, of sheets of coarse greyish paper, like the one she was holding now, on which she'd composed her self-criticisms and confessions. Or invented them.

'I can't believe Lily has lost all her convictions,' Grace said slowly. 'It would be like the Pope leaving the Church.'

'I imagine if the Pope had been through the Inquisition even he might find his convictions waning,' Patrick said. 'And the great proletarian Cultural Revolution, through the purifying fires of which my estimable mother has surely passed, must have been every bit as bad as the average Inquisition, I imagine.'

He said 'great proletarian cultural revolution' as though he were holding the words out at arm's length with a pair of tongs and dropping them in the dustbin. 'Wouldn't you say so, Mila?' he asked abruptly.

A ragged explosion of laughter carried across from the pool, then Alex's voice expostulating with the shame of a humiliated elder brother. 'Elena! Really!'

'She had a hard time in the camp,' Mila acknowledged in her remote cool voice. 'She had the—' she frowned, fingering through her mind for the English word ' — the *small number* several times. There was one time when a Catholic priest was being struggled against, as they called it. For saying mass while he was working in the fields. Just saying it to himself, I mean. Then we all had to shout slogans at him and, you know, that kind of thing. While he was kneeling there. And she just wouldn't open her mouth. So they pushed her down beside him, and we all had to shout at her, too. Then they both got the small number for a time.'

You know, that kind of thing, Dimitri repeated silently. But he didn't know. None of them did. What kind of thing? Kicking? Beating? Sermons from Mao's Little Red Book? She'd never told him.

'I did not know who she was of course, then.' Mila glanced at Michael apologetically. 'But it would not have made any difference. It was only a month before I came up for release. I would have shouted at anyone. I did not want another three years.'

They listened silently, and seemed to go on listening to the echo of it after she'd finished. Beyond them stretched the safe shadowed lawn, the dark calm humps of the shrubs, and the dim level sea below, on which a few ships' lights glided smoothly. Mila had never told anyone that before, except Dimitri, and not all of it to him.

Another burst of laughter drifted across to them. *The voices of children are heard on the green*, Dimitri thought.

'How did they find out he was saying mass?' John asked. 'If he was only saying it to himself?'

Mila pursed her lips, then shrugged. 'Somebody told them.'

'I rather wish I hadn't heard that story,' Patrick said dolefully. He shifted in his chair, took out another cigarette, then put it away again.

'Small number?' Stella said. 'What's that?'

'A cell that is too small to stand up in.' Mila looked down at the letter again, rubbing it absently between her finger and thumb.' I asked her once what she was in for. She said for having foreign connections. Like me.' She leant forward to hand the letter back to Michael. 'The priest's in Macao now. They let him out two or three years ago. Because he was half-French, I suppose.'

'Well, thank goodness that kind of thing's all over now in China,' Stella said almost breezily, like someone resolutely riding down a private doubt.

Mila said nothing, but her lips tightened as she tapped her toe on the ground.

Michael remembered, as he often had, the last time he saw Lily, a still-handsome middle-aged woman with an unquenchably zealous gleam in her eyes, walking onto the platform for Canton at the old Kowloon Station. She was carrying a scuffed brown leather suitcase that dragged her shoulder down with its weight, but she wouldn't even allow him to help her with it, let alone Ah Choi.

The swimmers were coming back along the path, walking Indian file behind the screen of tall bamboo. Michael folded the letter deliberately and slipped it into his shirt pocket.

Elena appeared first, wearing a green towel round her waist. She'd borrowed San San's bikini, and it had been too loose round the hips, half-falling off every time she dived in or hauled herself out. Peter couldn't take his eyes off her, and Alison had looked furious. 'The water was lovely,' she said gaily.

Thoughts would not have let her

It was nearly midnight when everyone left. Rachel went out on to the porch to say goodbye. Everybody shook her hand, except the English people, who seemed to think shaking hands was too demonstrative.

'So long,' Dimitri's daughter nodded casually. 'I'm Elena, by the way. In case you've forgotten.'

'As if anyone could forget who *you* are,' Alison said. She gave Rachel a half-hearted wave. 'The first six weeks are the worst — for culture shock, I mean.'

Patrick took Rachel's hand and kissed it theatrically.

'I hope I've got everybody's name and relationship right, now,' Rachel said.

'The main thing to remember is that all of us who look Chinese are actually bananas.'

'Crazy, you mean?'

'Yellow outside, white inside. I shall see you in the university no doubt soon,' he added vaguely, as though not anxious to make it very soon. 'Dimitri's the expert of course, but . . . . '

'Er, tomorrow?' Rachel suggested. 'Professor — *Dimitri* Johnston said he'd be there at ten-thirty.'

'Yes, yes, tomorrow, then, dear girl. Tomorrow morning.'

Rachel watched the cars leaving one after the other, their headlights flaring over the toneless leaves of the shrubs while the receding taillights glowed in the solid blocks of night behind them.

Her hair was still wet, moistening the collar of her dress. So was San San's; it hung like a jet waterfall halfway down her back.

'Guess I'll go to bed now,' she said as they went inside. 'I'm looking forward to meeting Paul tomorrow.'

'I'm sorry I can't say he's looking forward to meeting you,' Michael said dispassionately. 'I expect Jenny told you about him. He only lives from moment to moment, you see. An episodic sort of life.' But he glanced away as he spoke.

Grace looked at Michael appealingly, then at Rachel. 'Once he gets to know people, he's very fond of them,' she said.

As Rachel was going up the stairs, Michael called after her. 'Oh, by the way, did you bring that photograph? The one I sent you? No, no hurry, so long as it's safe.'

Sitting by her window later while she wrote her diary, Rachel tried to find the word for Grace's tone when she said that about Paul. *Wistful? Vulnerable? Remote?* she wrote. She left them all. She never corrected anything, and she tried not to compose. She wanted her thoughts to flow naturally, undistorted, uncontrived, so that one day she'd be able to read and rediscover herself raw, as she really was. Or had been.

She'd meant to sleep with the windows open — it was so quiet there after the noise of Bangkok — but she could hear a mosquito whining round her head and thought it might be malarial, so she switched on the air-conditioner. As she flossed her teeth (she'd brought six packets of Superfloss with her from the States) she could hear San San's violin faintly. She was playing the same few bars over and over, running up to and stopping at the same note each time. Rachel could hear her still after she'd switched off the light and lay with her hands clasped behind her head, gazing up through the closed window at the bright near stars.

Last night, in Bangkok, she'd seen nothing from her bed except a neon street-lamp and the grubby backs of buildings by the railway station, from which the whoop and grind of trains leaving or arriving had sounded all through the night. Scratched into the varnish of the bare cupboard jammed between the wall and the foot of the bed was a poignant quatrain from a previous traveller — some American hippy girl of the seventies, she guessed, long gone to other lands.

> *Smile when you're making it,*
> *Grin when you're taking it,*
> *Even if you're faking it,*
> *Nobody's gonna know.*

Rachel wasn't too sure what it meant, but she had an idea.

In Shanghai, Lily Denton, too, lay in bed. She was staring up at the grey flaky plaster of her perilously bulging ceiling. The radio was playing an opera behind the partition wall, muffling her neighbours' voices. Whenever she heard Shanghainese opera, she thought of the days when her mother was young and still acted. The clear clanging of a tram bell on Zhongshan Road cut a swath across the tinny waves from the radio, the very same clanging she used to hear in that house as a child, when Zhongshan Road was called the Bund and the Chinese Revolution hadn't happened.

Her Butterfly table-fan was broken again; it was too hot to sleep. But in any case her thoughts would not have let her.

3

Last picture taken

Rachel met Paul at breakfast the next morning. She came down late and ate alone, except for Ah Yee, the amah who had carried her luggage the night before, and who now kept coming in every three or four minutes to see if she wanted anything. After some time Rachel became pricklingly aware of something behind her — that knowledge that the skin has before the mind. She turned to see a large, somehow unfinished face silently observing her from the door. Paul stood as though poised for escape, safe in the distance between them. His expression didn't change when their eyes met. Or, rather, didn't meet — he seemed not to notice that now she was observing him, too. When she smiled, his eyes moved to her lips, but there was no acknowledging glimmer in them. It was like being stared at by a horse or a cow. Or an infant.

One of the amahs from the night before, a slight grey-haired woman, bustled in, giggling nervously, and led him unresistingly away with apologetic cluckings and murmurings. But he came back a minute or two later as Rachel was finishing her toast, and stood regarding her with that same watchful curiosity, as if she might suddenly sting or bite. This time she ignored him. After a while he moved nearer and touched her shoulder very gently. She noticed how long and supple his hand was. Then he started stroking her hair — or feeling it, rather, like someone fingering a new material.

'Hi, I'm Rachel,' she said, holding herself still. (Was that how animals felt when a stranger stroked them?)

He paused while she spoke, then continued stroking. She drank her coffee tensely. Yes, it was like being a nervous animal, she thought. But then gradually her tautened muscles slackened, as if he'd pacified her. But wasn't that the wrong way round? Shouldn't she be pacifying *him*? Well, then, perhaps she was, too.

Then he laid his hand softly on her wrist, led her to his room, and mutely showed her his paintings and drawings.

The trouble with Paul was that he had encephalitis at seven, which irretrievably damaged his brain — or so the doctors said. Until then he'd been, Grace thought, the sunniest of her children. Nothing ever seemed to trouble him for long; he never even caught any childhood diseases except chicken pox, which he scarcely noticed. You'd have thought he was charmed, but it was only Nature's stealth, to lull before she struck. Grace had to look at the photographs sometimes to assure herself her memory wasn't tricking her, or she her memory. And there he was as she'd remembered him, only flattened and faded on the card like a pressed flower, turning eagerly from the wire mesh of the birdcage in the Botanical Gardens, to tell her what he'd seen. Ah Mui, his amah, neat in her white tunic and black trousers, was holding his hand.

That was the last picture taken of him. (There were only seventeen others — none as good, though even this one was slightly out of focus. They weren't a picture-taking family). That very night Paul was delirious, and afterwards it would have been cruel to photograph him. You took snaps of ruined castles, not ruined people.

Only his love of drawing and painting had survived more or less intact, like a room miraculously and absurdly left standing in a collapsed house.

And Ah Mui, of course. She'd remained, too, still his amah twenty years later. With grey hair now, like Grace.

It was Paul's encephalitis, Michael believed, that had nudged Grace over the edge into the remote abstractedness in which she now lived. She'd always been private and inward. But after the shock and the waiting that was worse than the shock — so tormenting that, as it was prolonged, they'd both begun to want it over with one way or the other, just so long as it *was* over — she'd become almost a recluse.

Sometimes she wondered how it was that everyone didn't suddenly fall ill or get run over. It seemed another absurd miracle to her.

Keeping the ruin tidy

'With you on the committee,' Belinda Lai insisted, setting her tea-cup down with a decisive chink on the saucer, 'we would raise a lo' more money — *much* more than Melissa Chan raise' las' year.'

Grace smiled politely, gazing past her through the french windows. She'd been thinking of Paul's drawings before Belinda called, especially that last one of San San's violin. How much more alive it was than most of his paintings, despite all the colours he used, as if paints were something too complex for him to manage. And more alive than *her* paintings, too. And then somehow she'd drifted off and started wondering again why things happened the way they did — why did Paul and not Belinda Lai get encephalitis, for instance, and why was Belinda sitting there now with her small writhing lips and her greasy complexion all pasted over with powder and rouge, intent on outdoing Melissa Chan in raising money for a charity neither of them cared about? Was there some reason for all that, or did it just simply happen? She thought there ought to be a reason, and yet she was sure there wasn't. Yes, why was Belinda talking so urgently at her — Grace examined Belinda's little eel-like lips with sudden fascination, so that Belinda uneasily took out a tissue and dabbed them, her voice momentarily faltering — why were just those tiny rockets of sound and no others exploding there today? What a wonder it all was, that extravagant variety of beings: Belinda, herself, Paul, everyone and everything. Yet wouldn't it have been just as good if there'd been nothing at all? She tried to imagine nothing at all, and failed. All she saw was an amorphous grey mist, which after all was something.

Belinda was regarding her expectantly, holding the tissue daintily in her plump beringed fingers. The lipstick-smudges on the soft crumpled paper looked like blood. So did the stain on the rim of her cup.

'But I'm no good at committee work,' Grace said mildly, hoping committee work was still relevant. 'I never know what to say.'

Belinda's eyes widened reproachfully. 'But surely with Paul . . . I mean, surely you will want to help a charity for the mental' handicap'? I thought you will *specially* want to help a charity like this?'

'Oh, yes, I'll give you some money,' Grace said hastily. 'It's just the committee work I don't — '

'I saw him as I came in. He look' so clean. You do marvel' with him really.'

Sometimes Grace felt there was a dam about to burst behind her eyes. It happened suddenly, without warning, and it happened then, when Belinda commended her for keeping the ruin tidy and presentable for visitors. Yet there wasn't a constant flood of misery inside her; she wasn't unhappy, not even about Paul any more. She knew Paul himself wasn't unhappy, or no more so than any infant was. She just didn't want to be reminded, not like that; she didn't want trespassers, especially blundering ones.

'You could talk abou' how it's like to be a mother of . . . of such a chil',' Belinda trampled crassly on, impervious alike to grammar and to feeling. 'It would be very interest' for the normal member' on the committee.'

There was a shudder as if the dam was about to give way, then the sudden flood subsided. Grace took out her cheque book. 'I'm so hopeless at talking and that sort of thing,' she said with penitent stubbornness. 'Couldn't I just give you a donation instead?'

To atone for her absences, she added an extra nought to the cheque, thereby giving to a charity whose exact name she instantly forgot, a sum far larger than her husband's friend Dimitri's monthly salary.

Belinda's eyes glinted as she read the amount. She pursed her lips in a little grudging smile of acknowledgement, folded the cheque carefully, and put it away in her handbag. When Ah Yee came in to take the tea away, Belinda dropped her tissue negligently onto the tray and stood up. 'You are so wise not to have any Filipina maid,' she said approvingly. 'They are so unreliable. Melissa had one, you know, and when she came back one nigh' from dinner at Governmen' House she find the girl run away with all her fur'.'

Grace, having drifted off again, thought momentarily of Christmas trees and shook her head in vague amazement.

She sat there still after Belinda had gone, gazing out of the windows, waiting for the room to lose the echoes of Belinda's voice, the whiff of her perfume, the bruise of her intrusion. Gradually it grew quieter, calmer. She felt the stillness stealing back like a grateful animal to its lair, the room slowly composing itself again.

Yes, why wasn't there nothing at all? Wouldn't that have been just as good as all this that there was? She thought of people she'd known, who'd died and become nothing, of her father executed by the communists in Shanghai, of her mother, of her sister who died of cholera as a child. She thought of her own death, whenever that would be, and of Lily's, since she remembered Shanghai. Lily was older than she was. Would she die in Shanghai, or get out to Hong Kong or somewhere? When she thought of her own death, she often visualized the world just stopping, petrified in mid-flight, instead of carrying on as it would in the same old loop only minus herself. Did that mean she was egocentric? Well, anyway, wouldn't it have been just as good if none of them had ever existed? If there'd been nothing at all, as one day she assumed there would be? She imagined nothingness creeping like an enormous eclipse-shadow over the universe as the universe ran down. Only, it wouldn't be a shadow; it would be —

'Am I disturbing you?' she heard Rachel ask.

'No, not at all,' Grace lied pleasantly, turning after a moment to the plain young American woman standing uncertainly by the door. How unfeminine she looked in her blue jeans and white shirt, and with that unruly short flaxen hair as well. 'Have you had breakfast?'

'Yes, thanks. And I've met Paul.'

'Oh,' Grace said.

'And, er, I was just wondering what bus to catch for the university.'

'Oh, you couldn't possibly go by bus; you'd have to change, and it would take hours. I'll tell Ah Choi to take you in the car.'

'No, it's OK, thanks; I've got plenty of time.'

'It's such a hot day as well.'

'No, it's OK really. I'd like to try out the buses. I thought I'd take the Peak tram down — Dimitri Johnston said I could get a bus from the bottom. It only takes fifteen minutes, he said.' She'd been looking forward to the tramcar's spectacular slide down the side of the mountain.

'Are you sure?'

'Yes, really, I'm sure.'

'Well, Ah Choi can take you to the tram, then,' Grace acquiesced. 'He's just driven Michael to the Public Records Office, he must be back by now.'

'Public Records Office?'

'He's doing some research on the early history of Hong Kong.'

'I didn't know he was a historian.'

'Oh, not a proper one,' Grace said vaguely. 'He was going to be, he was going to go to Cambridge, but then the war came and . . . he had to give it up.'

'I see.'

'He took it up again a few years ago.' Grace's glance had slipped away to gaze past Rachel, but Rachel had learnt already there'd be no point in turning to look at what.

'He's writing something for the Royal Asiatic Society now.'

'Oh. What's it about?'

'Some early official.'

'I see.'

'Yes,' Grace said, still considering nothingness.

'Paul's been showing me his pictures,' Rachel said after a moment.

'Yes?'

'They're really good, aren't they? They're so . . . vital.' Listening to her voice, she was afraid it must have sounded patronizing, and cringed.

'*They're* vital, yes,' Grace said.

There was a pause. Rachel tried to fill it. 'Do you paint, too?'

'Not really — just now and then.'

There was another pause. The pause lengthened. Grace seemed unaware of it.

'Er, that Chinese lady I saw leaving just now,' Rachel fished up somehow.

'Mm?' Grace's eyes moved slowly back to her like people reluctantly returning from their holidays. 'Belinda Lai, yes.'

'It sounded strange, hearing you two Chinese people speaking English to each other.' Rachel suspected some kind of colonial snobbery was the motive, and her voice had risen in hesitant accusation.

'Yes, it's the only language we can communicate in,' Grace said detachedly. 'If we ever really do, that is. It's all rather complicated, I'm afraid. I mean, she doesn't speak Shanghainese, you see, and her English is better than my Cantonese. And neither of us speaks Mandarin very well, so it has to be English. Though I suppose we could just write everything down in Chinese characters without talking at all,' she added, thinking at least that would be quieter.

Rachel said she could see what Grace meant about it being complicated.

·

When there were barking deer

Rachel wondered why it was that she, who was so scared of flying, didn't mind being lowered down the hillside in a two-ton tramcar hanging on the end of a slim, quivering, greasy hawser. Was it just because it ran on a track instead of hurtling through the air, defying the laws of gravity? Well, there it was; she felt no tremor as the green, steeply sloping car jerked its way down through the trees towards the distant harbour, while the conductor apparently controlled their progress with a wooden stick he casually poked into some bit of machinery in the front. The car was empty apart from a few twittering Filipinas, a bearded tourist with a camera, and two neat grave amahs carrying large black handbags. Rachel looked down absorbed at rows of ships moored in the harbour, at white glittering apartment-blocks sliding past, at green asphalt tennis-courts, on which women in short white skirts silently ran and swung their rackets in a moving tableau of middle-class colonial wives at their morning leisure.

Leaving the terminus with its trashy tourist boutiques, she followed Dimitri Johnston's directions to a bus stop in front of a primary school, where English children in grey-and-white school uniforms were playing in their intermission. Where were all the teeming Chinese?

She waited in the shade of the flat-topped bus-shelter, her dollar thirty cents ready in her hand, while a four-lane stream of cars, lorries and buses rushed snorting past. The sky was a whitish blue, incandescent. The white walls of the building opposite dazzled her with reflected sunlight. A Union Jack hung exhausted from a tall white pole. She had walked no more than two hundred yards at most, but her skin was damp all over with sweat.

A blue double-decker bus with 3 on the indicator pulled into the stop. She dropped her money down the funnel as the bus jolted forward. 'University?' she asked the driver, who was listening to a transistor, one slippered foot negligently resting on the rattling engine-case, the other on the pedal.

'Uh?' He scowled at her behind opaque dark shades.

'Dai hoh tong?' she repeated in her first ever attempt at Cantonese. 'University?'

He jerked both his head and the pedal simultaneously, and she was sent staggering down the bus till she caught hold of a stanchion and swung herself into a seat. Silent Chinese passengers regarded her with obliquely swivelling eyes in straight unmoving faces.

The bus careered along a narrow road lined with shabby houses, shops, food-stalls, cramped apartment buildings and grimy hole-in-the-wall garages. Here the teeming Chinese were, then — only they weren't teeming, they were sauntering in twos or threes, haggling, drinking tea, hanging caged birds to sing out of dusty barred windows or from tiny verandas loaded with potted plants.

She counted the traffic lights — the first stop after the third lights, Dimitri Johnston had said. There'd be a bit of green and some trees on her left just before it.

The green appeared, shaded by spreading banyan trees. She stumbled to the door and jumped off, together with several young Chinese (students, she guessed), as the bus ground and jerked to a halt, then lurched away.

She looked up at the university. It seemed to be climbing step by precarious step up another slope of the very hill she'd just descended in the tram. An old spacious colonial building came first, veranda'd, pillared and towered, with tall palm trees along its facade. Then, on successive shelves above and round it, massive concrete blocks rose up, each one newer than the one below, hemming in the original leisurely building in what Rachel thought was a frowning, disapproving way. Still further up the hill, bulldozers were tearing out yet another site.

As she was finding her way up flights of stone steps to Dimitri Johnston's room on the top floor of the colonial building, she glimpsed bands of students in identical T-shirts parading on the paths outside, shouting slogans in response to some leader's commands.

Dimitri was watching, too, from the window of his room. 'Reminds me of the Red Guards,' he told Rachel, as she came in. 'Except that this is innocent, I suppose.'

'Is it a fraternity thing?'

'Sort of. An initiation rite for the freshmen. I don't think they quite realize they're imitating puerile English customs foisted on them in the twenties. *Ragging*, my school used to call it. It was supposed to make a man of you.'

'Was that a public school like' — she just checked herself from saying 'Professor Denton's' — 'like Patrick's?'

'Yes — that is, what Americans call a private school. But not exactly like Patrick's. At my school we weren't quite the sons of gentlemen, so they tried to teach us to behave as if we were. At Patrick's I suspect it was the other way round. As you may have noticed, Patrick's was no more successful than mine was.'

He gestured Rachel to a chair and sat down himself behind his desk. Keeping the barriers up? Rachel wondered. She'd read a book on body language in northern Thailand, discarded in a boarding house by some previous traveller.

'Well, I've been looking at your thesis proposal again,' he said, picking up the sheets she'd typed three months before. 'It's, er, very interesting of course, but' — hesitating, chewing his lip — 'well, I'm not sure Patrick wouldn't be more help to you than I would.'

'That's what he said about you last night.'

Dimitri gave a little twist of a smile, glancing away from her disturbingly unblinking gaze. 'In his case it's probably modesty; in mine it's realism.'

'But your book on Lu Xün was in the same area as my thesis.'

'Yes . . . well, the trouble with that is that some people think it's wrong of course,' he said uncomfortably. 'Besides, I haven't really kept up with all the stuff that's been written since then. Patrick has the advantage of comparative youth there.'

Or absolute youth for that matter. Through the window he could see a bulldozer savaging a mangrove tree on the gashed and rutted hillside where the next disfiguring learning-factory would be built. Watching the tree shuddering against the butting and shoving of the bulldozer's scaly prognathous jaws, he felt himself urging it to resist, glad of the way it swayed back and tossed its head after each rush. It was as if it was *his* life the tree was fighting for, not just its own.

The regimented freshmen had gone, but he could still hear them dutifully baying somewhere about the place.

'D'you mean you don't like my proposal very much? The way I'm approaching it?'

'Oh, no, it's not that at all. I think it's a perfectly good proposal. It's just that . . . . ' How was he to say that he didn't frankly think it mattered a toss whether she wrote it or not? 'It's just that I don't really think I'd be the best person to supervise it, that's all. You see, the thing is, apart from not having done any work on this period recently' — or any other, he thought, — 'the trouble is I'm out of sympathy with a lot of what's going on in the subject now, and, er . . . . '

'Well, I hardly know what *is* going on.'

'And in your own interests I mightn't honestly be the best person to act as your supervisor. I mean, people know that about me, and it might tend to colour their views when they came to examine your thesis. If you see what I mean. Especially if any of my scepticism has rubbed off on you.'

Rachel said: 'Oh.' Then: 'So you won't be able to help at all?'

'Oh, no, I'll always be pleased to talk about it and give you any advice I can; but, as I say, in your own interests — Look, why don't we talk to Patrick first and see what, er . . . see what he thinks about it? There's no need to rush things at this stage. I'll certainly do whatever . . . . ' His voice trailed as he led her to the door. 'Whatever, er . . . . '

Gives you the least trouble? she suggested in her mind.

But Patrick wasn't in his room.

'Well, he is a bit elusive sometimes,' Dimitri said, unsurprised. 'Never mind. We can go and have some coffee first. He's usually here after eleven.'

In the common room, beige-carpeted, with low rattan chairs clustered round glass-topped coffee-tables, only Chinese seemed to be sitting at some tables, only Europeans ('which in Hong Kong means Caucasians,' Dimitri said) at others.

She asked if they were always segregated like that.

'It's a bit like Catholics and Protestants,' he shrugged. 'There's a fair amount of seepage, but some people scarcely ever leave their own little sect. In either direction.'

'Do you?'

'Well, I have married outside my sect after all. Can seepage go further than that?' But he steered her away from where two Chinese were sitting to the only unoccupied table in the room.

'I meant here,' she said stubbornly. 'In the university.'

'I'm no good at social chat. I keep away from everyone.'

'Does that mean we're going to be silent now?'

He stirred his coffee for some seconds. 'Which would you prefer?' he said at last.

A wizened little Englishman with a jutting grey goatee beard joined them before she could answer. 'Hong Kong dollar's on the skids again, Dimitri old chap,' he said with confident gloom. 'Salary won't be worth the paper it's printed on by the end of the month.'

'I thought it had been more or less stabilized.' Dimitri's eyes flickered unsurely between Rachel and the man. 'According to today's paper.'

'Cosmetic. Give the big boys time to pull out. Soon as the hongs have got their money away to Bermuda or wherever — whoosh!' He glanced at Rachel quizzically and, when Dimitri reluctantly introduced her, leant forward, lowering his voice. 'Government's told department heads to prepare for immediate takeover. Fact.'

'Rumour, you mean. I've heard it, too.'

'No, fact. Chap I know saw the memo. Whole place'll go down the tube in a couple of months, mark my words. Well, only got themselves to blame.' He leant back, stirring his tea strenuously, slopping it into the saucer. 'They just don't understand how a capitalist society works.'

'Who don't?' Rachel asked.

'Hark at her. Tell she's not been here long, can't you? Peking of course. Or Beijing if you prefer. A rose by any other name. Some rose. Bloody commissars. Kill the goose and smash the golden egg as well, they will. Takes a genius to do that. Or a commie. They just don't understand. Hong Kong's a confidence trick, and they're taking away the confidence. Place is finished. Just a matter of time. Fact.'

He drank with the satisfied air of the messenger who brings bad tidings, then licked his lips and sucked on his beard.

'Well, Frank, I suppose you got your savings out long ago anyway?' Dimitri asked with what Rachel thought was factitious geniality. 'Before there was even a wobble on the exchange rate.'

'Bet your life I did. What about you?'

'I don't seem to have a head for money matters.'

'Have no bloody head at all if you don't watch out. Well, at least I'm leaving soon, that's one consolation. Like a bride on her wedding night, eh? Nine months, then I'm delivered. What'd you say you're doing here? Thesis, eh? Don't take any notice of me; I'm a nuts-and-bolts man myself. All the same, I'd go back to the States if I were you, double quick about it. Place'll be run by Reds before you've written a line, you mark my words.'

'Shall we see if we can find Patrick,' Dimitri suggested, 'while there's still time?'

They left the air-conditioned room and began to climb the steps again. The tiled corridors of the old building opened on to serene little courts, in which tall palm trees and flowering shrubs grew. In one there was a lily pond, goldfish gliding sinuously beneath the still green surface and the still green leaves.

'Hope he didn't scare you off,' Dimitri said.

'Not as much as you have. I don't see any sign of a crisis, though — except my traveller's cheques were worth more than I expected at the airport.'

'That's the way with crises,' he said. 'Till it's too late.'

'Are there many other eccentrics on the faculty?' Rachel asked, beginning to perspire again.

'Like Frank? He's the best. Or worst.'

'Because I can see why some people might prefer their own little sect to his.'

'Yes. Except that he's quite harmless. He might be right of course, about Hong Kong. Nobody knows. He's writing his autobiography by the way. Or claims to be. He couldn't make up his mind whether to call it *Exotic Nights* or *A Frank Account*. I told him to use both, so one's the title now and the other's the subtitle.'

'Is it any good?'

'I've managed to avoid reading it so far, but one can speculate of course.'

He didn't tell her Frank had come to Hong Kong twenty years before because he'd heard the tropics kept you randy longer. As an author he seemed to be aiming at a work in the Henry Miller genre, although that name had probably never passed Frank's lips or, going the other way, his eyes or ears. 'Who, when, where, how long and how often,' Frank had confided once, bleary at the bar. 'That's what people want to read. When you can't get it up any more, at least you can jot it down.' Frank used to be clean-shaven, till some woman told him his lips were too wet and fleshy, whereupon he'd grown a beard. But the beard only seemed to make them look even wetter and fleshier.

'Yes, he's quite an eccentric,' Dimitri said absently, relieved to hear Patrick's voice ringing out in the department office at the end of the corridor.

'By the way,' he asked Rachel as they went to meet him, 'would you like a ticket for the ballet next Friday? Only, Mila's got some complimentary ones; they're usually quite good seats.'

Consolation prize? Rachel wondered as she unenthusiastically said thanks very much, she'd like to go.

'I'll leave you to Patrick, then,' Dimitri said. 'For the time being.'

Back in his room, he went straight to the window, to see if the mangrove tree was still standing. It was, just, but many of its roots had been shorn away, poking white and splintered through the earth like broken bones. It wouldn't be long now.

And he could remember when there were barking deer on that slope. Ah Wong used to spot them from the kitchen window of the flat they lived in then, and call the children to see. Shy little rust-brown things, hardly bigger than a dog except for their long delicate legs. Helen never watched them. She was always playing the piano or crying. Or both. But he used to follow them with some tatty binoculars from one of the communist stores, taking turns with the children. Not with Ah Wong. She always claimed she couldn't see a thing with them. He'd never set eyes on a barking deer again since the day they moved, soon after Helen killed herself — he hadn't fancied the view from the old place after that.

And now the children were grown up, and Ah Wong's sullenly pretty niece, Ling Kwan, had appeared from China — swum across like Mila, most probably — and occasionally stayed the night, gossiping in a throaty voice that stopped secretively as soon as he entered the kitchen, where Ah Wong cooked elaborate meals for her. And gave her money, he assumed.

The mail had been laid on his desk. The annual record from his Cambridge college, and an invitation to the Hong Kong Students' Nite. From the sublime to the ridiculous — and he was equally distant from each of them. Every year, when the college record arrived, he felt an unstable blend of nostalgia and disgust for all that civilized cosy complacency which he'd deliberately abjured when he came back to work in Hong Kong, where he'd been born. There it was again: achievements in examinations and sports, a bit of college history, letters from old members, notes on the distinctions they were earning in public life . . . . A public school writ large, oleaginous with genteel smugness. Something curdled in him when he read it, yet he read it all the same. And he'd joined the college society and paid his subscription just so that he'd be able to go on reading it, year after year.

And the ambivalence went deeper. He'd approved Alex's decision not to apply to Cambridge, but secretly regretted it. The place was awful but good, awful because it was good. How he detested England sometimes.

The Hong Kong Students' Nites were another world. An underdeveloped world. He'd gone to them out of a sense of duty at first, but then irritation and embarrassment had got the better of him. He wasn't made for playing unselfconscious childish games — once they'd even had to sit in a circle and pass the parcel; another time it was finger-guessing and answering riddles, with fatuous penalties for failing.

'It is because you are too self-important,' Mila mocked him coolly once, meaning *you foreign-devils*. 'You are afraid to behave like children. See how Chinese always take their children along with them when they go out, and play with them? Not like you people with your pompous sense of being adults, too grown-up to play. You worry about face more than we Chinese do.'

'I hate you when you're on your We Chinese kick,' he'd said. 'Especially considering you haven't even got any children to take out and play with.'

'How can I help it if we are better?' she'd smiled, mocking herself now. But the barb about having no children had gone in, and he could tell it hurt. He felt instantly ashamed, but she never reproached him. She never blamed or, for that matter, praised him. She just accepted what came, like sunshine or rain.

He heard a shout outside, a rending of wood and a crackling crash. The mangrove had fallen. The bulldozer snorted triumphantly over the tree's crushed, still-trembling limbs.

Dragons rippling

'And what do I live on if you don't win?' Ling Kwan asked, brushing her hair in front of the little round mirror by the bed. She paused to watch Ah Keung's reflection in the glass. He was pulling on his Hell's Angels shirt, sucking in his belly as he tucked it under his belt. She thought of him laying his belly out along hers again, and then the great weight of him coming down on her breasts.

'Lucky to have a place like this,' he said, nodding at the bare plank walls, the bunk beds, the pitted cement floor. 'Not bad, ah?'

'If only I didn't have to share it with the others,' she pouted, smoothing the rush mat over the board they'd lain on. 'You could come here more often then.'

He started playing with her red fish-shaped moon-lantern, which she'd hung from the roof-beam over her bed after the Moon Festival. He kept tapping its snout with his forefinger, making it spin round and round, then watching it slowly unwind. She'd bought the fish-shaped one because the man said it was lucky for lovers, especially if you took it up high and the candle didn't go out. The other girls had all made fun of her, but she'd carried it up to the top of the hill anyway on Moon Festival night, and the candle hadn't gone out once. So she'd kept it ever since. And when he lay on top of her she could see it over his shoulder before she closed her eyes.

The corrugated-iron roof of the hut made little groaning noises when the sun heated it up. If you stood on the bed to touch it, it burnt your fingers. Like an oven, it was. Then in the night it made the same noises as it cooled down. She would lie awake and listen to it; it was all quiet and peaceful, like the creaking of the oyster-boats back in China. Only there wasn't the sound of the waves, just the others snoring and muttering. Sometimes she imagined Ah Keung lying there with her at night and them both watching the fish as it slowly swung in the hot heavy air.

Every time he tapped the lantern, it made a tight little drum sound, like a tambourine. 'Don't bust it!' she said. 'That's good luck.'

She knew she was going to give him the money; she only wanted him to say something nice about it instead of just expecting it as a matter of course, like he had a right to it or something. Staying away from the factory to be with him was costing her money as well, but he just took it all for granted.

'Luck,' he said. 'I'll show you some luck if you don't come out with that money.'

'Oh, you will, will you? S'pose I haven't got any?' She turned away, pulling the brush through her hair again. All the same, what he did to her today — she'd give him the money and stay away from work a week as well just for that. She loved it how the tattoos moved when he was on top and leaning back from his hips as he pumped into her, the dragons all sort of rippling like they were alive and the sweat all running down his chest in streams. And then the slippery panting weight of him as he collapsed all over her and she hugged him tight with both arms round his back.

She held the brush still, her head on one side, just thinking about it.

'Come on,' he said, snapping his fingers. Not impatiently — just to let her know. 'Don't keep me waiting.'

Someone was drawing water from the standpipe outside. They listened to the can banging and scraping on the stony path, and the changing pitch as the water level rose inside it. There was a smell of kerosene, too, from the next hut. Those people from Hai Feng, they were always cooking.

'And if you don't win?' she asked, handing him the money in a tight wad.

'It's fixed, isn't it, ah?' He peeled the notes back carefully, counting them one by one. 'Besides, you can always get some from your aunt, can't you? Working for a foreign-devil, she must make thousands.'

They left together, she locking the padlock carefully behind them, and picked their way down the hillside along the crooked uneven paths. The air steamed and shimmered over the iron roofs of the shanty village. Dogs yelped from empty huts as they passed, old women peered out at them from half-open doors, all shadowy themselves in the shadows. A younger woman was squatting in one doorway with a sleeping baby strapped to her back, chopping, peeling and scraping for the midday meal. A transistor radio stood on a stone beside her, with someone singing a catchy song. Ling Kwan started humming along with it.

'Like one?' Ah Keung said, nodding at the woman.

'Radio?'

He grinned. 'Baby.'

'Crazy!'

A blue and red Nationalist flag was still hanging from the roof of the old hut near the latrines, left over from the Double Tenth, when half the village flew them. What would happen to all those people if China took back Hong Kong? What would happen to her and Ah Keung?

They could see the traffic on the highway below them now, screaming along in double lanes. It was funny looking down on all those buses and lorries and cars. They looked so small. Like they were only toys or something, rushing along beneath you. Or like it must be from a plane, Ling Kwan thought.

'I'd like to fly in a plane one day,' she said. 'Wouldn't you? Go to America, ah?'

Ah Keung shrugged.

Wouldn't leave it too long

Michael met Yin Hong in a little Shanghainese restaurant in North Point. 'No one'll notice us there,' Yin Hong had said on the phone. 'Only don't bring your car. Take a taxi. There's nowhere to park.'

Michael was punctual — when was he not? — but Yin Hong was there before him, sitting in the back where he could watch the door. He gave a familiar patronizing, elder-brother kind of wave when Michael hesitated at the doorway, looking round. Michael made his way unsmiling towards him. The tables were small and close together, the chequered cloths stained, worn and faded. Yin Hong pushed a chair out with his foot and simultaneously offered his hand. 'How're you doing?'

'All right,' Michael said.

There was a thick steamy smell from the kitchen behind them, wafted out by the squeeching service-door, which flapped and swung irregularly like the valve of a leaky heart. *His own?* Michael wondered.

Yin Hong ordered noodles for both of them, and a bottle of beer. While they ate, he talked in spasmodic jaunty Shanghainese slang about the old days in Shanghai. For all his jauntiness, his age showed in his peachy eyes and the chicken skin beneath his jaw. And the buttonholes of his shiny double-breasted jacket were frayed.

After they'd finished, he came to business, speaking quickly and insistently like a salesman, his eyes alertly scanning Michael's face for signs of resistance or yielding. Only the salesman's deference was lacking — he belched and hissed as he busily picked his teeth. The restaurant was filling up, and Michael had to lean across the table to hear him above the noise of clerks, taxi-drivers and messengers, all shouting and laughing over their rice or noodles, arguing about the racing tips in their ink-smudged papers, while the agitated service-door squeeched and thudded without rest. Of course he could smuggle Lily out, Yin Hong said. He'd brought dozens out already. As for the cost, he left that vague. 'After all, we *are* old friends, aren't we?' he said with a lubricious grin. 'I won't push you too hard over the money. You can trust me for that, can't you?'

'When did you see her?' Michael asked, ignoring the smarm.

'About a month ago. Some people put us in touch.' He waved his hand airily. 'They knew I could help. Sat and talked to her like I'm talking to you now. Funny, isn't it, her getting fed up with the Reds after all these years, and she used to be so hot on them once? Mind you, she's been through a lot.' He gave Michael a you-don't-need-me-to-tell-you-this look. 'Prison and labour-camp. It takes it out of you, ah? And she's not exactly young any more, is she?'

No more are you, Michael eyed him silently. *No more am I.*

'It's taken it out of her all right. Wouldn't leave it too long if I was you, know what I mean?'

It was safety Michael worried about, watching the toothpick probe Yin Hong's broken worn-down teeth behind his curled lip.

'No problem. We've never lost a soul yet. Don't give it a thought.' Again the airy wave, familiar and patronizing. And the voice like a knife on the grindstone.

He wouldn't hear of Michael's paying for the meal, and left an extravagant tip.

'Going my way?' he asked outside. 'Share a taxi?'

Michael shook his head. 'I'm going to meet a friend,' he said, with a stress on *friend*.

Shadow lay across the path

The old Colonial Cemetery sloped gently up from the entrance-gates opposite the racecourse, a low green hill where dying crosses grew thicker than living trees.

Dimitri arrived a few minutes after Michael, as he usually did.

Michael pointed up the hill. 'The grave I want to look at is over there. It's mostly military people down here.'

Dimitri nodded, surveying the soldierly dead. Their graves paraded like Chelsea Pensioners, not quite in line, tottering and fading here and there, but decorated with confident allegories of eventual resurrection: angels, bibles and sundered chains. Death was a stage-point in those days, not a terminus where everyone got out. No wonder modern tombs were less elaborate.

He followed Michael along the erratic gravel paths, reading the inscriptions on the weathered headstones. *Died of fever, aged nineteen. Drowned off Hong Kong, aged twenty-seven. Called to rest, aged twenty-three. Aged thirty. Aged twenty-one. Aged thirty-four.* . . . He was glad Helen had been cremated. He wouldn't want to find a stone engraved *Killed herself because her husband had a mistress*. Not that he would of course. They'd be more discreet — but, all the same, it would remind him. Better where she was, her ashes scattered over the sea she'd died in.

Aged twenty-four years, he read. *In his thirtieth year*. At least her age would have suited. He glanced at Michael. 'If we'd been born in the East a hundred years ago, we'd have been dead and forgotten long before we were as old as we are now.'

'In my case, I could have been dead twice over,' Michael remarked matter-of-factly. He was panting faintly from the climb. 'It was malaria and cholera mainly.'

'Yes.'

'So far as one can tell from the records.'

'Yes.' Dimitri knew, but also knew that Michael couldn't miss things out when it came to history.

'Then dysentery and typhoid. Even plague occasionally.'

Dimitri nodded, and Michael thought of the little rat-bins you could still see about the place, from the last plague outbreak in the twenties. The Government had had them fixed to lamp-posts for dead rats to be put in, and a van would come round once a day to collect them for examination. But as the old lamp-posts were replaced the bins were vanishing. He felt an irrational regret at that. He'd have liked to see the past embalmed, nothing lost, not even the rat-bins.

'Whose grave are we looking for actually?' Dimitri asked.

'The Cantonese wife of a minor official called Caldwell, who came here about a hundred and forty years ago when Hong Kong was first founded. I need the inscription from her grave for the paper I'm writing on her husband.'

'Oh.'

'She's just up there, round the corner,' Michael said, as if they'd find the little old Cantonese woman waiting for them by her grave, bowing and smiling a welcome in her century-old clothes. 'Mary Ah Yow Caldwell, she's called.'

'Why Caldwell incidentally?'

Michael looked at him, puzzled. 'Why . . . ?'

'I mean, what got you interested in him? A minor official, you said.'

'Oh.' Michael stopped to get his breath back. 'Parallels with my father in Shanghai,' he said after a while. 'They both came out as junior officials. Both married Chinese women of rather dubious reputation — Caldwell got his wife from a brothel, and my mother was an opera singer, which wasn't considered to be much better. That caused them both a lot of trouble with the Europeans of the time. And they were both suspected of some sort of shady dealing.' He kept pausing for breath between short rushes of speech. 'Caldwell had his ups and downs like my father. Made money, nearly went bankrupt, made money again. And ended up being lionized by the very people who'd despised him in the beginning. I suppose my father did, too, in a way, sixty years later in Shanghai.'

'Sounds as though you should be writing about your father, then.'

'Yes,' Michael said. 'Caldwell's house was on the same site as mine by the way. Same foundations in fact. You can see them in the cellar.'

'That's the kind of thing that's supposed to send shivers down your back.'

'It does.'

They began walking again.

'Why don't you, then — or have you?'

'Write about my father? I might find out something I didn't want to know.'

About his opium deal, for instance, he thought, which saved him when he was nearly ruined. Lily, pure righteous Lily, used to cast that in his teeth before she left home. Was it legal or wasn't it? At best it must have been unsavoury. The shadow lay across the path. Did Michael want to cross it? Then there was that question about the ransom when he himself was kidnapped, the question his mother often raised in murky hints, especially when she was older and the chains of reticence or discretion were loosening; raised, but never answered. Could his father have paid the money earlier and thereby saved that excruciating mutilation of his finger? He felt the stump curling against his palm like a severed worm writhing, as the pain reached through his memory again. The concrete floor, the terror, the bloodstained quilt he'd lain on, the feeling of his joint being hacked through like meat at a butcher's. He imagined his father waiting for news, balancing his nine-year-old son's finger, or his hand, or his life, against a million Shanghai dollars. Even now, over fifty years later, he didn't want to know the truth. Perhaps Lily knew. He wouldn't ask her. Even if she came out of China, still he wouldn't ask.

They crossed a narrow stream that gurgled down beside the ossuary. Michael led the way into a secluded little clearing, unkempt and forgotten-looking, as though the graves there were too old, the dead too obscure, to deserve the same care as the rest.

But someone must have cared — there were lilies on Mary Caldwell's grave. They couldn't have been more than a day old; when Michael stooped to read the inscription, he smelt their rich heavy scent, the clinging sweet smell of funerals. Who had put them there? The thought of finding out filled him with a stolid joy.

He started copying the words down into his notebook. But the stone had worn and mouldered, and the leaves overhead threw flickering shadows across it. Some of the smaller letters were too uncertain for his eyes. 'Can you read that?' he had to ask Dimitri, who was gazing round at the collapsed, collapsing stones.

' "Dawn," ' Dimitri said. ' "Until the day dawn." '

' "Dawn," ' Michael repeated slowly, tasting it as he copied it down. The words looked hazy as he wrote; he couldn't hold the book far enough away to bring them into sharpness. How long before the fraying of his once-keen sight would spread to the rest of his mind? When would his memory begin to crumble, his hearing dull, his thinking soften? When would his heart send out another warning?

He shut it out and went on writing.

The first warning had been five years ago, and that was why he panted now, climbing hills. When he was fifty-nine, he'd fainted after swimming from the beach to his boat, no more than two hundred yards. Grace wasn't there; he couldn't recall why now. He'd been alone with Paul and Ah Man, the boat-boy. He came round slowly on the deck, to see Ah Man bending over him with anxious eyes, Paul leaning over Ah Man's shoulder with curious eyes, and behind them both the empty sky, which seemed emptier than he'd ever seen it before, like yet another eye, enormous, blank and staring. 'It's nothing,' he told Ah Man, and by the time they reached the harbour he did feel better. Yet he was still weak. When he walked he felt unsteady; when he spoke his voice was like an echo of his voice. He didn't tell Grace; he didn't tell his doctor son Peter — let alone consult him. He went to a heart specialist, a young Chinese from Harvard, who took down his history with a quiet, downturned, attentive face. Michael gazed at his long lean fingers curling supply round the pen. Were his parents still living? the doctor asked discreetly. 'No. My father died of heart disease, my mother died of cancer.' That wasn't quite true, but it was near enough. His mother had killed herself by swallowing opium, rather than undergo the disfiguring operation that might have saved her.

'What age did your father die?'

The doctor nodded when Michael told him. *That figures*, the nod said. Michael felt his heart thud briefly like a prisoner awaiting sentence.

After he'd examined him, the doctor said: 'Your heart isn't pumping quite enough. It wears out like a car engine — even a Rolls Royce, and yours isn't exactly that. Plus, there's liquid building up which it doesn't clear away. Your father probably had the same problem. I'm going to prescribe some pills to help. We can adjust the dose to suit you, but for one week start with two a day.'

'How long?' Michael asked.

The doctor shrugged, pursed his lips.

'I mean how long will I have to take the pills?'

'Oh, as long as you live. Which could perfectly well be a good many years.'

How many years made a good many? He didn't ask.

So it's the age to begin the medicines of age, he thought. At sixty they started treating you as a geriatric when you fell ill. He was only a year too soon.

'What are those?' Grace asked when she saw him take the pills that night.

'Heart pills.' He explained the symptoms and the diagnosis calmly, matter-of-factly, and she listened as calmly (He didn't know Ah Man had already told her about his fainting). She didn't say a word, but he supposed she was taking it all in whole, to separate and think about in her silences. He was glad she didn't comment. After all, what was there to say?

For a few weeks he woke up every night, and his first thought was death. Not the fear of death he used to feel when he was young, the first full realization that even he must end; not the terror he felt when he was kidnapped; not the terror he felt in '43 when the Japanese bombs entombed him in Chungking — because then there was always still the hope at least of an indefinite future — but the plain cold certainty of it. Yes, it was like being sentenced, only with a stay of execution. A good many years. And his father had died at seventy-two. He wasn't afraid, yet. But he felt as if he had two shadows now, a short one which was his own, and a longer which was death.

Then one night he told Grace of his death-thoughts and the feeling that he had two shadows. 'Doesn't everyone feel that?' she asked, surprised. After that he slept more easily. And he'd never had another attack. He almost forgot why he was taking the pills, though he never forgot to take them. He never worried about that other shadow any more, either. He'd grown used to it.

'I saw that man about my sister,' he said to Dimitri as he straightened up. 'The one who posted the letter to me. It looks as though it really is genuine. I thought so all along.'

'What are you going to do?'

'I'm giving him a letter for her. Then we'll see. It could be complicated, getting her out.'

'I imagine it could.'

Michael stood a moment looking at the grave. It was so quiet they could hear the leaves rustling and the flutter of birds' wings. It couldn't have been much quieter when Mary Ah Yow Caldwell was buried here, the Chinese wife of an enigmatic Englishman whose obscure descendants apparently still left flowers on her grave — as he still left flowers on his mother's grave, the Chinese wife of another enigmatic Englishman.

'A remarkable woman,' he said, turning away.

'Your sister, or Mary Caldwell?'

'Both, but I was thinking of Mary Caldwell.' Now, however, as they walked back, past the stream and the ossuary, he thought of his sister Lily. His mother, with her scorching protective love of her half-breed children, had made him promise before she died to do what he could for Lily. Now the promise was being called in. And, because he'd promised, he'd have to do it. But not only because he'd promised.

When he first opened Lily's letter and saw what it was, he took it out into the garden to read, as he did every letter that looked ominous. He wanted to be alone when he read it, so that nobody would catch the expression on his face. It was one layer of the thick protective shell which his Eurasian birth and upbringing, everything that had happened to him when he was young, had made him grow gradually round himself. He must not give himself away.

Preparing for the worst was another layer. He never let himself expect life to go well. Ever since his kidnapping, he'd been waiting for the next catastrophe, the next sudden dip of Fortune's wheel. He'd prepared for it as well as he could by making money — a good bit of money — but also by discounting its worth, devaluing it in his own eyes, so that he wouldn't fall so hard if, as somehow he was sure it must, it all deserted him in the end and let him drop alone again, onto a concrete floor.

In an ideal world, he would have been a historian. If the war hadn't come, perhaps he would have been one in the real world, too. But the war, and his mother's hectoring, settled it. *What use is history?* he remembered her demanding in that different time before the war, sitting in the house on the Bund, perhaps in the very bedroom that Lily had a share of now (No, it was the living-room; he saw it clearly in his head, a sepia photograph, misty at the edges — the evening sunlight sliding through the slatted rattan blinds). *You're a half-breed; you've got to make money. That's the only way you're going to get by.* She was still hectoring him when she followed him to Hong Kong after the war, where nothing pleased her much except mahjong, her grandson Patrick, whom she spoiled, and newly married Grace — *Shanghainese, good. You can't trust these southerners an inch.*

Well, by the time he was forty-five he'd made money, enough to live off and to take up history again, in the only, insignificant, way that was still open to him. It had gone against the grain, though, making money. As it had with his father. For both of them the real thing was elsewhere.

'My father really wanted to live in an English country house with a music room and a library,' he said abruptly as they walked slowly back towards the cemetery gates. 'Except that he was out of place in England in the end.'

'Don't we all?' Dimitri shrugged. 'Aren't we all?' He gestured at the ageing monuments of empire-builders, missionaries and adventurers all round them. 'Including this lot here.'

'Not my sister Lily. She never wanted an English country house. All she wanted was a revolution.'

'Well, she certainly got one.'

Communist's communist

No, not Lily. She'd been a communist's communist, inflexibly denouncing their father's leisured wealth, and later his own, too — though not above living off it when necessary. Or just convenient. But, then, he scarcely knew his stiff-necked and demanding sister any more (Only a grudging please, and no thank-you at all in her letter, he'd noticed, as if she'd got a natural right to whatever he could offer). He'd only really known her as a boy, and then only till the day he was sent off to school in England. While he was learning to become an English gentleman she was learning to become a Chinese communist. (Neither of them quite succeeded, though. Well, what could you expect of Eurasians?) When he came back she was pregnant with Patrick, or Pak Kay as she preferred to call him, after his martyred communist father.

Michael had never seen much of her from the time he was twelve, except for that brief period in Chungking during the war, when she was interpreting for the communists and he for the British. Since then he'd seen her just twice. First at their mother's funeral, when she'd already been purged and rehabilitated once, then immediately before the Cultural Revolution, when she'd tried to persuade Patrick, just down from Cambridge (on Michael's money, too — no word of thanks for that, either), to join her in China. *Building a new society* she called it, with no sense that she was mouthing slogans, still less that the slogans might be surrogates for thought. 'My dear mother,' Patrick protested, 'it sounds like bricklaying.' She didn't persist. Probably his decadence gave her a grim satisfaction, confirming her belief in the corruption and imminent collapse of capitalism. Besides, how could she really care about her son? She'd left him with her mother when she joined the guerrillas, and seen him only twice since in twenty-five years, during which she'd remarried and divorced — something she'd stated drily at her mother's funeral and never alluded to before or since.

He scarcely knew her any more than Patrick did, whom he'd brought up as his own son and given his own name. What did he owe her, apart from that promise exacted by his mother?

His life, unfortunately.

Deep in the back of his brain was a memory as vivid as a cave painting untouched by light since the day it was done. Yes, a cave painting, he thought wryly. As vivid as the memory of his kidnapping. He didn't visit it often, except involuntarily in nightmares. The Japanese bombs were falling in Chungking, falling nearer, shaking the earth like drunken giants stumbling clumsily towards them. The two of them had scrambled into one of those urine-smelling caves that everyone sheltered in during air-raids. He remembered the crash, remembered knowing instantly he'd been hurt, remembered coming round in utter darkness, bleeding, choking with limestone dust, his legs numb. It was the pitch-blackness that was worst, and the silence. And the terror that the invisible roof might come down and crush him at any moment, but not kill him outright, so that the rats would get to him before he died. He screamed and shouted, and his puny voice was smothered without an echo.

It was Lily who made them dig him out. They hadn't wanted to; they said it was a waste of time. Yet when they finally pulled him clear she was as brisk and impersonal as a nurse, as if to say, *I'd have done it for anyone. Don't think I did it because you're my brother.*

Why had she amputated all her feelings?

4

Like a landed fish

Yin Hong and Ah Keung followed Limpy down the lanes behind Jardine's Bazaar, where teeming Saturday-afternoon shoppers were picking over the bargains on the hawkers' stalls. After a time, Limpy stopped at a kerbside restaurant and sat down near the owner, who was frying fish balls in a great black sizzling wok. The place was crowded. Nearly every stool round the plank tables was taken. Worn-out old coolies with bony cheeks and bloodshot eyes hunched over their rice-bowls beside loud flabby taxi-drivers resting and gambling between shifts.

Yin Hong nudged Ah Keung. Ah Keung nodded; he knew what to do. Yin Hong waited until Ah Keung had slipped round behind Limpy, then he strolled towards him.

Limpy's eyes flared when he saw Yin Hong. He started up, but Ah Keung just laid his hands on Limpy's shoulders and pushed him down. It looked as friendly as could be.

'Surprised you're eating in a place like this,' Yin Hong said with a nice smile. 'With all that money of ours you've got, ah?'

'What money?' Limpy acted all surprised and innocent, but it didn't come off. 'I'm broke. I lost the same as you did.' He tried to shrug Ah Keung's hands off, but Ah Keung just dug his fingers in a bit till he winced.

'Thought you'd be eating somewhere posh,' Yin Hong said. 'Spend a bit of the loot.'

A bowed grey-haired coolie in dark shorts and a white singlet got up abruptly from the next table and shuffled away on his rubber sandals, like a man who didn't want to be a witness.

Yin Hong pulled his empty stool across and sat down opposite Limpy, watching him all the time.

'So what happened, Limpy?' He didn't sound so friendly now. 'You give us a tip, you tell us it's fixed, you take our money and the horse trots in last, farting like a pig. What sort of tip was that?'

'I know, I know. I lost money, too.'

'How do we know you lost money? Maybe you never put our bet on that carthorse? Maybe you put it on the winner, ah?'

'Now, wait a minute. I wouldn't do that; you know I wouldn't!' Limpy turned on the charm now, squeezing a smile out all over his face. 'I lost money, too. I'm just as sore as you are.' His eyes kept sliding from side to side, as if he'd forgotten he was lame and couldn't run fast anyway.

Ah Keung dug down into his shoulders till he yelped. A few heads turned to have a look what was going on, but they were careful so they wouldn't get mixed up in anything. When Yin Hong just stared at them they looked away, all except a big fat taxi-driver who held on to the finger-wide card he was going to play till his partner gave him a nudge.

'We want our money back,' Yin Hong said with a bit more edge. 'We feel like we've been taken for a ride. We want it back. All right?'

Limpy wriggled and yelped again when Ah Keung dug a bit deeper with his fingers. 'I don't have it,' he whined. 'I lost the same as you.'

'We don't give a fuck if you lost or not. *We* lost, didn't we? You gave us a lousy tip, and we want our money back. OK?'

Limpy nodded at last, and Ah Keung let go. Limpy went loose, rubbing his shoulders and sighing. The fat taxi-driver took another look and gave a little snigger like he thought it was funny.

'That hurt,' Limpy moaned, rocking to and fro. 'You didn't have to do that.'

Then — Yin Hong didn't see how it happened — Limpy had suddenly lunged sideways, grabbed a cleaver from the block on the stall, and was on his feet, slashing and flailing with it, shouting like crazy. 'Get off! Get *off*! Get *off*!'

The stall-owner ducked away, Ah Keung tried to grab Limpy from behind, dodging his clumsy swipes, and Yin Hong got a hand on the steaming wok.

'Look out, Ah Keung!'

Ah Keung jumped back just in time as Yin Hong tipped the boiling oil out over Limpy. It spattered his chest and legs. The fish balls rolled into the gutter, still sizzling. Then Limpy dropped the cleaver. And started screaming.

They could still hear him screaming after they'd dashed round the corner, thirty yards away. Nobody at the stall had moved. They'd all frozen, even the big slob of a taxi-driver, with the grin still stuck there on his face.

All except Limpy. He was moving all right, he was jumping and flapping like a landed fish.

In Hennessy Road they forced themselves to walk naturally. Well, Ah Keung forced himself; Yin Hong couldn't have run much further anyway. Then Ah Keung waved a taxi down. 'Where to?' he asked Yin Hong, cool as ice.

'Star Ferry,' Yin Hong panted as he slammed the door.

The driver nodded, palmed the flag down and turned his radio up louder.

Yin Hong's hand was burnt where he'd grabbed the wok. He sucked it quietly between breaths.

'You'll have some blisters there,' Ah Keung said, twisting round to peer out of the rear window.

'Not as many as he'll have, I won't.' He was still all wound up and excited, his pulse was going like mad, like it used to in the old days when they had the big triad fights. 'Anyone coming, is there?'

Ah Keung turned back, shaking his head. The driver was deep in his radio, he didn't notice a thing. Ah Keung settled down, his neck against the head-rest. 'Pity you didn't get his face,' he muttered casually, like he was talking about the weather or something. 'That would've really fixed him.'

'Never've thought he'd got it in him,' Yin Hong said, still breathing jerkily. 'Fancy a lame little runt like him trying that on, ah?'

Buggers jumping

The curtains parted hopefully yet again in the City Hall, although the patter of polite applause was thinning rapidly. The dancers pranced on to bow and curtsy one more time, all glittering eyes and painted smiles.

'I wish they wouldn't treat the curtain calls as part of the act,' Dimitri said. 'It only shows how vain they are.'

'No need to apologize,' Rachel said.

'Was I apologizing?'

'Weren't you?'

'I don't know, now.'

People were getting up, seats thumping back like ragged volleys of muffled rifle-fire.

'I have to go backstage,' Dimitri said as they edged towards the aisle. 'To collect Mila. Are you in a hurry or . . . ?'

'No, I'll come, too. I've never been backstage.'

Dimitri led, forging slowly through the upward and outward-flowing tide of mainly Chinese families with ballet-aged daughters wearing ribbons in their sleek ballet-braided hair. Rachel stepped in his wake.

'I enjoyed it,' Rachel said. 'Very much.'

'Can't really stand it myself.'

'Well, I haven't seen much ballet before — '

'All those tutus and tights and false simpering smiles. If you ask me, it's only suitable for children, imbeciles and lechers of either sex.'

'Well, I guess that just about covers everyone,' Rachel said.

A hand light as a canary's claw touched Dimitri's wrist before he could answer, assuming that he could have answered at all, which at that moment he doubted. He turned to see the ancient brittle figure of Osip Brodsky bearing the weight of a too-large suit as he waited to get out of one of the side-rows. The matron of the *Wayfarers' Home*, dressed in black skirt and ample blouse, was supporting his elbow.

'Osip! What are you doing here?'

'Came to see the ballet,' the matron answered loudly for Osip, as if he were a deaf child. 'He often comes, don't you, Mr. Brodsky, when you feel up to it?'

Osip's eyes were as bird-like as his hand, brown alert little buttons each side of his thin beaky nose. His scant fluffy white hair floated lightly round his head as he nodded at Rachel.

'This your daughter?' he asked in a wavery voice that still retained its strong Russian accent.

'No, Elena was on stage.'

'Oh, yes, of course, Elena, the blonde one.' He smiled and nodded. 'How she's grown. And your son's at university still?'

'He's finished now. He's a schoolteacher, here in Hong Kong.'

Osip nodded again and again, like a bird pecking up its seed. 'So long since I've seen them,' he said. 'I must drop in on you one of these days.'

'I'll drop in on you,' Dimitri said guiltily. 'I've been meaning to, only . . . . '

'You'd like that, wouldn't you?' the matron said to Osip, but looking at Dimitri with a level blue-eyed gaze. 'Not so easy to gad about these days, is it, what with the crowds and the traffic, when you're getting on?'

'No. I'll drop by soon.'

'Well, we'd better be moving, now the crush has gone. Don't want to be back too late, do we, Mr. Brodsky?'

Dimitri stood aside to let them pass. The matron helped Osip patiently up the stairs while Osip chattered volubly to her in his high feeble voice, fluttering his free arm as he slowly climbed.

'A friend of my mother's,' Dimitri said, still watching Osip. 'Did I tell you she was a White Russian? Osip was a rich White Russian once. Played the stock market. Now he's just a poor white. Lives in a home for expatriate flotsam. And jetsam.'

'There are poor whites in Hong Kong as well?'

'As well as in America, or as well as rich ones?' He went on towards the stage door. 'Either way the answer's yes. Hong Kong will surprise you, I can tell you that. It's not what it seems.'

'What does it seem?' Rachel asked, but he pretended not to hear.

They clambered over flimsy quivering flats and props, which stage-hands were already casually dismembering. 'Very good,' Rachel said to Mila and Elena, hoping she could deceive them at least. 'Of course I've never seen much ballet but. . . .' But really she agreed with Dimitri. The whole thing was just too pretty for her. Pretty music, pretty postures, pretty, silly stories. And Elena's larger-boned paler body (small though it was for a European's) had looked out of place alongside all those daintier Chinese figures.

'This is Tom,' Elena said, garish as a child's painting in her exaggerated make-up. 'He doesn't know anything about ballet, either; you've got something in common there. But he only came to see me anyway, didn't you, Tom?'

'Hi,' Tom said. He was tall, saturnine, and looked ten years older than Elena.

'He's a journalist,' Elena announced to Dimitri in a stage-whisper. 'Look at his hands, they're the best thing about him. Almost. He was in Vietnam.'

'Are you American?' Rachel asked, feeling abruptly she'd been away too long already.

Tom seemed to think that needed some reflection. He gazed at Rachel unfocusedly for two or three seconds. 'Nobody's perfect,' he said at last.

She glanced round at the ropes and curtains, at the debris of the illusion. 'How did you like it?'

'Vietnam, or the ballet?' Tom asked in a monotonous quiet voice, swaying faintly to and fro on his feet.

'I guess the ballet would get a shorter answer.'

Tom shrugged. 'Like Vietnam,' he said in the same dead level tone. 'Just dragged on too goddam long.'

Elena seemed not to have heard. 'Where's Patrick?' she called in her sharp British voice, craning her neck. 'Didn't he come? I'd've thought watching buggers jumping would be right up his street.' She ran off on her toes as if she were still on stage, to embrace one of the Chinese male dancers and gossip with him in Cantonese.

'I think I'd better be going,' Rachel said. Elena's artificial gestures, her mockery, her over-exhilaration — she found them all too much. And she guessed Tom was either drunk or drugged.

'We'll give you a lift,' Dimitri offered. 'Mila's just coming.'

Elena tripped back on her toes again. 'Tom, will you take me to supper and tell me how good I was?' she demanded as the others waved goodbye, picking their way to the stage-door. 'And drink champagne from my slipper?'

But in the taxi she drooped against him disconsolately. 'I was awful, wasn't I? I came off point twice and I missed a cue. Did you notice? Don't say you weren't looking.'

'Who cares if you came off point? It was your legs I came to watch, not your toes.'

'Honest? Were they pretty?' She sucked in her belly, took his hand and eased it down inside her skirt. 'You can't imagine how nice that feels. I'd know your hand anywhere. Even blindfold. Am I all sweaty? I'm too tired to eat. Just take me home and put me to bed and never take your hand away.'

'We'll be arrested,' Tom said, going exploring.

A woman's dulcet Cantonese voice declared after the chimes on the taxi's radio that the Chinese delegation considered the negotiations on Hong Kong's future had made no progress whatsoever so far.

'Couldn't say that about you, though, could they?' Elena murmured, wriggling lower down on the seat. 'You're making excellent progress, aren't you? Surmounting every obstacle on the way to your goal. D'you think I'm terribly lewd? I'm only like this about once a month, you know, so if you're really interested you'd better make the most of it.'

No one except herself

Why did Rachel keep on with her diary day after day, year after year? Who was it for? She had no close friends, let alone a lover. She'd never get married or have children. Why did she still sit down nearly every night (she knew why she'd started, but why go on?), recording the ephemeral banalities of her solitary life, when no one except possibly herself would ever read them?

No one except herself, the answer came echoing back off the walls of her single room, the long narrow corridors of her unaccompanied existence. Of course, that was why. If she didn't talk to herself in those pages, she'd never talk to anyone, and her life would pass unnoticed, even by herself. Her diary was the photo-album of her days. She rarely looked back in it, and never at the early agonies it began with — thank God they were over now — but at least it was there. Perhaps she would read through it all one day when she was old, revisiting her life in one long synoptic glance before she died. Like someone looking through old photos, assembling them in order, assigning each its time and place. Then perhaps she'd burn it. There'd be no one to leave it to after all.

Would she ever be able to read those earliest entries, though — those jagged silent screams of anguish scribbled in blue biro at the back of her school exercise book, when her mother had just walked out on her father and her? *The most terrible thing in the world has just happened,* she knew it began, in that large spiky scrawl which had never really changed since then, *the worst thing that could possibly happen.* And then again, later, when Jenny had appeared, brassy and loud, and married her father — how she'd resented that, without saying a word to him, keeping it all in, all in her diary anyway.

At least things were calmer now. She supposed they'd stay that way till the end of her life. She liked that; she hated turbulence.

She found during her adolescence that she wasn't interesting to boys. Nor were they interesting to her. There was little that was feminine about her. She had an angular sharp body and an angular sharp mind. Boys found both uncomfortable. She wondered at college whether she was lesbian; but girls didn't attract her, either. She'd attended a few consciousness-raising feminist sessions, but grim evangelical fervour, pimples and tufty armpits had put her off. She decided she must be neuter, something to do with her hormones. It didn't bother her.

There was a time when Jenny took a bossy interest, though, and compared her development unfavourably with her own grown-up children's — one just married, one already divorced. Having no boyfriends at seventeen seemed unnatural to Jenny, a matter for the analyst. But Rachel could be stubborn, and her father, with his mild owlish eyes, had stood, however meekly, by her side. Then Jenny lost interest. She was having trouble with her own analyst, whom she was consulting for what she called her stress syndrome.

'He asked me when I'd stopped masturbating,' she told Rachel with a measuring sidelong look.

'I don't want to hear about your analyst, Jenny.'

'Why ever not? Well, what d'you mean by "masturbating"? I said. Know what he said? I think he's really prissy. "Auto-stimulation of erogenous zones for purposes of sexual gratification," he said. I swear he was blushing. Oh, I said, I've never stopped that. What are *you* blushing for?'

Rachel came to think of her diary as her analyst — what else did analysts do anyway, except listen to you talking to yourself?

Her gaze was not as disturbingly direct as it seemed; it was partly myopic. All through her teens she'd worn glasses, then at college she'd tried contact lenses, but they made her eyes water. When she lost them in the swimming pool, she didn't replace them.

For years now she'd worn neither glasses nor lenses and was growing slightly round-shouldered from bending too close over her books. Often she didn't recognize people in the blur across the street, but she wore a perpetual, amiably wry grin, which compensated.

San San's been helping me find an apartment. I pick out ads from the Chinese papers and she talks in Cantonese for me on the phone. Usually, as soon as they find out it's for a foreign-devil they say it's already gone, or raise the price. But there's a place on Cheung Chau (one of the nearby islands) which we're going to see next week. The landlord speaks some Mandarin and English, luckily. Ah Yee heard about it from someone. It's about an hour on the ferry apparently.

(Later.) Grace, said she wouldn't dream of letting us go on the ferry, so we're going on their launch. How she imagines I'd actually live there if I rented the apartment I don't know.

Taken Dimitri Johnston's hint about the thesis. Patrick Denton will be the main adviser, with Dimitri in the background — doing nothing, I guess. Probably means he has no confidence in it. Or me.

Went there for dinner last night, with San San and Alex, Dimitri's son. He dotes on San San. I can't see why; she's just an ordinary girl, though quite pretty. I guess I'm colour-blind in that dimension, though. The best part of the evening was hearing about the ghost that's supposed to be there. Their amah joined in. Very lively, says she KNOWS there are ghosts, with such conviction you have to believe her.

They'd sat on the Johnstons' veranda, in rattan and bamboo chairs that were frayed and creaking, looking out over a band of moon-flecked sea to a fishermen's island opposite, where a few dim lights gleamed on the shore and a humpish hill blacked out the lower sky.

Rachel asked them about ghosts. Michael had told her a few days before of the ghost that the servants saw in his own house. They often saw a man standing by the door of Michael's study. When they spoke to him, he turned and disappeared. 'Always at night of course,' he'd said sceptically.

'Is it the man you're writing about, who first lived here?'

'Caldwell?' Michael had shrugged. 'Every old house is supposed to have its ghost. The servants wanted to have it exorcized, but I said I must see it myself first, before I spent all that money on a Taoist priest. Unfortunately I seem too prosaic to see it, though. Too preoccupied with other things.'

Rachel wondered what 'other things' Michael was preoccupied with. His historical research presumably. But every time she asked he just closed up.

'What about Grace? She's not prosaic, is she?'

'No, she's not, but I don't think she'd notice it. It would be the ghost who had to notice her. Otherwise they'd just pass straight through each other.'

She'd thought it a ruefully perceptive joke till she remembered he never joked.

Mila said there was supposed to be a ghost in their house as well.

'I used to hear it on the stairs,' Alex said. 'Because Ah Wong told me it was there.' He asked Ah Wong to show Rachel the place.

Ah Wong led her up two flights of stairs, smiling indulgently like a mother taking her child to a treat. 'Here,' she said emphatically, in her best pidgin, pointing to the top landing. 'Ghosty come boom boom same-same walky. You look see, no can see. Only hear boom boom.' She touched her eyes, her ears, and stamped on the floor, miming every word. 'No frighten, missy. Only naughty people frighten. People no naughty, she no hurt people.'

Rachel had taken a course in folklore and superstition for her master's degree.' How many people hear it?' she asked Mila.

'I don't know. But the cat does.'

'Hear it, she means,' Dimitri said. 'If you take the cat up there, it always bristles in the same place, on that stair Ah Wong showed you.'

Foreign numbers

Ah Wong cleaned the Johnstons' house, washed, shopped and cooked with tireless care and pride. Every morning she swept the fallen leaves from the courtyard and steps, and the swishing scrape of bristles over stone was often the first sound Dimitri heard when he woke. A fisherman-peasant's daughter, she grew plants, too, in the always-shaded strip of earth along the wall, and was nursing a puny papaya she'd raised from a seed in that inhospitable sunless soil.

She tended everything with fastidious care except her own room — that she treated with indifference, as if she were only briefly camping in it. Fluffy curls of dust collected in the corners, the curtains were merely tacked to the window-frames, and the only decoration was an old calendar hanging from a nail in the wall, with glossy gold lettering on it. *Scenic Beauties of China*, it proclaimed in English and Chinese, neither of which could she read. The top sheet, for January 1976, was a colour print of the Altar of Heaven. She never turned to the sheets below. The varnished teak table and bare cement floor — she refused to have a carpet — were half-covered with tightly bound plastic bags containing clothes, blankets, quilts and toys she'd bought for her China people. Every new year she took large bundles of them across the border, but in the following months she always bought more than she'd taken, so that her hoard continually increased while her floor-space diminished.

On the edge of the table were two orange moon-lanterns, old and partly burnt. They were Alex's and Elena's, abandoned with their childhood. She used to keep them for them from year to year, and kept them still.

Most of her own possessions were in a narrow unpainted wardrobe: a few clothes, two pairs of shoes, a large shopping-bag, some photos in an old envelope (cockroaches had long since licked all the gum off the flap), her gold and jade ear-rings, her seal and the pass-books for her substantial savings and gold accounts at the Hongkong Bank (she bought gold whenever the radio announced a dip in the price, but never sold an ounce).

She carried her radio with her wherever she happened to be working, and listened to it incessantly. On the dressing table Dimitri had installed for her she kept her hairpins, soap, toothbrush and a giant metal alarm clock from China, painted a bilious green, with two silvery bells on top that clanged like a fire alarm. She wouldn't have a television set; she believed the flickering light damaged your eyes. Besides, it made you lazy. At night, when she'd finished her work and eaten, she would sit in the dark in her room — in the dark to protect her eyes — and listen to her radio, immobile as a nun at prayer. But, though she heard ghosts and sometimes saw them, she had no altar in her room and burnt no joss sticks.

She had lived like that for twenty years, and Dimitri had never seen her take a broom to the place. Normally she ate in the kitchen, listening to operas or ghost stories on her radio, but when her niece Ling Kwan, her only visitor, came, they would carry their food down into her room and eat there. If Ling Kwan stayed the night, Ah Wong gave her the trestle bed, sleeping as comfortably herself on a straw mat on the floor.

Ling Kwan usually phoned before she came, but this time she just turned up without warning, clacking down the steps to the courtyard in her plastic sandals.

'Eh, Ah Kwan!' Ah Wong turned from the oven. 'Why didn't you phone? I'd have got some pig's trotters from the market.'

'Couldn't get through,' Ling Kwan muttered throatily. She sat on the only chair and started examining her toenails, lifting first one bare foot from its sandal, then the other. Her skin was quite brown — not just her face, even her legs and feet which scarcely got the sun. It was a pity, Ah Wong often told her, because she was good-looking otherwise. But with dark skin like that they'd have a hard job finding her a husband, even if she was a good worker and the factory had taken her on at once. Ling Kwan only shrugged.

Ah Wong quickly fried some fish and rice while Ling Kwan went on silently examining her feet. She was wondering what they would look like if they were bound and small like in the old days. She scarcely noticed when Dimitri came in, and wouldn't even have greeted him if he hadn't spoken first. Ah Wong, embarrassed by her bad manners, tittered uneasily, saying Ah Kwan was very tired. Ling Kwan only drooped her lids, coolly pushing down the quicks of her toenails, her cheek resting on her raised knee.

'All the time worky worky,' Ah Wong apologized in pidgin, so that Ling Kwan wouldn't understand. 'Stupid girl, too tire', no can talky.'

Dimitri smiled unbelievingly. Ah Wong's pouty niece was wearing flimsy cotton polka-dot trousers and a matching blouse which were almost like pyjamas, the cheap kind that people from the mainland bought before they'd made enough money to move up-market. Although she was ignoring him, he sensed from the way she held her head and occasionally glanced up at him under her lids that she wanted him to notice her. Which he did. The tightened thin cloth of her trousers fitted the thigh of her provocatively raised leg like another skin, and she knew it.

'Why didn't you say something?' Ah Wong hissed as the door closed. 'What's he going to think of you?'

'I know what he thinks all right,' Ling Kwan said in her harsh sulky voice. 'See the way he looked at me?'

'Ai-ya, he doesn't want you, crazy girl!' Not that she'd have minded if he did. She expected a man to have more than one woman.

Ling Kwan shrugged. Taking some cotton-wool out of her purse, she pushed little wads of it between her toes.

'What's wrong? What's happened to your foot?'

'Nothing. Just painting my nails.'

'Painting your nails? What kind of girl does that? Toenails, too! Like a Filipina!'

Ling Kwan's tongue peeped between her full lips as she carefully stroked on the scarlet. 'Everyone does,' she said calmly at last, stretching out her leg and turning her foot to consider the effect.

It wasn't till they were downstairs and had finished eating that she took the cotton-wool wads out and dropped them in her empty bowl. 'They're raising the rent,' she said, wiggling her toes. 'I'll have to leave if I can't pay.'

'Come and live here. I'll ask if you can.'

'Too far from the factory. All that way to Kwun Tong.' She was admiring her toes, her head on one side, circling her feet from the ankles. 'If you could lend me some money, till the end of the month . . . ?'

'Ai-ya, Ah Kwan, I've lent you three thousand already!'

'Only till the end of the month. It's only two weeks.'

Ah Wong hesitated, then laid her chopsticks down. She took her savings-book out of the wardrobe, peering uncertainly at the printed figures. All she could read or write was the foreign numbers, and even so she had to work at them.

Whenever she ate, she took her denture out — biting on it made her gums sore. Without the teeth to support them, her cheeks fell in slackly. Ling Kwan watched her aunt mouthing the figures with mumbling lips. She reminded Ling Kwan suddenly of her grandmother in China.

'How much, then?' Ah Wong asked, narrowing her eyes as she frowned down at the little printed marks that she could never quite be sure of.

Or life imprisonment

Michael felt out of place in his lawyer son's office, like a man without a jacket at an executives' luncheon. Up on the thirty-fifth floor, with its muted colours, silent air-conditioning, concealed lighting and sealed port-hole windows looking down on to the harbour, it was like the business-class section of a jetliner, its only character to have no character at all. Apart from the self-effacing law-reports along the wall, the place might just as well have been, and in a couple of hours he supposed could easily become, a dentist's waiting-room or a travel agent's. And John blended with it like a quiet tie.

Michael hardly ever visited the place, but when he did he realized how featureless John's life had become, how wide and empty the space had grown between them.

A girl neat and synthetic as an air hostess had placed a cup of instant coffee beside him. A plastic cup of course. At least the spoon was metal. He sipped the coffee and put it down. Non-dairy creamer — naturally they wouldn't have the real thing. All that was missing was the piped muzak and the in-flight entertainment.

'If your sister entered Hong Kong illegally,' John was saying detachedly, 'which appears to be what you're asking about at present, anyone assisting or abetting would be liable on conviction to a maximum fine of five million dollars or life imprisonment.' He drummed silently with his fingertips on his cheek, as he used to when he did his homework at primary school, before he went to England. No one would guess, just looking at him, that he wasn't fully Chinese, except perhaps from the slightly longer face. Yet he never used his Chinese forename. None of them did except San San, though they'd all been given one. And San San never used her English name. Well, Susan wasn't very exciting; they should have thought of something better. 'Susan wouldn't help me with my concert career,' San San had said when she went to America. 'But San San will. They've got a thing about Chinese names now.'

'They must mean business, then,' he said to John. 'With penalties like that.'

'They do.'

Michael recalled a little boy swinging his feet under the desk, frowning down at his book and drumming on his cheek as John was now. 'Life imprisonment,' he repeated slowly.

'The maximum, yes.' John turned the page. 'There are other possibilities, of course though. Apart from illegal entry, I mean. If she were a political refugee, for instance. But she'd have to prove she was likely to be persecuted if she was returned to China. Which in the present circumstances isn't very likely.'

'Quite apart from the fact that with these rather tricky negotiations going on the Hong Kong government certainly wouldn't want to alienate China just now — assuming Britain would allow them to.'

'It occurred to me she might be able to claim British nationality, since her father was British.'

John had said 'her father' quite impersonally, as though the man wasn't his own grandfather as well. Keeping him at a distance, Michael thought. And Lily as well — John wouldn't call her his aunt. It made him feel held at arm's length himself. But he'd felt that for years. Perhaps he deserved it. Even with his children he couldn't wear his heart on his sleeve.

'But the question would be whether she could prove that, too. Since I gather she was . . . illegitimate?'

'As I was. It made no difference to your grandfather. He married your grandmother as soon as he got his divorce.'

John flushed. 'I mean there'd have to be some documentation,' he went on hastily, like a man trying to ignore another's gaffe. 'And I imagine that might be difficult. And then there's the complication that she's certainly a Chinese citizen, and has been for forty years.'

'Nearer fifty.'

Their father would have been careless about certificates, Michael knew; at least at the time Lily was born. Michael himself had only become British because he needed a passport to go to school in England. But Lily had never left China (*never* — so what conception could she possibly have of the world outside, the world she wanted to join?). For her there'd been no point, until it was too late. 'You didn't need documentation in Shanghai in those days,' he said. 'Anyway, I don't suppose it would have survived all these years even if there was any.'

'If she made an application under that section, it might take years,' John continued, tapping the paragraph with his middle finger. 'But, legally speaking, it's probably the only way. There don't seem to be any strong compassionate grounds for a quick decision. But I gather she's in a hurry.'

'At seventy, you probably are.'

'And I suppose there's no chance at all of her applying for an exit visa from China in the normal way?'

'There'd be no point, would there? In the first place, it would take years; and, in the second, they don't let people out who are going to give them a bad press.'

John drew his lips together in grudging acknowledgement. 'Have you heard from her again?'

'I'm expecting another letter before long. If Yau Yin Hong's to be trusted.' Yin Hong reminded him of his mutilated finger. He began massaging the stump, not because it ached — not in the drier weather — but as a kind of solid memory. He'd always thought Yin Hong was mixed up in the kidnapping; it was soon after he'd gone off to join the triads, after all.

'Do you remember her at all?' he asked John. 'When she came to Hong Kong the last time?'

John shook his head. 'Not much. She seemed rather . . . grim?'

'She did give that impression, yes.' Michael decided not to tell him what else he'd done about Lily. Not yet anyway. John wanted to keep his hands clean; even hearing about it would bother him. 'She isn't a comfortable person,' he conceded, getting up. 'But, then, I don't suppose idealists ever are. By the way,' he added with studied casualness, 'are you coming on the boat on Saturday? Your mother wanted to know.'

John glanced down at his desk. 'I was going to ring today as a matter of fact. The, er, the trouble is I've got a case coming up on Monday. And Stella's going to this meeting about a deputation to Beijing. I don't honestly see how we can, I'm afraid.'

'Never mind.'

'She's very involved in it,' John went on quickly. Too quickly.

'It really doesn't matter, John.'

'She thinks we can Do Something.'

'Let's hope she's right.' He paused by the door. 'Do the phones here chime a little tune incidentally? When they have to keep a caller waiting, I mean.'

'Yes, that's right.' John looked surprised. 'Why?'

'Nothing. I was only wondering. I thought they would, but I don't remember hearing it.'

As the plastic-padded elevator whooshed him down, he recalled the clanking lift in the old Central Building, long since demolished, where he used to have his office. Typewriters clattered noisily, phones didn't sound like musical boxes, people had wooden desks, and he drank real coffee with milk in it. And the clerks and typists had dim-sum at lunchtime in twenty different restaurants, instead of burgers in identical garish fast-food stores. Was it really better then, or was he just indulging sentimental nostalgia, like a doddering old man wishing he was young again? He knew of course; it was better *and* worse. But had Lily even tried to think what kind of world it was she wanted to come to? Let alone what kind of risk he'd have to run getting her there?

He glanced at the closed-circuit camera's patient eye in the elevator's soothing ceiling, as if people were watching him already.

And they'd have reason to if they were. Because he'd gone further than John knew; he'd taken the first, uneasy step. He played the scene through his mind again, watching the floor-lights flash on the indicator.

'Certainly we can get her to Taiwan once she's here,' old Ma had said in his genial Shanghainese, in for a business trip from Taipei. 'There are always ways and means. No problem. The question is whether the Government will want her.' His lips never quite closed over his large, unevenly protruding teeth, so that he seemed to be constantly smiling, a smile that was both benign and cracked. Ma remembered Lily well, he said, from St. John's University, where they'd always been on different sides. Lee Li-li he kept calling her, using her communist husband's name to emphasize the problem. 'You see, on the one hand she's not exactly a big catch for us, and on the other she's never been — shall we say *well disposed?* — in the past.' He had a loud jolly laugh, but it came and went to order. 'You know, I remember her in a debate at St. John's before the war. I was on the other team.' The hard breezy laugh visited his mouth again, revealing several gold-crowned molars. 'Quite a firebrand in those days, she was. Oh, yes, quite a firebrand.'

'Naturally she'd be self-supporting,' Michael had hinted. 'She wouldn't be a drain. Quite the contrary; I'd make sure of that.'

Ma had polished his glasses and said he'd see what he could do. He'd talk to one or two people, but it would take time of course, it would take time. His lids sagged, and his eyes looked woebegone and watery without the thick ramparts of his lenses. Like a sad spaniel's. 'Yes, quite a firebrand,' he said. 'She wiped the floor with us — then.' His crumpled face remade itself as he placed his glasses firmly back in place.

With casual grace

In his flat, on the lower slopes of the Peak, Patrick relaxed at last, untangled, and fell apart from Chung Yan. Panting and slippery with sweat, they lay exhausted on the bed for several drowsy minutes.

Gradually Patrick became aware of the phone ringing in the living-room, of his own regular breathing, heavier and slower than Chung Yan's, of the deep purring of the air-conditioner that insulated them from the street-noises below, of his leg sprawled over Chung Yan's thigh, and his hand resting on Chung Yan's smooth round shoulder.

At last the phone stopped.

He stirred and nuzzled Chung Yan's ear, then moulded himself more closely to the still, prone body. Chung Yan breathed evenly beneath him. Patrick felt the shallow peaceful rise and fall of Chung Yan's side against his chest, inhaled the tang of Chung Yan's sweat mingled with his own, and opened his eyes finally to see the half-pouted lips, the gently dilating nostrils, the closed long-lashed eyes beside him on the crumpled pillow. Next to the bed stood the almost empty wine-bottle and his wholly empty glass.

'I'm cold,' Chung Yan murmured in Cantonese.

Patrick pulled the sheet over them both. 'Shall I turn the air-conditioner down?'

Chung Yan's head shook faintly. He sighed, wriggled away from Patrick, rolled on to his back and stretched, eyes still closed. Patrick started tracing the brown aureole of his nipple lightly with his forefinger.

Chung Yan's lips twitched. 'You're tickling.' He pushed Patrick's hand away and opened his eyes at last, gazing at Patrick with a faint frown.

'What is it? Did I hurt you?' Patrick reached across him to pour the last of the wine. Chung Yan watched, wrinkling his nose. Despite being a waiter, he disliked even the smell of wine, let alone the taste of it.

'Did I hurt you?' Patrick asked again.

Chung Yan shrugged, reaching up to finger the bite-shaped bruise on his shoulder. 'Why can't I stay all day?' he asked. 'My only day off this week?'

Patrick drank. 'You know I have to go out, dear boy,' he said in English.

'You promised,' Chung Yan accused him, still in Cantonese.

'Nonsense, dear boy. Poppycock.' He spoke more affectedly than usual, to smother the uneasy recollection that Chung Yan was right. 'I merely promised to get out of it if I possibly could. But I couldn't. It isn't a holiday for me, you know.'

Chung Yan frowned, translating as he listened. It gave Patrick an advantage, and they both knew it.

'You don't care how I feel,' he muttered sulkily when he'd understood. 'Because you pay me. You think you own me.'

'Oh, don't be tiresome, Chung Yan! You're talking like a soap opera heroine. Really! I don't pay you, and you know it. I give you presents. And I take you to Macao. That's an entirely different matter, dear boy.'

Chung Yan listened carefully, then shrugged, a light ripple of his shoulders, meaning: *What's the difference, then?*

'But I do have to go to the university. I have to earn my modest living, too.'

Chung Yan strained to follow, then gave up. 'You only speak English to me to make me feel stupid,' he said sullenly.

Patrick finished his glass. 'Don't you want to improve your English?' he said, in Cantonese now. 'You said so yourself, didn't you? You asked me.' Whenever he spoke Cantonese, he dropped his affected manner, part-camp, part-Edwardian. Not that he meant to deliberately — it simply wouldn't go into Cantonese. 'Come on, let's have a shower. I've got a new shirt for you.'

Chung Yan's watchful eyes stirred and glistened, although the discontent was still there at the back of them, shadows in the pool.

In the shower, with the water spraying over him, Chung Yan soaped himself with casual grace, knowing by instinct how to stand and move seductively. Patrick embraced him suddenly. The water rained down on their faces, one Chinese, one almost Chinese, and their clasped bodies. Chung Yan leant his head back, watching him through half-closed lids. 'Are all your family rich?'

'All except my mother. Why?' As if he didn't know.

'The communist?'

'*Ex*, dear boy, more likely.' Speaking English again, he resumed the customary affectation that for him belonged to England as much as strawberries and cream or cucumber sandwiches did.

Chung Yan laid his head against Patrick's chest and slipped his arm round his waist, pulling him closer.

They were back on the bed, wet and slippery, when the phone rang again. This time it rang determinedly, and at last Patrick answered it.

'Rachel Martin is waiting for you,' the department secretary's voice said dispassionately. 'She says you were supposed to see her half an hour ago.'

Habitual lonely tune

The news came on. Lily switched it off. She never listened to it any more, not even the news about Hong Kong. But the same words drifted through the partition from her neighbours' radio.

At least they were muffled, easier to ignore. She imagined a billion people eating their evening rice to the sound of those sanitized announcements. Well, perhaps it helped the digestion.

She was eating her own evening rice at her unsteady folding table, her chopsticks chinking their habitual lonely tune against the rim of her bowl. Sometimes, while she ate, she reckoned up all her possessions after a life of seventy years. They didn't mount to much, even counting her clothes and hairpins. Her eyes slid familiarly as a worn hand over the blue Thermos, silver peeling off the top, the table, two chairs, bed, Butterfly fan (still not working), and the single shelf of books, mostly medical. And a rented room, shared toilet and kitchen. Michael's amahs must own twenty times as much. And as for money . . . . She glanced up at the cobwebs hanging from the cracked bulging ceiling, untouched, she guessed, since her parents had lain and gazed up at it forty years ago.

But that wasn't what had soured her. Not at all. The Party would have arranged a larger room for her now, if she'd asked. Probably a separate kitchen and toilet, too. But she'd never asked, and she never would. Hardship still appealed to her. Or, anyway, luxury didn't. No, it was the other things that rankled: humiliation, injustice, betrayal. She could never forget them; they were burning her steadily away, a slow smouldering fire that nothing could ever put out.

5

It's all relative

'I do like coming on your boat,' Elena said to San San. 'It's the luxury of it. I don't think I'll ever marry for love. He'd be bound to be poor, and I'd get varicose veins from babies and shopping bags and things. I'll just have a succession of sugar-daddies.' She was leaning over the rail between San San and Rachel. 'By the way, have I been invited for Paul?'

'Paul? Why?'

'Well, you've got Alex, and Alison's got Peter — at least I suppose she has — so that leaves Paul for me.'

'Or me,' Rachel said, when San San said nothing.

'Oh yes. I'd forgotten you.' Elena glanced at Rachel with raised eyebrows, as though after all she was pretty forgettable. 'We can take it in turns, then.' She turned back to San San. 'There's a lot to be said for sugar-daddies. You can twist them round your little finger for one thing. And they're too old to be pulling your knickers off all the time for another.'

San San blushed beneath her almond skin.

'Which category does your friend Tom belong to?' Rachel enquired distantly of Elena's half-turned shoulder.

'Tom?' Again the raised eyebrows, the amused glance. 'He's got a foot in both camps. He's just another mixed-up American really. I'm off to change. Coming, San San?'

'In a minute.' San San knew she couldn't leave Rachel alone like that.

'You *must* invite Tom on the boat some time, San San, really. Promise you will. He's quite well-behaved for an American.'

San San considered the heavy block of silence that Elena had just dumped between Rachel and herself. 'You mustn't take Elena too seriously,' she began propitiatingly. 'She doesn't mean half of what she says; she's just joking.'

'Oh, I wouldn't take her seriously even if she meant all of it,' Rachel said in a tart voice. 'Is that an island we're passing?'

'Lamma Island, yes. It's the one we saw from the Johnstons' house last week.'

They stood watching the coastline. It was empty except for an occasional cluster of houses along the shore. The bulging green hills hung over the houses like drowsy lids over eyes dazed by the sun.

'Think I'll go and change, too, then,' San San said after a time. 'What about you?'

'Oh, I'll just watch the view a bit longer,' Rachel said, thinking: *Two's company.* She turned to look at the other side now, at the blurring grey granite cliffs and steep hills of Hong Kong. In the folds of the hills, tower upon tower of tall white apartment-blocks reached up, windows glinting occasionally in the sun like sparks struck from petrified forests.

Yesterday, walking from the university to the post office nearby in Sai Ying Poon, she'd suddenly come upon narrow old streets with sidewalk workshops, fruit and vegetable stalls, crumbling houses with steep dark staircases and crooked paintless wooden shutters. The cramped decaying district might have been as old as Hong Kong itself. And in the post office, below a stern dusty portrait of the Queen, a long serpentine queue of patient men and women waited at the worn wooden money-order counter, each one looking old enough to have been born under the Manchu. Toothless, with sparse grey hair, fading eyes and clawed hands, they shuffled slowly forward to cash the postal orders, which she guessed their well-off sons, and daughters sent them from Chinatowns in England, Canada or America.

Not one of them could write. They presented their orders humbly to the clerk, watched the notes being officiously counted, tapped and recounted, then gave their receipts with feeble thumbprints, wiping their hands clean afterwards on the rag tied to the counter before they fumbled the money laboriously into their pockets, their mouths working with the effort. She imagined them stumbling and dragging their way up those steep blind stairways afterwards, to their dingy roach-infested rooms.

That was yesterday. But today there she was on a gleaming launch, gazing across the gleaming sea at the gleaming mansions of the rich — she could see Michael's house quite clearly on the Peak — and what did the slums of Sai Ying Poon mean to them?

'My turn first,' Elena's voice sang out behind her.

Rachel turned. Elena was climbing the ladder to the sun-deck, wearing what appeared to be no more than three handkerchieves and some string.

'With Paul,' Elena called out. 'Remember?' She waved as though they were the best of friends.

When San San rejoined her, wearing a slightly more extensive swimsuit, Rachel asked if she didn't sometimes find the contrasts in Hong Kong kind of hard to take.

'Contrasts?' San San glanced at the sea, the brilliant sky, the land. 'No, that's what I like.'

'I mean between the very rich and the very poor?'

'Oh.' Tilting her head, San San reflected, as if for the first time. 'Well, I suppose as long as they're getting richer themselves people here don't mind if others are getting richer still. In fact it encourages them.'

'I saw a bunch of old people in Sai Ying Poon yesterday, and *they* sure didn't look as if they were getting richer.'

'Richer than, you or richer than before?' Michael asked behind them. He held a book under his arm, his finger keeping his place. 'They're almost certainly richer than they were before, and richer than they'd be in China, otherwise they wouldn't be here. Not that it's easy here — it's just better than where they came from, that's all.'

'It's all relative,' San San said. 'Isn't it?'

Sometimes till the dawn

Peter Denton had taken the wheel from the 'boat-boy', a middle-aged man with sun-withered cheeks, who was smoking and chatting beside him. Peter held the wheel casually with one hand, a glass of orange juice in the other. His longish hair fluttered in the wind above the dark sunglasses that concealed his eyes. He was wearing white trousers and an elegantly coloured silk shirt, half-unbuttoned.

'Want a go?' he gestured to Rachel.

She shook her head. He was dressed to kill, but she had no wish to be the prey and assumed she wasn't really meant to be. Alex Johnston had just joined San San, so she climbed up to the sun-deck. Peter's English wife, Alison, was lying in her swimsuit face down on a towel, her generous shoulders and thighs glistening with suntan cream. Elena, astonishingly true to her word, was playing stone, paper, scissors in the shade with Paul, who was chortling delightedly as his slow fingers mimicked her fluttering hand. Grace leant back motionless against a cushion, gazing musingly ahead.

The boat was heading south now, round the western tip of Lamma Island. Rachel glanced first at the harbour behind her, anchored ship marshalled after anchored ship, then at the open sea ahead.

'Would you mind putting some sun-cream on my shoulders?' Alison asked drowsily. 'This sun's beginning to make me sizzle.'

Grace closed her eyes, considering with relief that Rachel, compliantly squirting sun-cream in white splotches over Alison's reddening skin, had taken up the burden of conversation also. Sometimes she listened to people talking — Alison, for instance, talking now to Rachel — with detached amazement. Not just at what they said (although that, too), but at the apparent ease with which they said it, always finding the word they wanted with such unthinking assurance. For her, words were flimsy and shadowy things; they hovered so often just out of reach. People smiled and waited while she groped for them, till as often as not she gave up and let her voice trail resignedly away, smiling with an apologetic wave or shrug. There were so many thoughts and feelings and images crowding inside her head, but she could never catch them with the insubstantial net of language. For everything except the simplest everyday affairs, silence, or silent gestures, seemed less distorting.

Besides, just then she was tired. Often she would wake up in the middle of the night with some scene from her childhood fresh in her mind, as fresh as the day it happened. And then she knew she wouldn't sleep again for a long time, sometimes till the dawn when Michael woke. She would lie still, reliving that fragment of her past for hours until at last she slept again. And then it would be a heavy dreamless sleep, often till nine in the morning.

That night it had been the house in Shanghai where she was born. Not the house but her bedroom. Not even the bedroom exactly, but the window and its purple curtains, and the foot of the bed with the sun slanting across it — she could even feel the band of warmth across her legs. That was all, but it was as real as her own waking heartbeats, and she knew she'd never recalled it before. She couldn't tell what year or what time of year it was, or what day or what happened on that day. But it was real, it was *there*. Perhaps in some other night she would recover another fragment.

After a while she'd got up and gone to check Paul. Sometimes he woke very early and was a nuisance; the pills didn't always hold through the night.

It was first light when Michael found her sitting beside Paul's bed, watching his drugged but restless sleep.

When Michael asked her anxiously, 'What . . . ?' she only shook her head, smiling, and went back to bed.

'Your turn now,' Elena called out to Rachel. 'I'm going for a prowl, see what I can pick up.' She walked past Alison, miming sinuous cat motions behind her back.

Alison raised her head suspiciously, watched her down the steps and then shrugged. 'That's Cheung Chau over there,' she said. 'God, I hope I haven't had too much sun.'

Her own plants flowering

The launch slid round the stone wall of the typhoon shelter and glided down a lane of still water between moored sampans and fishing-junks. Plastic bags, rotting fruit and waterlogged rattan baskets gently nudged the shining hull and wallowed in its wake. Children were diving and swimming off the stern of one junk, watched by a barking dog and an absorbed glistening-eyed infant tethered to the mast by a rope round his waist.

At the wooden jetty, only San San and Rachel went ashore. The waterfront was a noisy crowded jumble of tiny houses, shops, stalls and open-air restaurants, smelling of fish, smoke and cooking-oil. Peeling garish Chinese characters sprawled across every house and shop, advertising 7-Up, Coca-Cola, Oyster Sauce and what Rachel deciphered as the Cheung Chau Residents' Welfare Association. Little alleys led off through crevices in the crumbling facade, to cut across other streets and other alleys, all narrow, teeming and littered. Along each alley ran an open drain with greyish water swilling down it.

'This way,' San San said, stepping past a woman in pyjamas and wellingtons who was squatting beside some plastic bowls. As Rachel passed, the woman pulled an eel out of a bowl with rubber-gloved hands and decapitated it with a couple of strokes on a bloody fish-scaled block. The eel was still squirming and thrashing as she casually fed it into a plastic bag and handed it to her customer, a slight and frail old woman dressed in black, with thin grey hair caught in a straggly knot at the nape of her neck.

'I'm glad I'm a vegetarian,' Rachel said.

'Oh, they don't feel anything,' San San answered lightly.

They found the place easily, halfway up a tree-lined hill behind the village. A boy pushing a trolley up the path showed San San the door, shouted for the landlord, then wedged the trolley against a tree to watch what would happen.

'Is that the only kind of traffic here?' Rachel asked, nodding at the trolley.

'Apart from drugs, I expect,' San San said, viewing the boy, now joined by two others, unfavourably. The three boys stared back at the two strangers frankly, as if at the start of a play. When Rachel tentatively smiled, they grinned — not at her, but at each other and muttered amongst themselves.

A stout, bald, affable man ambled round the corner of the building, drying his hands on a towel. He was wearing blue shorts, a white singlet and grey ankle-socks rolled down to the tops of black patent-leather shoes.

'Mr. Chan,' San San said. 'Miss Martin.'

Mr. Chan nodded. 'Come see fla',' he instructed rather than asked them, and led them up two flights of tiled steps to the top floor. On each landing, Rachel saw, through open doorways barred by metal grilles, intense groups of mah-jong players, men and women, shuffling the pieces round and round on plastic tables. On the wall of each room was a little red wooden altar with a red bulb glowing above it. One or two of the players glanced incuriously at them as they passed. Unregarded radios were booming pop music or commercials.

'Holiday,' Mr. Chan said as he led them up, raising his voice above the scraping, clacking and blaring. 'Wee'-day have quie'.'

San San stood by the door while Rachel followed Mr. Chan round the small apartment. He threw doors open with a flourish, and stood proprietorially beside them, so that it was only round his immovable bulk that Rachel could survey the rooms displayed. Whenever she spoke in Mandarin he answered in English.

'Very bik,' he declared by the shelf-sized kitchen, flicking his towel like a ring-master's whip. 'Have plenty roo'.'

Rachel squeezed determinedly past him to try the faucet.

'Have lot water,' he asserted in the tone of a man whose integrity, unjustly doubted, is about to be vindicated. 'Have water-pipe ah.'

The water flowed, first rusty, then cloudy, then clear.

Anticipating Rachel's other doubts, Mr. Chan ran the water in the bathroom, flushed the gurgling toilet and went round switching on lights and fans.

'What do you think?' Rachel asked San San, gazing from the narrow balcony over the roofs below, down to the harbour.

'It's what *you* think,' San San said with a little shrug that meant *Not for me*.

Rachel could see the long white launch, elegantly aloof among the shabby browns and greens of the fishing-junks, a thoroughbred amongst mongrels.

'It's two thousand a month?' she asked tentatively, in English now.

'Two fi.'

'But you said two thousand on the phone!'

'Have roof, two thousn' fi' hundre'. Have roof more betta.'

Rachel frowned perplexedly at the ceiling, while Mr. Chan shouted at San San in amicable Cantonese.

'You get the sun-roof as well,' San San interpreted.

Mr. Chan, sighing, took them up a final flight of steps on to a flat red-tiled roof with a low wall round it. Flowerpots of various sizes stood forlornly about, with brown withered plants trailing miserably over their rims.

Rachel looked across to the neighbouring roof, on which a large Chinese family, dressed, by descending generations, in pyjamas, shorts or swimsuits, were eating loudly under a blue and white canopy. On the other side was the harbour; a triple-decked black and white ferry was just approaching the jetty.

'Flowerpot' can have,' Mr. Chan offered largely. 'No pay money.'

Rachel imagined her own plants flowering in the parched earth of the forsaken pots, imagined more flowers blooming all round the wall, imagined herself serenely working amongst them under her own cheaply installed canopy. She felt the vertigo of decision upon her, and then she leapt — or fell. 'I agree to your honourable proposal,' she announced in one more brave attempt at Mandarin communication.

'Two month' deposi',' Mr. Chan said. 'Mus' pay now.'

She felt uncertain again as soon as they started walking down the hill into the crowded warm smells of the waterfront. But at least she would really be in an authentic Chinese environment, she thought. Wasn't that what she'd come all that way for?

How small everyone seemed, though, in the alleys and behind the tiny stalls — as if they'd grown just tall enough to fit their diminutive houses, and then deliberately stopped. But they had such quick, alert gestures and expressions, as though compensating in energy for what they lacked in size. She'd never seen so many slight quicksilvery Chinese.

'Oh, these people aren't Chinese,' San San said carelessly. 'They're Tanka. Gypsies really, boat-gypsies.'

'Not Mr. Chan?'

'No, he's Chinese all right. He's Ah Yee's cousin. Expect she'll get a cut from your rent, by the way.' She contemplated the crowd shouting and jostling at the turnstile to the ferry. 'I hate people in the mass, don't you? They always seem so raw. Still, now we can go somewhere quiet and have a nice swim.'

They sped back, shearing through the hard low waves, to the eastern shore of Lamma Island, which lay (Rachel saw from the map) like an out-flung hand against the massed coast of Hong Kong. Skirting the red and black flags that marked the nets of a little fishing-junk, they anchored in a deep-set bay with a sabre-shaped blade of sand between the sea and the thick vivid-green shrubs of the hillside above it. In the breeze-cooled shade of the boat's awning they ate the picnic lunch that Grace's amahs had provided. Rachel drank a glass of wine despite the noonday sun; it made her sleepy almost at once, and she lay down on the deck while the others swam or skied from the little speed-boat they'd towed behind the launch. The splash of water, the distant whine of the speed-boat's engine, the intermittent slither of skidding skis and the light hollow thud of waves against the gently rocking hull lulled her as she dozed.

The day my childhood ended

'Remember the first time we came here?' Alex Johnston asked as he rowed San San ashore in the dinghy.

'I've been coming here as long as I can remember.' She was scooping water up with her hand, listening to the plash of the oars, the squeak of the rowlocks, the chatter of the water rippling under the boat.

'No, I mean we — you and me. It was the summer after my mother died. I must have been eleven. You rowed Elena and me to the shore and showed us your cave. At least, you said it was yours.'

'Oh, then. I always thought of it as my cave, yes.' She scooped up some more water and watched it trickling, bright as sunlight, through her fingers. 'I didn't mind sharing it with Elena, though. And you.'

But it was Elena who'd been her friend. They were in the same class at school and went to the same ballet lessons, taught by Mila. One day Elena didn't come to school, and some of the kids said in hushed voices that her mother had killed herself. Everyone made big eyes and pretended to know how she did it. She'd drowned herself, cut her throat, shot herself, hanged herself, stuck her finger in a power-socket, and heaven knew what else. The most dramatic story was that she'd jumped off the top of the high-rise block she lived in and landed on some railings underneath. Children who knew there were no railings at all were adamant they'd seen the firemen cutting the railings away with the body still spiked on them. It was a let-down when it turned out Elena's mother had merely taken an overdose after a party on the beach.

Then Mila left the ballet school, and the other teachers wouldn't say why. Someone else took her class — someone not as good, San San remembered distinctly. And the whisper went round that Mila had left because she'd been Elena's father's girlfriend.

Years afterwards Elena told her she couldn't recall what she'd felt when she learnt of her mother's death. 'Must've blocked it out,' she shrugged. 'It was a lovely funeral, though. I looked terribly fetching.'

That was in the days when they used to meet in London. San San was at Cheltenham Ladies' and Elena at the Royal Ballet. They would meet for tea at the beginning and end of San San's terms. They always met at the Connaught — San San because she was born to it, Elena because she wasn't.

'You took my hand to help me out of the boat,' Alex was saying. 'You must've thought I was a terrible wimp.'

'Me take a grubby boy's hand? Never!'

'Well, you did.' He sounded mildly injured.

The dinghy rasped along the sand. He dropped the oars with a dull clatter and jumped out. They hauled the boat up together. 'Was it terrible for you when your mother died?' she asked as they turned to walk as a matter of course towards the cave.

Was it terrible? He looked inward. His father had woken them late, too late to go to school. When Alex asked, he shook his head, smiled — sadly, it seemed later, but not at the time — and said: 'You needn't go today.' They knew there must be some special reason, but something about his bearing, his face, made them uneasy, and they didn't ask what. Ah Wong gave them breakfast. She was grim-faced, but he didn't think anything of that — she was often grumpy in the mornings. His mother frequently slept late, too, so he thought nothing of her absence, either. Then, when they'd finished, his father sat down and smiled again — again, it was only afterwards that Alex realized it was a sad smile, and that his father's eyes were tired and red-rimmed, his face worn. Alex couldn't remember the words now, halting and hesitantly chosen, in which he'd told them. He didn't say she'd killed herself; that only leaked out later. He made it sound like an accident. 'Too many sleeping pills,' he said. Alex couldn't remember the other words, but he could recall the first tremor of fear after his father began, then the pounding shock and disbelief — he tried to pretend it was just some terrible grown-up game, and she would come out of the bedroom smiling and laughing in a minute, saying, 'You didn't really believe it, did you?' Only, she hardly ever smiled or laughed. His most lasting memory of her was of her sitting at her dressing table, with slumped shoulders, head turned away. When, avoiding their eyes, Dimitri had said, 'Too many sleeping pills,' Elena had giggled, as though she, too, thought it was a game. And the smile had hung there lop-sided on her face when she realized it wasn't. He himself had felt a tic in his cheek, which still sometimes came without warning.

He didn't know when he started crying; he believed it wasn't till that night. But he knew he was grateful he didn't have to go to school; he was afraid of everyone staring at him if he gave way and cried there. To have people pointing and watching while he cried — that seemed at the time the most fearful thing of all. That night he'd begun sleeping with the pillow over his head, and, no matter how hot it was, he'd done so ever since. It shut out the world.

When the suicide verdict was returned at the inquest, he tried to persuade himself they were wrong. For years he pretended secretly, against all the evidence that she'd done it by accident. He fabricated fanciful theories in his daydreams to explain away her suicide note and the calm and methodical way she'd gone about her death. Of course the self-deception failed, and eventually he gave it up. He wanted to tell San San all this, which he'd never yet told anyone.

Was it terrible?

'It was the day my childhood ended,' he said.

They were walking through the dark wet sand at the water's edge, sinking up to their ankles and leaving deep sucking footprints, which the incoming sea quickly puddled. It was harder going, but the scorched dry sand would have burnt their feet.

'I suppose it sort of closed me up,' he went on uncertainly, dragging the words out as laboriously as he dragged his feet out of the clutching sand. 'I mean I felt ashamed somehow, dirtied by it. Kids used to come up to me at school and say: "Did she do it because your dad had a Chinese bird?" I suppose they'd just picked it up from their parents, they hardly knew what it meant. But I could imagine how they picked it up — you know, the little sneers and sniffs. It made me feel unclean, disgusting. And even more so when Miss Cheung said she couldn't give me piano lessons any more.'

'Miss Cheung?' San San laughed. 'But she was awful! You were lucky there.'

'I didn't think so at the time,' he said drily, not wanting his sufferings made light of. He'd brooded on them for years, they'd given him a sense of his own distinctness and importance, and he wanted her sympathy, her respect for them, not a smiling dismissal. He was baring his soul to her after all.

'Why didn't your mother teach you?' San San asked. 'Before, I mean?'

'She couldn't handle beginners. I suppose she couldn't handle anything really.' He thought of Miss Cheung, a woman with a frozen face and a voice as brittle as ice, who seemed to have always been old. Before each lesson she would wipe the keys with a moist cloth and examine your fingers for signs of sweat or dirty nails. She was a stern Catholic. A crucifix hung on the wall above the piano, as if to remind you that you, too, were there to suffer. And you did suffer

— wrong notes earned a rap with a ruler on the guilty finger. He'd hated and feared her lessons; but when, at the first lesson after the inquest, she abruptly told him she couldn't teach him any more he felt shocked, like a boy expelled from school for some unmentionably obscene misconduct. He sensed he'd become morally tainted in her eyes; and he assumed she must be right. He'd scarcely touched a piano since that day. 'She must have heard the gossip about Mila,' he said. 'I suppose in her book suicide was bad enough, but adultery must have been unforgivable. I used to see her sometimes in the town after that; she always stared straight through me.'

'And yet Elena was hardly touched by it at all,' San San said, feeling almost guiltily that she herself had never been touched by anything.

'Well, everything's always been a game for her.' He compressed his lips in both envy and condemnation. 'All she ever does is play.'

'That's all I ever do,' San San said a little wistfully. 'Play the violin.' Sometimes, especially when with Elena, she felt obscurely afraid that all those long hours when she just shut herself away to practise and practise were warping something in her, stunting its growth. The muscles of her hands were strong and agile, but what about the muscles of the heart?

They climbed over the smooth brown rocks at the end of the beach. Beyond them was the cave San San had first shown them, a great slab of granite resting on two boulders, covered at high tide by the sea. They used to go and lie in its shade on the wet, ridged, sandy floor, or sit and cool off in the shallow pools the tide had left — sometimes there would be schools of tiny fish trapped in them, dark shadows darting away when you stirred the water with your hand or foot.

I will kiss her there, Alex thought. It was there that he'd seen her changing into a fresh swimsuit once, when he'd swam eagerly to the shore to fetch her at the twilit end of a long summer afternoon. He must have been about sixteen at the time. He'd watched with guilty enchantment as she swiftly, shyly slipped first the top on, then the bottom. When she'd wriggled snugly into it, he pretended noisily that he'd just arrived. 'You've changed your swimsuit,' he remarked in mock surprise. She blushed. 'The other one's got oil on it,' she said, rolling it hastily in her towel. In fact it was blood from her copious period.

He never told her of course that he'd seen her changing. He'd merely carried the picture of her naked body and her black hair streaming down her pale back — carried it about with him in his mind as others carried photos in their wallets — and it had been the focus of all his adolescent fantasies. I'll kiss her there, he thought again. He imagined telling her one day, when they were lying in bed. If only he knew when and how.

But he couldn't kiss her there. When they reached the top of the rocks, they saw a Chinese man and woman in black wet swimsuits, embracing on the floor of the cave. The sand coated their glistening brown bodies like yellow fur as they rolled giggling from side to side, squirming and groping.

'And I always thought it was my cave,' San San said in a strained voice as they climbed back down to the beach. She was thinking how gritty they must feel, and wondering if they'd got sand in their mouths. How animal it was! Like a couple of cats mating. Almost inadvertently she started her exercises.

'What on earth are you doing?' Alex asked with forced interest.

She was holding up her hand and crooking each finger in turn. 'Finger exercises. Haven't you ever watched a violinist's left hand?'

Neither of them mentioned the two writhing sand-furred bodies they'd just seen, but the image of them filled their minds like a boulder on a narrow path, which they must cautiously edge round without disturbing. With their thoughts on that unacknowledged looming boulder, there was nothing they could say now that wouldn't sound constrained. So Alex wasn't really surprised that San San slipped away when they reached the water's edge.

'Let's swim,' she said a bit too blithely. 'I'm baking, aren't you?'

The Million-Dollar Finger

An unsteady clinking noise woke Rachel — Alison, emptying a wine-bottle into her glass.

'Now I've really bloody well burnt myself,' she said as Rachel stirred. 'That sun-cream's absolutely useless, look!' Her face and shoulders were an angry red, and the thin white stripe she revealed when she pulled her shoulder strap down was so sharp-edged it looked as though it had been printed on her skin. There were pale shadows round her eyes, too, where her sunglasses had been, giving her a goggle-eyed, even more indignant look. 'I'm so thirsty as well,' she said, swallowing the wine. 'We just can't take the sun like you Chinese.' She jerked her head disparagingly at Grace and Michael as if it was all their fault.

Grace smiled distantly. She probably hadn't heard. Michael, reading in a corner under the awning, placed his finger on the line and looked up reluctantly. 'There's some more sun-cream in the cabin.'

'Useless on fair skin like ours,' she said peevishly. 'This always happens when I come on the boat.'

'*I'm* not sunburnt,' Rachel said mildly.

'Well, you didn't lie in the sun, did you?'

'That's what I meant.'

Alison sighed impatiently. 'But I *did*, didn't I? Can't even swim now. The rays pass straight through the water. Might as well change, I suppose.'

Rachel expected Michael to return to the reserved privacy of his book. Normally he would have done so. He found the forced intimacy of launch-parties suffocating, and never came without a book he could retreat into, often opening it at the beginning of the trip so that his guests would know politeness didn't require them to badger him with small-talk — and even required them not to. And when he invited them he usually warned them to bring along something to read. This time, however, liberated though he was from Alison, he didn't go back to his book. He laid it face-down on the cushion beside him and nodded past Rachel at the deep curve of the bay.

'See those ledges along the hill? Rice-terraces. They were still growing rice here when we first started coming. There's a village behind those trees. Empty now, except for a few old women. The young people have all gone.'

'Where to?'

'Factories in the new towns. Or abroad. The villages are dying all over Hong Kong. Yes, they even had buffalo when we first came here. I miss all that. I wonder if they do.'

It was the first time he'd ever said anything personal to her, and the words seemed to come hard, like bits of a glacier broken off from some denser mass inside him. She traced the blurred lines of the terraces, softened by thick climbing grass, along to the cluster of trees at the foot of the hill. 'What are those trees?' she asked.

'Papaya and mango,' he said without looking. 'And the tall one with the light green leaves is a flame of the forest. You should come in June, when it's in flower. We always used to come here in June when the children were young. It's different now, of course.'

'You're very fond of it, aren't you?'

He nodded, remembering the first boat they came on, a little junk that slithered and rolled on the waves, and took over an hour to reach the bay — it was all they could afford then. They'd always come to that bay because he'd wanted to plant it in his children, to grow it in their bodies, in their brains, like bone and muscle, that blue-grey water and brilliant sky, that strip of sand beside the grass and trees, those long, careless, tranquil afternoons. With a stolid obstinate passion he'd wanted all that to grow in them, like a farmer planting trees that he knew might not bear fruit till long after his death. He wanted it for them because he hadn't had it himself, and he knew the harm the lack of it had done him. They must have it; it must be rooted in their memories, to strengthen them against the day, whenever it might come — but he was sure it *would* come — when things went wrong and the ground just slid beneath their feet.

How could he, so staid and mundane, have thought such quietly passionate thoughts?

'The children needed it,' he said opaquely. 'Especially when they were young.' He drummed his fingers on the back of his book, uneasy that he might have given too much away, made himself vulnerable, even if only to this innocuous American girl. No more feelings, then. He glanced down at the shortened finger on his left hand and held it up, to deflect them both from more vulnerable regions. 'I used to tell them stories about how I lost the tip of this finger,' he said inconsequentially. 'I expect you know how.'

'Jenny did say something about it. It was when you were kidnapped . . . .'

'Yes. I was nine at the time. They cut it off to encourage my parents to pay the ransom. A million dollars.' He waggled the stunted finger, gazing at it meditatively while he spoke; then, seeing Rachel wince, explained. 'It was a regular thing in those days. One Chinese banker had his son posted back to him piece by piece when he couldn't pay the ransom. Or wouldn't. And of course Pak-kay — that's my sister Lily's first husband, Patrick's father — the Japanese chopped his head off before the war and left it on the doorstep.'

'Ugh.'

Michael shrugged. 'Life is cheap in this part of the world. And it was cheaper still then.'

'At a million dollars it sounds kind of expensive for some.'

Michael paused, then nodded. 'Yes, I suppose you could say that, too,' he agreed without a flicker of a smile. 'Anyway, I used to make up stories about this little finger when they were young. But they were never really as good as the truth. I'm afraid I haven't got much imagination.'

'The Million-Dollar Finger we used to call it,' San San said, hauling herself suddenly aboard with a swoosh of water. She shook the sea out of her ears and pulled back her hair. 'Aren't you going in, Rachel?'

Rachel said she was, but she'd keep her hat on, so she wouldn't get burnt. And she dabbed a white blob of sun-cream on the tip of her nose, too. Michael said he wouldn't swim. He hardly ever did swim now. And nobody imagined Grace would. She'd sat in the same position for more than an hour, her eyes half-closed, her head leaning back against the rail. But nobody imagined she was asleep, either.

'Look out for jelly-fish!' San San called.

In brighter colours

'Your costume's a better fit than San San's was,' Peter said, with a glance that stayed too long on Elena's hips. 'Which was the last one I saw you in.'

She was pulling the ski-belt round her waist. 'Meaning you want to see the top half fall off now?' she asked, pulling the buckle tight.

His eyes discreetly indicated the boat-boy at the wheel, and Paul sitting beside him encumbered in a bulky orange life jacket.

She glanced at him with a taunting little smile. 'Respectable, are we? Observing the decencies?'

'Observing everything,' he said.

She gave the buckle a final tug and slid over the side, a ski under her arm. 'You're quite well hung yourself,' she said, shaking her wet glistening head. 'Don't cross your legs — you'll squash it.'

The white ski-rope lay snaky on the water beside her. She let it slip through her fingers as the boat moved gently away.

'Ready?' Peter called.

She gripped the handle, set her feet on the ski, and crouched in the water. Then she nodded. 'Watch carefully, OK? Watch the birdy.'

'Is that Elena skiing?' Rachel asked Alex, peering at the blurred shape skidding behind the speed-boat.

'Where?' Alex was swimming beside her, tugging the dinghy along by its painter.

'Over there, waving something.' When she put her ears underwater she could hear the speed-boat's engine singing beneath the sea.

Alex trod water and watched the speed-boat planing across the bay, watched the skier swinging far out to the side, whirling a strip of cloth negligently above her head. He flushed suddenly beneath his tan. 'That's Elena all right!' he said gruffly, turning to swim again.

On the launch, Alison was shading her eyes. 'What on earth's Elena shouting about out there?'

'She's laughing,' Grace said, not opening her eyes.

Michael, holding his book at arm's length, turned the page.

San San raised her head. She had the keenest sight of them all. She saw Elena throw away the ski-rope and glide gracefully below the water, both hands above her head in a ballet pose, her swimsuit top held delicately as a sash between her elegantly drooping fingers. The speed-boat swung sharply round to retrieve her, its bow rearing out of the water like a shark.

'Whatever is she up to?' Alison demanded querulously. 'Making all that racket!'

'Would anyone like some tea?' San San asked loudly. 'Alison?'

'All right.' Alison turned back. 'Honestly, the way that girl carries on, always drawing attention to herself! She's just a little exhibitionist if you ask me.'

San San filled the kettle in the galley, ransacking the cutlery-drawer noisily for teaspoons.

'I'm rather fond of her,' Grace said unexpectedly. 'She's so full of life.' She thought Elena painted the everyday in brighter colours. Grace painted, too, but her colours weren't bright. Nor did she paint in her life like Elena, but merely with ink and brush on rice paper. Her paintings were of bamboo and flowers, always graceful, always fading from stroke to stroke. She felt they lacked life. Not that she minded — so did she, and she didn't mind that, either. But life was what Elena possessed. And Paul's drawings, too, in their way.

Constellations and galaxies

Michael laid his book aside again, to watch the sun setting behind the hills. It went quickly. In only a few minutes it was gone and the long-armed shadows were stretching smoothly out over the beach, fingering the water, stroking the boat. The light ebbed from moment to moment. A puff of cloud glowed above them briefly, and then that, too, faded into the grey of the dusk.

The beach, the rocks, the trees grew indistinct, and what was bright and cheerful under the sun became desolate in the twilight. A dog barked in the invisible abandoned village, then another and another. Then they all came loping across the sand, scavenging dim shapes like wolves. San San, watching beside him, thought of the two furry bodies in the cave.

The boat-boy started the engine as the speed-boat returned. Alex fastened the dinghy's painter, Peter the speed-boat's. The anchor-rope slackened as the launch eased forward, and the boat-boy hauled in the anchor. They moved smoothly out to sea.

Alison was the first to speak. Turning Michael's book towards her, she bent low over it to make out the title. *'The Campaign against Footbinding in China,'* she said. 'Fancy reading about that!'

Rachel said she'd seen an old lady the other day with feet so small in her black slippers that they must have been bound once. She was hobbling along, supported on each side by a teenage girl. Granddaughters, Rachel guessed.

'But why did they bind girls' feet?' Alison demanded. 'It's not as if it made them beautiful. Really I can't understand you Chinese!'

Nobody answered at first. Rachel noticed Peter's eyelids droop, his lips tighten.

'One theory is that it prevented women from running away,' Michael said detachedly at last. 'But people did find it attractive, too, as a matter of fact.'

'It was a turn-on,' Elena said blithely. 'Like garter-belts. Even the smell. I expect it was quite cheesy.'

'Well, really!'

'Wasn't it supposed to affect the way they walked, too, and that tightened the muscles inside and made them a better fit for men?' Elena asked Michael.

'It has been said so, yes,' he conceded uncomfortably.

'Better fit? What on earth do you — ?' Then Alison thought she did know what Elena meant after all. 'And to think when I first met Peter in England he said the Chinese were the most civilized race on earth!'

Peter sighed audibly, and went to talk to the boat-boy.

'Tried getting him for misdescription of goods?' Elena asked Alison. 'There's a law against that, you know.'

The launch began to pitch in the open sea as it slipped past the black rocks at the mouth of the bay. The boat-boy switched the navigation lights on and turned towards Hong Kong.

Elena came and sat between San San and Rachel in the stern. Rachel stiffened, but Elena seemed oblivious. She let her long wet hair flutter loose in the thick salty wind, not yet cool enough to chill them. 'He's Ah Choi's brother,' Elena told Rachel, nodding at the boat-boy, between whose lips the tip of a cigarette glowed and faded. 'You know, the Dentons' driver. See the likeness? They were both jockeys once.' She nudged San San. 'Remember how Ah Choi used to give his girlfriends lifts when he was driving us back to your place after our ballet lessons?'

In the summer time, the drivers all used to lie across the front seats of their cars, parked in the shade outside the studio, reading or snoozing beneath their newspapers, occasionally calling out racing tips to each other. Ah Choi was the most respected tipster. Then, when the girls came running from class, skins glistening with sweat, the engines would start up, the doors slam. Every driver would switch the air-conditioner on, except Ah Choi. They'd catch cold, he maintained adamantly; it was the same with horses if they got in a lather. Grace would tell him it was all right, he should switch it on in future, but it was no use — they always had to ride back with the windows open and the hot exhausted breath of the city panting all over them.

Ah Choi would pretend the air-conditioning was broken if San San insisted, and even fiddled with the switch so that it really seemed not to work. To mollify them, he would tell them stories about the horses he'd ridden at Happy Valley, about how the triads drugged horses and fixed races, about the illegal bookmakers and their signals. Scarcely taller than they were, he could only just see over the steering wheel, but he never had an accident. Horses were harder to handle, he used to say. And women. When he polished the car every morning he had to stand on a box to get at the roof. There was a bluish dent in his temple where he'd been kicked by a horse once, but he never told them about that. Couldn't remember, he used to say.

San San and Elena often had tantalizing glimpses of Ah Choi's various love affairs. Strange women would be loitering from time to time beside the car when they came from the studio, and occasionally one or another would ride part of the way home with them. 'I'm just giving a lift to this aunty,' he would say sheepishly, and they would drive in proud majestic silence till the young aunty got out somewhere along the way and ran off, giggling at something he'd whispered in her ear, throwing a little thank-you glance at San San as she went.

Ah Choi's wife had a vegetable-stall in Causeway Bay, where she lived with their three children. But Ah Choi rarely went home to them, preferring the freedom of life on the Peak.

'Does he still have all those women?' Elena asked San San.

'Getting a bit past it now, I should think.'

'Some of them were a foot taller than he was. I used to wonder how he managed it. Stood up in the stirrups, I suppose.'

San San glanced uneasily at Rachel.

'Think I'll go upstairs,' Rachel said abruptly.

'It's called *aloft* on the sea,' Elena called after her.

She climbed the steps to the sun deck.

Michael, Grace and Paul were silently gazing towards Hong Kong, Paul still in his ungainly life jacket. Alex lay on the deck, looking up — disconsolately, Rachel thought — at the first pale pin-pricks of the stars. When she turned towards Hong Kong, she understood why they were all so silent. The hills were black against the violet sky; below them, towers, slabs, columns, rows, constellations and galaxies of lights glittered in every hollow and along the shore, throwing a faint luminous halo into the sky above them. Here and there beads of orange lamps threaded the hillsides, the headlights of cars silently moving along the roads they marked.

The sea splashed, beat and hissed against the hull. Here and there the lights of other boats gleamed, and a lighthouse sent out its patterned brilliant pulses. My God, Rachel thought. I can see why they're fond of this place.

Paul took her wrist in his soft trusting grasp and pointed wordlessly at the lights, his eyes shining like a child's.

Shadow people

As they rounded the headland and made for the typhoon shelter, they came upon a police boat that had intercepted a shabby brown junk. The beam of the police boat's searchlight lay rigid across the sea, pinning the junk like a butterfly where it fluttered its sails on the swell.

They leant over the side of the launch, watching the grey police boat drawing slowly alongside the junk. A rope whirled across and was made fast, a loud-hailer blared out metallic orders, several policemen in khaki uniforms dropped on to the junk's deck and went below. Torches flashed. There were shouts. A solitary fisherman in old blue trousers and shirt watched resignedly from the wheelhouse. In the stern a woman squatted indifferently by a kerosene-stove, cooking.

'What are they looking for?' Rachel asked. 'Drugs?'

'IIs,' Peter said. 'Illegal Immigrants.'

The launch cruised slowly past, leaving the police boat and the junk wallowing in their suspicious embrace.

Michael watched still. How often had he seen newspaper pictures of captured IIs, rounded up by the police or the Gurkhas as they tried to sneak over the border from China? Nearly every day, nearly every summer. With blank peasant faces, in blank peasant clothes, they squatted stoically on their hunkers, waiting to be sent back to China and whatever fate awaited them — beatings, labour-camps, or only a lecture; even nothing at all. Nobody could tell, from one district to the next, from one month to the next, what the policy would be. They came with nothing but their clothes and their hopes, their unreal hopes, and perhaps an address of some relative already in Hong Kong. Those that got through became shadow people, working in shadow jobs for shadow money, living in huts or shadowy slums, shadows in the crowd, afraid of the policeman on the corner, the sudden checkpoint on the road. Yet they kept on coming, because they preferred the shadows there to the substance where they came from.

There was one woman, he remembered, who'd been caught six or seven times; she had her photo splashed in all the papers, a record-holder, smiling timid and bemused at the lens beside her large and smirking captors. Would he open a paper one day to see a photo of his sister Lily — seventy, grey, obdurate and stern — surrounded by police with dogs or by club-swinging Gurkhas?

He watched the disappointed policemen returning to the police boat. The searchlight snapped off, and in the deepened dark the two vessels drifted slowly apart. The junk began to make way towards Aberdeen. The police boat settled down to wait.

'No luck this time,' Peter was explaining to Rachel, who couldn't make out what was happening. 'Helping IIs — they treat it almost like murder here.'

'Well, we'd be swamped with them if they didn't, wouldn't we?' Alison said indignantly. 'The whole bloody country would come across if they could.'

The Fourth World

The sun was milder in the afternoons now. Lily's room didn't get so stuffy, and she didn't miss the still-unmended Butterfly fan. But she'd been in all day since getting Michael's letter from Yin Hong, and she was restless, elated. She decided to go out.

It wasn't till she'd gone down the worn stairs, out into the old garage of the house, and was unlocking the heavy padlock on the heavy chain of her heavy bike that she thought where she'd go. Of course, she'd call on Chu Wen-li again. 'Things are moving,' she'd tell him. 'Things are moving.' He'd know what she meant.

As she wheeled the bike out, a memory of her father's car slid into her mind. The Rolls used to stand there, where all those untidy bike-racks stood now. That dark oil-stain probably came from it. Probably she could find some other relic — a broken valve-cap or a burnt-out headlamp-bulb — if she searched through all the dust and litter. Nothing usable, of course; that would have gone long ago. For a moment, as she passed between the doors, unpainted and warped now, dragging on their rusty fallen hinges, she could see the car standing there gleaming and splendid as it was before the Japanese came, with the driver — what was his name? — flicking the dust off with a feather duster. The image dissolved as she wheeled the bike out towards the street. Yes, what was his name, though? Man? Lai? Chung? For a communist — or an ex-communist now — she'd always had an uncomradely tendency to forget workers' names. And a rather imperious manner as well, she had to admit. Not that they were ever the faults she'd been criticized for. Better, fairer, if they had been. She could have accepted that.

She mounted cautiously, and after a few wobbles was pedalling steadily with the tide of cyclists flooding along Zhongshan Road. No, her crime had been her blood, not her character. Even now, after all those years, she still woke up to the memory of it, the pulpy throbbing in her stomach. *Lee Li-li, British spy and reactionary authority!* The poster had shivered slightly in the wind, the thick red characters daubed like blood. *Report to the organs of mass dictatorship at eight o'clock tomorrow morning for criticism and denunciation! This order must be promptly obeyed!* They'd written her name upside down;

she knew that meant real trouble. And she went, promptly at eight. That was the madness of the time; you went.

Now, cycling anonymously in this silent sea of cyclists, she recalled again that quiver of shock and fear, which she first felt when she read the poster on the hospital door, when the crass crude characters seemed to thud into her like punches. Of course, she'd known it was coming. Everyone had. You knew when people started avoiding you in the canteen, when you found yourself sitting alone, when the nurses ignored your instructions and the doctors you'd worked with for years didn't recognize you in the corridors. All except Chu Wen-li, and he knew he'd soon be a fellow-victim anyway. She'd known what to expect long before that, though, or she should have done anyway. Back in the Anti-Rightist campaign in 1957, when Fung told her he wanted a divorce. Drawing a line, he called it. 'Your complicated background — I must draw a line.' Always had a nose for trouble, he had. And for advantage, too. After liberation (she no longer thought of it with a capital L), sniffing the advantage of marrying the widow of a communist martyr. Then, in the fifties, sniffing the danger of her Eurasian blood, her foreign connections. So off he'd gone. What a nose; no wonder he'd done so well in the Party! Yes, his nose. She remembered the little dents his glasses left when he took them off at night. And the garlic on his breath, mingling with the stale smoke of his Front Gate cigarettes — he'd no nose for that. Fung's kisses never gave her any pleasure; but, then, they were never meant to, she supposed. His lips were always dry and hard, unlike Pak-kay's, the only other man she'd ever kissed.

She circled a white-uniformed policeman who'd left his traffic-pagoda to scold a docile peasant holding a bike piled high with rattan baskets. Already a mute blank-eyed audience had formed around them. Anything for a show, a bit of excitement. She pedalled on, breathing harder now. At the bus-terminus, she read some of the handwritten notices, glued to walls and lamp-posts, as she passed. *Lathe operator in Shanghai wants exchange jobs with one in Canton, to be with his family. Hospital worker in Tsingtao wishes exchange with similar in Shanghai. Electrician in Hangchow. Office worker in Chungking. In Lanzhou. In Wuhan. . . .* Had the authorities sent everyone to the wrong place? Couldn't they get anything right, or was it just perversity?

'China,' she said in English, puffing and slightly giddy as she entered Chu's apartment. 'China is really on the move. It's a land' — she sat down gratefully — 'a land where everyone wants to be somewhere else. People in Tibet want to be in Canton, people in Canton want to be in Shanghai, people in Shanghai want to be in Beijing. And university students everywhere want to be in America. Yes, China's really on the move. Or at least it wants to be.

And in my case' — she lowered her voice — 'perhaps soon I really will be.' At home in her room (some bare room or other had been home to her most of her adult life), she was often depressed, but whenever she met Chu she brightened with acid humour and became sardonic, belligerent even. His bland, genial, self-effacing tolerance, his incurable optimism — even after what they'd done to him — always set her off. She wanted to shock him out of it, to infect him with her own disillusioned cynicism. Besides, he was the only person she could ever talk to.

'I guess you've heard from your brother?' Chu asked in his hooting voice. They spoke English partly as a precaution, partly for practice. Chu's American accent came from seven years in Boston in the forties, which he'd paid for with seven in a barn in the Cultural Revolution. 'At least the Red Guards didn't charge me interest,' he would say with his wide unrancorous smile. Now he eked out his pension by teaching English to students who were themselves applying to study in the States. So forty years after the revolution they were back where they started. And the English Chu taught them was back there, too, larded with forties' college slang that he imagined was standard language in constant use. For all Lily knew, it might be.

'Yes, I've heard from him,' Lily answered. 'By special messenger.'

She didn't say any more, and he didn't ask. The Public Security Bureau would be bound to question him when she'd gone (when, not if, she thought); so she pretended she'd applied for an exit permit quite legally, and he pretended he believed her. But they both knew she'd never have got one. Fung, with his nose for trouble, he'd certainly have seen to that. And once she'd applied they'd have kept an eye on her, and that would have been that.

Wai-chung brought them some tea, then left. She had a pupil waiting, she said. But she wouldn't have stayed in any case. She never did. She wanted her husband to have only safe friends now, and Lily wasn't safe. Wai-chung was always cool when Lily came, and always left the room with some excuse about housework or a student. If Lily had been more sensitive, or just weaker, she'd have taken the hint. But who would she have talked to then in the city of her birth? Chu used to remonstrate with his wife at first. Lily had heard them muttering in the kitchen or the bedroom where he'd followed her. But then he'd given up and let things be. In fact, after all, they both preferred it when she wasn't there. Her glacial caution froze their talk; it even froze their thoughts. They'd sit there exchanging safe banalities, when she was there, like a couple of strangers in a train.

'Wai-chung had a worse time than I did in the Cultural Revolution,' Chu had apologized obliquely once in his hoarse voice. 'Shucks, she just wasn't made for carrying night-soil.' The hoarseness came from a beating the Red Guards had given him; a blow on the throat had damaged his larynx. That was why they had a large flat now, with their own bathroom and kitchen. As if that could make up for it. Being head of the chest unit must have helped a bit, too.

Wai-chung hadn't been made for carrying night-soil; she'd been made for playing the violin. But who did what they were made for these days anyway?

'And what will you do in the West, if you do go?' Chu asked, putting his cup down and leaning back with a sigh.

'When.' She knew what she would do. She'd do the thing at last that all those wasted years had fitted her for, so that they wouldn't be wasted after all.

'If or when.' He didn't believe she'd go in the end, and he didn't want her to. For one thing, he'd miss her. For another, her going would be unsettling, a silent rebuke to him for staying. And he'd had enough of unsettling thoughts. 'What will you do, a woman of your age? Have you really thought about it seriously?'

'That's how you used to talk to your patients,' she answered sharply. 'Avuncular and patronizing.'

'Avuncular? Hey, what does that mean?'

'I'm going to write a book about the Fourth World.'

A hesitant pupil was struggling painfully through *Twinkle, Twinkle, Little Star* on a squeaky violin in the next room. Nearly all Wai-chung's pupils were beginners.

'It means like an uncle,' Lily added.

'Like an uncle, ha. And what is the Fourth World, then?'

'The Fourth World is you and me. It's our world. Or it was. The world of the camps.'

6

As a sparrow trapped

Rachel got out of the taxi at the gate, forgetting that in Hong Kong there would probably be a steep drive leading up the side of a hill before you reached the apartment-block itself.

Sure enough, when she turned round she saw a narrow concrete cut winding up between hacked-out walls of rock. She sighed and started walking. A drill ruptured the air behind her, the afternoon sun glared off the whitish cement, and a delivery-van grinding past in first gear spouted black diesel smoke into her face while its clattering engine, amplified in the little canyon, battered her ears.

At the top of the cut, beside arrows pointing sternly to the *Upper Carpark, Lower Carpark* and *Visitors' Carpark*, was a patch of fatigued brown grass, which a Filipina maid in a blue uniform was half-heartedly patrolling with a little blonde girl who was pushing a doll's pram. 'So you do not like water?' the maid asked in a bored parroty voice. 'Why you do not like the water?' A dachshund sniffed the grass around them with scarcely more interest, occasionally cocking an unenthusiastic leg.

Rachel negotiated the empty bays of the *Upper* and *Lower Carparks*, each one splotched with the tarry spray of petrol fumes, and found a lobby at last, where a morose hollow-cheeked caretaker was reading a newspaper at a grey metal desk. He didn't speak Mandarin, or at least didn't understand hers, but when she showed him Patrick's address he gestured her to another lobby further along. She was passed on from that to the next and the next until at last a caretaker in the fourth one pointed silently to the elevator. She pressed the button for the seventeenth floor and turned on the fan to dry her sweat.

The elevator let her out into a marble-tiled vestibule. A waxy-leafed rubber plant stood opposite her, inadequately masking a large red fire extinguisher. On either side of these were identical metal grilles covering identical blank teak doors. Checking the address she'd been given, she went left to 17A. It sounded still and empty behind the door. Not hoping for much, she pressed the bell, and heard it buzzing far inside.

There seemed to be a deeper stillness now, a stillness like held breath. She was about to press the bell again when she heard a chain rattle and a lock click.

Patrick stared at her through the grille.

'You weren't in your office,' Rachel begun accusingly.

'Oh God, was it today?'

'So I thought I'd drop this draft round here for you. They gave me your address in the department. I'm sorry to bother you at home, but I can't get on until we've discussed it.' She was still sweating and she wasn't sorry at all. Nor did she sound it.

It was only when she'd finished that she fully took in what he was wearing: a long pale-grey Chinese gown and black Chinese slippers. One hand held the door, still defensively half-closed, the other a pi-pa by its narrow neck. He looked like the conventional portrait of a Chinese scholar, only too young; and too unwelcomely disturbed.

'My dear girl, I do apologize most profusely.' He affected his brittlest British accent, more incongruous than ever with that Chinese gown and that Chinese instrument. 'I fear I must have mistaken the date.'

'Again,' Rachel said.

'How very tiresome for you. I'm most terribly sorry, dear girl.'

'Maybe I can leave it with you now, and we can fix another time?'

'Of course, of course.' He came round the door, unlatched the grille and offered to take the large brown envelope from her.

'Hadn't we better fix a time now?' She clasped the envelope firmly. 'If you've got your diary?'

'Oh, yes, my diary,' he repeated, thinking behind his eyes.

Rachel waited.

'But do come in,' he said at last, with sudden loudness — over-loudness, she realized later. 'I'm always confusing dates, alas. I was just whiling away the time on my pi-pa with, with . . . . a very indifferent performer, I'm afraid, but still . . . .' With elaborate flutters of hand and voice, he ushered her into the living room. 'But still one tries, one tries. What else is one to do?'

A slim youthful Chinese sat on a blackwood chair, leafing through a thick glossy magazine of Chinese ceramics.

'Oh, that's Chung Yan,' Patrick said casually, as if he were a dog. He didn't introduce Rachel. 'He's just leaving.'

Chung Yan looked up with shuttered eyes. The top two buttons of his white silk shirt were undone, revealing a gold chain lying on his delicately smooth chest.

'Pleased to meet you,' Rachel said.

Chung Yan allowed her a soft hand to shake.

'Rachel,' Rachel said. 'Rachel Martin.'

Chung Yan said nothing, glancing enquiringly at Patrick.

'Well,' Patrick said.

'I hope I'm not disturbing you?' Rachel said unconvincingly.

'Oh, no, not at all, dear girl. Chung Yan's just going. He just dropped in to — '

Chung Yan interjected something in Cantonese, swift and familiar, with a nod at Rachel. Patrick answered uneasily. Chung Yan spoke again, then stood up, eyeing Rachel with mildly hostile curiosity. They went together to the door. Chung Yan was wearing trim-fitting dark trousers and built-up shoes. He tossed his hair out of his eyes like a girl as he walked. Rachel heard them speaking hurriedly, quietly, by the door, then the grille clashed shut, the door closed.

'Now, dear girl, would you like some tea while I just find my diary?' Patrick plucked a crumpled towel off the back of a chair with an exasperated gesture. 'Simply *terrible* of me to miss you like that again. I can't *imagine* how it happened.'

'Can't you? Yes, if you've got some. Don't make it just for me, though.'

'No, there's some in the kitchen. We were just . . . . ' But his voice always faded when it came to what they were just . . . or what Chung Yan had only dropped in to . . . and all the time he was flitting round, touching chairs and vases, plumping cushions, darting anxious glances everywhere except at Rachel, as if searching for some tell-tale sign he must cover up before she saw it.

'Mind if I sit down?' Rachel asked.

'What? Yes, of course, please do, what am I thinking of?' he flicked the towel nervily, started folding it, then crunched it into a ball. 'Now, let me just find a cup.'

'Are you sure you've got some tea?' Her irritation was beginning to dissolve. It was hard to stay mad at someone who was as flustered as a sparrow trapped in a room. She felt she ought to open some window and set him free.

'Yes, yes, of course I have. It may be a trifle cool, but . . . . Patrick went into the kitchen, and she heard the chink of china.

She picked up the pi-pa he'd laid on the table and touched the strings. 'Is it hard to play?' she asked as he came back with some green tea in an eggshell-thin white cup.

'Quite.' He seemed to have got a hold of himself somehow in there. 'Is the tea all right? It's been made some time, I'm afraid, dear girl. I was just going to throw it away. It's not too positively disgusting, is it?'

It was tepid and bitter, but it slaked her thirst. 'It's fine,' she said. 'What does a pi-pa sound like? I've never heard one live.'

'It sounds exquisite, dear girl. Simply exquisite.' He plucked a few strings. 'Even in my clumsy hands.'

She sipped the bitter tea again. 'Were you playing before I came?'

'Playing?' He glanced at her under his lids. 'Yes, I was, actually.' But it was his lips that were playing now, with an ambivalent smile which she studiedly ignored.

She put the cup down and leant back. 'Can I hear some, then?'

'Very well, if you can stand it,' he shrugged, not displeased. 'But you must remember I'm only an amateur.' He said *amateur* with a French *r* at the end, very pronounced.

He began to play, sitting half-turned away from her, gazing out over the balcony, only occasionally glancing down to watch where he placed his fingers. In his long gown and Chinese slippers he reminded her still more now of one of those old black and white photos you sometimes saw of Chinese intellectuals in the twenties. Was it self-conscious, just another pose like his British blazer and extravagant Edwardian mannerisms? Or had he been dressing up for his friend? She knew people did things like that, but only in the way she knew people lay on beds of nails — what they got out of it was a mystery to her.

She glanced round the room. Everything was Chinese — furniture, scrolls, porcelain, carpet. Even the bitter tea. Well, he certainly blended with the scenery. Perhaps that was the reason.

'I liked that,' she said when he stopped. She had, although she hadn't really been listening.

'Would you like some more tea?'

'What's your Chinese name, by the way?'

'Pak Kay. After my father.'

'The man who was . . . ?'

He drew his hand like a blade across his throat. 'The same. Before I was born.'

'Pak Kay suits you better in these surroundings.'

'I know. Now, dear girl, shall I pour you some more tea?'

'Hadn't you better find your diary first?'

Private study of his heart

Where the mangrove tree had fought so stubbornly against the bulldozer, a concrete mixer stood now, feeding a moving band of wheelbarrows, which coolies were trundling to the gaping foundations of the new building. Dimitri half-watched them from the window of the seminar room, half-listened to the department's preparations for its international conference on Third World culture.

'Will you be giving a paper?' Rachel had asked him in the corridor that morning.

'Neither giving nor receiving. I don't care much for conferences of any sort,' he'd added as Rachel waited, questioning him perplexedly with her short-sighted gaze, 'and least of all for conferences on culture. But, if we must have one on that subject, I'd have thought the Third World culture that had the greatest claim on our attention was agriculture. Which, apart from spreading bullshit, this department seems quite unable to promote.'

Rachel's freckled brow had wrinkled even more perplexedly.

Well, there they were anyway, sitting round the long oval table, debating which well-paid savants they should fly in for a few days from Europe or America, paying their fares and their hotel bills and giving them parties, just so that they could air their dotty theories which people could read about anyway if they were mad enough to want to — and not a soul thought how much better off the Third World would be if all that money went into feeding the buggers instead of alternately patronizing and lionizing them.

Robert Smith, who couldn't read more than three words of Chinese, proposed in his arid grating voice that one of the themes this year should be the *Treatment of Female Sexuality in the Popular Chinese Novel.*

'Dear boy, you make it sound like a medical conference,' Patrick commented lackadaisically. 'Besides, you'll only get the shabby-raincoat brigade coming to that.'

'Putting it crudely,' Smith grated louder, 'you think they'll just come to masturbate and fall asleep?'

'Well, it is the normal sequence,' Dimitri observed to the window-pane.

'What has all this to do with Third World culture?' Faustus Yu asked, blinking with embarrassment behind his lenses. When they sent him to a Catholic school, his parents had equipped him with the Western name Faustus, supposing that Faustus was a Christian saint who had wrestled with the Devil. They thought it would please the fathers. Luckily for him, the fathers were Irish Jesuits who enjoyed a joke, and sent him on to some well-known American academies from which he'd evolved nine years later with a PhD. Ever since then he'd been compiling a twenty-volume anthology of world poetry, and had reached the letter P. 'What has all this to do with the conference?'

'About as much as anything else we're likely to say, dear boy,' Patrick said. 'Or possibly more, since the conference itself is simply self-abuse in a literary form.'

'If that's your attitude to literary theory, Patrick,' Smith sniffed exasperatedly, 'I really don't see how you can claim to be interested in literature at all.'

'Oh, why not, dear boy? One can be interested in a well-cut suit without wanting to read the drivel in the fashion columns, surely?' Patrick took an ostentatious interest in his own well-cut suit, flicking an imaginary speck of dust off its immaculate cuff.

Dimitri smiled, recalling the sly stiletto Smith had slipped into him years ago, when Smith had just joined the department and he himself was groping through the black year of Helen's death and Mila's return to China. His book on Lu Xün had just come out, the one glimmering beacon in all that dark, and Smith went out of his way to tell him how little he'd enjoyed it. 'Not very taken by it, to be honest,' he'd said with a wry little cough of a laugh. 'Found it a bit dated in its theoretical approach. Of course I shouldn't be saying that really, should I? You want to hear how wonderful it was and so on, but . . . .' His lips had puckered into a withered rueful smile. 'But I think candour is kindest in the end, don't you?' Dimitri had shrugged and grinned sheepishly, as if to say: *Why are we even talking about such trivia anyway?* But he winced when the blade went in, as he winced remembering it now, and it was a wound that disabled as well as rankled. Ever since, he'd felt as though Smith had a hold on him, and could make him squirm whenever he chose, just by saying 'Not very taken by it' in that complacent, desiccated, wrinkled-nose voice of his.

But that was his trouble: he'd always bought disparagement at face value, and discounted praise. Even the old Chinese scholar Chen's, for instance, who had written him a kind complimentary letter about the book; correcting a couple of errors, but generally favourable. And *he'd* met Lu Xün in the twenties; he knew what he was talking about. But still it didn't weigh with Dimitri against a piss-artist like Smith's sniffy dispraise. In the private study of his heart he suspected and would always suspect that Smith was right.

'When are you going to write another book?' people used to ask him.

'I've learnt my limitations,' he would answer.

Did Smith ever peer uneasily inside himself, to discover his? Not bloody likely. What would he find there but gears and chains?

On the downward stairway

They agreed on *Female Sexuality*. Patrick said they should sell conference raincoats at the entrance. They could get them from Oxfam — authentic shabby ones.

Stuck to Dimitri's door by a piece of clear tape was a folded message: *Please phone Mr. Denton.*

As he dialled he gazed out of the window at the ever-moving coolies trundling their barrows full of glistening sludge from the concrete mixer to the foundations, like figures on a revolving belt.

'I was wondering if Mila was going to Macao with the ballet company next week,' Michael began indirectly, his voice strangely hesitant and guarded.

'She's going on Thursday. I thought I'd go, too, on Saturday, and stay for the weekend as a matter of fact.'

'Only I've had this letter back from my sister.'

'Ah. So it was genuine — the other one?'

'Yes. She remembers that incident with the priest. In the labour-camp, I mean. And I was thinking perhaps I ought to meet him . . . .'

'I see.' Dimitri had wanted to be alone with Mila in Macao. 'Well,' he said, trying not to sound grudging, 'why don't you come along?'

'The thing is, I have to go to Macao anyway, to meet the man who . . . the man who's been acting as postman. He's got someone there who might be able to arrange some, er . . . .'

'Transport?'

'Yes, transport. And I wondered whether Mila could possibly introduce me to this priest. I think she said she knew where he was now. If it's not too much trouble?'

'I'll ask her. I'm sure she could.' Although she might not want to, he thought a second later. She liked to keep the hatches down on all that heavy cargo.

'My sister asked me to look him up. He might be able to help a bit. Or fill out the picture. If Mila really wouldn't mind?'

'We'll be at the Boa Vista,' Dimitri made himself say. 'Why don't you stay there as well?'

'Oh, no, I'd only come for the day. Just to meet this man, and the priest if possible. And there's something I want to look up in the Leal Senada library as well, for this paper I'm doing on Caldwell.' His voice was becoming easier, as if, now that he'd got his request out, he could relax. Well, he was more accustomed to giving favours than receiving them.

'No problem,' Dimitri said, relieved it wouldn't be much of one. 'Let's meet for lunch on Saturday. One o'clock on the veranda?' He didn't suggest they should travel together — too much arranging. Besides, Michael would go first class.

His eye was distracted from the cyclical procession of the coolies round the foundations of the new building, to a flock of cockatoos swooping and screeching above the trees outside the window. Replacing the receiver, he watched them sweep down the last tree-green valley of the Peak like a school of white fish diving through a great shimmering pond of air. People belly-ached about them stripping the foliage, but he'd always thought of them with their sulphur crests and alert knowing eyes as symbols of hope and liberation. One of his earliest memories was of a cockatoo perched on the roof of a hut in the camp at Stanley, where the Japanese had interned British civilians during the war. It was eyeing him watchfully, head tilted, with a bright unwinking gaze, while his mother told him the war was over. The Japanese were supposed to have brought the birds as captives, and released them from their cages at the end, just before entering their own. Well, it was a nice story.

Anyway, freedom had suited them; they'd multiplied. Often, now, the birds settled like giant snowflakes on the trees round his house, and he would watch from the veranda as they clung to the swaying bauhinia branches and plucked the long green seed-pods, clutching them in their claws and gnawing them with their hooked yellow beaks, occasionally pausing to utter their shrill triumphant shrieks of joy. It seemed appropriate that he should see them now, too, talking to Michael about his sister's bid for freedom.

A mile away, Michael was replacing his own receiver, thinking that his integrity was crumbling already. He was no longer his own man. Yin Hong had phoned him from Macao, so he must go to Macao. Yin Hong said they wanted money, so he must take money along. And handing it over would commit him, the first irrevocable step on the long downward stairway. After that, he'd begin to belong to them. Already on the phone Yin Hong's voice had sounded more familiar, more assuming. He thought of Caldwell, that minor colonial official a hundred years ago, whose life he was uncovering now. He thought of his own father in Shanghai. Each of them had been tainted by shady dealing. Was he to be tainted himself in the same way?

Stay in the woodwork

Patrick didn't miss his next appointment with Rachel (she phoned to remind him the day before), and afterwards he took her to lunch in the senior common room. Talking at ease with her in his room, he dropped all his Edwardian camp affectation, as he had, in the end, a fortnight earlier, after he'd played the pi-pa for her in his apartment. But as soon as they were out in the corridor, in the public world again, he put it all back on like a fancy dress or a disguise. Some *disguise*, she thought.

The dining room was cavernous and noisy, reminding Rachel of her father's office canteen, where she'd always felt exposed and out of place whenever, imagining it a treat, he took her there. 'Hal, this is my daughter. Jack, remember Rachel?' he'd say eagerly to earnest preoccupied men, his moist brown eyes shining with meek pride. The preoccupied men would nod and smile absently, returning to their low-caloric plates and their low earnest talk. After a while her father would give up and sit in subdued silence, and she'd sit there, too, squirming inside, swallowing her food down quickly, listening to the scrape of their knives and forks, knowing her father was a loser in the Great American Game.

Affected or not, Patrick never wilted before an audience. He found an empty table, had the girl change the soiled chequered cloth, ordered in his ringing head-turning voice and loudly summoned Dimitri to join them when he appeared at the door.

'How's Cheung Chau?' Dimitri asked her. 'Settled in yet?'

'It's a whole new world,' she said without thinking, like a gushing Midwestern widow on her first coach tour of Paris or Rome.

'An old one, I'd have thought,' he said drily, unfolding his napkin. 'Personally I can't stand it.'

Well, what can you stand? she wondered. *Not ballet, not conferences, not Cheung Chau. What's left?*

'To me it's just a grotty little village paved with dog turds,' Dimitri went on. 'Where affected expatriates mingle in affected harmony with affected fisher-folk who are in reality ripping them off for all they're worth.'

'Excepting Rachel of course, dear boy.' Patrick waved a deprecating hand, the fingers long and slim as a girl's. The wide band of a gold ring gleamed on his little finger.

'Meaning I'm not affected or not being ripped off?'

'I'm sure you're not affected,' Dimitri said, snapping his chopsticks like crocodile jaws.

'Rachel dear girl, you must absolutely forgive Dimitri his cynicism,' Patrick intoned episcopally. He sipped his wine. When he put the glass down again, it cast a little glimmering amber pool on the red and white squares of the table-cloth. 'As he in turn forgives you your youth.'

'Youth?' Dimitri said, snapping his chopsticks again. 'I can forgive the young anything except that.'

'Wow, so many fireworks,' Rachel said, 'Do you practise for the show?'

Dimitri eyed her askance, then smiled wryly, like someone accepting a justified rebuke. 'Spontaneous, I assure you,' he said mildly. 'In a habitual sort of way.'

Rachel chewed her toasted cheese sandwich ruminatively. It sounded like crunched ice in her ears. Yes, it *was* an old world she'd meant all the same. Old with cobwebs and grime and a life that was like a stubborn stain that electricity and refrigerators and colour televisions just couldn't bleach out. The Pak Tai temple, for instance, which she'd visited several times, with its stone-flagged courtyard stretching down to the sea. It was still a playground and meeting-place now, as it must have been for centuries. Old men sat and smoked there and played chess. Old women and young girls — everyone else was presumably out fishing or farming — brought young children and gossiped there while the kids played. Inside the temple, thick incense-sticks clogged the air with sweet-smelling smoke, dropping their grey ash like perfectly formed powdery ghosts of themselves into the holders below. Tiny frail women with cropped grey hair knelt before the main altar, casting fortune-spills on the stone floor in front of several candles that threw a flickering light over the fierce red face of the god. And what they knelt on, one after the other, was a battered car seat, pinkish sponge rubber leaking through the rents in its plastic cover. That was how they made the new things serve the old, Western things serve Chinese.

Little, hardened splashes of candle-wax and incense-ash and rotting fruit-offerings lay all around on the unswept floor. The stone carvings in the roof were broken, smoke-grimed, veiled in clinging black cobwebs. Electric cables trailed amongst them, leading to naked bulbs, feeble and dusty, hanging like dying men on trembling cords over the fortune-tellers' tables.

And yet the old life flourished in that untidy mess — flourished untidily and scruffily, but it flourished. The temple was always busy. Old men shuffled from side to side throughout the day, offering fortune-spills and incense-sticks, and people came in to pray at all hours, making their requests and departing as matter-of-factly as people filing telegrams at *Cable and Wireless* — which, spiritually, she guessed they were.

On the hill above the temple was an old people's home. Ancient men and women sat mute and docile on benches under the dappled shade of still more ancient trees, until summoned to their meals by a stentorian tannoy. But even the modern tannoy seemed to have gathered a patina of antiquity there, the worn speakers hunched under the eaves like old metallic bats. Michael had told her the place was built near the site of an old death house, where the aged and sick, whose families couldn't or wouldn't care for them, used to go to die. Maybe that was the function of the old people's home, too. Now she thought of it, death house might be a more honest title than old people's home. Chinese was a pithy language.

She realized Patrick was addressing her, and refocused her eyes.

'The thing I should detest most about living on that remote little island,' he was saying, 'apart from the almost total absence of civilized society, is that positively nauseating ride on the ferry every day. There's a stretch about halfway across when the beastly boat simply rolls and rolls in the most disgusting manner. Very queasy-making, I must say.'

'I haven't noticed,' Rachel said. 'The only thing is, the last ferry back is kind of early, if you've gone to a film or something.'

Dimitri said if she ever needed somewhere to stay the night she could always use their place. Alex and Elena were hardly ever there and, anyway, there was lots of room even when they were. He raised his tea-cup at the same time that Patrick lowered his wine-glass, and Rachel viewed the contrast of his broad nail-bitten fingers, dark hair fuzzing the knuckles, with Patrick's smooth, pale, manicured hand.

'Are you sure?'

'Of course. In fact, next weekend you'd be more than welcome. We'll be in Macao, and we want someone to look after the cat.'

'Ah, Macao,' Patrick sighed. 'And the jetfoils are as smooth as silk. One scarcely knows one's on the beastly water.'

'It's Elena's cat really, but if she ever has children and treats them like that they'll all be taken into care. Not that she doesn't like it; it's just that when she's got a boyfriend she forgets.'

'Will Elena be there next weekend?' Rachel enquired warily.

Dimitri smiled. 'Have no fear. That's why I'm asking you. The ballet's performing in Macao. And you wouldn't have to worry about feeding the cat. Ah Wong does that. It's just a question of emptying the litter-box . . . .' He regarded Rachel's freckled face and short flaxen hair hesitantly.

'Oh, I wouldn't mind doing that.'

She was picking up toast crumbs with her fingertips and then fastidiously licking them off. Her tongue, pink between her even white teeth, reminded him of the cat's.

'Why doesn't Ah Wong do the litter-box?' Patrick asked, dabbing his lips with his napkin. 'I thought that was what servants were for?'

'To cut a long story short, she thinks it would poison her. In some ways she's as dotty as a domino.'

He'd found the cat eleven years before, in a plastic bag hung on the garage gate. It was only a few days old, its eyes still closed. The bag was a pink and swanky one from Lane Crawford. 'Must've been some rich Chinese threw her out,' Elena said, feeding her with a dropper. Why Chinese? Because they weren't sentimental about animals. Ah Wong would have nothing to do with the cat at first. Bad luck to bring a stray cat into the house, she warned sourly. But the bad luck had happened already. Helen had killed herself, Mila had disappeared into China — what else could befall them? Gradually Ah Wong had thawed, but only after a bitter campaign over the litter-box, conducted with savage silent fury over several weeks. He'd wanted it to be in the basement; she claimed the smell was poisoning her (though it was nowhere near her room). Although Elena at that time cleaned the box every day, Ah Wong insisted she could smell it everywhere, and wore a cloth over her nose, answering in curt monosyllables if at all when spoken to. 'Put it upstairs in the bathroom,' Elena had begged him tearfully at last. 'Otherwise she'll kill the cat.' So he had to give in. He did so sullenly, without a word. Ah Wong pursed her lips triumphantly and put away her cloth. But she was magnanimous in victory. The next morning she bought some kau yi from the market, his favourite fish, which for weeks she'd insisted was unobtainable. 'It's no use fighting them,' he remembered Helen used to say wearily. 'They always win in the end.' That defeat provided him with a sobering perspective on the domestic history of the British Empire. He began to see it as a varied and ulcerous series of guerrilla skirmishes, in which domineering servants in the kitchen exacted a lasting revenge for their country's battlefield submissions.

That was before Elena went to England. When she left, a few months later, she implored him to look after her cat; and he did. He even grew as fond of her as Elena was. They never gave her a name; she was too composed and elegant to answer to any of that Tinkerbell or Fluffy trash. Just Mau Nui — Cat Girl — as Ah Wong called her. When he was sweaty she would lie beside him on the chair and lick the salty moisture off his skin with her harsh dry tongue. And often, when she was washing herself, she would wash his hand as well, sweaty or not. Ah Wong came to like her, too.

She would feed her and talk to her endlessly, but never touch either her or her litter-box.

Whenever she came back for the holidays, Elena would stand in the hall and call, and for her alone the cat would come running, rippling down the stairs to meet her. Then, one summer, when he met Elena at the airport, Dimitri sensed a change. Was it her manner, her expression, the scent of her skin even? Something indefinable but unmistakable proclaimed she was a woman now. She was just eighteen. When she entered the house, for the first time in years, she didn't call the cat; but the cat came running anyway. Elena picked her up and fondled her, but the single-minded devotion was gone.

Now that she'd joined the ballet company she was as often away — he never asked where — as at home, and the cat had to put up with erratic and divided affection, as he did himself. It wasn't too hard for either of them. The cat withdrew into regal indifference, and he had Mila back. 'Sex has got a lot to answer for,' he said to Mila once, as he carried the litter-box up the back steps himself. 'You should know,' she answered, with her eyes that almost smiled and her lips that almost didn't. He supposed he did know by now. And Rachel — glancing covertly at her as he drank his tea — he judged Rachel didn't.

'Mind if I join you?' a sing-song voice enquired behind them. A large, sudsy beer-glass was placed carefully at the vacant place beside Rachel, then the bearded wizened Englishman she'd met in the common room before — Frank something or other — eased himself with equal caution on to the chair. 'I know. Don't tell me — you're the girl who's doing a book on Chinese literature,' he declared, regarding her with filmy brown eyes.

'Not a book exactly. Just a thesis.'

'Admire you literary chaps. Nuts-and-bolts man myself. Have a beer?'

'Alas, we've just finished,' Patrick said with distant civility. 'If I may speak for the others.'

'Writing a book myself, matter of fact,' Frank said. 'Nothing highfalutin', mark you, not like you literary chaps. Story of my life. Or love-life. Comes to the same thing really, doesn't it? Strong stuff, some of it. I've put my prick in some pretty rum places, I can tell you, in my time.'

'Where most people wouldn't put the tips of their umbrellas,' Patrick murmured, wrinkling his nose.

'Where d'you put *your* prick, then?' Frank asked pleasantly. He swallowed a long draught of beer, his Adam's apple moving up and down in the undergrowth of his beard, like a half-plucked turkey gobbling. 'Hear you're having a conference next term? What's it on?'

'Oh, the usual rubbish,' Dimitri said. 'As we have nothing to say to ourselves, we invite a lot of people who have nothing to say to themselves to come and say it to us. The Hong Kong dollar seems to be holding up, I notice, despite your prediction?'

'Can't last. Sino-British talks are getting nowhere. Chinese are going to make a unilateral declaration. Fact. And that'll be that. Down the tube. If you've gone in for that readership, I can assure you, you won't enjoy it for long.'

'I won't enjoy it at all if I don't get it.'

Readership? Rachel wondered. *Is he writing for the newspapers?*

Patrick pushed back his chair. 'Well, if you'll excuse us, dear boy . . . . '

'One thing, though,' Frank said solemnly to Rachel as she was about to follow the others. 'At least the commies'll keep the pansies down. Credit be where credit's due, they won't be drafting a Queers' Charter in Hong Kong now. Wouldn't dare walk into a gents' again if they did. Specially here.' He nodded at Patrick's receding back, attempting a wink which, not quite closing his eye, gave him a momentarily demented look.

'You mean it's against the law to be gay here?' Rachel asked incredulously, yet with a sense of illumination slowly stealing over her.

"Course it is. Where have you been all this time? Consenting adults, privacy of their own homes, the whole lot. Place may look like San Francisco, but the poofters stay in the woodwork here, my girl. And long may they do so, too.'

Worse, my catamite

'Like many poets, East and West, ancient and modern,' Emmelina Wu read out in her plain and serious voice, holding her essay close to her plain and serious glasses, 'Li Po's main theme was the impermanence of life.'

'The lightness of being,' Patrick murmured, his eyes closed.

Emmelina Wu looked up uncertainly.

' "The lightness of being" is a more striking phrase, which perhaps catches your meaning better than "the impermanence of life". It does a little more for the imagination, I mean. It's from a novel.'

Emmelina Wu frowned, testing the phrase dubiously in her head, then pencilled a note in the margin of her essay.

'Just a thought,' Patrick said. 'It's not important. Let's go on.'

The lightness of being. And the weight of it, too. Just now it was the weight he felt, the weight of Frank's boozy sneer lying like a lump of lead on his chest. He'd half-heard it as he left, half-guessed it from Rachel's thoughtful expression afterwards. He was pretty resilient — bouncy even — but that was the one taunt he couldn't answer, the one gibe that infallibly brought him down. He pretended he hadn't heard Frank, he produced an imitation of himself for Dimitri and Rachel to laugh at, but inside him there was lead. And Dimitri and Rachel smiled only out of politeness, like an audience whose mind was no longer on the show.

The remedy, he knew, now that he was alone — with Emmelina Wu you were as good as alone — was imagination and self-illusion. He had to wind life back in his mind, and play it through again, but with a better ending. So, while Emmelina Wu read dully on, he played scene after vivid scene against the background drone of her voice, scenes in which he put Frank down in mid-beer-swill with crunching retorts and rapier one-liners. He saw Frank's face gaping in bleary sheepish humiliation, he saw respectful looks on every side, he saw himself walk out triumphant and unruffled. The one thing he couldn't do was find the words that did the job — they always lurked on the edge of his mind, just out of reach.

It was only a fantasy, a painted curtain that he drew across reality. One poke of the real, and it tore. But it was better than nothing. It compensated. It helped him through. And, if it didn't give him self-respect, it gave him a taste of it.

'Yes, imagination is a great consolation,' he said inconsequentially to Emmelina Wu, who had finished reading her essay and was waiting patiently for his comments. 'In Li Po, I mean. For the, er, the weight of being.'

'You said "lightness of being" before,' she said reproachfully.

The remedy hadn't worked perfectly of course — it never did. Although Patrick had tried several replays, each with a different twist at the end, fact was always stronger than fiction, and he went back to his empty flat with the memory of Frank's sneer, and many others, too, still weighing him down. He felt grey and heavy.

He unfastened the grille and slotted the key into the lock. As he pushed the door open, something moved in the hall, and he felt a leap and flutter of alarm before he realized it was Chung Yan. Chung Yan, wearing Patrick's grey silk gown, much too long for him, and mincing towards him in a burlesque of a model on a catwalk, holding the gown up like a skirt. He'd hung his gold chain round the collar. It gleamed and shook as he swung his shoulders extravagantly, his eyes shining, lips parted, free hand patting his hair.

'How did you get in?' Patrick exclaimed in Cantonese, holding him close as the door swung shut behind them. The world remade itself as he heard the latch click securely home. This after all was the only cure, feeling

Chung Yan's body moulding to his, feeling Chung Yan's hair against his cheek. 'Thank God you did, though.'

He'd pinched the spare keys of course, and had copies made. 'Now I can come and go as I like, can't I?' Chung Yan said, parting his full moist lips temptingly. 'Unless you change the locks.'

'I won't change the locks,' Patrick said, with the sense that he was promising more than just not to change the locks. 'For better or worse, my catamite,' he added in English.

'Let's go to Ocean Park,' Chung Yan pleaded later when Patrick had slaked his desire. 'I want to see the killer whales.'

'You know that beastly place bores me to death,' Patrick objected, knowing perfectly well he'd go anyway in the end.

7

With a musical laugh

Michael found Yin Hong feeding the one-armed bandits just outside the main hall of the circular Macao Casino. A young man with a strong body lounged against the machine beside him, tattooed arms folded over his chest. The place was half-empty — it was ten in the morning — and coins dropped, levers clunked only desultorily around them, like turnstiles in an unfrequented seedy subway station.

Yin Hong nodded casually, yanking the lever with a bandaged hand. 'I love to play these things,' he said in Shanghainese. 'Better than roulette or cards. You're nice and early. Meet my friend Ah Keung. Want to play? No?' He fed more coins in and yanked, fed and yanked. 'What about cards, then, inside? Some people playing for high stakes if you're interested, rich man like you.'

'Not that rich,' Michael said perfunctorily. He glanced into the dim and tatty circular hall, where a few apathetic girl croupiers with etiolated eczematic skin sat facing scatterings of tense devoted players. Most of the tables were empty, the girls sipping tea or dozing upright on their chairs. Later, in the evening, he supposed, it would be different — crowded, lively and bustling. Now it was only desolate and gloomy.

'I'd like to get our business settled.'

'Sure, sure, let's just finish, ah?' Yin Hong squinted at his watch, long-sighted like Michael. 'Plenty of time anyway. Old Snakeboat Wong's not expecting us for another half-hour.' He fed and yanked, his last handful of coins.

Suddenly the machine clanked and coughed, then spewed out a stream of dollars, as if it had finally been sickened by all it had swallowed.

'Look at that! Must be my lucky day.'

The coins clattered out for a quarter of a minute. Other players came to watch, but none of them spoke. They gazed with mute patient envy, until the stream ended with another clank, as if a metal jaw had clamped shut inside it.

Ah Keung gathered the coins up in a red plastic bowl which the listless girls at the counter gave him, and exchanged them for notes.

'Right, then,' Yin Hong said, pocketing the money. 'Let's take a cab.'

He stopped the taxi near the Rua Das Lorchas, leaving Ah Keung to pay.

'Down here,' he said. 'We can walk the rest.'

Michael glanced over the wooden piers of the Porto Interior at China, half a mile away. A dull grey Chinese gunboat was patrolling the channel, its bows scabby with rust. He imagined his sister Lily standing amongst the few drab figures he could see on the other shore, imagined her gazing longingly past the same gunboat at the decayed grandeur of Macao and the distorting enticement of its freedom.

'This way,' Yin Hong called.

He led Michael under the crumbling colonnades, the facades of once-elegant colonial houses, now run-down ship's chandlers, godowns and rice-stores, and stopped at a godown near the end, beside a shop selling kerosene. The cracked paint-starved doors stood open, but the tong mun had been drawn across the entrance, thick round wooden bars like the rungs of some enormous ladder. Yin Hong called out, peering into the long dark innards of the godown.

After a while a grey-haired paunchy man in a white singlet and black shorts shuffled out of the gloom towards them. Scowling against the dazzling light, he glanced suspiciously at Michael, then questioningly at Yin Hong.

'My friend,' Yin Hong said. 'Come to see the boss.'

The man slid back the tong mun just enough for them to pass through, then closed and fastened it again.

My friend, Michael repeated silently. He felt as though Yin Hong had just linked arms with him or slapped him on the back.

They followed the man into the gloom, past piles of bulging sacks, timber and packing-cases. The man's rubber sandals flip-flopped over the uneven floor without ever wholly parting from it, like a pair of slobbery lips kissing.

Up some unplaned wooden stairs into a loft. Four men in singlets and shorts, playing mah-jong at a flimsy collapsible plastic table. In the corner, a little crude red altar with a joss-stick smouldering in front of it.

'Our friend,' Yin Hong said. 'Finish your game. No hurry.'

Our friend, Michael repeated silently. *No hurry.*

The grey-haired paunchy man poured them some tea and brought them folding wooden stools, while the players, after cursory nods at Michael, continued slapping and sliding the pieces on the table. A fishing family, he decided. And smuggling presumably. And whatever else. The older player, about fifty, who was facing him across the table, must be the father, the others his sons. The father kept glancing up at Michael while he considered his pieces, or pretended to. He had tight thin lips, but his eyes were frank, good-humoured even. A dumpy woman with iron-grey hair chopped off at the neck brought in some fresh tea — the mother, he supposed. She wore a grey floppy jacket and trousers, and swayed slightly as she walked, as if she were on a rocking deck. He noticed a gold earring. She, too, glanced at him assessingly.

When the game ended, they made room for Yin Hong and Michael. The father slid one of the pieces to and fro on the table with his forefinger. 'Mr. Yau says you want to see the boat,' he begun formally in a strangely light tenor voice which carried like a singer's.

Michael felt four pairs of eyes examining him. The mother had gone, the paunchy old man was fiddling with the teapot, Yin Hong was slurping his tea with elaborate indifference.

'Well, if it's going to cost so much, it's a good idea to see what you'll be getting,' Michael said peaceably. He caught a whiff of dried fish through the barred open window above his head. 'And I'd like to know how you'd arrange things, too.'

The father's finger paused and tapped the mah-jong piece. 'It doesn't cost so much,' he said lightly, in the same musical tone. 'We're giving you a very good price. Don't you trust us?'

'It would be bad business to buy something you'd never seen from someone you didn't know, wouldn't it? Whatever the price.'

The father smiled faintly with the corners of his narrow lips. He started moving the piece again, to and fro, to and fro. 'We don't want a lot of people knowing about it,' he said slowly, frowning down at the cube sliding below his finger. 'We'll be taking some pretty big risks after all.'

'So will I.' He glanced at Yin Hong. 'So will my sister.'

Yin Hong shrugged, meaning: *Suit yourselves; it's between the two of you, nothing to do with me.*

As if to emphasize the risks, a police siren started wailing some way off. Their eyes swivelled to the window as the wobbly shrieking approached, passed, grew lower, smaller, fainter. For a moment it seemed as though they'd all been holding their breath. Then the father, who had smothered the mah-jong piece with his hand, as if it might have given them away, moved it thoughtfully again, glancing round the table at each son in turn. The sons looked woodenly at each other, looked woodenly back at their father. Michael caught no hint of expression, got no clue.

'And then you pay the money?' the father suggested, returning to Michael. Michael hesitated. 'Ten per cent now.'

'Ten per cent?' the tenor voice repeated with a musical laugh. The sons all grinned and chuckled with him.

'If he's satisfied with everything, he'll pay a bit more,' Yin Hong said quickly, turning to Michael. 'Won't you? To hold your booking, ah? Like an airline ticket.'

'Half now, half when it's done,' the man said, holding the piece still again.

Michael performed a show of considering, a show of giving way. 'Twenty-five per cent now,' he offered, 'Twenty-five per cent before you start, the rest when it's done.' It's just like any other business deal, he thought with mild surprise. Crime ought to feel different; this is too ordinary.

Again the old man glanced at his sons, reading each face in turn. He refilled Michael's cup deliberately, then all the others. Michael tapped the table with his finger in ritual acknowledgement. Somewhere outside, the mother muttered to a child, scolding it, then raspily hawked and spat. If he'd been buying a load of rice, Michael thought, it would have been no different. Or timber. The muddy water of the dock outside reminded him suddenly of a godown in Mandalay, where he'd bought some timber once, in the afternoon of a distant New Year's Eve. Distant, so very distant, now.

'All right,' the father said at last, drinking his tea. 'You can see the boat from here; we'll go and have a look at it later.' He stood up and went to the window. 'Take a look, come on.' Now he spoke with a kind of jocular condescension, like a man reassuring a doubting child.

Dead now, of course

'Now let's eat,' Yin Hong said afterwards. 'Your turn to pay, isn't it?'

'I have to meet some people.'

'Know that place where they have pigeons?' He waved to Ah Keung waiting in the shade across the road. Ah Keung nodded and sauntered across. 'Shall we go there?' Yin Hong said. 'It's not far.'

'I can't,' Michael said curtly.

'Suit yourself, suit yourself. Next time, then, ah? Your turn to pay, don't forget. Can we drop you off somewhere?'

Michael shook his head and turned away. But as he turned, Yin Hong put out his bandaged hand and Michael saw himself taking it automatically, before he could think. His fingers felt the soft thready texture of the bandage.

'Not too hard, ah?' Yin Hong grinned, pretending to wince.

'What happened?' Michael asked perfunctorily.

'Cooking accident.' Yin Hong grinned at Ah Keung now. 'Spilt some boiling oil over it. Still, better than getting your finger chopped off, ah?'

'Yes,' Michael said, then: 'What would you know about that?'

'Know about it? I could tell you who chopped it off! Dead now, of course. Know why you were kidnapped, don't you? Your pa owed Pockmark Chen some money, on an opium deal. Didn't he ever tell you? It was Pockmark Chen getting his money back, that's why they kidnapped you. You couldn't put one over Pockmark Chen. Nobody could. Ask your sister, ask Lily. She was old enough to know. Ask her when she comes out.'

No, Michael thought. *I won't ask her. That's one thing I never want to know.*

'We'll keep in touch, OK? I'll give you a ring next week.'

Michael walked off without answering. No need to answer. No point. Whatever he might say, he knew Yin Hong would keep in touch. As a spider keeps in touch with a fly in its web.

He turned left into a small street, which led into a tangle of little alleys, themselves like threads of a web. When he realized he was lost he stopped a taxi. If only it was always so easy.

So his father *had* been as shady as Caldwell, he thought dully, if what Yin Hong had just told him about his kidnapping was true. He gazed out at the crumbling houses and locked abandoned churches sliding past the taxi window. And he himself was becoming equally shady. It was as though they were all fated. He wondered if it was some little act of loyalty that first snared his father and Caldwell, too, some simple thing they couldn't refuse, as he couldn't refuse Lily.

Galloping inflation

Tom was lolling on a bench under the trees, watching a patch-sailed junk making its slow drowsy way up the muddy channel.

'You're late,' he said, reaching for Elena's hand. 'This reminds me of the Mekong.'

'I couldn't help it; the rehearsal just went on and on.' She drew her hand away and stood in the shade, wrinkling her nose at the smell of the mud-flats.

'Sit down. Admire the view.' He gestured with a wide sweep of his arm from the low green shores of China across the water to the doomed colonial buildings of Macao all round them. 'This is history.'

'I'm sweaty and tired and I want to rest before the performance,' she said definitely. 'Let's go. Besides, it's hot and smelly here.'

A passing trishaw coolie slowed his pedals and clanged his bell, eyeing them invitingly. He was an old, stringy, round-shouldered man, with a shallow dun-coloured straw hat tilted raffishly forward to keep the sun out of his eyes.

She bargained him down in Cantonese from seven dollars to five for the ride along the Praia Grande to the hotel. 'Two people,' the old man kept saying, wiping his glistening face and neck with a grubby strip of towel. 'Two big people such a long way.' But he nodded at last and dismounted to let them in.

Starting with a run and a push, he stepped on to the turning pedal and leant forward to thrust down on it with all his puny weight. Elena gazed at his thin sharp shoulder blades, sticking out beneath his greyish singlet like amputated wings, and at his scrawny muscular legs below his shorts. A long mauve vein ran like a knotted cord down each calf. She felt suddenly uneasy, being drawn along by a grey-haired old man as if he were a human horse.

'He's like a pony in a trap,' she said.

'Ever seen a pony pedalling?'

She would have tossed her head, but her temples were throbbing. She leant back under the shade of the tattered canvas canopy instead, and half-closed her eyes. 'Well, you needn't be so damned complacent about it anyway.'

'Got a horror story this afternoon,' Tom said. 'About one of the snakeboats smuggling kids in from China. They looked like getting caught, so they tied the kids up and dumped them overboard with stones in their pockets.'

'Kids?'

'Yeah. Got rid of the evidence.'

'I realize that. I'm not thick.'

At last the coolie changed gears with a clank of the lever on his crossbar, and sat down now to pedal. He was breathing hard and coughing. The towel he'd draped round his neck looked limp and moist.

'Why don't you nose out a happy story for a change?' Elena asked, glancing out over the slack brown water of the bay. 'I think my brother's a virgin by the way.'

'Why?'

'Why what?' The spokes clicked, the pedals heaved the chain round, and a missing tooth on some cogwheel made a sudden grinding jolt on every orbit. She felt each sound and movement in her head like blows from a hammer that had been muffled in black cloth. 'Why do I think he's a virgin, or why should you nose out a happy story? Explain yourself!'

'Take your pick, kid.'

She considered while they passed two men playing chess on the sea-wall, watched intently by several others. She couldn't think now why Tom should find a happy story. You only got misery in the newspapers after all;

people must like it that way. So she settled on Alex. 'Because San San said *she* is; and, if she is, he probably is, since he's never thought of anyone else, poor mutt.'

'The first time for a girl's supposed to be deeply significant,' he said sententiously.

'Oh, don't be soppy.'

'Whereas for a man it's more like a driving test. Like after that you've got your licence.'

'You're not drunk, are you? Already?'

'Why?'

'Because you don't usually say "like" like that unless you're pissed as a newt. It makes you sound like an ageing hippy.'

'Not a drop since last night.' He raised his great hands palms up, and let them fall expressively in his lap. 'You're not like near your time, are you?'

'I really hate you sometimes,' she said through her teeth.

Round the bend the shore-fishermen were hauling their vast net up from the sea. Raining glistening showers of water back into the bay, the net swung slowly up on two long bamboo poles, sagging in the middle like a Buddha's bulging belly with its load of frantically suffocating silvery fish.

Suddenly she felt contrite. She slipped her hand into Tom's. 'If you promise not to get drunk while I'm dancing, you can wreak your will on me tonight if you want,' she said penitently. 'Only once, mind; I couldn't stand more. Now, I can't say fairer than that in my condition, can I?' She glanced up at him wide-eyed. 'Well? What d'you say?'

Tom closed his hand easily round hers and held it tight. 'How long is once?'

She shrugged. 'As long as you can make it.'

'Guess I can make it pretty long.'

All she really wanted was to be liked by someone with strong hands. That was why she always went for older men. Except that first time in London, which was with a student hardly any older than herself.

'The first time wasn't a deeply significant experience for me,' she said. 'At least, not in a nice way. It was just messy.'

She felt Tom squeeze her hand, saying 'There, there,' in sign language.

'Mark you, it was nice the second time. And most of the others. Look, there's Michael Denton. In that taxi.'

Tom twisted round. 'He looks Chinese to me. I thought only his wife was?'

'He's half and half. He's very nice in a dull sort of way, and terribly knowledgeable about Hong Kong. I'll get you an invitation, shall I? I've been meaning to for weeks.'

The coolie braked and climbed off the saddle, panting heavily.

'Give him ten dollars,' she said as she stepped out.

'I thought you said five?'

'They've got galloping inflation here.'

The old man coughed and wheezed in long racking spasms as he watched Tom counting out the coins.

'Galloping consumption, too, by the sound of it,' Tom said.

But Elena was already walking up the steps to the hotel.

Class of '72

They sat at the corner table on the veranda, Michael, Dimitri and Mila, beside a vivid mossy patch of mould that grew triumphantly through its anaemic whitewash camouflage. Michael was abstracted throughout the meal, talking only with an effort, frequently staring away over the balustrade, across the bay to China.

'What exactly do you expect to get from this priest?' Dimitri asked him when the coffee came.

Michael shrugged, tipping his heart pills out from their little silver box into the palm of his hand. 'I don't know *exactly*,' he said, swallowing the pills with a gulp of coffee.' You see, my sister's a bit of a blank to me really. I'd just like to find out what's happened to her, what she's been doing, what she's really like now. I hope this Father . . . Father . . . ?'

'Ignatius,' Mila said.

'I hope he can just tell me something, that's all. It seems they got quite friendly in this camp they were in.' He glanced at Mila.

Mila shifted cautiously on her chair, so that Dimitri knew her back was hurting. 'I would not have thought they had very much in common,' she said, looking out at the long curve of the bridge that joined Macao to its outlying islands. 'Except being victims, of course.'

She imagined the bridge as an arching backbone, arching as hers no longer could, supple and pain-free.

The others were looking at her expectantly. 'Father Ignatius was always, well, patient, mild. You know, Father-forgive-them. Whereas your sister seemed to be bursting with resentment.' As she let the bridge fade out of focus, she could visualize them both, Father Ignatius and Michael's sister, kneeling on the muddy ground, and herself chanting slogans with the rest. She could hear a ghost of the dutiful shouting, feel a ghost of her own hope and fear. And shame.

'Well, shall we go?' Dimitri said, waving for the bill. 'We can walk down to the Praia and pick up a taxi.'

'Let's get the hotel to call one here,' Mila suggested quietly. Sometimes walking, especially walking downhill, made her feel as though her back was splintering.

They sat silent and preoccupied in the taxi. Up and over the hump of the bridge, down to Taipa, past the drab ostentation of the Hyatt Hotel, past the shoddy new buildings of the university, along the pot-holed causeway to Coloane.

'I used to come here in the summers when I was a boy,' Dimitri said. 'No bridge or causeway then, you had to take a boat. We used to go to Bamboo Beach, nearly every day. Or Black Sand Beach. They were always empty then. God knows what they're like now, with all these roads and bridges. Haven't been there for years.'

'You went with *me* once,' Mila said, as if he'd forgotten.

But he hadn't. 'Before the bridge was built,' he said. When they were young and hot-blooded and couldn't get enough of each other.

At least the village had scarcely changed. It was still almost a Portuguese village, grafted on to a reluctant China a couple of hundred or so years ago. Somehow the transplant had taken, though the symptoms of rejection were always there. As they drove round the tree-bordered square, past the tea-house and the shops, he realized he could find his way without difficulty, the place matched the map in his memory exactly, down to the trees, the hibiscus and the noodle-stall where the taxi stopped, a few yards from the low embankment. A little further on, he knew without looking, was a sprawl of brown wooden huts, limping unsteadily on stilts out into the sea. At his back, the church and the two-room library. Across the estuary, China began — a few buildings, a red flag, and no people. The tide was out, fishing-junks and sampans lay in the mud, wallowing like water-buffalo. In the narrow stream a launch — Portuguese or Chinese, he couldn't tell — chugged slowly past.

'This way,' Dimitri said. 'Isn't it?'

They walked back along the shore to the little square. At the opening of the square, by the sea, stood a stone monument commemorating the *Combates de Coloane, 1910*. He'd forgotten that.

'It was a skirmish between the Portuguese and some pirates,' Michael said precisely, feeling the stump of his little finger. 'They'd kidnapped some children for ransom.' Twenty years before he was kidnapped himself in Shanghai. And it still went on.

They walked across the sun-bright square towards the little whitewashed church. 'Funny, this priest choosing to come to a place like this,' Dimitri said. 'Only a couple of hundred yards from China,' he glanced back at the shore.

Two figures in dull olive-green uniforms stood watching them. 'You'd think he'd prefer to be somewhere else, after what he'd been through.'

As he spoke, one of the figures trained his glasses on them. Mila turned her back. 'Usually priests do not choose; they are sent,' she said coolly. 'But in my case I don't think it is funny exactly.'

Of course, Dimitri thought, she was familiar with the faith and understood its curious forms and practices. He'd forgotten she'd been sent to a convent school in Hong Kong. Even now she could still recite the Paternoster, without understanding a word of Latin. He almost expected her to cross herself and genuflect when she entered the church. But she didn't.

It was small and bare inside, austere enough to be a Protestant chapel except for the extravagantly bleeding Jesus at the altar, and the life-sized Virgin, moulded in that curving pose of the Chinese goddess Kuan Yin, with whom she'd gradually merged. All she needed was a pair of slit eyes and a different hairstyle, and she'd do in a Chinese temple. Plus a few joss sticks and a dozen coats of dust.

The door closed behind them with a soft echoing thud. They stood uncertainly. Michael examined a glass case in which a fragment of greyish bone was proclaimed to be the elbow of St. Francis Xavier. As Mila walked hesitantly down the aisle between the few rows of wooden benches, a young boy came out of the side-chapel, followed by a short light-skinned Eurasian priest with stiff grey hair and a straggly beard. He sailed towards them in his white cassock, beaming. 'You've come to see the church, the martyrs' bones?' he asked, first in Cantonese, then, glancing at Dimitri, in Gallic English.

He looked younger than Mila remembered him, though it was eleven years now. And he'd plumped out. She'd forgotten his genial eyes, darting curious glances at each of them in turn. Perhaps they weren't genial before. 'Where are you from? Hong Kong? We do not see many tourists here.'

'Do you remember me, Father Ignatius?' Mila asked in Cantonese.

He looked at her quizzically, speaking Cantonese himself. 'Are you the lady who came last year, or . . . ?' His eyes hazed uncertainly. 'Or was it somewhere else?'

When she said the name of the camp, he looked at her sharply, then smiled. 'Were you there, too?' he asked, as if it had been a boarding school. Which in a way it was, Dimitri thought. And probably taught them more than most.

'I was there for three years,' Mila was saying in a quiet subdued tone. 'I remember you, but you wouldn't have noticed me . . . .' Was it the convent school that had made her so uncharacteristically demure before a priest? She was like a girl at confirmation class.

'But of course I was the only priest there,' he laughed, sliding a questioning glance at Michael and Dimitri. When did you leave?'

Leave school, Dimitri thought.

'Soon after . . . .' She baulked at saying it. 'In April '72.'

'Ah. And now you are married to this gentleman?' Father Ignatius smiled at Michael.

'No, me,' Dimitri said, 'I'm afraid.'

'Excellent, excellent. The good Lord has protected you.' He rubbed his hands together. 'How many children?'

'Father, my friend would like to know about someone else who was there at the camp. His sister.'

'Ah.' Father Ignatius tilted his head alertly at Michael. 'Come,' he said, crossing himself before the altar. He led them into the cramped sacristy and switched on a fan. The bearings were loose; the blades pinged regularly against the wire guard. Or perhaps it was the guard that was loose. A bowl of rice stood on a little table in the corner, chopsticks resting on the rim.

'Sit down, please, sit down.' Father Ignatius indicated some upright wooden chairs, which looked like relics from some ancient schoolroom, and sat down himself at the table. The vestments stirred and fluttered in an open cupboard along the wall.

'Does the name Lee Li-li mean anything to you?' Michael asked awkwardly.

'Lee Li-li? Of course!' He clapped his hands delightedly. 'She is your sister? I don't see the resemblance. We had some interesting conversations. Very interesting.'

No bitterness at all, Dimitri noticed. He treated it like a school reunion, Class of '72.

'What has become of her? She was still there when I was' — he made a shovelling movement with his hands — 'expelled.'

Michael sat upright and uncomfortable on his upright and uncomfortable chair. 'She's in Shanghai now,' he said, as if afraid of giving too much away. 'But she wants to come out.'

'Ah.' His eyes shone with cheery comprehension. 'But they won't let her? Of course not; her husband is too important.'

'Her ex-husband,' Michael said.

'By communist law perhaps.' Father Ignatius poured some tea from a red Thermos into a tumbler, looked round for others, sighed and handed the glass to Mila. 'Unfortunately I have only one glass.'

Mila drank. The tea was lukewarm and very weak. It must have been in the flask all day. As she put the glass down, some switch of memory clicked, and she could feel the thin tepid camp soup in her mouth, with its greasy aftertaste.

'I wondered if you could tell me anything about her, Father,' Michael was saying brittly. 'I hadn't heard from her for years, until a couple of months ago. I've no idea what happened to her, or why she was sent to the camp. When I last saw her she was a dedicated communist — she had been all her life.'

'What happened to her? What happened? My friend, the whole of China is full of people who *were* dedicated communists.' He shrugged again. 'Of course, she lost her faith, what else? How could anyone keep it? Unfortunately she had not found the true faith — then. But' — he raised his hands to heaven half-humorously — 'God will send an angel before she dies.'

'Do you know why she was sent there?' Michael asked, unamused.

'The whole country went mad, my friend. You could be sent there for anything, or nothing.' His eyes narrowed with sudden shrewdness as he leant forward across the table towards Michael. 'But how will she come out? If they don't want her to? She is quite old, I think. As old as me? Older?'

Michael, elbows on knees, pressed his fingertips together. For a moment he seemed to be praying. 'I have heard from . . . a certain source of someone who has a junk, here in Macao,' he said gravely. 'I wonder if you have come across him?'

Father Ignatius reached deep into the pocket of his cassock, pulling out a scratched metal glasses-case. 'Would you write the name down for me, please?' He snapped the case open and placed a pair of rimless lenses on the end of his nose, watching Michael write on a blank page of his pocket diary. Twisting the diary round, he frowned down, pushing out his under lip, then slid the diary back across the table. 'Wong, Snakeboat Wong. I have heard he is trustworthy,' he nodded. 'But expensive.'

'Expense is not the problem.'

'I don't know more than what I hear, of course,' Father Ignatius warned. 'But how did your sister know I was here?'

'From another source,' Michael said, slipping the diary back into his pocket.

Michael's Holy Frail

Michael posted a hundred-dollar bill into the offertory-box when they left. Father Ignatius' eyes gleamed gratefully. He pressed pamphlets upon them, and gave them each a little key-ring with a medallion of St. Christopher attached to it. 'You *are* Christians, aren't you?' he asked with sudden misgiving.

'Er, not Catholics,' Dimitri answered tactfully.

'Not yet,' Father Ignatius corrected him with a confident smile. He gave Michael one more medallion. 'For your sister,' he said. 'For a safe journey.'

Then Mila, about to leave, turned back and briefly crossed herself, bobbing down as if she did it every day.

Outside in the still sun-bright square, Dimitri looked at the key-ring in the palm of his hand. It must have been made of tin, he could bend it so easily. *She'll need more than that to get her out*, he thought. Aloud, he asked Mila lightly: 'Why did you cross yourself? Did the old boy convert you?'

She shrugged. 'Don't you English say when in Rome do as the Romans?'

'I almost felt I was watching a confirmation candidate in there. Or a young girl at her first confession.'

'Confession,' Mila repeated, listening to the sound.

'I wonder where he comes from? His Cantonese was odd.'

'He's half-French. I suppose that's why they let him go in the end. After twenty years.'

Their shadows stalked before them across the square. Dimitri wondered aloud how Father Ignatius' child-like faith could possibly have survived all those years in a communist prison.

Michael shook his head, thinking of other things.

'How would *he* have survived *without* it?' Mila said tartly.

'Did you feel you got much out of him?' Dimitri asked Michael as they climbed into the taxi — the same taxi; the driver had parked in the shade and stretched out on the sea-wall to doze.

'A bit.' He felt like a man who'd lived in an earthquake zone all his life. In a nook of his mind he'd always expected a catastrophe, and talking to that priest had been like feeling the first faint far-off tremor of the earth. 'About the snakeboat-owner, for instance,' he said. 'Though I'd checked that already.'

Mila asked what Grace thought about it all. Nobody asked what Patrick thought — they knew he disliked the whole business and wanted as little to do with it as possible.

'Oh, Grace doesn't let things intrude too much.' He gazed out at the pine-covered hills, the slashed red earth, the old flaking-plaster houses and the tawdry new villas. 'That's why she never travels; that's why she didn't come with me today. She's got everything she needs inside her head.'

He spoke dispassionately, as though about some distant acquaintance, not his wife. But for the glances that occasionally flickered between them, nobody would ever have guessed he cared for Grace at all, except in the worn habitual way in which husbands usually cared for their ageing wives. Not that there had ever been much passion between them. He'd never felt he really possessed her. Even when he used to quiver inside her warm body, he always felt she was remote, he hadn't really entered her essentially at all. It wasn't that she'd ever shrunk from him, or resisted. When he wanted her, as he had urgently at the beginning of their marriage, she'd accepted him willingly, even with warmth. But he knew she never wanted him; she'd have been just as contented if he'd never touched her at all. Yet her passive smiling detachment hadn't troubled him — on the contrary, it fascinated. Even now he always looked for her first in a room, and hated to be away from her. On his business trips, early on, when he'd occasionally slept with a woman, it had always been joyless. It was only Grace he ever really wanted. But after San San's birth his always moderate desire began to wane. She seemed too fragile and too delicate to be touched in that clumsy way. And soon it became unimaginable that he'd ever do so again. Yet it was her very fragility and remoteness that attracted and absorbed him, her always being just out of reach. 'Grace is Michael's Holy Frail,' Patrick had remarked once.

All this he kept to himself, as if to acknowledge it would humiliate him. His feelings showed only in an occasional unguarded tone or glance or gesture, just as the vivid metaphors of his secret thoughts flashed out only rarely through the disciplined plainness of his speech.

'I'll let you out at the Boa Vista,' he said as they rode over the bridge. 'There's something I want to look up in the Leal Senada library.'

'Won't it be closed?' Dimitri asked. 'On a Saturday afternoon?'

Michael said he knew the caretaker.

As if his blood had spilt

First they'd eaten, then they'd played mah-jong, and then, since he'd won, Yin Hong was eating again. 'Come on, Ah Keung,' he said, picking the pigeon's eyes out with his chopsticks. 'Eat up, ah. What's the matter?'

Ah Keung watched him crack the bird's skull open and take out the brains. The split battered head lay on the dish with only the little beak intact. He wrinkled his nose. 'Not hungry.'

'Not hungry, why? Don't you like 'em?' Yin Hong crunched the brains busily, spat out a tiny fragment of bone, sucked the grease off his lips, and swallowed some more brandy from his half-full tumbler. 'If you're not going to eat that one, I will.'

Ah Keung shook his head, and the old man went to work on the last skull, too, scattering more bits of bone and chewed gristle all round his bowl. Ah Keung looked away out of the window, down into the narrow cobbled Rua Da Felicidade. A shiny black taxi was squeezing its way past a couple of trishaws, their seats piled high with newspaper-bundles. A coolie, squatting between the long shafts of his rickshaw, was smoking a cigarette through a wide bamboo funnel, his eyes heavy-lidded and dreamy. Some old men were picking through the stuff on the junk-dealer's stall opposite. Women walked slowly past, lugging bags full of vegetables and fruits. Watching a young girl's receding back, he was reminded of Ling Kwan — something about the way the girl's hips moved. He imagined Ling Kwan in her hillside squatter's hut. He imagined her hips moving.

'Make you think better, Ah Keung, these will,' Yin Hong was saying knowledgeably. 'Like monkey brains. You should try them, too.' He belched and chuckled. 'Wouldn't do you any harm to think a bit better, either.'

'When're you going to phone them about Limpy, then?' Ah Keung turned back abruptly as the girl disappeared. 'We've got the money now. Let's get it settled.'

'All right, all right, take it easy, ah? When we've finished eating. Thought you liked it in Macao?'

'I'm getting bored.'

'Miss the girl, ah? What's her name again?' Yin Hong winked and nudged him. 'Not getting enough of it, ah?'

'I'm getting bored, I said.' Ah Keung stared out of the window once more.

'What's her name again?'

'Ling Kwan.'

'Good-looker,' Yin Hong said, through a mouthful of munched brain. 'What's she do to fill her bowl?'

'Factory.'

'Factory, ah? Electrics?'

'Knitting.'

'Knitting, ah? How much she bring in, then?'

Ah Keung shrugged. ' 'bout two thousand a month,' he said grudgingly.

'Only two thousand?'

'Well, she'd get more if she'd got an ID card.'

'But she hasn't, though, has she?'

'Good one costs a lot, doesn't it? I'm working on it.'

'Thought of putting her on the game, have you? She'd bring in ten times that much.'

The muscles in Ah Keung's cheeks stirred and tightened, and a dark flush flowed out beneath his skin as if his blood had spilt. It spread down his neck, all the way to his hunched powerful shoulders.

Yin Hong grinned. 'Like that, is it, ah?'

The flush deepened. 'Like what?' His voice was thick as mud.

Yin Hong, watching his downturned sullen face, suddenly felt uneasy, like with a dog that snarls when you're teasing it. Better back off a bit, he thought obscurely. His tongue gently probed the broken tooth in his lower jaw, the one he broke in that fight with the Wo Hop years and years ago — never bothered him once, except he caught his tongue in it now and then. Yes, back off a bit, he thought, sliding the tip of his tongue over the wet jagged edge. 'OK, don't want to share your meal, ah?' he said easily. 'Wait till you've had enough, ah?'

'Right,' Ah Keung said. 'Right. And when are you going to phone about Limpy?'

'When we've finished eating, OK?'

'I have finished, haven't I?'

Well fuck you. What about me? was on the tip of his tongue, but somehow Yin Hong couldn't quite get himself to say it. He'd got a real feeling he'd better back off where Ah Keung's girl was concerned. So he pretended he hadn't heard and just went right on eating. He finished in silence, swallowed the last of the brandy with a gulp, and called for the bill.

'And I want to use your phone,' he told the foki loudly, so everyone would hear, laying an extra twenty dollars on the tray. 'Three minutes to Hong Kong, all right?'

Ah Keung lounged in the doorway, watching Yin Hong shouting into the receiver. 'Listen, that business with Limpy. We're willing to make a settlement, all right?' He listened, frowning and picking his teeth, then flicked the toothpick away as he shouted again. 'Let's drink tea and talk about it, ah? Just the four of us.'

8

Latter-day rice-Christian

When Dimitri asked if she was tired, Mila paused, head tilted, the brush's bristles deep in her hair, and glanced at him in the dressing-table mirror as if she sensed another meaning — the other meaning — in his question. 'No.' She resumed her slow steady brushing. 'My back hurts a bit, that is all. It is Elena who should be tired. *I* wasn't dancing.'

Through the open veranda doors he could see the lamps on the bridge and the gleam they cast on the black water below. On the shore the glitzy lights of the round Casino, like a giant kitsch wedding cake, were reflected on the mud-flats beneath it, and magically metamorphosed there into insubstantial beauty. 'Where did Elena go? I didn't see her afterwards. She was rather good tonight, wasn't she? As far as I could tell, which isn't much of course.'

'Yes. She said she might go to the Casino with Tom. Or to the Bluebell Girls, if she wasn't too tired.'

'The Bluebell Girls? What on earth would she want to see a leg-show for?'

'It is more than legs, isn't it?'

'Whatever's on display, I wouldn't have thought it'd interest her. Tom perhaps, but . . . .'

She glanced at him again in the mirror, as she pulled the brush whispering through her hair. 'But your daughter is not very like you, Dimitri, is she? For one thing, she does not brood. For another, she is dedicatedly frivolous.'

'I wouldn't have thought that was another thing; I'd have thought it was the same.' He didn't dispute her judgement — Elena *was* frivolous, she made light of everything. As though she was simply oblivious of starvation and cancer and torture, of people cutting each other's throat for a belief and murdering for a flag. She blotted them all out, as she'd blotted out the memory — he'd tested her often — of those weeks after her mother's death when she'd never said a word, day after day, sitting pale and stony-faced, without a tear, until quite suddenly she'd stirred, returned to life, like someone slipping out of a coma. It was Alex who'd grieved normally and could be normally consoled. But Elena — he sometimes felt that all those forgotten, unfallen tears must still be there, petrified inside her, and one day she would have to shed them.

'That only shows how brooding confuses your mind,' Mila was saying.

'What?'

'If you think that not brooding is the same thing as being frivolous.'

'I'm not such a brooder anyway,' he said, turning away.

They'd been jarring like that all day, and he knew it was because of the night, the distance between the twin beds, this room with its memories. He shouldn't have booked it. He of all people should have known that, even though the past may be recaptured, it is never repeated.

She laid the brush down deliberately, got up with a little wince as her back moved, and went to the bathroom. He stepped out on to the grubby tiled floor of the veranda. It was nearly midnight, the bridge was empty now, the solitary lamp-posts offered their sad unwanted bouquets to the sea. Some of the lamps had gone out, leaving stretches of the bridge darker than the sea below. Macao.

He didn't want to be in the bedroom when she came out. He didn't want to know at once whether she was wearing a nightdress or naked, as she used to be when they came there before. The question had been flickering in the air all the time, a little electric charge jumping the tense gap between them, and that was why (he realized now) he hadn't moved the beds together as he used to. He wanted her to give the sign.

Her body when they'd first come here. He'd lain beside her stroking her skin — the pale smooth inside of her thigh, he remembered — with a delighted wonder, murmuring — a bit self-consciously, it was true, but still — murmuring, 'If there is paradise on earth, it is here, it is here, it is here.' And she had smiled and, mistaking the allusion, called him Aga Khan. Or was that not the first time they came here, but the first time after she escaped from China? A long time ago anyway.

It occurred to him he could check his old passports (he'd kept them in the bottom drawer of his desk) and work out every single time they'd come here in those days. But no, he didn't want to see those blank youngsters on each page three, successively reminding him of time's tireless erosion.

He heard the weary plumbing grumble, the bathroom door open, a second's silence, then her bare feet on the tiles. She came and stood beside him. In her nightdress.

Her hand rested on the stone balustrade an inch from his. Light from the bathroom window gleamed on her wedding ring. They'd got married properly, in the City Hall Register Office. Elena had giggled, Alex looked solemn.

'Hold my hand?' she asked quietly.

'Faute de mieux?'

She didn't know any French, but his tone carried the meaning. Or more than the meaning; he hadn't intended it to sound so chill. She shifted her hand away, paused, then went inside.

The bedroom light went out like a face swiftly turned away. He heard the bed creak, the one nearest the veranda. A car was passing across the bridge. He made himself watch it all the way over, until its lights fell into the empty dark the other side, like a swimmer diving. Then he, too, went in.

She was lying on her back, gazing up at the ceiling. She didn't move or look at him. There was a dim twilight in the room — seeping in from the moon, he supposed — and he could see her eyes glistening faintly. He hesitated, then lay down on the other bed, in the towel he'd wrapped round himself after his shower. *If there is paradise on earth*. He clasped his hands behind his head and gazed up, too, watching a little rippling lizard on the ceiling as it darted, froze, darted again. When they first came, to that same room with the same decrepit air-conditioner which they never used, the same musty carpets, the same curtains falling off their runners, the same faded gilt-framed prints of Napoleon at Austerlitz — when they first came, a little green lizard like that one, glued to the ceiling, had watched them as they lay together.

'How long do lizards live?' he asked suddenly. His voice sounded hard and sullen, despite the effort he made to curb the resentment or self-pity or whatever it was he felt.

'About a year, I believe,' she said with her maddening cool detachment. If only she would shout or scream, just once. 'That's quite a young one up there.'

'One of his ancestors watched us, years and years ago.'

'Mm.' She knew immediately what he meant. Probably she'd been thinking the same thought, but chose not to express it. Typical. Preserve harmony. Never mind truth. Her damned Chineseness.

'And now that one's descendant is watching us, lizard generations later,' she said musingly.

'He can't be getting as many kicks out of it as his forefather did, though.'

She didn't answer. Of course not. Harmony. Calmly counting up the lizard generations, most likely.

'Why didn't we move the beds together?' he heard himself ask in a dull toneless voice.

Her bed rustled as she shrugged. 'I don't know. It doesn't matter.'

'Not to you evidently. Sometimes I think you'd be just as happy without me as with me. You're content when I'm there, and you're equally content when I'm not there.'

'Wouldn't you want me to be happy all the time, then?'

He couldn't quite tell from her voice whether she was smiling or not. Perhaps she hadn't decided herself.

'Brooding,' she said chidingly. 'Brooding, brooding.'

Was she smiling at him? 'Contented whether I'm there or not. That makes me a zero.'

'I do not think so,' she said thoughtfully, as though pursuing the arithmetic rather than the emotion. Still he couldn't tell whether she was smiling. But in any case he was beginning to feel ridiculous, like a boy that's being teased out of a childish grievance. If she'd laughed at him then, he'd have had to laugh with her. Or else work himself up into a temper. But she didn't laugh. She simply slipped quietly into his bed and curled up against him, her back against his belly. He put his arm round her, with a show of reluctance at first, then gratefully, feeling her body through the nightdress. She held his hand still against her breast. 'See? This is nice, too,' she murmured. 'You don't have to be doing acrobatics all the time.'

Her hair tickled his nose, but he didn't want to move, he liked the smell of her skin. 'But you do have to sometimes,' he said.

'You are not broody with other people, are you?' she asked drowsily. 'You're quite witty and ironic then. The trouble is you let yourself go with me, don't you? I'm not sure whether that is a compliment or not.'

He blew at her hair, but it still tickled. 'Well, you only married me to get a British passport, didn't you? You're a latter-day rice-Christian, so I have the right to let myself go.'

When his hand cupped her breast, she held it still again. 'But think of all the Englishmen I could have married for their passports, and I chose you. You ought to be proud.'

She was always quicker than he was, always skipping one step ahead.

Acquainted with that hour

It was the main door of the hotel slamming shut that awoke him. He recognized it at once through some long-sunk memory stirring on the sleepy sea-bed of his mind. And he knew at once, too, that Mila wasn't beside him. For a moment of stabbing alarm he thought she'd walked out into the night, but then he saw her asleep in the other bed, her face turned away from him towards the veranda.

He lay still, listening to footsteps climbing the stairs, passing down the corridor towards Elena's room. Then came Elena's suppressed whispering giggle and the deep slurred answer of Tom's voice, which she instantly shushed. He heard the key grate in the lock, then, a few seconds later, the latch click as the door closed. There was something definite and final about that click echoing down the corridor, as if it was more he who'd been locked out than they who'd locked themselves in.

Would they push the beds together?

He turned his head. If he was very still and quiet, he should be able to hear Mila breathing. He raised his arm cautiously and peered at his watch. Nearly two. He was acquainted with that hour, the hour he used to wake up regularly night after night, after Helen's suicide, after Mila had gone back to China. And it was the hour of Helen's death, too, or at least the hour he found her drugged dead body on the beach, wallowing like a waterlogged tree-stump, which was what he thought it was at first, wallowing to and fro in the nudging wavelets of the incoming tide.

It was in that period of his life that he first heard the phrase *lightness of being*, not knowing its source (it was Patrick who lent him the book, years later); and he applied it to himself, especially when he woke at night, always around two. Because his whole life seemed to be light, weightless, then, floating endlessly away in dead empty space, turning slowly over and over like the lost astronaut in that space-odyssey film, nothing but deep chill silence and distance all round him, silence in the bed, in the room, on the stairs, in the whole flat (the sleeping children were silence, too, remote in their dreams); silence everywhere except in his chest, where the muffled pounding of his heart shoved the silent blood along his arteries and veins. Yes, he was acquainted with that hour.

Everything he did then when alone, day or night, echoed and re-echoed itself. Every cough or sniff resounded hollowly, every little act or gesture reflected reflections of itself. He let the children go to bed later and later, just so that there'd be some other sounds about him besides the sounds he made himself, staying pointlessly alive. But then eventually the inevitable silence would rebegin, in which he heard only the reverberations of his own breathing, his own heart, and saw only the hollow vastness of his own room, his own walls, his own bed, which he felt he'd never share with anyone again. And it was then that words started forming in his head, metaphors, rhymes, broken images. Like voices whispering to him, but they were his own voices.

The incurable lightness of being.

Not that he'd missed Helen. When the shock and all the harrowing business of inquest and funeral were over, he'd felt only a sense of release, as if all his life till then he'd been living with his nerves and muscles too taut. He could let go at last. But when Mila went back to try her luck in China, and he thought he'd never see her again — that was the desolation.

And then she'd come back. Five years later she'd come back, when he'd given up thinking of her, when he slept through the nights again, when he'd somehow assuaged the incurable lightness of being with one thing or another, and grown accustomed to it, to life in the void.

He knew her voice on the phone from the very first word, which was his name. She said it without any inflection, stating rather than asking, as she always had. His stomach had lurched with . . . with what? Disbelief? Fear? Hope? Love? All of those at least. She was phoning from a fishing village near the border, and she'd had trouble getting his number — he'd moved from the old flat, and the phone company kept changing the numbers anyway. But eventually, about midnight, she'd reached him. The second thing he remembered her saying into the stunned silence of the line was 'I was afraid you might have left Hong Kong.'

'Where would I go?' he'd asked. And then: 'Where are you?' He drove out to fetch her at once, afraid the police patrols would get her first and he'd close his hands on nothingness once more. But 'You needn't have worried,' she said in her cool way. 'I still have my Hong Kong ID card; they couldn't have sent me back.' He wasn't so sure. On the drive out there, he'd had time to compose himself, to adjust to the fact of her return, and when he saw her, thin, worn, but still with that imperturbable delicacy of feature, it was as though she'd only been away a week. She was wearing an old T-shirt and baggy shorts which she'd pulled along in a plastic bag behind her, swimming the four miles from China. Her hair was still wet. He drove with his hand on hers all the way back and took her straight to bed where she fell asleep at once in his arms. She smelt of the sea.

Everything was the same then as when he first knew her, or so he thought. But later he realized she had changed. A part of her never came back. It was as though she'd had an organ out and somewhere inside she was still numb.

At first he'd tried not to ask her about the Red Guards and the struggle meetings and the public-security people and the camp; then he'd tried to ask. But she never let much out. Once she'd laid her finger on his lips and said, with a faint smile: 'It is like being dead. Before it happens you cannot understand what it is like, and afterwards you cannot explain.'

He'd wanted her to have a child, but she'd said: 'No, no children.' Too numb. But sometimes he still wanted it. It wasn't too late.

He got up, walked stealthily to the bathroom, watched his pee tinkle against the cracked stained toilet-bowl, went out on to the veranda. The casino lights were still burning furiously, their insubstantial reflection still glimmering magically on the muddy shore. But the street-lamps on the bridge looked wan and tired. A jetfoil was leaving for Hong Kong, rising darkly off the water like a black sprinter from his blocks.

When he tiptoed back, he saw that Mila was watching him. Perhaps she'd been watching him all the time. He stopped by her bed.

'It was I,' she said in her punctiliously articulated, over-grammatical English.

'What was you?'

'Who gave Father Ignatius away. They kept telling me I'd got to show my attitude had changed if I wanted to get my release. They said there must be something I could tell them. So in the end I told them he was saying mass to himself. I thought otherwise I might never get out. They asked me how I knew it was mass, and I said because I went to a Catholic school in Hong Kong. And they said: "That's right. That's why you're here."'

She spoke in that level dispassionate tone of hers, as if she were talking about someone she barely knew, someone she mildly despised. But when he sat beside her she took his hand in hers and held it tight. 'When I told them about him, they said they'd known all along; they just wanted to see if . . . if my attitude had changed.'

He shook his head slowly, raising his eyebrows. Gazing out at the lamp-posts drooping over the bridge, he tried to imagine the scene, and failed. His mind filled up with television villains and the clichés of Hollywood B movies. *Before it happens you cannot understand.*

'That is how they do it,' she went on in the same detached monotonous voice. 'After that they have you.'

He lay down beside her, slipped his arm round her waist and held her close.

'I didn't want to go there, to Father Ignatius with Michael, did you realize that? Because I was afraid he might have found out, he might have known. But he didn't know, did he?'

Still that clear composed tone, as though she were speaking of someone else. If there was any agitation, it was in her hand, rapidly stroking the back of his.

'No, he didn't know,' Dimitri said.

You-know-what

'You could've stayed here,' Alison said. 'Those old houses must be crawling with cockroaches. Not to speak of rats.'

'It was just that they wanted someone to look after the cat,' Rachel said mildly.

'Well, what've they got an amah for? Surely she can look after a cat while they're gone for a few days? Really!' She edged round the coffee table and sat down with an exasperated sigh. 'If she can't even look after a cat, what *can* she do? Sorry I'm still in my dressing gown, by the way. Would you like a drink?'

It was ten past eleven in the morning. The observant Filipina maid, neat in her blue uniform and white apron, was clearing the breakfast-table, which Alison didn't seem to have touched. 'Coffee?' Rachel asked hesitantly. 'You sure you can spare those flowerpots?'

'Don't mind if I have a little freshener, do you? It is nearly lunch-time after all.' Alison poured some vodka, splashed orange into it, and leant back with another sigh, this time of satisfaction. 'Yes, why not? *I'll* never use them.'

Through the open balcony doors, Rachel viewed the harbour spread out below, still and vivid as a child's scissors-and-paste picture. Even the smoke from a great yellow container-ship's stack looked as if it had been cut out and stuck on to a blue-grey paper sea. In the dry November brilliance the Kowloon hills and Lion Rock were another cut-out, jagged and brown, pasted on a light blue sky. What was it like in the countryside beyond the hills?

'What a wonderful view you've got here,' Rachel said politely.

'Yes, it's all right.'

'Patrick's promised to take me round some of the villages soon.'

'Patrick?' Alison sniffed. 'Well, you'll be safe with him all right. No, I just can't imagine what that amah of theirs does if she can't even look after a cat. It's not as though they can afford to keep a lot of idle servants like Peter's parents can.' She drank, dragged some cigarettes out of her pocket, and offered one to Rachel. 'No? It's my first today. Not that Filipinas are any better, mind you.' She jerked her head significantly towards the maid. Beneath her pink dressing gown a full sunburnt shoulder and heavy breast showed. She twitched the terry cloth closer round her. 'They're all the same if you ask me.'

'I like Ah Wong,' Rachel said pacifically. 'She's real lively.'

'Maria! Maria!' Alison waved her hand imperiously. 'Ashtray, please! If you mean she talks a lot, I dare say she is. I can't understand a word she says, myself.'

But Rachel was fascinated by Ah Wong's talk. While Alison complained between sips and puffs about the unreliability of Hong Kong servants, Rachel, behind a fixed and inattentive smile, recalled her return to the Johnstons' house from the theatre the night before. Ah Wong had been standing in the kitchen, sipping a cup of instant coffee — she never drank tea, she said — and dunking biscuits in it, which she was nibbling with toothless gums. Her little radio stood on the draining board beside her, and she was listening to it raptly as it gave out weird wails and groans, curdling shrieks and spooky music. Ah Wong had stood entranced, eyes clouded, smiling satisfiedly, while the cat mewed unregarded round her feet. She didn't even acknowledge Rachel till the programme faded with the tones of faint eerie lute music. 'Gu sih,' she'd explained then. 'Kwai gu sih. Ghosty story.' She never fully accepted that Rachel couldn't speak more than a few words of Cantonese, having seen her reading and speaking Mandarin with Dimitri. So every time she came Ah Wong started in Cantonese, switching only reluctantly and incredulously to the pungent telegraphic pidgin she'd acquired in her early life of service to foreign missies. 'Gov'men' radio talky ghosty story every nigh'.'

Rachel, who could never go to a Hitchcock movie because they haunted her for weeks afterwards, had asked her if she wasn't scared.

Ah Wong chuckled, shaking her head. 'Only bad people frighten ghosty, missy. Ghosty never mind good people. When I little girl, my big sister go home die. I see her some time after. I never mind, very pretty. No hurt, missy, no hurt.'

'How did she die?'

'I no know missy. I too small. Japan people come, many people go home die. My mummy no talky me.'

Alison was slopping some more vodka into her glass. 'Sure you won't have something to drink?'

'Er, coffee?' Rachel asked tentatively again.

'Maria! Ashtray!'

'I went to the theatre last night. The Asian Arts Festival. Have you been?'

'No. What was on?'

'Peking Opera.'

'God, no!'

The Filipina placed a glass ashtray on the table with a faintly sulky gesture. Alison tapped half an inch of ash off her cigarette and swallowed half an inch of vodka. 'No, it beats me why they keep her on. What's she called? Ah Wong? They can't have all that much money. I mean, she's practically made herself one of the family. Rules them, if you ask me. Still, as Mila's Chinese as well . . . . ' Birds of a feather, she implied with a dismissive shrug.

'She was telling me about the ghost there last night,' Rachel said evenly. 'And other ghosts. She really believes in them. I mean, I guess it's still part of the culture.'

'Well, what d'you expect? Wouldn't be surprised if Peter does, too. Except the only thing he really believes in is you-know-what, as far as I can see. Wouldn't be surprised if that's part of the culture, too, if that's what you want to call it. He's got a bar-girl, you know.' She dropped her lids disgustedly. 'I don't let him have it any more. God knows, he may be a doctor, but you'd think he'd never heard of VD. I've learnt a thing or two about Chinese men since I married him, I can tell you. Or three-quarters Chinese if it comes to that.'

Rachel realized that Alison's face wasn't merely fat, but puffy-eyed and bloated, whether from drink or crying, or both. And her show of indifference was belied by the little spurts of venom she kept injecting into her voice.

'Talk about inscrutable orientals, I've seen through *him* all right. A common or garden bar-girl. You'd think he'd have more taste. I suppose she does it the way he likes or something. The things he's asked me to do — well, I'd be ashamed to tell my best friend.'

Afraid she might nevertheless tell her, Rachel asked quickly why Alison didn't get a divorce if she felt like that.

'He'd screw me with the lawyers. I'd end up without a penny. You know the law protects the man out here. This isn't the UK, you know. Well, thank God we didn't have any kids at least. That's one problem off my mind.' Now that Rachel had given up resistance, Alison rambled at leisure through the misery of her marriage. Peter ignored her, never took her anywhere, his friends all spoke Cantonese anyway — 'Disgusting language, sounds like a lot of fishwives squawking' — he stayed out all night sometimes and didn't even bother to lie any more . . . .

Rachel listened uncomfortably, wondering if it was drink that made Alison miserable or misery that made her drink, and whether she was only miserable or also enjoying her misery. She could easily imagine Alison revelling in the role of the ill-used English wife of an unfeeling Chinese — 'Well, as near Chinese as makes no difference' — before a clutch of martyred expatriate women at some consciousness-raising coffee-morning. Only, it wouldn't be coffee.

'So you can thank your lucky stars you're not married,' Alison ended. 'To one of *them* anyway. I can tell you one thing, though: I certainly won't be here when the Chinese take the place over, even if *he* will, which I frankly doubt. Enough's enough. Oh, I completely forgot — you came for those flowerpots, didn't you?'

'If you can spare them, yes.'

'They're on the back balcony. Why don't you stay to lunch?' She started to get up, then sank back again. 'Maria! Maria!'

'Ma'am?' replied a subtly insolent voice from the kitchen.

'No, I think I'd better not stay, thanks very much,' Rachel said firmly. 'I must get to the library and do some work. If you really can spare those pots, though . . . .'

Alison leant forward, rolling her eyes towards the kitchen.' And I've seen Peter giving *her* the eye, too,' she whispered, mouthing the words exaggeratedly with widely parted lips. 'Just let me catch them at it, that's all I say. Just let me catch them at it!'

Old lady now

After spending most of the afternoon in the library, where students piled books on the desks and fell asleep over them just as they did in the States, Rachel went to a mainland movie about the Cultural Revolution with shy prim Cheung, the only communist student she'd managed to meet. The movie was a howling ideological melodrama — nearly every character wept, beat his head against the wall and died. 'It was kind of like an American soap opera,' she said cautiously to Cheung afterwards, 'only it had politics instead of sex.' Besides, she could only get about half the dialogue. Cheung blinked at her gravely behind his lenses. 'Bourgeois aesthetic standards are irrelevant to Marxist art,' he declared. She tried to see the film differently, as an instance of art serving the masses. But it was no good; the masses weren't even there. The theatre was almost empty — maybe fifty people at most, she reckoned — and none of them seemed too interested. They were all talking loudly throughout the movie, wrapping and unwrapping crackly plastic bags, eating and drinking, while the lethargic ushers switched their torches off and dozed. The houselights went up before the last scene had faded, and the audience filed out at once while unintelligible images flickered on the already-drawn curtains.

No, the masses were all in the theatre just across the street, where a slash-cut-and-kick kung fu movie was playing to a full house. A milling crowd was blocking the foyer and spilling out on to the road, buying noodles and fish balls from cooked-food hawkers. Cheung gazed at the scene as if it were Sodom and Gomorrah. 'You see how Western bourgeois values corrupt the people,' he said.

I thought kung fu was Chinese?'

'Ideologically it is Western,' he assured her earnestly.

She was glad he didn't have time to eat dinner with her. *It would have been kind of stodgy, she wrote later in her diary. He reminds me of the Mormon missionaries from the States you see about the place, with their buttoned-down shirts and their buttoned-up minds.*

After eating a vegetarian meal in a crowded Causeway Bay restaurant, she rode a tram all the way to the western end of the island, sitting upstairs on the wooden seat ('Beware of Pickpockets') for three-quarters of an hour. She got off at the last stop, where the night market merged with the docks, and the streets were all narrow and crooked, lined with old, cramped, decaying houses.

Walking up towards the university, where she'd left the flowerpots Alison had at last given her, she explored once more the century-old district she'd stumbled across in her first weeks in Hong Kong — the crumbling houses of Sai Ying Poon with their steep dark stairways, ornate balconies and crooked unpainted wooden shutters. She'd never walked there at night before. The streets were almost empty, and she could hear people talking in doorways or playing mah-jong behind shuttered shop-fronts, through the gaps in which the red lamps of little altars glowed, and the bluish light of televisions. Here and there the old houses were being pulled down, and bleak concrete apartment-blocks rose from the ruins, neater and cleaner, but faceless, like parking-lots for people. Yet in other streets she felt she was walking through a village that had scarcely changed in a hundred years. How come she didn't mind the litter and decay so much now? Was Hong Kong getting to her?

She wandered into a block, only a street or two wide, where all the lamp-posts were decorated with ribbons, and paper figures stood outside a temple, one at least twelve feet high. There were offerings of fruit at little street-side altars and at the feet of the paper statues. She watched two old women praying at one altar, and a taxi-driver stopping to pray at another, leaving his engine running and his passengers waiting till he'd finished and drove on.

Rachel tried to discover from a young girl, first in Mandarin, then in English, what festival it was. The girl shrugged. 'Old people custom,' she said indifferently. She was listening to a Walkman and wearing Levi jeans.

It was nearly midnight when she arrived at the Johnstons' house.

'Yam cha, siu je?' Ah Wong asked when she heard her coming down the back steps. 'Cuppa tea?' She believed every foreign-devil visitor required a cup of tea whenever they came, morning or night. No one entered without being offered one, except at the hour she abandoned herself to her radio ghost-stories, when nobody could get anything out of her at all.

'Thank you, Ah Wong.' Rachel set the flowerpots carefully down in the courtyard and came in past the fly-screen door, which Ah Wong was holding open for her.

'I cook you something?'

'No, thanks, I've eaten already. Ah Wong, do you know what festival it is today?' she asked, picking up the cat. 'In Sai Ying Poon?'

'Sai Ying Poon?' Ah Wong shook her head. 'Festival' wasn't in her pidgin vocabulary.

'Religion? Temple? Celebration? You know, like party?'

'Oh, you go party Sai Ying Poon?' Ah Wong's eyes gleamed with comprehension. 'Go party Sai Ying Poon! Very nice! Go party!'

Rachel gave up. She wondered how often in her life Ah Wong must have seen her employers go off to parties that the word had been so instantly familiar. The cat, purring with throaty joy, was licking her neck, its rough tickling tongue sending little shivers of unfamiliar pleasure down inside her.

Ah Wong had been looking at her pictures before the American girl came. She hated being alone in the house, hated quietness and emptiness. Not that she was afraid. Ghosts didn't bother her, and, as for robbers, there was the watchman outside, an old man who muttered, chuckled, shouted and argued with himself all night, who sometimes sang snatches of Peking or Cantonese opera, sometimes spoke in English, but just stared stupidly at her if ever she spoke to him in Cantonese. His sad old face with its bloodshot baggy eyes reminded her of someone — she couldn't think who. But, anyway, he stayed awake all night — and often kept her awake, too, with his muttering and chanting — so she didn't have to worry about robbers. It was just the quiet she couldn't stand, and being alone. She liked it best when the house was full of people talking and eating and shouting, as it was before the children grew up, even though it meant more work for her. So now, with everyone gone except this quiet American girl, she'd taken out her pictures to give herself some company.

'You looksee my picture', missy?' she invited Rachel, stirring the tea.

There was no album; just a bundle of different-sized photos, mainly black and white, which indirectly told the story of her life. *Like my diary tells mine*, Rachel thought. They were nearly all sun-shot curling prints of blond babies and infants, now strapping men and women presumably, on one veranda after another, in one garden after another. Sometimes the mother or father was there, too, sometimes Ah Wong herself, holding a baby in her arms, smiling with dazzled eyes into the sunlight and the lens. All the other figures changed — dark, fair, tall, fat, bald or bearded (once) — but Ah Wong remained the same, always dressed in her white tunic and black trousers, her hair braided in a queue or, as she grew older, coiled round her head.

She pointed to a picture of Dimitri's first wife, Helen, holding the young Alex and Elena, one on each hand, and to others taken by Helen of the children and herself. In one, Ah Wong held the infant Elena proudly, under the shade of a tree on some beach. Birthday parties with balloons and candles, beach parties and picnics — no wonder she knew the word 'party' — from those photos you'd think her whole life had been one long party. There were even some of Helen and the two children a few days before she killed herself.

'*Killed* herself!'

'Yes, kill,' Ah Wong said calmly. 'Takee medicine, go sleep by sea, no more wakee.'

'But why?'

Ah Wong shrugged. 'Jealousee.'

Helen had asked her to take the photos, told her where to look and how to press the button, then given the film to her to have developed. Ah Wong had got the pictures back after Helen died. She'd never shown them to Dimitri or the children.

Rachel studied them respectfully. They were traces after all left by the light that bounced off a woman who'd decided to kill herself. But they looked no different from the others. Or, if they did, it was that Helen was serene, even smiling, in some of them, whereas in the earlier photos she often looked strained and wretched. As if the decision to die had brought her peace. You could see the likeness to Elena, too, though she guessed their characters must be poles apart.

There were no pictures of Ah Wong's own family — of her parents, her brother and sister, her numerous nephews and nieces. They didn't have such things as cameras in her village in those days — they were only peasants and oyster fishermen — and she'd never wanted one since. 'Old lady now, no need.'

How long had she been with Dimitri? Rachel asked, leaning against the dresser as she drank her tea. Ah Wong wasn't sure. She'd come when Elena was a few months old. The previous amah, and the one before, had left after a few weeks, finding Helen too nervy to get on with. The man from the Domestic Agency had warned Ah Wong before she went, but Ah Wong liked to make up her own mind. She walked in, took the introduction note out of her large black handbag and offered it to Helen politely with both hands. But Elena was fractious with colic on her mother's shoulder, so Helen couldn't read it. 'You looksee letter, missy, I hold baby,' Ah Wong had said, and Elena, perhaps out of sheer astonishment, quietened immediately. Ah Wong had known at once the missy was difficult, but also known she'd take the job. She had scarcely inspected the flat, or questioned Helen closely about the work, as she would usually have done. She hadn't even haggled about her wages, or her New Year lai see. She'd just accepted after a quick glance round — there was no doubt it was she who accepted Helen, not the other way round — and said she'd start work the next Monday. 'She'll never come, she just didn't want to say no,' Helen had muttered audibly as she left, but on Monday she came, carrying all her belongings with her in two plastic bags.

The note from the Domestic Agency, for which Ah Wong paid half her first month's wages, read *'This is to introduce Maid Wong Chau Yee'*; but Helen, who didn't understand then — or ever — how Chinese names went, called her Ah Wong instead of Ah Yee. She didn't mind; she was used to being mispronounced, miscalled, misunderstood. Alex called her Ah Wong, too, and in the end Dimitri did as well — Elena grew up with it. Ah Wong had stayed, the only servant they ever had who could manage Helen's edgy moods and tempers.

'This picture Elena young gir',' Ah Wong said. 'Very beauty young gir', ah?'

'Alex looks like his father, doesn't he?' Rachel said deliberately.

Ah Wong gave the cat some milk and watched it drink. The cat crouched down, purring loudly as it lapped, its ginger tail flicking slowly from side to side. 'You hear ghosty upstair' las' nigh', missy? No hear boom boom?'

She was disappointed. 'Maybe you hear tonigh'. You never mind, missy, ghosty no hurt you, only hurt naughty people.' She took her teeth from an old broken-handled cup on the window-ledge and fitted them into her mouth. Her face looked fuller and several years younger now. 'People no naughty, ghosty no hurt,' she kept repeating.

When her teeth had started aching a few years before, she'd gone to China on an impulse and had them all out, getting a replacement denture the same day. But her new teeth hurt so much when she ate that she always removed them, and mumbled the food patiently with her gums. She laughed when Rachel asked her why she didn't go to a Hong Kong dentist. 'Spend money, missy! Hong Kong dentist very spend money! I old lady now, never mind. Ten years go home die. Young gir' spend money OK, old lady no good. I old lady now.'

Yes, my China

It was past midnight when the phone rang, Ah Wong answered in careful toneless English, then 'Eh, Ah Kwan!' in vivid Cantonese, growing louder and more excited as she went on.

First she stood, then she squatted on her heels, finally she sat on the floor in the hall, listening and shouting into the phone.

'My China people very naughty!' she declared to Rachel when at last she finished.' Number one man my China talky my brother, say where you get money make housey more big?' My brother say my sister give money.' She stabbed her chest with her forefinger, eyes indignantly wide. 'Me give money my brother makey housey big, now number one man say where he get money!'

'Your brother in China?' Rachel asked uncertainly. 'He's made his house bigger — more big?'

'Yes, my China! Number one man talky my brother say where you get money! Ling Kwan talky me telephone say me go China talky number one man, say *me* give money. Lot money, missy! Me give lot money! What for number one man my China talky my brother where you get money? Ai ya!'

'Were you talking about a boat, too, Ah Wong?'

'Boat? Me no talky boat. What for talky boat?'

But Rachel was sure she'd heard the Cantonese for boat. It was one of the few words she'd learnt.

And now Ah Wong says she'll have to go and prove the money came from her, not from smuggling, as far as I can understand her, Rachel wrote in bed, resting her diary on her knees. *She seems to think it's just a way of asking for a bribe. So maybe it will all be settled through the back door, as they say in China.*

She gazed ruminatively across the room at the bookshelf, in which Elena's erratic tastes were revealed like a drawer full of untidy clothes. *Anna Karenina* and *Jackie Collins*, *The Story of O* and *Black Beauty*, *Tales from the Ballets* and a dog-eared copy of *Woman's Own*.

The cat lay on top of the bookshelf, its head on one paw, the other paw hanging loosely over the edge, regarding her peacefully through slitted eyes. Again Rachel hadn't heard any steps on the stairs, but when she carried the cat up to the litter-box it did bristle and spring out of her arms at exactly the place Ah Wong had shown her. She listened to Ah Wong still muttering indignantly to herself downstairs as she locked and bolted all the doors.

Bitter through and through

It was just before the struggle meeting against Father Ignatius that Lily realized she had lost her faith. She dated it now to one of those weekly harangues on Marxist-Leninist-Maoist thought, given by that spectacled woman cadre with sparkling eyes and rosy cheeks — that was when the realization had come to her like the slow paling of the dawn. The woman, sincere, earnest, dogmatic, was parroting all the usual jargon about correcting your thinking and admitting your errors — jargon that had stultified Lily's own mind for forty years — when something about the tone of her voice or her air of certitude chimed with a distant memory, hazy and dim. What was it? Who was it? A voice, a face, a manner from years and years ago. But where? And when? She let her mind empty, just hearing the convinced voice drone in her ears, just seeing the blind faith shining behind the blandly glinting lenses. And then suddenly it came to her. Miss Pulham of course! The missionary in Shanghai who'd nearly converted her when she was a young girl! *She'd* spouted her jargon-ridden faith with the same certainty, the same naive misplaced trust and zeal, that the cadre was spouting hers with now. Miss Pulham, whose life was spent in good works while her mind atrophied in a childish superstition! And she, Lily, had escaped, a trembling adolescent, from the bonds of that mystical mumbo-jumbo only to shackle herself in the fetters of another just as bad. She had believed all those years just as religiously as simple deluded Miss Pulham, just as blindly and naively; believed in another faith, another promised land, another saviour, another church — but all equally illusions, all equally false. They preached different messages, but there was no real difference, the two faiths reflected each other precisely. Communism was just another universal church with another scripture and another pope, another ritual of creed and confession, another liturgy — the political meetings — and another inquisition for the heretics.

She felt a sense of liberation, but simultaneously of self-disgust. At last in her sixties she'd outgrown religion, both the sacred and the profane. But why had it taken so long?

Of course her faith must have been decaying secretly for years, beneath the thinning crust of certainty that formed the surface of her mind. Like water seeping through a worked-out mine, her unacknowledged doubt had found its own slow way, filled up every shaft and every tunnel, until in that single moment the whole thing had simply subsided under its own rotten weight. She went into the camp a communist despite everything; she left with every belief in it destroyed. She felt she'd been swindled, and it inflamed her bitterness to think she'd colluded in her own deception. As bitter or worse was the thought that Pak-kay, her first husband, after whom her alien son in Hong Kong was named, that he, too, had been deluded, had been martyred for a faith with as little sense in it as the faith for which that sincere, well-meaning, bird-brained missionary Miss Pulham had lived and died. Pak-kay, the only warm memory in her whole life — he, too, had been the dupe of an illusion! They all had.

She was emptied of every feeling except bitterness, a rancour which devoured her and which she devoured. No wonder she refused to shout those puerile slogans at Father Ignatius. Their clumsy stupidities stuck in her throat. Better the small number. Soon after she came out, when they were both put to sweeping out the kitchens, 'The two faiths are just the same,' she'd whispered harshly to him. 'These people and your people — there's nothing to choose between you.' She didn't want him to suppose her silence at the struggle meeting had been in the least for his sake. To her astonishment, he'd only laughed.

Although she'd been released, rehabilitated even, the bitterness flowed just as strongly, only sometimes in a more sardonic form. 'You see things too black,' her friend — her only friend — Chu kept telling her comfortably in Shanghai. 'Times are changing.' 'Stop dosing yourself with analgesics,' she'd reply. 'Even if you don't feel the pain, the disease is still terminal.' She resented communism for not existing.

A more sardonic form. That was how she evolved an exact ecclesiastical code for talking about the Party, a bitter little game which Chu, too, though unrancorously, sometimes enjoyed. 'I hear the cardinals are sitting,' she'd say of a Politburo meeting; or 'It seems the one true church is dwindling', of the falling Party membership. 'The Pope has issued another edict on birth control,' she said of the one-child policy; and 'The bishop's been summoned to Rome' when the mayor was called to Beijing. 'I wonder how long the Holy Father will live,' she'd say of Deng Xiao Ping. It was startling how pat it all fitted; the party simply was the Church, with everything inverted. What did the house-warden make of it when she listened in to her phone calls or eavesdropped in the shabby halls? 'You're crazy.' Chu said placidly. 'They don't do that kind of thing any more.'

'You think the lay sisters are getting slack?' she retorted, speaking loudly for the old woman to hear. 'Neglecting their religious observances these days?'

The old woman would nod and smile perplexedly across the hall, a wary dimness in her eyes.

Old? No older than Lily herself. But, unlike Lily's, her feet had once been bound, and after liberation (*Liberation!*) she'd become a 'small-foot policeman', an informer.

Sometimes Lily thought of her abandoned faith as another kind of foot-binding, one that moulded and deformed her mind. The bindings had come off at last, and she was free to walk where she would; but she could only hobble — the flesh was still raw, weak, misshapen. Perhaps it would never heal and grow firm again.

Outside the canteen on Maloo (she still thought of Nanjing Road by that old name), her eye was caught by a blurred photo in the outspread *People's Daily*. She put on her glasses to examine it, bending nearer to read the caption. Yes, it was her second husband, Fung. Leading a delegation to Europe now. He'd like that; he'd eat himself sick as soon as he got there. What about his table manners, though, how would they go down at the banquets? He'd always eaten like a pig. In the early years she tried to persuade herself it was a sign of his freedom from bourgeois artificiality and inhibition. She even tried to emulate him for a time, to shovel and slurp as he did; but that didn't last, it disgusted her too much. To think that her disgust had made her feel guilty and, as a penance, she even used to give him some of her own rations like a traditional dutiful wife! That was one feudal custom she never heard him complain about.

She folded her glasses and put them slowly away.

Inside the canteen she queued for her ticket, queued for her bowl of noodles, queued for a place at the bare littered wooden tables. All round her people ate swiftly and silently, each immured in the cell of his own cautious solitude, against the bars of which the clatter of bowls, the scraping of chairs, the officious voices of the cooks and servers rattled like gaolers' clubs. *We are an imprisoned people*, she thought.

She recalled that winter evening in Datong when Fung said he'd have to draw a line. They'd both looked like beetles, bundled up in their thick worn padded jackets, wearing even their caps indoors. They were sitting, he at the table over his bowl, she on the other chair by the window, gazing out at the street. Snowflakes fluttering down created an illusion of wide graceful space in the dusk, before they melted in the mud, coal dust and garbage of the unpaved road. The first snows always turned to yellow slush there, stained by the sulphurous grime of that city of coal, and it wasn't till the really heavy falls that the snow briefly got the upper hand and covered the muck with smooth white drifts which the soot and coal dust soon besmirched. City of coal? But there were two of the finest temples in China there, so Chu told her years later in Shanghai. She'd heard of them, but never gone inside. What did such things mean to her?

'We must consider our relationship,' Fung had begun abruptly, she remembered. 'In the light of your unsatisfactory class background.'

Abruptly, but she could tell it was a rehearsed speech. He'd peered into the corner of the bare darkened room as if he expected to find her guilty class background skulking there. 'In the light of your unsatisfactory class background.' How did people get such slabs of verbiage into their mouths — or out of them for that matter? But she herself had done it for years, and believed she was making sense with them as well.

Fung looked almost the same then as when they'd married seven years before — balding, earnest, and with sedulous attentive eyes. Yes, his eyes. They'd be all over your face while he was talking to you, assessing, calculating, gauging, behind his wire-rimmed lenses. Sometimes he forgot to take them off when he turned to her in bed.

'Your unsatisfactory background is becoming a problem,' he'd gone on, lighting one of those expensive Front Gate cigarettes — there were always little luxuries he allowed himself. 'It's making things difficult for my work.'

His eyes were crawling like spiders over her face, and she'd turned her head away to avoid seeing them. A woman had gone trudging down the street wearing a coal-sack for a coat. What else did they have? Lily had wished she was that woman; she'd have been less desolate, less cold inside.

'Tang called me in this afternoon.'

He'd waited expectantly, but she'd held herself quiet and still. She, too, was waiting after all. He wanted her to make it easier for him, but something stubborn rebelled in her. He'd got the gun against her head, but she wasn't going to pull the trigger for him; he could do that himself. She'd watched the woman, hunched together under her coal-sack, tramp stolidly by. So the party secretary had called him in. Well, then.

'My work requires me to draw a line. My personal feelings are different of course, but . . . .' As a doctor might say clinically: 'You are infectious, a menace to public hygiene, and we must isolate you. Our personal feelings are quite different of course, but . . . .'

Always that leprous taint of her Eurasian birth and her class origin. Could she never be cured of it? She realized he must have scented trouble coming. He always had such a nose for it. In the hospital, at that time, nobody had breathed a word, no one had even begun to glance at her askance or look the other way in the corridor. But Fung had got his snout up and sniffed the breeze.

Yet how assiduously he'd pursued her before, when the glory of Pak-kay's martyrdom was still reflected on to her. The little gifts, the attentions at meetings, the watchful eyes that always found her face from the platform. Did she marry him because of all that, and because he was a good speaker, like Pak-kay? Well, there was no one else. Certainly he'd never attracted her physically. But she'd persuaded herself personal feelings were a bourgeois anachronism; they must never stand in the way of the political ideal. *'My personal feelings are different of course.'*

Whenever she visualized his face, it was always the livid little dimples his glasses left on the bridge of his nose that she saw first.

As she was leaving the canteen, a bright-cheeked girl came in with glossy black hair braided down her back, and eyes shining with laughter, as though the wretched state of China had never cost her a moment's thought. Lily could scarcely believe that she herself had once been young and bright with hope — a different hope — here in Shanghai with Pak-kay. Sometimes she cycled down the street where they'd lived before he was killed. The building itself had gone in the war, but she knew the spot exactly.

It was all so long ago, and everything that had happened to her since then had made her hard and cold. She was bitter, bitter all over, bitter through and through.

There was a crowd of people waiting for the tram. She wished she'd come by cycle now, in spite of that giddy turn that had decided her not to. Blood-pressure; nothing much at her age. Over-exerting herself pumping up her tyres in the garage, and bending down, too. She'd had to sit when it happened, breathing heavily, gazing greyly at the cement floor until it passed. It was strange, looking down from a couple of feet at the little pits and flaws in the concrete and the tiny smooth slices of flint sticking in it; things you'd never noticed in your life before, however often you'd walked across it. Like suddenly seeing something familiar through a microscope and realizing what it was really made of. Like seeing the first glorious forty years of communism in China as just a heap of barren sand.

She was suddenly itchy to make a start on the Fourth World, as though, if she delayed, she might not have enough time.

9

Help and comfort

Of course, he'd have to go and see Lily, he thought, waiting for the sun to rise. Unlike Grace, who slept most heavily after daybreak, Michael always woke early, often before first light. He could sense without looking at his watch that it would soon be dawn. It wasn't from the sky — that had no glimmer in it — but from the still freshness in the air, the breath-held expectancy, as if the earth checked itself and paused a moment before turning on towards the sun. In Chungking, in the forties, he'd grown used to early rising before the morning raids came in; and he'd never lost the habit. He used to watch the dawn from a hill near the British military mission, watch the day slowly peeling the night off the sleeping city like someone gently lifting a blanket off a sick old man. First the muted paling of the sky, then the muffled shapes of boats appearing in the river, of buildings on the banks, then the wasted body of the whole city stretched out stark before him.

Sometimes, when he'd had to travel to the front, he would get up in the small of the night, when the world was still as death and the moonlight shone like black lacquer off the silent roofs and silent water, and he would feel a stirring of that desolation and terror, which ever since his childhood kidnapping had lain buried in the deepest layers of his mind. He was afraid of the journey to the front with the British officers who only half-accepted him, afraid of raids, shells, wounds and mutilated limbs. He was afraid, and afraid to show it.

It was in one of those low small hours, on the hill by the British mission, that he'd decided he must marry Grace, whom at that time he'd scarcely spoken to and hadn't seen for eighteen months or more. Not decided; realized. It was partly in the dim hope of quietening that uneasy fear for good; or at least of never having to face it alone again (but of course he'd had to all the same). If there was one clause in the marriage ceremony that caught his imagination more than any other, it was *'for the mutual society, help and comfort that the one ought to have of the other'*. Society, help and comfort. And that, too, was why he'd wanted his children to have those serene summer days planted early in their minds, a help and comfort on the day their own desolation came. As he sensed it must.

So he realized he must go and see Lily, just as he'd realized he must marry Grace. He never really decided such things; he merely waited to find out what he was going to do.

He was sitting at his desk with his work on Caldwell neatly arranged before him — his patient reconstruction of the fragmented, faded, scratched-out story that Caldwell's life had been. But he hadn't switched on the lamp; he was waiting for the day to break before he went back to his laborious absorbing task of reassembly.

Soon there came some faint cheeps from the trees outside, then with a shrill rush the excited babble of all the birds. A few minutes later the night was ebbing; he could see the shapes of the bushes in the wan returning light and the feathery elegance of the bamboo nodding round the pool. As the light strengthened he heard Ah Choi muttering to the dogs as they whimpered eagerly round him. Ah Choi was always the first of the servants to wake, as though he still had to go for his crack-of-dawn gallops in Happy Valley. Then Ah Yee's voice sounded, quarrelling as usual with Ah Choi about what and how much to feed the dogs. 'Oats, oats, always oats. You think they're horses?' Then the scraping of the spoon as she ladled out cold rice on top of their meat. The dogs whined and snuffled. Soon she would waddle splay-footed to the bottom of the garden to do her morning exercises, overlooking the sea.

The kitchen noises came next, then a little commotion in the hall, and Paul strayed in, staring blankly, his shirt-tail hanging out, his fly undone. *He'd be better off in an institution, he'd be better off in an institution.*

Paul gazed at him as at a wall, then let Ah Mui lead him away. Michael watched the back of his head as he left, and imagined it filled with all the thoughts and feelings of the complete person he might have been. It was hard to turn to Caldwell after that, and at first his mind dragged against his will. But gradually, as he read through what he'd written, the enigmatic man took hold of him again. He could see him now, not quite English-looking, not quite a gentleman, fluent and supple in the court, translating from Hindi as easily as from Cantonese while the crapulent Chief Justice, lolling beneath the punkah, stared with arrogant cod eyes at the abject fawning witnesses; then walking back afterwards to the house — *this* house — that he could scarcely afford, to the Cantonese wife and half-breed children he could hardly support, meeting her dubious brother with his schemes for shady ventures that would enrich them all . . . .

Soon after seven, Ah Yee brought in his breakfast and the newspapers, one English, one Chinese.

'I'll have to go and see Lily,' he told Grace when she came down at nine.

Her eyes widened apprehensively. 'Will I have to go, too?'

'No. Why should you? In fact it's probably better I go alone.'

It wasn't, but he knew what she was thinking.

'There's a letter from San San,' Grace said. 'She says everyone in America thinks China's going to walk in and take Hong Kong over any day.' Her eyes questioned him mutely.

'Everyone? How does she know?' He recalled the *Ming Pao* and *Morning Post* reports he'd read a couple of hours ago. 'The only thing everyone *knows* is that the two sides are still talking in Beijing — everyone who reads the papers, that is.' The nearest he came to irritation with her was that she never did read them, and was always amazed by world events when she happened to hear about them a week or a month or a year later. Grace looked down, chastened, and he felt guilty immediately — it was because he, too, was worried about the talks that he'd hurt her with that uncharacteristic flick of sarcasm. 'It's true they don't seem to be getting anywhere,' he added contritely.

'Oh.'

Which may mean we shall all have to get out, he silently warned himself. He watched her eat. Or, rather, not eat. After only a few bites she seemed to forget there was more food there. Her plate and cup were always half-finished at best. She returned to San San's letter.

'Paul looked rather . . . glazed this morning,' he said after a time.

'I know.' She laid the letter down.

He glanced at the thin blue paper with San San' s firm black writing on it, only three or four words to a line. He liked the way she wrote, bold and assured, so different from his own minute tight script. Did she write to Alex Johnston? He supposed he wrote to her.

'Perhaps we ought to adjust the dose?' Grace said. 'Shall I phone Dr. Tsui?'

He'd be better off in an institution.

'Let's wait a bit,' he said, shrugging.

She handed him the first page of San San's letter. As he started reading it, tilting his head back, it occurred to him that he was now nearing the age in Hong Kong that his father had been when the communists took Shanghai over. Unlike his father, though, he was prepared. He'd put enough money abroad to live on, although most was still invested in Hong Kong, and each day worth a little less. But he didn't want to be a refugee again. If he had a life to lead, it was there in Hong Kong. Anywhere else he'd be an alien pensioner. And Grace and Paul — what would it do to them? And the servants? He'd always thought of life for as far back as he could remember — perhaps from the day of his kidnapping — he'd always thought of life as a protracted struggle in which victories were temporary and defeat the only end. But he wanted to hold out where he was, not scuttle away to a foreign bolt-hole, leaving the servants behind. Despite his fear, he wanted to hold out.

'You will be careful, won't you?' Grace asked anxiously. 'In China? You won't get yourself put in prison?' She was thinking of her father and mother, of half her family.

'I'm only going to talk to her, Grace.' He hadn't taken a word of San San's letter in. 'I'm not sure Lily really has any idea what she's letting herself in for. I just want to tell her, that's all. It'll be perfectly safe. I've been there before, after all, even if it was a long time ago.'

Nevertheless, he felt uneasy. Was that why, when he put the letter down, he still hadn't taken a word of it in?

'I'd better see what Paul's up to,' Grace said as she left the table.

It was his ambitious daughter-in-law Stella who'd unwittingly slipped the idea of seeing Lily into Michael's head. He'd met her with John in the Mandarin lounge, while a suavely black-suited trio poured soapy music over the brittle chatter of the Happy Hour.

'Perhaps she's being Set Up?' Stella had suggested in English, hesitating self-consciously over Set Up, as though not quite sure whether the idiom was proper. She flashed the gleaming dishes of her lenses at him. 'Suppose someone wants to incriminate her? Does she really know she can't get out legally? It's very risky.'

As usual, John dwindled to an embellishing echo. 'Yes, it's pretty dicey,' he agreed.

They had their own reasons for playing up the dangers of course. They brought up every objection they could think of because they wanted to protect Stella's political career. It was transparent — anyone could see through it — yet they never acknowledged it, probably not even to themselves. Ambition gave them the motive, and ambition made it opaque to them. Stella wanted to be in at the start of the new Hong Kong, whatever that would be like — and he doubted whether she really cared — in and running without a handicap. And Lily escaping from China would be a handicap.

'Steely Stella waxes eloquent about Preserving Freedom and Civil Rights now all right,' Patrick had sighed one evening. 'But wait till the commissars actually come. She'll be shining their shoes with the best of them then.'

Presumably John would be a shoe-shine boy as well. Sometimes, quite often, Michael felt he didn't really know his son, as though a different person had slowly devoured the old one and occupied his skin. Was this uneasily distant lawyer, dominated by his calculating wife, the boy he used to watch sitting chin in hand over his homework, swinging his crossed heels under his chair, eyes dreaming out of the window? No, of coarse he wasn't; he was a different person altogether, a remotely connected descendant of the child, as distant as twenty generations.

'Besides, she must be rather old now,' Stella had gone on. 'Could she take the journey? Or the change?'

'She must be seventy,' John chimed.

'Seventy-one and a half,' Michael said drily. 'May the twenty-first. I suppose I ought to find out whether she can or not.'

Stella was dressed expensively in her irreproachably severe office-suit. Her smoothly made-up face seemed mask-like to Michael, as though if she laughed she'd crack. But she did smile and nod (ingratiatingly, he thought) at a squat silk-suited Chinese as he passed.

Michael had vaguely recognized the face. 'Who's that?' he asked. He remembered at once when John told him. 'The property developer? He's a crook, isn't he?'

'Very influential,' Stella had said, without disagreeing. 'He's well in with the Canton Authorities.'

Half-aloud in the box-room

Standing in the box-room where she kept her painting things, Chinese ink in one hand, brushes in the other, Grace looked up at the topmost shelf. They'd had the shelf fitted there years ago, running the whole length of the wall, and on it they'd stored all Paul's toys, hoping that one day he might grow back into them. After his illness, he'd never played with any of them again. He'd scarcely even touched them; and, when he did, it was without recognition. But they'd kept them all just in case — one of them might have tugged some memory one day and pulled him back into the world. Some he'd already outgrown when it happened, like the blue wooden engine; others, like the eagle-shaped kite, still in its plastic wrapping, he'd never grown into. But the days passed, and he passed the age of toys, and no memory ever tugged him back.

She ought to clear it all out; she ought to give it to Oxfam or some children's home. But she could never quite bring herself to do it — it would be like throwing away the photos of his childhood. She'd given most of her jewellery away to charity, and her wardrobe was only half-full (Michael had stopped buying her either jewels or clothes years ago, when he realized where they all went). But she couldn't give away those toys. *Not yet*, she thought, not yet. No more could either she or Michael bring themselves to take Dr. Tsui's reiterated advice to place Paul in an institution. 'Much less strain all round; he'd be better off,' Dr. Tsui would say in a voice that seemed as smoothly white-coated as he was. 'After all, he'll have to get used to it one day.'

She let her eyes travel slowly over the crammed, untidy, cobwebbed shelf, as if she were fingering each toy in turn. *One day*. Ten years ago they'd gone to look at institutions in the States and Britain, where Paul, Dr. Tsui said, could be 'socialized' better than at home. 'No painting or drawing for a time,' one doctor had said blithely. 'That's what makes him withdraw into himself still further. We need to bring him out of all that. We've got to socialize him.'

Grace only hoped Paul would die before they did.

She collected a sketch-book and some watercolours from the lowest shelf. She'd sit and paint beside him. Perhaps he'd do something, too. He often did.

She wondered sometimes why she kept on trying. Wasn't he all right as he was in his wild solitary world? Did she really want to lure him away from there, and cage him in the normal one?

But at other times she sensed he knew that he was maimed, he dimly knew it. And she felt obscurely guilty for it all. She realized some people thought she was almost as remote as Paul himself, and they probably wondered whether she, or her genes, were not at least partly responsible for the vaster remoteness of Paul. Sometimes she wondered herself.

'But it was encephalitis,' she protested half-aloud in the box-room.

Woman from the other tribe

Elena walked out, slamming the door. He could lie there drinking till he puked and choked on it for all she cared. How she hated Tom when he was drunk, with that damned expressionless drawl and those damned glazy eyes.

She was in the best week of her cycle, too, the one time when she really wanted him, and when she phoned he'd promised to come back early. After her shower she'd put on nothing but her bracelets and necklaces — all of them — and dabbed perfume in all her best places; then, wrapping herself in her dressing-gown, she'd stood by the window, waiting impatiently for him to arrive. They'd have a couple of hours before she needed to leave for the theatre, and she'd just throw the gown off when he came in and let him do whatever he wanted with her.

But he was late. And then he was very late. She grew more impatient and then, as the time passed, more cool. When at last he did come, she saw he was swaying as he climbed out of the taxi. She turned away from the window hard and cold.

She heard the lift hum in its shaft, she heard the doors slide open, she heard Tom's key scraping about at the lock until at last it slotted in and turned. She waited, arms folded, at the other end of the hall, her lips set, her eyes narrowed.

'Welcome home,' she said levelly. 'At last.'

'Guess what?' He leant against the jamb, peering at her as through a mist. 'Beijing's threatening to make a unilateral declaration about Hong Kong if the Brits don't come to heel. Just came through on the telex.'

'Do you know what time it is, by any chance?' she asked glacially.

He shook his head like a sleepy bear. ' 'bout six o'clock. Why? Stock market's dropped seventy points. Brits might as well take the flag down now.' He pushed the door shut with his foot and lumbered deliberately towards her. 'The party's over. Take down the flag.'

She ducked away from his lunging whisky-scented kiss. 'Take the key out of the door, too, while you're about it.'

'What?'

'Or are some more of your drunken instant-comment cronies coming up?' She turned and walked into the bedroom, sat down in front of the dressing-table and started putting on her clothes.

When he followed her a minute or two later he had a whisky in his hand. 'Getting dressed?' he asked.

'I'd be taking my things *off* if I was getting *un*dressed.' She flashed a dagger glance at him in the mirror, turning her head to put on her ear-rings. Usually she enjoyed the cool smooth feel of her ear-lobes, but nothing could please her now and, if it could, she wouldn't've let it.

He drank obliviously. He seemed to be rinsing the stuff round his mouth as if he were at the dentist's. She almost expected him to spit it out instead of swallowing it. 'Kind of early, isn't it?' He slumped on the bed, easing off his shoes. 'What time's the performance?'

She drew a stocking carefully over her left leg.

'What time's the performance?'

'Midnight! Quarter to six! Three in the morning! When is it usually?'

'Disgusted by the drunkard, huh?' He rinsed and swallowed again. 'Well, let me tell you something. So am I.'

She pulled on the other stocking and straightened the seam.

'So we do have something in common after all?'

'But the reason is Veetnahm,' he went on in that same dazed, grey, monotonous voice. 'That's when it started. Either you took drugs or you took drink. But in Veetnahm you had to take something.'

'Actually I call it Viet Nam,' Elena said, stepping into her shoes. ' "Veetnahm" sounds like a depilatory cream to me. If there's one thing I hate more than drunkenness, by the way, it's maudlin drunkenness.'

'What the fuck would you know about it?' Tom asked amiably. 'You uptight little British bitch.' He swallowed the last of his whisky, leant back on the pillow and closed his eyes. 'Yeah, Veetnahm,' he sighed. 'Take down the flag.'

She could hear him still muttering as she walked away down the hall.

It was raining. The first rain since August, and it had to be today. The sky was covered with featureless cloud, and everything, even on the mid-levels, looked grey and shabby. The pavement was greasy with drizzle, and the walls of the high-rise blocks lining the road — a road she could still remember as a shady lane — were blistered and stained with mossy mildew. Elena waited for a taxi, but it was the rush-hour and several went past full, tyres sizzling on the dark wet surface. One slowed at last, almost stopped, then drove past to pick up a middle-aged Chinese who had only just appeared on the kerb a few feet further along.

'Racist!' Elena said loudly in Cantonese.

Driver and passenger laughed, shaking their heads at each other as if she'd told them a joke they'd never heard before.

While she was still staring truculently after them, a blue Mercedes drew up beside her. Peter Denton leant across from the driving-seat, pointing enquiringly down the road.

'I'm in a terrible temper,' she warned him as he lowered the window. 'I'll probably say something hateful. Wouldn't you rather I didn't . . . ?'

He opened the door. 'Just tell me where you're going and you needn't say another word.'

'Somewhere in Central. Is that on your way?'

'It is now.'

He watched her reaching for the seat-belt, his eyes slipping in one clinging glance from the knee not quite covered by her skirt, up along her body (no bra, he noticed), to her tightened lips and the little angry points of colour on her cheeks. He thought of her water-skiing in the summer.

'Very kind of you,' Elena muttered through almost clenched teeth. 'Only better not talk to me; I'm feeling very shrewish.' She gazed stubbornly away from him, out of her window.

He kept an eye on her as he drove, thinking: *Alison had that fair complexion once; they don't last long. I ought to divorce her now really.* The trouble was he'd married her straight after Cambridge, simply dazzled by the glamour of a blonde English wife. It was a picture he'd married really, not her. A picture of himself returning triumphant with a woman from the other tribe, striking and rare. But Alison had soon bored him once they'd settled into Hong Kong. Her Englishness seemed crude and graceless beside the delicate pretty Chinese women he met at parties and dinners — and more so when Alison began drinking and running to fat in her disorientated unhappiness. Before long, with his money and his looks, he could have his pick of would-be models, aspiring starlets and nightclub singers — it was the women of the home tribe that allured him now. In everything except their shared apartment, he'd left his wife within a couple of years. It didn't trouble him that he was the main cause of her discontent. She was miserable and boring, so he took his pleasures elsewhere — as he would have done if she'd been happy and exciting, only not so soon perhaps, and not so often.

For that matter, nothing troubled him much, except the occasional failure of his erotic pursuits. He was startled when someone asked him once if it was Paul's illness that had led him to take up medicine. The idea had never occurred to him. He'd taken it up because he thought he'd be good at it and it could make him a lot of money.

He'd driven almost as far as the Botanical Gardens before Elena spoke again. 'Could you drop me near a coffee-shop, please?' she asked, still gazing out of her window. 'I feel starving sometimes before a performance.'

'Just what I was thinking.'

'You're not going to perform tonight, are you?'

'You never know, do you?'

She smiled in spite of herself, and turned to observe him. He gazed ahead at the traffic, a faint smile on his own lips, ready for some pert retort. He assumed, also, that she was admiring his profile — most women did. But 'You've got quite strong hands, considering,' was all she said grudgingly. 'I suppose it's because you're a surgeon. You can buy me a meal if you like. I'm starving, but it won't cost you much. Besides, you're loaded, aren't you?'

She said she was starving, but when they sat down at a corner table she wouldn't order more than a slice of toast and some tea, and she left half of that.

He sipped a glass of wine.

'Look!' she said suddenly. 'Isn't that Patrick's fancy boy? That waiter over there?'

'No idea.' Peter glanced uninterestedly at the epicene youth standing by a table in the other corner.

'Yes, I'm sure it is. I wonder what they actually *do*.'

'The same as us,' he chanced it. 'With a few adjustments.'

'Speak for yourself.'

But the game was on. Her eyes began to glisten. She let her foot occasionally touch his beneath the table, or his hand brush hers, or held his eyes with a sly smiling invitation. This was the bit she liked best, the bit that was only play and teasing.

'Shall I take you to the city hall?' Peter asked. 'Is that where you're performing?'

'Can you drive one-handed?'

'Why?'

'I might let you put your hand on my knee.'

But she didn't of course. She only agreed to meet him for supper after the performance. 'I might give you another chance then,' she said as she slipped out of the car. 'Depends how I feel. Ten-thirty, all right?'

Peter waited by the stage-door from twenty past ten till eleven, when the stagehands locked it and all the lights went out. Elena had left by the other door and hurried anxiously back to Tom, without even cleaning off her make-up. In the middle of *Scheherazade* she'd suddenly imagined him lying unconscious on the bed, his eyes staring up startled at death.

But he was sitting at the typewriter, blurry-eyed and frowning, yet perfectly articulate. *Time to Strike the Flag?* she read over his shoulder.

'How'd it go?' he asked, reaching behind to take her hand. 'I've got to go to Beijing tomorrow — '

'Oh, Tom, you nearly lost me and I wanted you so much and you know I only feel like that once a month and I was afraid you'd be dead like my mother when I got back and now I'm too tired.'

'Jesus, don't ever become a journalist. Sub-editors have a hard enough time with *my* stuff.'

Half an hour later he was holding her hand again, but they were horizontal now, and her face was flushed and sleepy. 'You know I don't have favourites, don't you, Tom?' she murmured. 'But, if I did, you'd be my very best. It's your bear's paw I go for, and your furry chest.'

Snakeboat business

'No problem,' Comrade Pang told Ah Wong cheerily, leaning back in his chair. 'All you have to do is make a statement.' He tapped a cigarette up from an American packet with his thumb, dragged it out thoughtfully with his lips and lit it with a Japanese lighter, closing his eyes against the smoke. Then he pulled a sheet of paper towards him. From his tunic pocket he unclipped an American ballpoint pen and begun writing, pausing every few characters to consider, frowning and drawing deep, on his cigarette. 'I suppose you still can't read or write?' he chuckled as he wrote. 'No literacy campaigns in Hong Kong, ah?'

Ah Wong, sitting deferentially on the edge of her chair, tittered and shook her head. She watched the pen's quick strokes making characters and the characters making long rows across the thick ruled paper. On the bare shabby wall behind Comrade Pang's head was a large pale oblong patch, exactly the size of the coloured picture of Mao Tse Tung that used to hang there. She remembered seeing the picture last time she was called to the office, about the television set. But that was years ago. Outside, through the cracked open window, she heard people passing, talking, a man grumbling about the price of a broom. Then someone coughed and spat.

The Japanese camera she'd taken out of her bag lay untouched where she'd placed it on the corner of the desk. It was a good one, Ling Kwan had told her when they went together to buy it. So it should be at that price, too.

Comrade Pang's cigarette was getting moist and squashed. He just let it hang there from his lip between puffs, and she kept watching to see if it would fall off, but it never did. Every now and then he'd lift it away between his finger and thumb and take a long deep drag on it, screwing his eyes half-shut as the smoke curled up round his face. Then down it would hang from his lip again. She'd never seen anyone smoke like that before.

Looking through what he'd written, he sucked the cigarette down to the wet flattened end, squashed it with his thumb in an old tin-lid, and sighed the smoke up all over his face as if he was washing in it. He had a round friendly face with yellow sticking-out teeth that reminded her of a goldfish.

He cleared his throat and read the statement out to her, pausing to sip tea from a white enamel mug with a chipped blue rim. She tried to listen carefully, but he read so fast she only got mixed up.

'All right, ah?' he ended. 'Make your mark.'

'Is it all there about the three payments?' she asked uncertainly.

'Course it is. We're not a bunch of sharks from Hong Kong, you know.'

She made a cross where he pointed, and he wrote something beside it, chopping it with an oval blue stamp.

'If your brother was more careful, he wouldn't have all this trouble,' Comrade Pang said, placing the paper carefully in a green cardboard file. 'First there was that business with the TV set, then his daughter going off to Hong Kong. Think we didn't know where she ran off to, did you? And now the money for that house of his . . . . '

'But it was a present from me. So was the TV.' She nudged the camera a little further towards him.

'I'm not saying it wasn't. But people talk, don't they? And then we have to look into it. It's trouble for everyone. Just tell him to be more careful, all right?' He grinned suddenly, his eyes popping wide open just like a goldfish. 'If he hadn't had someone to put a word in for him, he could have really landed in it, right up to his neck, couldn't he?'

He took the camera at last, turned it over in his hands, then put it carefully in the bottom drawer of his desk. 'Right, then,' he said, locking the drawer.

She left the office smiling and nodding gratefully, but her face set hard as she walked down the uneven rutted lane, spattered with pig droppings, towards her brother's house. She ignored the children who gathered and followed her, staring, whispering, giggling, nudging each other, some of the older ones pestering her to change money or asking for a Hong Kong biro. She didn't recognize most of them anyway. Every year it was the same; there were more kids she no longer knew in the village. She didn't even know the woman who greeted her by name from the door of old Tsang's house, although she recognized her face and gave a grimly polite smile back. One side of the house was still in ruins, the wall propped up with bamboo poles. It didn't look as if they'd ever mend it. And she could remember when it was the best house in the whole village, before old Tsang was thrown out after the revolution for being a landlord — him a landlord, because he hired that lazy devil Chan to help him work the land that he couldn't work all on his own! Nor did she know the young man with two heavy rattan baskets balanced on his bamboo shoulder-pole, although he gave her a friendly nod, eyeing her Hong Kong clothes, as he passed. The baskets were full of pig food, judging by the rotten smell.

The children dropped away as she went on. Soon there was nothing but the rice-fields with their narrow grass banks, and her brother's newly extended house, the last in the village. Behind the house was the sea. Her brother's grey junk was anchored further out with folded sails, and a man and woman were fishing from a sampan close inshore, the man rowing from the stern while the woman beat the water with her weighted stick, scaring the fish into the nets they'd laid. Ah Wong wondered if she knew them, but she couldn't see their faces under their wide dun straw hats. The regular thump and splash of the weighted stick carried across to her as she walked towards the house.

Her mother was sitting where they'd left her in the sun, twisted hands still resting limply in her lap, her small eyes squinting peacefully across the empty fields out of her crumpled face. Her grey hair was so thin now, you could see her scalp through it. It looked as if you could blow it away with a puff of breath.

'You've come, then,' her mother said, as though she hadn't seen her only a couple of hours before.

Ah Wong went inside without answering. The house smelt of oysters, even the new room they'd built on the back, still bare and empty.

Her brother was drinking tea at the table. He looked round, raising his eyebrows without speaking.

'Pang wrote it all down on a paper,' she said, setting her black bag on the table. 'And I had to make my mark. And he still remembers the TV set. Said you ought to be more careful.'

Her brother glanced at the colour television in the corner. Young girls in swimsuits were parading across a stage dazzling with lights. Fine thing for him to be watching.

'The sound's gone,' he said. 'It's always like that when you try to get Hong Kong.'

It was the first colour set in the village. Even now there were only two others, and one was Comrade Pang's. Did anyone make trouble for him?

'What did he say about the camera?'

'He said you were lucky you had someone to put a word in for you. Otherwise you'd've been in it. Up to your neck, he said.'

'What did he write on the paper?'

'How do I know? I couldn't understand it.' She was angry with herself for being scared of Comrade Pang, for having to give him a present and say please and thank you just because she'd given her brother some money. Whose money was it anyway? She could do what she liked with it, couldn't she? She was angry with herself and she took it out on her brother. None of it would have happened but for him. She'd given him the money. Did she have to have all this trouble as well? When her brother poured her some tea from the old metal thermos, she pushed it aside irritably. 'Give me some boiling water,' she said, taking her little instant-coffee jar out of her bag. Through the back door she watched her brother's wife spreading manure round the roots of the young greens. Her brother's eyes had strayed to the girls on the screen again, although the picture kept snowing. They'd got long shiny evening gowns on now; the things they did, parading about in public like that.

'A good worker, your wife,' she said sharply, stirring her coffee. 'Does as much as the rest of you put together.'

Her brother looked away from the screen guiltily and gazed at his wife bending double over the dark wet earth. He sighed and nodded as if he couldn't help it that he wasn't out there working, too, then sipped his tea.

'She's a good worker,' Ah Wong repeated. She'd been telling him that for years, but what was the use? You kept pouring water over the duck's back, and still the duck's back was dry. 'Well, what about this other business with the boat?' she asked. 'Snakeboat business?'

Her brother rubbed his chin. 'We've had an offer,' he nodded at last. To take some people across.'

'When?'

'In the new year,' her brother said. 'They come here at night and we take them out to sea' — he glanced through the doorway at his junk — 'and hand them over to cousin Siu Kong near Macao. And he takes them on to Hong Kong.' He paused to let it sink in. 'Five thousand Yuan. They call him Snakeboat Wong in Macao.'

Ah Wong took a McVitie's biscuit out of the roll she always carried in her bag and dunked it in her coffee. 'How much does Siu Kong get?' she asked suspiciously.

Her brother shrugged. 'Says his risk is bigger.'

Ah Wong nibbled her sodden biscuit. Five thousand was a lot of money, but she couldn't swallow her anger just like that. Besides, they'd never done anything like that before, apart from bringing in a few cigarettes and radios. 'You'd be running risks, too,' she said coldly. 'Just the same as him.'

Her brother's wife had come in, wiping her hands down her tunic. 'If we do it for this price at first,' she said gravely to her sister-in-law, ignoring her husband, 'we can ask for more later.'

'What about Pang?'

She shrugged, rubbing her back and stretching. 'We'll give him a cut,' she said.

Ah Wong never stayed to eat the evening rice with them; she wanted to get back to her radio and her room in Hong Kong. But she expected to be asked, and as usual her brother's wife pressed her to stay. She shook her head, drank another glass of coffee, nibbled another biscuit and left to catch the last bus.

They'd carried her mother in when the sun went down, and sat her in front of the television. She nodded and smiled, lifting her one good hand to wave goodbye, then turned back to the flickering screen.

'When she dies I won't come,' Ah Wong told her brother. 'I'll send money for the funeral, but I won't come.' They'd got the funeral clothes and the coffin already: all she'd pay for was the food and the gravestone. Her brother could do his bit, too, instead of expecting her to pay the lot just because she came from Hong Kong. Especially if they went through with that snakeboat business with cousin Siu Kong.

There were a dozen or so people with baskets and boxes tied with twine waiting at the bus-stop. And nearby, leaning against the wall, she saw old Chan. She glanced away quickly, but not before she'd seen his face was blotchy red from drinking, and that he'd recognized her, too.

'Ah, here's the capitalist Madam Wong from Hong Kong,' old Chan jeered. 'Come to feather her brother's nest again, ah?'

A few people glanced at her, but nobody spoke. She tilted her chin and gazed steadfastly down the lane. She could see the bus-lamps bouncing towards them, half a mile away.

'Explain away the money for brother's house, then, did you?' old Chan called out hoarsely behind her.

She sensed eyes turning towards her now, curious watchful glances beneath their lids. To think her mother had wanted to marry her off to that drunkard thirty years ago, even after that business with old Tsang! Everyone knew it was Chan who'd gone to the party secretary and denounced old Tsang as a landlord. Thought he'd get the house for himself — well, they weren't as stupid as that at least. She felt the heat rising behind her eyes. 'Better feather your brother's nest than foul up someone else's,' she said loudly to the evening air.

Old Chan laughed, but she could tell he was worried. Things weren't the same now as they used to be, and he knew it. He laughed again and belched. 'She wants the landlords back now, ah?' But he moved away as the silent glances switched back attentively to him. He knew she could say more if she chose. Drunk he might be, but he wasn't too drunk for that.

10

Depraved tastes

'It's still breathing,' Rachel said. 'Can't we do something?'

Patrick said: 'Don't touch it. It might have rabies.'

Chung Yan turned away, grimacing with disgust.

The animal was lying across the track, unable to move, one leg twisted up under its body, its small head turned grotesquely round on its neck. The thin black lips curled viciously back from its perfect white needle teeth, but its pale green eyes were dulling. Its striped black and grey fur and bushy tail were dirty and caked with reddish mud. Its flanks were moving faintly and slowly, as if it needed all its failing strength just to struggle for one more breath.

'What is it?' Rachel asked in a small voice.

'A civet cat,' Patrick said. 'Probably smuggled in from China, and escaped. They often have rabies.'

Everything about the animal was deathly still, except that slow laborious breathing. And the dimming eyes that feebly strained to follow each of their voices.

'Smuggled? Can you make pets of them?'

'Pet!' Chung Yan snorted.

'I don't know,' Patrick said blankly. 'But you can certainly make a meal of them.'

Rachel shuddered. 'Can't we do something for it? Get a vet or something?'

'Really, Rachel! A vet!' Patrick glanced expressively round the bare hillside. They must have walked three miles from the road already, and hadn't met a soul.

'Only animal,' Chung Yan said impatiently. 'Never mind she die.'

Rachel wondered if it could have been bitten by a snake.

'Snake?' Chung Yan stepped quickly out of the long grass on to the stony path. 'Snake? Crazy!' He glared at Rachel accusingly. 'Crazy!'

'Oh, do stop being hysterical!' Patrick snapped. 'You said you wanted a day in the country, didn't you?'

They left the civet to die, Chung Yan indifferently, Patrick regretfully, Rachel with guilt. She knew she should have killed it swiftly, not left it to suffer. But she didn't know how; she was afraid she'd only make a mess of it, and it would suffer more. Besides, she was squeamish. The thought of hitting it with something, the thud of wood or stone against the base of its skull, the shock travelling up her arm — it unnerved her. She was ashamed.

The track led upwards from the coast, over one treeless slope after another. Behind them the sea grew hazier with every fold of the hill.

It had been edgy from the start. Patrick hadn't warned Chung Yan he was bringing Rachel along, and Chung Yan bridled when he saw her in the car, especially when he realized he couldn't sit in front. Then he kept moaning: about the distance, the heat (it really wasn't too hot even at midday now — Rachel slept with a blanket at night), and the detour Patrick made to show Rachel one of the old walled villages — though when she stepped inside she understood his sniffy feelings about that.

'So dirty,' he said, wrinkling his nose at the muddy path, the goose droppings, the smell of rural garbage. He tossed his head when a solid young man in jeans, paring his toe-nails with a knife on the threshold to the courtyard, grinned up and muttered something to him.

Rachel gazed at the dismal ancestral hall with its rows of progenitors' tablets like miniature gravestones, and at the surrounding damp dark corridors breathing lassitude and decay. A few old men stared at them sourly. She felt the place was rotting resentfully away.

'Watch out for rats,' Patrick said, stepping over a ledge. 'Things are getting run-down here, too.'

'Too?'

'Wait till you see Chung Yan's village. At least some people are still living in this one.'

Rachel wondered whether they should be. It seemed to her more like a dilapidated stable than a village.

The young man muttered to Chung Yan again as they left, and again Chung Yan flung his head away.

'What was he saying?' Rachel asked.

Patrick unlocked the car door before he answered detachedly. 'He was asking Chung Yan whether he was your boyfriend or mine.'

Rachel climbed determinedly into the back seat this time. Patrick made only a token attempt to dissuade her, but it didn't improve Chung Yan's mood. 'Not very nice,' he commented at the Sai Kung restaurant where they stopped for dim-sum, eyeing the worn table-cloth and commonplace bowls distastefully, and only picking at the food. And when they parked off the road further on, to begin the long walk to his village, he became still more sulky, making Patrick still more solicitous, still more oblivious of Rachel. But coaxing only encouraged him to pout and moue the more. The path was too rough or too steep, he was too hot, he was tired of walking, the sun gave him a headache . . . . '

For God's sake! Rachel thought.

At last Patrick himself grew irritable. 'Don't you *want* to see your ancestral village again? Doesn't it mean anything to you?'

Chung Yan only shrugged his slender silk-shirted shoulders. 'Old people care,' he said sullenly. 'I don't care. I don't like.'

Often they argued querulously in Cantonese, leaving Rachel to walk alone. She listened uncomfortably, picking out occasional words, knowing from Patrick's suddenly lowered tone and Chung Yan's overtly hostile glances that they were quarrelling about her.

After a time the quarrel lapsed into sultry silence. Chung Yan lagged behind, his face blank and sullen; and Patrick, giving an exasperated shrug, went on with Rachel. 'Really, he's so *difficult* today,' he sighed apologetically, as if over some fractious child (*Well, isn't he?* Rachel thought).

Since he'd acknowledged he was gay, Patrick rarely performed his extravagant Edwardian act for her. He staged it only for others, as if he could deflect them with his unflagging theatre from the reality he was caricaturing. With Rachel he had no more need.

She'd been almost as astonished as he was when she'd suddenly confronted him with his homosexuality, one afternoon in the university a few weeks before. They'd finished discussing the plan of her thesis, and she was just putting her papers away when she looked up and asked: 'Patrick, are you gay?' Perhaps it was because she'd seen him in Central that morning, walking with Chung Yan, and he'd only given her an embarrassed distant wave — perhaps that was why she asked him then. It was on her mind that if he knew she knew and knew she didn't care, he wouldn't be so jumpy. But, though she heard herself ask quite naturally, as she might have asked if he was left-handed (after all, that was all it was, really, wasn't it?), she realized at once she'd put it to him too directly. He stared at her as if she'd stabbed him, then looked quickly away. She'd never seen him so flustered since that day months ago when she called at his apartment and found Chung Yan there.

'Dear girl, what a question!' he prevaricated when he'd recovered. But he was flushing, and his eyes looked scared. 'Do you make such personal enquiries of all your acquaintances, or am I specially singled out — ?'

'I just wondered.'

'Or are you perhaps conducting one of those ghastly American surveys? Sexual mores of the cosmopolitan Asian male?'

'I just wondered.'

'Ah, you just wondered. I see . . . . ' He hesitated, twiddling his pencil between his finger and thumb. 'You just wondered, did you? Well . . . . ' He glanced huntedly round the room, from bookcase to picture to door, but never once at her candid expectant gaze, as if searching fugitively for some evasion to hide himself in. Then he gave a little resigned shrug and smiled warily at her. 'Let's just say I love my fellow-men, dear girl. Why?' He was still twiddling the pencil, a black one with a silver clip. His eyes were fixed on that now.

'I don't know. I just assumed you were, I guess.'

'An assumption which did not perhaps require positively the most strenuous leap of the imagination to make?'

'You don't have to try so hard with me, Patrick.' She was astonished again to hear herself speaking like that. 'I mean, it's no big deal, after all, is it?'

'Well, one doesn't exactly care to *proclaim* the truth in Hong Kong, dear girl — '

'Do you *have* to keep saying "dear girl"?'

He checked himself, then went on, smiling wryly. 'One doesn't exactly care to proclaim the truth in Hong Kong. One has to observe what are quite indecently called "the decencies". One can talk like a queer and nobody minds, but one mustn't proclaim one behaves like one.'

'You'd rather have people snigger about you behind your back? Like that awful man Frank . . . whatever he's called?'

He winced. 'One has no option, alas,' he said quietly, laying the pencil down at last. 'One would rather not be *harassed*. You do realize homosexuals are criminals here? Do you know what the penalty for buggery is in Hong Kong? Oh dear.' He held up a floppy foppish hand, relapsing into his extravagant camp style. 'Now I suppose you're going to become maternally sympathetic in a juvenile way and ask how it all happened and so on. Was I perverted by a paedophile prep-school pedagogue, and all that odious canting stuff? How absolutely tiresome.'

'I don't understand these things.'

'How very modest. How evidently true.'

'I seem to be kind of neuter.' She felt suddenly that she was blushing.

'No, dear girl — dear Rachel, I mean. You're transcendent. You're above the battle, beyond both the splendour and the squalor, so to speak. You are, if I may say so, a female eunuch, inhabiting the regions of eternal sexless calm.' He watched her putting her papers tidily together, clipping them into her folder with her neat pale fingers; and he saw her lips were set and the blush was spreading, right round to her neck. His irony drained away at once; he felt emptied. 'As a matter of fact,' he sighed, speaking in a tone that, being natural, seemed at first unnatural for him, 'I wasn't buggered by anyone, if you really want to know.'

Rachel had never grasped exactly what buggery was. The dictionary was inexplicit but, anyway, she wasn't really interested. 'I don't specially want to know as a matter of fact.' She stood up.

'I developed my depraved tastes quite spontaneously. I wasn't a flower whose growth was blighted; I was just a rank and noxious weed all along. Though why the first person I should tell this to — apart from my catamite, of course — should be a woman, and you in particular, I really can't fathom.'

'Because I'm transcendent?'

She'd almost reached the door when he asked her, naturally again, to go and have some coffee with him. Since then he'd rarely camped it up with her, except in deliberate parody when someone else was there. And then she felt he was doing it with a wink at her, so that instead of cringing for him in the stalls she could enjoy his burlesque from the wings. But she still detested it when, as occasionally he still did, he put on an act for her alone.

Smuggling people

They'd been walking for more than two hours over the bare hills before they came to a saddle, on which a large derelict stone building stood.

'School,' Chung Yan said. 'Very dirty. Very poor. No more now.'

The windows were all broken, the roof fallen in, the rubble-strewn floor blackened here and there from campers' fires. Names and dates, in Chinese and English, had been scratched on the walls and gouged into the blackboard that still hung askew behind the teacher's dais.

'Why do people always do that?' Rachel asked, deciphering some of the characters. *Lam, Tang, Wu, Chan, 1970, 1974, 1980.*

'Vanity. No doubt some American astronaut has defaced the lunar surface with his puny initials, too, just to brag to the universe that he's been there.'

But she thought it was more because people didn't like to pass and leave no trace.

Along the outside wall crude characters had been daubed in red paint, and partially erased. Rachel struggled to reconstruct them.

' "Death to the running dogs of British imperialism," ' Patrick read aloud. 'A hangover from the red and heady days of the Cultural Revolution, I suppose. If they ever come back . . . . ' he made a throat-slitting motion with his hand. 'The news is not encouraging, I need hardly say. Britain will surrender and leave us to our fate in the end.'

Rachel said she couldn't imagine her communist friend Cheung cutting anyone's throat. 'He's just very shy and very prim.'

'I believe Robespierre was, too. Which way, Chung Yan?'

There were three tracks wandering off from the schoolhouse. Chung Yan nodded at the most overgrown. It zig-zagged steeply down the side of a narrow valley. He refused to go first, for fear of snakes; so Patrick led.

As they stumbled down the path, the long thick grass swishing round their legs, their feet tripping over roots and stones, they passed under the shade of trees for the first time since they'd started. Through the branches, across the valley, the tiered ledges of disused rice-terraces showed like ribs beneath a smooth green skin.

The path grew steeper, they heard water running, then they came suddenly to a stream, a stone bridge, a broader path; and then a minute later they were in the village — a row of abandoned stone huts with ruined walls and broken lop-sided doors. Papaya and mango trees were growing wild, creepers had smothered every building; fragments of plates, cooking-pots, bottles, even cheap red plastic toys lay half-buried beside the path. In one hut Rachel saw an ancient iron treadle sewing machine lying on its side. Outside another, a loose stone wall still stood, enclosing a vegetable patch gone to seed. The path ended abruptly at the last hut. Beyond was nothing but grass and trees. There was no sound except the forlorn trickle of the stream past one derelict hut after another.

Patrick asked Chung Yan which hut was his home.

'All same,' Chung Yan answered with a shrug.

Resting her hand on the loose rough stone of a tumbled wall, Rachel wondered how many generations of peasant hands had rested there, feeling the rough texture against their palms as she did then. She knew she'd be a gardener herself one day. 'Why did they leave?' she asked aloud, meaning it was a pity that they did.

'Money,' Patrick said. 'Escape from rural idiocy. Ask Chung Yan; he was born here, dear girl. After all, what would you do on a Saturday evening here? On every Saturday evening of your life, that is?' He called her 'dear girl' to mock her, but a second later his mood changed. 'Of course it's sad in a way to see it go back to the jungle,' he said. 'Did you know they used to grow the emperor's rice near here? A few more years and there won't be a paddy-field left in Hong Kong. Or a village, I shouldn't be surprised. Not that Chung Yan cares of course.'

Then abruptly, as if that thought had released another which he'd been keeping down beneath it, 'I'm so worried about him,' he said in an anxious low voice. 'What will he do when China takes over? Can you imagine him surviving under a communist system?'

Not very well, she had to admit. 'Homosexuality is a social disease,' she recalled Cheung saying the other day, viewing her earnestly through his glasses as they stood on the red-tiled Sun Yat Sen steps outside the university library. 'When China recovers Hong Kong, such problems will be solved. As they have been in China since Liberation.' Along with drug-taking, prostitution, pornography and what he called 'Rap.' Socialist values would be introduced and spiritual pollution cleaned up. 'Sounds hygienic,' Rachel had remarked.

'He'll be in his early thirties in 1997,' Patrick went on. 'I'm trying to get him a UK passport, but you can't imagine how difficult it is. And he doesn't understand; he thinks I ought to be able to manage it just by clicking my fingers.'

Chung Yan, hearing his name, had begun to listen alertly, hovering on Patrick's other side.

'I've even thought of finding him a job in Macao. It's easier to get Portuguese citizenship, and then at least he'd have an escape route that way. But he won't hear of going there.'

'Macao,' Chung Yan repeated, pleased at being talked about. 'Not nice, too dirty.' He took Patrick's arm and spoke to him in Cantonese.

'Chung Yan thinks we ought to go now,' Patrick said. 'Otherwise it'll be dark before we get back to the car. He's petrified of stepping on a snake. You'd hardly believe he'd been born here, would you? Besides, they must be hibernating now.'

Chung Yan still hung on his arm, so Rachel went ahead, leaving the love-birds to coo in Cantonese together. Near the first hut, its shape blurred by a blanket of grass and creepers, she found a little hexagonal spirit-mirror, the glass speckled in its thin red frame.

'My house,' Chung Yan said quickly when he saw it. 'This glass come my house.'

'You want it?'

He took it from her, examined it, then gave it back disdainfully. 'You keep. I don't want.'

'You sure?'

'Too old.' He tossed his head, meaning unmistakably that it wasn't good enough for him, but it might do for her. 'Can frighten ghost away,' he said grandly. 'Old people believe.'

She dropped it in her shirt-pocket.

'He half-believes it himself,' Patrick murmured fondly. 'He's so superstitious.'

She made a secret grimace and went on. The love-birds followed slowly.

Somehow she must have taken a wrong path beyond the bridge. After some time the track petered out, although the long grass ahead had been flattened recently. She paused, waiting for the others, but there was no sound of them. She went on a little, round the curve of the hill. The flattened grass, thick and dark green, led to another deserted stone hut.

But it wasn't deserted. A man appeared at the doorway; then another, younger, with tattooed arms. She smiled, they didn't; and on the instant she felt a flutter of alarm. She tried in meagre broken Cantonese, then in flowery Mandarin, to ask where the path was. They stared at her expressionlessly, neither friendly nor hostile, more as if she were a thing or a stray animal.

She became suddenly aware how small and alone she was, aware of the helpless emptiness behind her, all round her, aware of the bleak calculating expressions in the two men's eyes. She sensed they didn't want her there, were considering what to do about her, and wouldn't care what they did. Then she saw a movement behind them in the hut, and realized there were others there, too, peering at her. She glimpsed blank sunburnt faces and drab blue cotton tunics in the gloom.

Nobody spoke.

The older man pulled the door half-shut, without taking his eyes off her. The hinge creaked across the afternoon stillness, and the stillness grew stiller after it. Then the old man muttered to the younger one. The younger one nodded.

Nobody moved. They continued watching her with their flint eyes, assessing and cold.

Don't be absurd; they just don't understand, she told herself. But that sickening butterfly of fear still fluttered in her stomach. She smiled again, shrugged, turned and walked deliberately back the way she'd come, her neck taut and prickling, listening tensely for the thud and slither of running footsteps behind her. She knew she mustn't run herself, and she mustn't look round. Then she thought she heard the swish of grass at her back, and a scream started surging up her throat. At the same moment Patrick called, quite near.

She shouted back unsteadily; it was only then she noticed how hard and rapidly her heart was thudding against her ribs. Patrick appeared twenty or so yards below. She dared to look back now. The younger man with tattooed arms was halfway between the hut and her. He was standing watching them, still with that flat cold look in his eyes. She thought she caught a glint of metal as he put his hand behind his back. And simultaneously she thought quite detachedly how strange it was that your limbs really did go watery when you were terrified.

'Not that way!' Patrick called. 'The path's down here!' Then his face changed — a sudden tightening — as he glanced past her, and he began speaking volubly in Cantonese, calling to Chung Yan, who appeared nervously behind him.

The older man started walking down the path towards the younger one. Neither of them spoke.

'Oh God, this doesn't look good,' Patrick muttered.

Then the younger man, the powerful one with tattooed biceps, seemed to recognize Chung Yan, speaking to him with a brutal kind of familiarity. Chung Yan answered quickly, in a high timid voice, gesturing at Patrick and Rachel.

The older man muttered a few gritty words, then Chung Yan turned away.

'Come on,' Patrick said. 'Let's go.' He pointed to the path. 'Don't run. Just keep walking.' As they clambered breathlessly up the hill — no fear of snakes now — Rachel suddenly remembered, or thought she remembered, where she'd seen the older man before. Wasn't he the man on the plane when she first arrived in Hong Kong, the man who spoke to Michael in the airport and somehow disturbed him?

'I think I know one of those men,' she muttered, turning round.

'Keep going. For God's sake, just keep going!'

At the old schoolhouse they looked back, panting. The path behind them was still and quiet, the leaves motionless on the trees.

'It's all right,' Patrick said, breathing heavily.

'Quicker, quicker,' Chung Yan kept saying, his smooth young face still tense and pale.

'D'you think the young guy had a knife?' Rachel asked, 'He kind of put his hand behind his back when he saw you.' She felt absurdly secure now, as she'd felt absurdly fearful before. She guessed at most they might have taken her money. And the fact that she'd seen one of them before was strangely reassuring.

'No idea. But I wouldn't be surprised. He comes from the village. He knew Chung Yan, lucky for us.'

'Quicker, quicker!' Chung Yan was almost crying. He started off by himself.

'Yes, perhaps he's right,' Patrick said. 'Perhaps we'd better . . . . '

The sun was sinking steadily behind them, their shadows loomed ahead as they walked. They followed the curves and folds until at last they could see the sea again, blue and tranquil as ever. A cargo-ship lay on the horizon, its white superstructure gleaming. Near the shore, some yachts were drifting peacefully out of the sunlight into the shadow cast by the hills.

'What d'you think they were up to?' Rachel asked, breathing easily now. 'They gave me a real scare.'

'They gave us all a real scare.'

'What were they doing there, though?'

'Smuggling, I imagine.'

'Smuggling?' She laughed, and the laughter took hold of her as if she might become hysterical. 'Smuggling civet cats?'

'Smuggling people.'

'I *said* not come here!' Chung Yan glared furiously at Rachel. 'Crazy! Crazy!'

'He's overwrought,' Patrick said, putting his arm round Chung Yan's shoulder. Chung Yan spoke rapidly to him, almost sobbing.

'He's afraid you'll tell the police,' Patrick explained. 'In which case those triads would be after him.'

'Oh, I wouldn't tell the police,' Rachel said. 'They didn't do anything after all.'

She went on. Her limbs felt light and springy, as though the energy that fear had pumped into them was still there, buoying her so that every step was effortless. Yet she wasn't sure any more that there'd really been anything to be scared of at all.

The sun had nearly set when they came upon the civet again. It was dead now. The mellow light shone full into its stiffly staring eyes, giving their harsh green a milder, deeper tone. And the black and grey stripes of its fur seemed softer, too, almost lustrous despite the mud. But when she looked closer Rachel saw legions of tiny black ants swarming all over it.

Frozen memories

They took an early train from Shanghai to Soochow, sitting in the soft seats Michael had arranged through the China Travel Service. He'd asked for return tickets, but the clerk, a young man who stooped and hunched himself round his narrow chest as if to protect it, said you had to get the returns in Soochow, they couldn't book them from Shanghai.

'Will the trains be crowded coming back?'

'The trains are always full.'

'I may not be able to get tickets, then?'

Shrug.

So things haven't changed much, he thought.

Lily had scarcely ever travelled soft before — at first only on principle, but later of necessity as well. She sat on her upholstered window-seat, glancing at the cadre opposite her — the other passengers were overseas Chinese — with a kind of wondering scorn, like a Catholic spinster who'd caught the priest tippling the communion wine.

She'd met Michael at the Peace Hotel, and she'd never been there before, either — at least, not since the pre-Liberation years when it was the old Cathay. Then it was reserved for the rich, now for Foreign Friends. It came to the same thing: in both cases ordinary Chinese were excluded. When she walked in and wrote her name in the book, it was like slipping backwards in time. The reception-counter, the chandelier, the carpets, even the flowerpots — everything seemed familiar, everything shook some sleeping memory awake. She felt she could have found her way to the bar, the restaurant, the ballroom (not that she'd ever frequented *them*) without a second's hesitation. Yes, it was just the same, only mildewed, aged, cracked and worn. Like her. The carpets were threadbare, the chandelier dim and dusty, the marble chipped.

'Who do you want to see?' a security man said, tapping the empty space on the page with his little finger. 'What's your unit?'

She wrote *M. Denton* in English, and *brother* in Chinese.

'Unit,' the man said, looking over her shoulder.

She wrote the hospital's name and then *Retired Person*.

The man turned away. She asked the clerk for the room number. He finished adding a column of figures, then checked them through, before off-handedly telling her.

Michael was standing by the window, gazing down at the river. They smiled at each other awkwardly — ruefully, almost, like people making up after a long quarrel. 'How are you?' he said in English, uncertain whether to shake her hand or kiss her. She gave him her hand, laying the forefinger of her other hand over her lips.

'All right. How are you?' she said.

'All right, I suppose.'

She went to the dressing-table and wrote swiftly on the back of the envelope she'd brought along in her pocket: *Don't talk about it here.*

He shrugged and smiled, as if humouring a child who was playing some game. Perhaps she was; she'd never done it before. But Yin Hong had warned her on his last visit.

For some reason Michael spoke in a louder voice now, as if to make sure whoever might be listening heard him. 'You haven't changed,' he lied. 'Shall we go and have a drink?'

'We've both changed,' she said bluntly, shaking her head. 'Let's go for a walk; it's quite nice out now.'

Before they left she tore the envelope into little pieces and flushed it down the wheezing rusty toilet.

They walked slowly along the crowded Bund, Michael in his coat, she in her quilted jacket — Shanghai was cold in late November. 'It's called Zhongshan Road now,' she said.

He nodded. They were walking towards their old house. Nothing seemed to have changed except that everything had grown scruffy and decrepit, like the hotel.

Soon it was evening. The listless street-lamps came on, pale and bilious. It was safe to talk, but they were still too constrained, wary of each other if not of being overheard. They asked stilted questions and answered them stiltedly. He told her Patrick sent his love and was looking forward to meeting her. She gave a frigid smile and told him drily that she'd spent six years in labour-camps, but was 'what they call rehabilitated' now. They nodded, cleared their throats, glanced surreptitiously at each other, walked on silently. Like two acquaintances meeting unexpectedly at an airport, struggling to make polite conversation while their eyes and ears were straining for their separate boarding calls. He noticed how flushed her cheeks grew as they walked. She thought his face was lined, but of course she looked more worn than he did — she'd been through more. When he mentioned Mila, she scarcely remembered her. 'There were so many people,' she said indifferently. 'Always coming and going. I only remember Father Ignatius really well. We were both Eurasians after all.' She said 'Eurasians' with a little shove in her voice, as though it still hurt to get it out.

And both inclined to martyrdom, Michael thought.

It wasn't till they came to the house, and looked up at it, dilapidated and unpainted, that they began to talk more freely. The familiar shape of the building, with weak yellow lights shining dimly in its windows, thawed their frozen memories, and they talked more easily at last, standing there at the entrance, while passers-by stared curiously at Michael, trying to make out who he was in his luxurious foreign clothes.

So they decided to go to Soochow the next day. She would show him round, and he would pretend to be nothing but a tourist.

He didn't want to go into the house.

'I'll take you in if you like,' she offered grudgingly. 'But it'll attract attention. The small-foot policeman . . . . '

He shook his head. 'After Soochow perhaps.' He preferred not to see the changes. 'Shall we go back to the hotel and eat?'

Lily said no, she'd got some work to do, and she didn't like the atmosphere of the hotel anyway. Besides, she'd have to get up early to queue for tickets.

'Oh, no, I'll arrange them with the China Travel Service.'

'I suppose you'll want to travel soft,' she said with a little resigned grimace of disapproval.

He didn't ask about the work she'd said she had to do.

Thin-lipped little smile

So they sat next to each other on the train, arms involuntarily touching — it seemed too close — watching the silent faces silently watching theirs.

A Hong Kong woman — Lily guessed from her smart clothes and make-up, — sat by the corridor, with one of those earphone things over her head, her finger tapping her knee rhythmically, in time with her private music. The cadre opposite Lily watched, fascinated and envious, but Lily glanced away out of the window indifferently. That wasn't what attracted her about the West: there was only one thing she wanted there. As the train clanked through the level countryside, past nondescript villages still huddling in the morning chill, through colourless stations, their shabby platforms a blur of patient peasant faces, Lily contemplated the transparent reflection of her own set face, and behind that the reflections of her memories.

She remembered the smell of rain on the baked earth in Shaanxi, the meek averted eyes in the meeting-hall, the hangdog face of the cadre who denounced her. *He* had some sense of decency still; or did he see his own denunciation coming? She recalled the rough cement walls of her first detention-centre, and the stunned cowed faces of the prisoners who couldn't believe what had happened to them (one, an old schoolteacher with crooked glasses, was crying) and shunned each other's glances out of shame.

She remembered the notice of her release in '58 — *Allowed to practise under the supervision of the masses* — and her fatuous gratitude at being pardoned for having committed no crime. Only, then she didn't see the fatuity, she still believed.

She remembered Chu's teenage sons in '66, just back from Beijing, their faces shiny with dangerously innocent, self-important exaltation after seeing Mao in person in Tien An Men Square. A few weeks later she saw those same faces in the crowd condemning her, still innocent, still self-important, shouting with the rest of them for the ropes to be tightened, ecstatic with the joy of power and self-righteousness. Surely they must have known their own father would be next?

She remembered her arms being jerked up behind her as the rope tugged them, and the scream of pain that even she let out before she fainted.

And still she believed, believed like some imbecile priest being burnt by the Inquisition — believed it was only an aberration, the Party would correct its errors, she'd be rehabilitated and truth would prevail in the end.

Not till her third year of labour reform did her faith crumble. And then in a moment it had collapsed and gone.

After her rehabilitation they'd begun suggesting she should rejoin the Party. 'You're the kind of person the Party needs,' plump old Ho had said, eyeing her with his mild bovine gaze. He'd kept that gaze throughout his own purging and reinstatement, like a docile ox that had somehow ambled through the slaughterhouse unharmed, and still tamely followed the slaughterers who led him there.

'My thinking is not yet correct,' she'd said, in a voice so expressionless that poor Ho, gazing at her in sad perplexity, couldn't tell whether she was being serious or not.

Chu had gone one better when they asked him. 'The honour is too great,' he'd said with a modest bow.

Well, they hadn't bothered either of them since.

Lily realized she was giving herself a thin-lipped little smile.

The cadre opposite her began pouring tea from a leaky metal Thermos into a large enamel mug. The tea trickled down the side of the thermos on to the floor and ran in a little rivulet towards her.

She shifted her feet.

Appalling confidence

Gazing inattentively at the streams and bridges of the old Humble Administrator's Garden in Soochow, Michael told her she'd have difficulty getting British citizenship. 'They've tightened things up, you see; and, anyway, it would take a long time. The only realistic place for you to go to at the moment would be Taiwan.' The loose stones on the path crunched beneath his feet. 'Of course, they'd expect to get something out of it in return.' He glanced askance at her. 'Propaganda, I mean.'

'Taiwan,' she repeated sourly, compressing her lips.

'Remember Ma? The Nationalist at St John's University?' He saw she did. 'He's in with the Government in Taipei now. I've spoken to him about you. He remembers you of course.'

'Ma!'

'Well, you can't keep your hands absolutely clean, you know,' he said mildly, 'once you start this kind of thing.'

'Is Hong Kong really impossible?' she asked, as if she didn't believe he was trying hard enough.

Did she imagine she could just walk into the 'free world' and be welcome anywhere? 'They send everyone they catch back to China,' he explained once more. 'About two hundred a week. They'd send you, too, as you could hardly prove you were being politically persecuted now. No, just not liking the system isn't enough. And they put people who, as they say, harbour illegal immigrants in prison. For quite a long time. In your case that would be me. Besides, it'll be going back to China in a few years — or earlier, for all we know. I suppose it's absolutely out of the question for you to get a normal exit visa?'

She shook her head impatiently, as if to say: *How can you ask?*

So he might be taking a few risks — exaggerated, she suspected. Wouldn't she do the same if she knew it was right? And she had something serious to do out there; she didn't just want a retirement home. Besides, she'd had a harder life than he had, it wouldn't matter if the balance swung a bit the other way. She resented it; it was unjust that she, who'd always been the cleverer one, the idealist, had ended up on the wrong side after all, while he, the dull pragmatist and temporizer, had prospered. Anyway, hadn't she suffered enough for her 'overseas connections' in China? It wouldn't do them any harm to run a few risks for her now in Hong Kong. But 'Well, if it has to be, then,' she said ungraciously.

'Be what?' he insisted in his patient pedantic voice. 'I have to make arrangements, you see.'

'Taiwan! Taiwan!'

His lips puckered slightly. They walked on in needly silence for some time.

Then the garden began to seem familiar to him. Wasn't it one his father had taken him to, before he left for school in England? At each turning he came on views he seemed to have seen in some far-off past, though he could anticipate none of them. 'I think I've been here before,' he said propitiatingly. 'It must've been with Father, before the war. It doesn't seem to have changed.'

'They probably smashed it up a bit in the Cultural Revolution,' she said indifferently. 'And then restored it, more or less.' She didn't care much whether it was restored or not. What was a garden? 'It's the people they smashed that matter.' She paused to let a group of Japanese past, led by a Chinese woman guide who looked both bored and dutiful. 'It isn't so easy to restore people. Though *they* think it is.'

'But things have changed, haven't they? Is it really so bad still?' he asked carefully. 'I mean, the whole world's full of people struggling to get by; it isn't only China — '

'It's not *that*: it's not the struggling to get by! D'you think I'd go to all this trouble just to get away from a bit of poverty? To buy myself a refrigerator and a colour television? It's all the other things. Secret police. labour-camps, controlled press, controlled thoughts, controlled people — d'you think *that's* all stopped now? D 'you think *that* will ever change?'

He didn't know. He only knew he wished he didn't feel he had to help her; he wished she'd just resign herself to her present disillusionment instead of preparing another for herself in the West. He wished she'd just left him alone and not burdened him with her demands for help. And not even a word about the risks she calmly expected him to run for her. Every time he thought of John reading from the statute, 'Five million dollars or life imprisonment,' his stomach curled with fear.

'Have you really thought what it'd be like for you outside China? You've never been in the West after all. It wouldn't be easy.'

She didn't answer at first, and when she did it was an accusation. 'Are you trying to put me off, because you don't want to help? You're scared?'

'No, not at all — '

'You'd better say so if that's what it is.'

'Not at all. It's just — '

Just what?

They had come to the gate. The Japanese tourists were clustered attentively round their guide, a few on the fringe glancing curiously at the silent elderly couple as they passed. They'd probably take us for man and wife, Michael thought. Except for the difference in our clothes. Ahead of them was a hump-backed bridge over the canal.

They walked towards it. 'If you need my help, I'll give it,' he said stiffly. 'I just hope you won't regret it, though, that's all. It's not what it may seem from here, living in the West.'

'I won't regret it,' she said with appalling confidence. 'I won't regret it for one minute.'

He sighed, pausing at the top of the bridge to get his breath. *Yes, like husband and wife,* he thought, gazing down at their two heads reflected side by side in the placid water. 'But how are you going to live? I don't mean money; that's not a problem. But have you thought what you're going to do? You'll be cut off from everything you know.'

'I have my work.'

He glanced round at her. She'd said that in the tone of someone who announces a vocation. As he might have spoken about his own work, for that matter.

'I'm going to write a book about China.'

'Lily, every survivor of the Cultural Revolution who gets to the West writes a book about it. There must be a thousand of them already.'

'Have you ever heard of a book called *The Gulag Archipelago*, about labour-camps in Russia?' She didn't notice that he smiled faintly as he nodded. 'Well, this will do the same thing for China. This isn't just a book about the Cultural Revolution. It's about China's labour-camps.'

She'd got the idea from a copy of the Russian book, which she'd found under the seat of a tram, dropped presumably by some Western tourist — the name on the flyleaf was *Michael T. Birne*. She'd read it, curiously at first, then avidly. Somewhere, towards the end, she'd realized she must do the same for China; and at the same time the title had occurred to her. *The Fourth World*, the world one step below the Third. It was then that she knew she had to leave China instead of simply living on in the husk of her life and eating bitterness until she died.

Michael didn't know, seeing the clear zealous glint in her eye, whether she awed or repelled him.

'*You've made indignation a way of life*,' he nearly said; a little tug of shame restrained him. Instead he murmured inconsequentially: 'Of course you could apply for British nationality once you were out. If you didn't want to stay in Taiwan, I mean. Only it's not clear whether you'd get it — '

'I don't want to turn into a Briton. I'm still Chinese.'

Down the wrong road

They could only get hard seats on the way back. The compartment filled up with peasants and their baskets, soldiers, workers, students. When the seats were all taken, they sat in the aisles, stolid and weary, yet all staring inquisitively at Michael. Uncertain what to make of his foreign clothes and nearly Chinese face, a few began discussing him amongst themselves. One of them asked Lily who her companion was — *she* passed for Chinese — but she merely answered tersely with the ritual 'A foreign friend.'

The air in the swaying, jolting carriage slowly thickened with drifting layers of coarse stale cigarette-smoke and the smells of lukewarm rice, fish and beans. Across the aisle, a large brown bottle of beer went round. Somebody stretched out to sleep on the littered floor.

A young man — a student, Michael guessed — glancing at him tentatively for permission, eased a book out of Michael's shoulder-bag, and a group of them huddled round it, turning the pages with careful fascination. It wasn't the content — rural life in early Hong Kong — but the quality of the print and paper that seemed to absorb them. After twenty minutes or so, the young man replaced the book with a barely perceptible nod of thanks, or perhaps it was merely acknowledgement.

'In China nobody has a private life except cadres and criminals,' Lily said distinctly in English.

The eyes all turned to her now, watching with patient attention for what might come next. But she only leant her head back and dozed, or pretended to.

Outside the gloomy ill-lit station, people were waiting uncomplainingly for the next day's long-distance trains. Families, couples, solitary travellers, all with their roped shoddy suitcases, baskets and striped plastic bags beside them, they were eating cold food, smoking, spitting, sleeping with their heads on their bundles, like a crowd of wartime refugees. Only where was the war?

'Now you know what they mean by a mass movement in China,' Lily said, stepping over sprawling legs and bulging cardboard boxes. 'A million people waiting for trains.'

Michael said they must eat dinner somewhere. If she didn't like the hotel, there must be somewhere else. Somewhere reasonably good.

She hesitated a few seconds, then said she'd like to bring a friend. She'd call at the hotel in an hour.

Her friend, who waited inconspicuously outside the hotel while she went in to fetch Michael, was a genial old man with a hoarse booming voice that he seemed unable to modulate. 'Chu Wen-li,' he introduced himself in English. 'My wife couldn't make it.'

'Your wife?' Michael said. Then: 'Oh, I'm sorry.'

Chu took them to what he called the best place in town, a restaurant with garish neon lights and drab walls, where, like Michael, Overseas Chinese were treating their mainland relatives to meals the relatives themselves could never afford. Lily looked round unfavourably while Chu ate and ate, washing the food down with glass after glass of the dark local beer, which Michael thought tasted like aerated Guinness. 'We guys hardly ever come here,' Chu said, explaining his gusto unashamedly. 'It's right outside our price range.'

'He lived on scraps for six years,' Lily said dispassionately. 'He's still trying to make up for it.'

'How do you find your sister, Mr. Denton?' Chu hooted. 'After all this time.'

'A very determined woman.'

'I'll say.' He took another dumpling. 'But she doesn't know how to enjoy herself. She'd never have found this place without me. That's why she asked me along, eh?'

Lily only raised her eyebrows.

'Look at her — she's hardly touched her food!'

'No,' Michael said. 'She doesn't let herself go enough.' He was wondering if she'd always been so chilly and severe. Even as a young girl before he was old enough to remember her? Had she ever felt any real sympathy for a single one of all those peasants and workers she was supposed to be working for as a young communist? He doubted it. It was only the thought of her own purity that really moved her.

'Can I ask you a favour?' Chu boomed at the end of the meal. 'Got any books on teaching English, or Mozart violin scores you could spare? Lily can give you my address.' He hesitated, then beamed guilelessly at each of them in turn. 'Only old stuff. I couldn't pay for it.'

He left them at the restaurant door, gripping Michael's hand like an American.

'A nice man,' Michael said as he waited with Lily for the tram. 'He seems to enjoy life here, despite everything.'

'He makes himself enjoy it,' Lily said tartly, resisting the insinuation. 'He knows he can't get out.'

The crowded tram took them jerkily through the streets Michael knew and no longer knew to the house of his childhood.

'I won't come in,' he said again. 'You must be tired.'

'I'll see you tomorrow, then.'

They were both looking out over what used to be the Public Gardens, now Huang Pu Park. How familiar the trees and shrubs seemed to him — and yet how remote.

'You can't imagine what it feels like', she said abruptly, 'to realize you've wasted your life travelling down the wrong road.'

'Who takes all the right turnings? I knew I took a wrong one when I went into business instead of going to Cambridge. But I had to do it, until I was nearly fifty. Everyone takes the wrong road at some time or another. You just have to find your way back to the right one somehow.'

'That's what I'm doing.'

'Well, I hope so.'

She hated that sceptical tone. What right had he to preach to her about wrong turnings? What had he ever given up in comparison with her? He gave up Cambridge and got a fortune in return, but she . . . she gave up everything and got nothing in return at all. She gazed out bleakly over the darkened gardens, the darkened river, the whole darkened country. 'At least you knew what you were doing,' she said bitterly. 'And you got something back. But I got nothing. And I feel I've been tricked. It was a gigantic fraud.'

Anxiously in their cages

Michael wasn't tired. After he left her, he wandered through the streets of the old international settlement, as he'd wandered once as a boy, just before Pearl Harbor. At first he felt the world had stood still there without a single change. He found he could find any place from his childhood that he wanted, following the same streets with the same buildings and ending unerringly in the very same spot. True, the street-names were different, but nothing had been torn down or rebuilt or altered — at least, from outside. But then he began to register the subtle gradual changes of time and neglect — worn stones, uneven pavements, unpainted woodwork, broken iron gratings. Everything was there all right — the Shanghai Club, from which his father had been expelled for marrying a Chinese, the Customs Building where his father had first worked as a young official, the banks and hotels — but decayed and put to different uses, like an abandoned imperial palace taken over by the serfs. Which he supposed was roughly what it was. And yet he felt that, unlike himself, all the buildings needed was a wash and a coat of paint to restore them to their prime.

He found his father's grave, unkempt and overgrown — Lily had warned him she never visited it — and recalled the last time he saw it twenty years before, when his business had brought him to Shanghai, and his father's old amah had led him to the place. He'd paid Ah King an annuity until the Cultural Revolution, when he'd got a message to stop — it was causing her trouble. And then he heard she'd died. He walked on past the cathedral. Through the partly open doors, under a dim yellow light, he saw half a dozen people in the nave. Old people, praying or gossiping or holding a meeting — he couldn't tell which.

It was just ten o'clock, and the streets were nearly empty.

Out in the back alleys of Hongkew, where before the war Japanese sentries had searched and humiliated him, he came upon a peasants' free market, lit by the hissing kerosene-lamps he remembered from his childhood. Most of the stalls were closing, but a small crowd still stood round one, a crude restaurant with three or four folding wooden tables and stools. In front, wire cages like large rat-traps were piled on top of each other. Slithery green and grey snakes were coiling and uncoiling themselves uneasily inside them.

The fat moustached hawker looked over the cages consideringly, touching them lightly one after the other, then settled on a four-foot snake, olive green and lithe. He took it deftly behind the head and drew it slowly out, a bit of a showman, holding it up for display to all the silent onlookers. Then he clamped its neck with a large metal file-clip, clamped its tail in the same way, and hung it by its head from a rope between two poles. The snake, half-throttled by the clip at its throat, weighed down by the clip on its tail, could only writhe weakly, hopelessly, it seemed.

Michael knew he should leave then, and knew he couldn't.

The hawker ostentatiously felt the snake's body, stroking his fingers down the peach-smooth skin, until he felt what he was searching for, somewhere about a third of the way down. Then he took a pair of scissors out of his pocket, snipping them like a barber, and coolly slit the snake open, about a couple of inches. The snake made a sudden thrashing convulsion like a silent shriek, lashing its weighted tail. But the man soon held it still with one hand, bending it double at the wound so that the blood poured out, red and dark, into a thick glass tumbler which he held in the other.

The snake quivered and writhed still, but more feebly, lashing its obscenely tethered tail in laboured dying sweeps, while the smiling hawker raised and lowered the tumbler as if showily pouring tea. When the flow diminished, he began to coax the blood out, squeezing and caressing the long agonized body with proud casual skill.

The glass was three-quarters full. He set it down carefully on the nearest table, letting the snake dangle, its tail flicking like the feet of a man being hanged. Then again that gentle thoughtful caress with his fingers till he found the second place he wanted, about a foot from the tail. The scissors were in his other hand again, blood-stained blades clicking, and he snipped out a little bulb-shaped organ. The snake writhed spasmodically once more, then hung limp, only twitching. Dropping the organ in the tumbler, and stirring with the scissors, the hawker took it to a young man sitting at the furthest table, his back resolutely turned on the butchery. Occasional drops of blood splashed from the snake on to the muddy ground.

The hawker offered the tumbler with a flourish, like a waiter in an elegant hotel, and the man paid him. It looked like thirty Yuan — four or five days' wages. Then, while the hawker attentively watched, the man leant back his head and drank it all down in one long gulping draught. A few feet away, the last blood was still oozing grudgingly from the dying snake. The crowd gazed at it all with that same hushed fascination with which people used to watch public executions, and probably still did.

The empty glass knocked on the table, the hawker relaxed in satisfaction, and the man got up to leave, pushing self-consciously through the crowd. Shoulders hunched, eyes down, he glanced neither at his victim's still feebly twitching body, nor at the awed spectators, parting before him as before an executioner. His face looked sullen, sheepish, defiant, proud. He wore the usual padded jacket, patched at the elbows, and thick blue denim trousers.

Michael imagined him licking his lips, clearing the warm, thick, salty taste off the back of his teeth.

'It's for virility,' a man muttered to the woman beside him, eyeing Michael at the same time with guarded curiosity. The woman giggled, and Michael realized nobody had spoken till then, not the hawker, not his customer, not a soul in the crowd.

He turned away and walked on to the end of the alley. When he came back ten minutes later, the snake still hung there limply, but the crowd had gone, and the hawker, humming a tune, was folding his tables and stools together. The other condemned snakes slithered and stirred anxiously in their wire cages.

No, he thought numbly, nothing had really changed. The old China was still there. Beneath all the slogans and the politics, it was still there.

Yellow with sunlight, grey with rain

He left at dawn two days later. Everything that had to be said had been said, and neither Lily nor he had more than that to say. They parted the evening before in the hotel lobby, shaking hands undemonstratively again like mere acquaintances, yet awkwardly because each felt they should have been more.

The plane, tumbling, creaking and quivering, hurtled clumsily down the runway, then soared gracefully at last into its own element. Looking out of his window, Michael saw a long glowing orange streak, bulging at the centre, the sun rising over the eastern rim of the world. Below it a few scattered lights glimmered on the dark earth. Above it a few scattered stars glimmered in the dark sky. As the plane rose and turned, he watched the orange bulge steadily growing, rising second by second above the horizon. He leant forward to watch — the seat-belt was as slack as a rubber band. How mysterious the sunrise was, he thought, how immense. For a few minutes he seemed to be floating in space, watching creation.

But in half an hour the sky was pale and ordinary, and his thoughts were as pale and ordinary as the sky.

The stewardess offered him a paper cup of lukewarm green tea and a packet of dry biscuits.

Near Hong Kong the pale ordinary sky began to change again. Enormous castles of cumulus cloud rose up in the distance, tower after tower, yellow with sunlight, grey with rain.

11

Stay a bloody private

'I was really scared for a moment,' Rachel said, holding an overfull glass of orange juice with both hands. 'I felt *menaced*.'

'Oh, your colour would probably have protected you,' Dimitri said carelessly. He was glancing round the palm-decked hall at the knots of newly-graduated students talking tightly with their teachers or loosely with each other. Up in the balcony, the white-tunicked police band began banging out tunes from some musical. Smiling and nodding at a student whose name he couldn't remember, Dimitri wondered how many times he'd gone through the Graduates' Reception ceremony. More times than were left anyway. Two and a half more times at least he reckoned. And every time the police band had been there, playing the same dreadful tunes.

'A white skin's a sort of violent-crime insurance policy in Hong Kong,' he said, drifting back to Rachel. 'Up till now at least. I wouldn't bet on the future of course.'

'It didn't feel like it at the time, out there in those hills.' She sipped her juice carefully and licked a shred of orange off her lip. 'I'm not sure I believe those stories about foreign-devils being less at risk than Chinese.'

'You would if you were Chinese. Ask Faustus; he'll tell you.'

Faustus Yu smiled genially as he left three of his students. Holding a sausage roll delicately in an orange napkin between his finger and thumb, he had the air of a conjuror about to produce a rabbit. 'Sorry to hear about the readership, Dimitri,' he said. 'No justice, eh?'

'There probably isn't, but I wouldn't say *that* showed it. However, while we're on the subject of justice, would you say that criminals in Hong Kong tend to leave foreign-devils alone? What is that terrible music they're playing up there, by the way?'

Annie Get Your Gun, Rachel said.

'Because they think the police will be tougher on them if they attack foreign-devils,' Faustus agreed, peeling the napkin away from the sausage roll with a deft magician's flourish.

'And are they?' Rachel asked, almost surprised that the roll hadn't metamorphosed.

'The question isn't whether they *are* tougher,' Faustus said, taking a careful bite, 'but whether criminals *believe* they are.'

'It's *Anything You Can Do I Can Do Better,* isn't it?' Dimitri said. 'Unfortunately not true in my case. Or theirs, by the sound of it.'

'You sound pretty fiesty,' Faustus said, chewing deliberately. 'Considering.'

'Yes, I suppose I am, considering. What does "fiesty" mean exactly? I've never really known.'

'It means full of fight, gutsy,' Rachel said. 'Just what I wasn't out in Sai Kung last week.'

'So what happened in Sai Kung last week?' Faustus asked her, looking for somewhere to drop his napkin.

'Oh, er, nothing much. I just had a sudden feeling I was going to be mugged or something.'

'But you weren't?'

'No, I wasn't.'

'There you are, then,' Faustus said didactically. 'Because you're a foreign-devil.'

Dimitri listened to the band crashing into, or possibly out of, another tune.

Faustus turned to him in a quiet interlude while a tuba moaned affectingly above them. 'I didn't see you at the degree congregation this morning.'

'No.' Degree congregations, with their crush of proud shining relatives, reminded him of speech day at his dismal English boarding school. 'I only come to the receptions these days, and even then you can't get a decent drink.'

'Patrick wasn't there, either.'

'Doubtless he had something better to do — or at any rate more enjoyable.'

Faustus hesitated before allowing himself an embarrassed smile. Rachel, knowing Patrick had gone to Macao with Chung Yan, examined her glass. She wondered if the orange juice had been diluted with water. 'The band's playing *South Pacific* now,' she said. 'In case you didn't know.'

'I don't suppose the composer would, either. As a matter of fact, I had something better to do, too, this morning. Visiting some poor white trash.'

Faustus' eyes stirred bemusedly behind his glasses.

'Poor White Russian white trash?' Rachel asked. 'The old man we met after the ballet?'

'What a memory you have.'

'Hallo, Mr. Johnston,' a voice said politely behind him. 'Do you remember me?'

'Vividly,' Dimitri answered the dark-suited young graduate, foraging through his mind for a name to match the earnest face. 'Er, what are you doing now?'

'I'm starting a thesis under Dr. Smith.'

'Oh, yes, that's right,' he said convincingly. 'What was the topic exactly? Something about . . . ?'

'Culture and literary theory.'

'Oh, yes, of course. It would be.'

'I think you are not so much interested in literary theory, Mr. Johnston?'

'I prefer the beer to the froth.'

The still anonymous graduate glanced uncertainly at Dimitri's half-full glass. 'Shall I obtain another drink for you?' he offered courteously.

'Oh no. No, thanks. It's quite all right.'

Faustus relieved the puzzled graduate of the burden of eccentric conversation with Dimitri, leaving Dimitri himself free to recall his poor White Russian trash. Osip had sat in the Wayfarers' Home that morning, scanty white hair floating like dandelion fluff round his head, chattering excitedly about his plans and ambitions as though he thought he was never going to die. Past and future got confused sometimes as he slipped from the gigantic stock-market killings he'd made in the fifties to the ones he was going to make next month or next year. It was only the inglorious present that never intruded; he was oblivious to that, except at the end. Osip kept slithering from Russian to English, too, often in the same sentence, waving his hands about, mottled and skinny as turkey's claws. The last trembling thread to Dimitri's childhood, Osip had known his mother as a girl in Harbin. When that thread snapped, his own childhood would finally be cast adrift, to sink in the wake as his ship ploughed on to wherever it was heading. The breaker's yard presumably.

Osip read him some of his autobiography, page after page of flowery Russian, handwritten in a bundle of ordinary notebooks, their covers torn and crumpled. He wanted Dimitri to find a publisher for it — that was how he'd finance his triumphant return to the stock market. Dimitri promised to look into it. Then, as he got up to go — the matron was firm about mealtimes — Osip had clutched his arm with both his frail hands. 'I'm worried about 1997,' he'd said urgently. 'If Hong Kong goes back to China,

I'll be stateless. What about Australia or Britain, would they take me?' Dimitri had glanced away at the fresh-cut flowers on the window-ledge, and said he'd look into that, too. In 1997, Osip would be nearly a hundred. Still, why shouldn't he be worried? Everyone else was.

'Such a lively old gentleman, isn't he?' the matron had smiled as Dimitri left. 'And sharp as a needle still, most of the time.'

Dimitri finished his beer. 'Ah, there is your supervisor,' he said to the nameless graduate. 'Holding court over there.'

'Dr. Smith? So he is. I would go and say hallo to him.'

'Yes. Say hallo for me, too.'

'He has just been given a readership, I think?'

'Yes.'

'He is young for that, isn't he, Mr. Johnston?'

'Yes.'

'He is very young, I think?'

'Quite. Not so very very.'

'What is a readership exactly?' Rachel asked as the young man bowed and left.

'It's a sort of penalty for academics who publish too much. They're forced to read what they've written. Isn't that *West Side Story* they're playing now?'

'It's supposed to be in recognition of scholarly distinction,' Faustus said, tapping his glasses higher on to the bridge of his nose as if he were about to deliver a lecture. '*Supposed* to be.'

'Like a campaign medal,' Dimitri said. 'Only, you get a pay-rise, too.'

Faustus edged off towards the food-table with a little wave.

Rachel still hadn't finished her orange juice, but Dimitri had found another glass of beer. 'You seem more cynical than usual today,' she said.

'Yes.'

'And more monosyllabic.'

'Yes.'

'How was your White Russian friend?'

'Rotting gently away without realizing it. Like the rest of us, I suppose, only in a more advanced stage of decomposition.'

'Overdoing it a bit, aren't you?'

'I shall probably think so tomorrow morning. Speaking of decomposition, I'm afraid Frank Browning is making a beeline towards us. Tell me if you see Mila, by the way. I'm beginning to get drunk.'

'Is she coming?'

'I hope so. She's got the car, and I haven't got the bus money.'

'Well, Dimitri,' Frank said, swaying slightly and eyeing him with befogged eyes, 'I hear I have to commiserate with you. Robert Smith's got that floating readership, is that right?'

'Do readerships float as well?' Rachel asked.

'Some do, some don't.' Frank turned slowly to focus on her. 'Floating readerships are up for grabs by anyone.' He went on struggling to keep his eyes fixed on her face while he tried to expound the arcane complexities of the British system of academic advancement. 'The other kind we called "structural," which means they belong to a particular department and only people in that department can apply for them. Dimitri here was in for a floating one — '

'The upper windows in this hall are rather attractive,' Dimitri said studiedly, gazing up at the roof. 'I never noticed before. Like quartered port-holes.'

'Are they?' Frank peered up unsteadily, his mouth slackly agape in the forest of his beard. 'So they are. Isn't that what they call "scalloped"? Well, floating or structural, they'll all be scuppered when the commissars come, if that's any consolation to you, Dimitri my boy.'

'It isn't, as a matter of fact.'

Rachel said floating readership reminded her of floating kidneys.

'Well, they are quite similar,' Dimitri remarked detachedly, glancing across at Robert Smith. 'People who get either of them are usually full of piss.'

But when Smith joined them a few minutes later Dimitri only smiled wryly and said 'Congratulations.'

'Thank you. I must say it's rather gratifying,' Smith said in his neighing nasal voice, smoothing down his lank black hair with an air of modest complacency. 'Of course, it must be awful for you. Especially at your age,' he smiled tightly. 'Still, perhaps you'll get the next structural one in the department. There won't be so much competition there.'

'I appreciate the sentiment, but I fear it's a trifle optimistic. Piss-artistry is everywhere these days.' Dimitri returned to his contemplation of the windows. 'If you want my honest opinion, Faustus Yu should have got that readership, and he didn't even apply.'

'Ah, Doctor Faustus.' Smith cackled briefly as if he'd said something original and amusing. 'Burrowing away at his anthology of world literature. Excellent scholar no doubt, but no interest in post-structuralist theories.'

'Not *but*,' Dimitri said. '*And.*'

Frank touched his arm. 'Here comes your good lady. Is that your daughter with her?'

Elena was wearing a tight black leather dress, long leather boots, and earrings like giant safety-pins hanging down to her shoulders.

'I told her she would embarrass you if she came in,' Mila said equably. 'But you know what an exhibitionist she is.'

'Is everyone staring at me?' Elena asked. 'I don't want to look; it would spoil the effect. You don't mind really, do you, Dimitri? It won't ruin your career prospects or anything, will it?'

'You're just too late for that. But, yes, they are all staring. Dribbling at the mouth, many of them.'

'Only at the mouth?' Elena enquired demurely.

'But I thought you did not care about the academic rat race?' Mila asked in the car when he told them about the readership. 'You didn't even tell us you had applied.'

'Wanted to surprise us all, didn't you, Dimitri?' Elena said. 'Like Christmas.'

'We could have done with the money. Besides, even if you don't like being in the Army, wouldn't you still rather be a corporal than stay a bloody private?'

Try the cakes

A strange voice answered on the entry-phone first, then that bitch Lai Ying's came on, breathy and crackling, telling him to come up. Sounded a bit nervy, too, and so she should.

The metal gate buzzed beside him. Yin Hong pushed it open and went inside. Powerful springs all right, it clashed shut behind you like a ton of metal trays.

Nice lobby. Lots of room, palms, real marble tiles by the look of it. Shiny brass numbers on the letter-boxes, too; someone looking after things there all right. Wouldn't mind a place like that himself one day, might get it, too, if things worked out. Mercedes in the carpark as well. Like that place he had in Shanghai in the old days, on Maloo. Yes, he was somebody then all right, working for Pockmark Chen.

Lift wasn't bad, either: nice thick carpet, big mirror — get that tie straight, that's better — went up smooth and quick, too. So it was chat about things, was it, now? About time, too. Make that bitch Lai Ying give him some face at last. No wonder she sounded breathy, she was dead worried all right.

Yin Hong licked his finger and smoothed his eyebrows down, stretched his neck, patted the loose chicken-skin under his jaw.

So what if he was getting on? He wasn't past it yet. Never mind the old belly turning over a bit. Years since he'd had a chance of talking to a 432 or a 435, let alone a 426, bound to feel a bit tense. Even in the old days he would have done, those people were big planks and no mistake.

The lift stopped with a faint judder, the shiny doors slid back. Yin Hong stepped out, buttoning his double-breasted jacket.

A young 49 he didn't know nodded him towards a black iron grille over a panelled wooden door.

'Nice place you've got here, brother,' Yin Hong said courteously, giving the hand-signal.

The 49 pressed the bell. They waited silently. Yin Hong thought he could have answered at least.

Something moved behind the spy-hole, then the solid door swung inward and another 49 looked him over before opening the heavy metal gate. Yin Hong remembered that old iron door up those concrete steps in Shanghai, the day he hung up the blue lantern, swore his triad oath. Well, he'd kept that oath all right, how many years ago, though — they should show him some respect at least.

'Go on in, then,' the man beside him muttered as if he was a novice, and Yin Hong seemed to hear the years fluttering past like a pack of cards falling through the dark as he followed the other 49 down a dim soft-carpeted hall into a large room. Or like a flock of bats' wings in a cave. God, how he hated bats.

There she was, the bitch, sitting at one end of a long table between two men dressed in expensive business-suits. Papers and files open in front of them. At the other end was the altar with incense burning, a rice offering below it. And a plate of cakes as well, he hadn't seen that before.

The older man took off his glasses to look him over with watery tired eyes. 'Where are you from?' he asked in the proper way, but when Yin Hong said he was from the east, from the five-finger mountain, the man just gave a bored kind of smile and said all right they could cut all that out, they knew who he was anyway, otherwise he wouldn't be there, would he? But Yin Hong felt uneasy, he didn't know if the man was 432 or 435. How should he speak to him? It bothered him. The man was older than Lai Ying and the other man, but still years younger than Yin Hong himself. Ten, fifteen years younger. That bothered him, too. Made you think, that did.

The man waved him to a chair near the altar, while Lai Ying went on talking to the other man in a low voice, tapping a file with her long lacquered nail, then doing a sum on a calculator while the man nodded and rubbed his chin. Yin Hong perched uncomfortably on the edge of his chair. When Lai Ying glanced up at Yin Hong at last, the jewels that crusted her glasses glittered and flashed. He hated seeing women amongst the top people like that. Especially her. He ignored her. He wished they'd been wearing their robes, he'd've known who was who then, he'd've given them face and they'd've given him face, too — he wasn't a nobody himself after all.

'So you settled that little business with Limpy Ng, then, did you?' the older one asked pleasantly. 'Go ahead, make yourself comfortable.'

'Should've known better than to trust a cripple like him,' Yin Hong said, easing himself back gratefully in the chair. 'Crooked legs, crooked mind, I say.'

'Lie down with dogs, get up with fleas, ah?' the old man smiled, glancing at the younger one.

Yin Hong didn't like the way Lai Ying smiled, too, as if they'd got some private joke going. And why didn't they say what their titles were? It wasn't like that in the old days, people took more care, you knew where you were.

'Must've cost you a bit,' the older man went on. 'I hear he was badly burnt.'

'Well, he wouldn't have much to show the girls now,' Yin Hong said. 'Not that he'd got much before of course.'

They waited then, the younger one looking down and rubbing his chin as if he was puzzling out what it all meant. Lai Ying's glossy scarlet nails did a little tap-dance on the table.

He didn't like the silence, the waiting. And Lai Ying's nails tapping like claws.

'Hope it didn't make any trouble — I mean inconvenience — for you?' he asked respectfully.

They all smiled and glanced at each other and chuckled, and the older man waved his hand as if to say *How could small fry like you bother big fish like us?* 'Still,' he said, 'we don't like trouble between brothers. Better to settle things peacefully, isn't it?'

'Oh, I did settle it peacefully in the end — '

'Unless someone's broken his oath of course,' he smiled again.

Yin Hong smiled, too, but he didn't feel right. Been a brother longer than any of them after all, he deserved a bit of face, too. And what did he mean, unless someone had broken his oath?

'Fifty thousand dollars, wasn't it?' Lai Ying asked casually, switching her smile on and off again like the neon light over a brothel. 'Bit much for you to find, wasn't it?'

He gazed at the wall above her head as if he hadn't heard a word. There was a picture there of a foreign-devil woman with bare tits playing a flute. She had long golden hair falling over her shoulders, all in a gold-coloured frame. And there was a real clock in the corner of the picture, he noticed; he could see the second-hand jigging round. He looked at the older man and said it was a nice clock. Nice picture, too.

'Was it fifty thousand?' the younger man asked.

He felt them all gazing at him, even the 49 behind his back. He stirred in his seat and said that wasn't much for him, he'd done all right in Macao. Besides, he'd got a few irons in the fire. Always had.

'Like the snakeboat syndicate?' the older one suggested, all friendly again. He seemed to like that, he gave a little nod. Showed he'd got a head for business, he said.

Then he leant forward, putting his glasses on again. 'I hear you think things could be improved at the Bangkok end?'

Yes, that was what they'd like to talk about, the younger man said, taking a cigarette out of a silver case. The Bangkok end.

Yes . . . well, bound to go wrong sooner or later, using foreign-devils like they were, Yin Hong told them, giving Lai Ying a little stare. She was fiddling with the keys on her calculator now, avoiding his eyes probably. Worried now, all right. 'They're just the kind to get picked up, aren't they?'

'Conspicuous, ah?'

'Right, conspicuous.' That was what he'd told Lai Ying, he said, giving her another stare. Only she wouldn't listen. This time she stared back at him coolly, so coolly that he had to look away before she did. Customs didn't take long to find the stuff, he said, once they'd decided to search you. Did they?

'Don't they?' Lai Ying said, raising her plucked smooth eyebrows.

Nobody else spoke. The room just seemed to grow stiller and stiller like they were all waiting for her words to fade away. Well, he wasn't going to answer them anyway, he'd pretend she wasn't there.

'The problem is,' the younger man said at last, leaning back till his head rested on the back of his chair. 'The problem is we *have* lost some stuff, but no one's been caught by the Customs.' He blew a long stream of smoke out and watched it slowly spreading into a cloud.

'Not the Customs, ah?' Yin Hong repeated slowly.

'And we wondered if you knew anything about that' the old man added, still very pleasant and smiling. 'We just wondered if you'd been on the take.'

'Me?' Yin Hong felt as though his stomach had just dropped right out of his body. 'Me on the take?' He stared at them, injured, astonished, angry, scared. And they were all staring back at him, like snakes at a frog. His pulse was suddenly rushing in his ears. 'I didn't even know where they were carrying it!'

'Didn't you?' Lai Ying said, looking at her nails, first one hand then the other.

A whole lot of faces tumbled through his mind — large sunburnt Australians, Americans, Germans, all in their frayed jeans and sloppy leather sandals. Bearded, freckled, smiling, scared great stupid idiots with dirty sweatshirts and smelly skins. What would he have to do with *them*? 'Not me,' he said weakly. 'You must be crazy!'

'How did you raise that fifty thousand, then?'

His neck prickled as he heard the 49 move behind him. His heart was thudding unsteadily. His voice wobbled as he rushed out explanations and tripped over them. He kept telling them they'd got the wrong man, he didn't know anything about it, he'd never broken his oath in all the years he'd been a brother, he'd got the money from a down-payment for a snakeboat-trip. But his fear made him sound guilty even to himself.

They just looked at him thoughtfully as though they couldn't quite make up their minds, letting him tie himself up, stumble, make a fool of himself. The younger one blew out another long stream of smoke, leaning his head against the back of his chair. Lai Ying watched him like a cat, her claws just clicking on the table.

The older one pushed his glasses up at last and massaged his eyes gently. 'Well, we'll try the cakes, then,' he said in a tired voice. 'That should settle it.'

Lai Ying got up, took the plate of cakes from the altar, and put it in front of Yin Hong. Three little round brown cakes, like moon cakes.

'What's this, then?' he asked fearfully.

'If you're lying,' the older man explained in his weary patient voice, 'the cakes will kill you. If you're not, you'll be all right. Now eat.'

'Of course, if you're lying,' the younger man added, 'you'd better not touch them. It's a very painful death. You'd better just tell us now.'

'Your guts shrivel up,' Lai Ying added. 'It's like being on fire. Go ahead. You said you didn't know anything about it.' Her face was as smooth as her voice, she was almost purring.

Yin Hong sensed the 49 moving behind him again, and saw the older man signal him with a faint flutter of his lids. The younger man got up, walked to the altar and scooped up a handful of the rice, absently letting the grains sift through his fingers back into the bowl. 'Well?' he said softly. 'You eating or not?' And he just glanced at the 49 as he spoke, like he was telling him to wait a minute and then he could get to work.

Yin Hong's arms were trembling. His voice was trembling. It wasn't himself he heard meekly pleading, but a broken quavery old man. 'You . . . you . . . you wouldn't cheat me, would you? They won't hurt me if I'm telling the truth?'

'If you've kept *your* oath,' the younger man said, brushing his hands lightly together over the rice-howl, 'we've kept ours.'

Lai Ying gave a little snigger.

Nothing to pay?

Peter Denton placed the films on the smooth, milky screen and switched on the light. Leaning forward, chin in hand, he gazed at the shadow pictures of Mila's spine for more than a minute, comparing one sheet with another, going back, going forward, pausing and frowning. Then he spun slowly round on his revolving chair and took a rubber backbone deliberately down from the shelf beside his desk.

'Your spine should be like this,' he said, letting the springy thing, a dull orange colour, hang down like a playful eel. 'But the discs are wearing thin and the vertebrae are damaged down here, see?' He leant back to tap the lowest silhouette on the translucent screen. 'That's the cause of the pain — some nerves are trapped.' Now he squeezed the two spongy vertebrae together on the rubber spine, so that Mila almost winced.

'Wear on the discs is a common problem,' Peter went on, jerking the spine to make it dance again. 'Normally we'd just fuse the vertebrae together and that would take care of it . . . . '

It had been a lecture till then, she realized, one he gave routinely to his patients, the words coming off his tongue of their own accord while his mind rested. But now he had paused, he had hesitated, thinking what to say, how to put it.

'So I am not normal?' she prompted.

He dropped the model backbone on the desk. It quivered there like a spiky blancmange. 'In your case, I'm afraid the bones themselves are degenerating. As a result of your injury. They're gradually crumbling away.' He rubbed his fingers and thumb together eloquently. 'Like chalk.'

'And you cannot fuse them?' She glanced at the X-rays again, thinking: *That is my back there; those are my bones.*

'It wouldn't hold.'

'I see.'

'There isn't much we can do about it,' he said, pursing his lips. 'Eventually you may need a wheelchair, I'm afraid — not at once, but eventually, as the bones degenerate.'

'How long is "eventually"?' she heard herself ask as coolly as if she were asking him the time.

He shrugged. 'Ten years? Between five and fifteen, say. Depends how well you look after them. Pity they didn't throw you on your hip really. If they had to throw you, I mean. We can give you a new hip, but a new backbone's a bit beyond us.'

He was fingering the rubber model absently while he talked. She watched his nimble fingers manipulate the supple spine. *I will think about it later*, she thought. *When I'm alone. Not now.*

'Physiotherapy may help a bit,' he said dubiously as he conducted her to the door. 'And avoid jarring it of course.'

'What about acupuncture?'

Peter shrugged and smiled.

The silent patients in the waiting-room glanced up from their magazines. She imagined them eyeing her back as she walked to the receptionist's counter, eyeing those little chalky knobs of bone. She opened her handbag.

'Nothing to pay,' the receptionist smiled.

'Nothing to pay?'

In an aquarium beside the door, goldfish wiggled their spines effortlessly through the gently babbling water.

She waited for the lift, feeling her bones were already grinding together, crumbling away. Two clerks carrying heavy files chatted while they, too, waited. In the lift itself sober businessmen stood with shiny black briefcases and shiny black shoes. *Not now*, she thought. *I'll think about it when I'm alone*. But as the lift started with a little judder that made her wince, the image of a wheelchair slid into her mind. She saw herself in a wheelchair being pushed into crowded lifts, pushed along corridors, pushed into doctors' waiting-rooms, pushed by . . . .

She couldn't see who was pushing.

Well, she was young, too

'It's not a real performance,' Elena said in the coach that evening. 'I'm not going to try.'

Mila gazed silently out at the concrete acres of Yuen Long; new high-rise estates, half-finished flyovers, gallows-pylons and rubbled lorry-parks.

'Especially in a hall like this,' Elena said as the coach drew up. 'It's like an aircraft-hangar.'

She was right. The place was as bleak as its surroundings: a bare cement box with a bare cement floor and row after row of clattering wooden seats. Forbidding, over-life-size busts and over-realistic paintings of stern long-dead community-leaders stared censoriously down from the walls. The District Office had tried to decorate the hall with a few coloured ribbons, but they looked woebegone and self-conscious, like wilting flowers. The audience came in free, factory workers, shop assistants, old people and young children, only faintly interested, just to find out what was going on. District Office officials bowed and smiled them in, handing them programmes headed *Yuen Long Cultural Week*. Young administrative officers fresh from the university, they looked as uncomfortable there as the shy rosettes they wore on their lapels and the limp ribbons they'd hung from the walls.

The music was so distorted through the blaring speakers that you could hardly tell whether it was *Swan Lake* or *Coppelia*. The dancers were lost in the shadowy stage-lights. People crackled plastic bags, ate and gossiped. Children ran up and down the aisles. The wooden chairs scraped, slammed and creaked. And the smell of wet cement floated in through the open doors.

Mila was watching from the back of the hall when she was struck by a jagged electric charge of pain and had to sit down. Not just the pain then, but the gloomy hall, the harsh metallic speakers, the barren dinginess of the whole place — they all brought that other hall in China back to her. It was exactly the same, she realized, except in China the busts and pictures were of Mao. Even the smell of wet cement, that was the same. She gauged the height of the stage from the floor. Yes, that, too. *Pity they didn't throw you on your hip.*

Rocking and swaying gingerly until the pain eased, she watched Tse dancing the *pas de deux* with Elena. When he'd got out of China and joined the company, he'd come up to her with tears glistening in his eyes — he always did cry easily. 'I didn't know what I was doing,' he'd said, taking her hand in both his. 'I was so young. What can I say?'

Well, she was young, too. So were they all.

All she could do was shake her head, and she shook it again now. She neither forgave nor hated him. She only wanted to bury all that, to leave it behind.

Watching Tse now, as he wobbled landing from his final leap, she remembered those large expressive eyes, now momentarily anxious, blazing at her in that other hall in Shanghai. Did he help to throw her? He said not, but he'd say that anyway. He was strong enough, though; that was why he partnered Elena. Perhaps it would be good to hate him. But there was nothing there; she was empty.

Only a falling dream

'Might just as well have danced to a Chinese railway-station announcement,' Elena said of the music afterwards. 'No wonder we were all off. Lucky it was only a demonstration.'

On the coach back to Central, she held up a scrap of vermilion silk and lacy black ribbon. 'See the knickers Tom gave me before he went to Beijing? Aren't they shameless? He says he'll keep me in knickers the rest of my life.'

'The material will not cost him much.'

'Ah, but the style. I can't wait to put them on; they'll feel like a man's caress — better.' She slipped her arms through the legs as far as her elbows and walked with them on her knees, raising and lowering her palms as if she were going on point. 'They were meant to be for my birthday, but I made him hand them over before he left; he's hopeless at remembering things like that, even though he is a journalist. He can't help it, it's because his mind was fucked in Vietnam. Pardon my language, I've been reading Jackie Collins. I'm going to wear them in bed tonight. *Far* better than a caress.' She hugged herself in anticipation and did a little leap with her hands, twinkling her fingers. 'The gusset's sheer, see? Absolutely shameless! I don't know whether I'll go to that party tonight. I think I'd rather just go to bed in these.'

Mila watched the back of Tse's head as he talked and laughed in front of her.

For years after her release she used to wake up in the small of the night, half-dreaming still, panic throbbing through her veins, feeling herself falling, falling, falling from some enormous cliff-like stage. She would see blurred faces gazing down at her, blurred faces gazing up, as she tumbled, cart-wheeled, somersaulted down through the rushing air. The faces above were laughing, the faces below were scared. She always knew she was going to land on her back, she knew her spine was going to split and break like a snapped twig, she could foresee the splintered white bones poking through the lacerated skin. And, though of course she always woke before the impact, her heart would still continue thumping wildly, as though the dream still gripped her body after her mind had struggled free.

Whenever she awoke like that, her pulse pounding with terror, she was lying on her back, moaning. It was that pulpy choking in her throat that woke her.

The nightmare never came while she was in the camp — only after her release, when she had more to lose again, further to fall. But gradually, after she escaped to Hong Kong, the dream faded. She hadn't had it now for years.

The coach let the dancers out by trickles of twos and threes in the glittering lights of Causeway Bay, Wanchai and Central. Elena, Tse and

Mila were the last to leave, at Statue Square. Elena said she'd go to the party after all, and walked off chattering to Tse.

Did Tse avoid Mila's eyes?

She waited alone for a taxi.

The cat was lying on an old pair of Elena's ballet shoes in the hall. She got up, stretched and rubbed her flank against Mila's leg, purring welcome. Mila, stroked her slowly from head to tail. How that perfect spine rippled under her touch! Upstairs Dimitri lay asleep, the bedside lamp shining on his open book.

She undressed slowly, half-hoping, half-afraid that he would wake up. But he slept on oblivious. She lifted the book from his chest, switched off the light and lay down beside him. He sighed in his sleep and turned on to his side, away from her. She thought of Father Ignatius and Michael's sister, kneeling in the mud. Even though her back had been injured before all that, she sometimes felt as though her pain was a punishment for betraying Father Ignatius. How often, since, the words had floated through her head.

'He says mass to himself while he's working.'

'How do you know it's mass?'

'I went to a convent school in Hong Kong.'

'That's right. That's why you're here.'

Yes, that was why she was there. She'd written it in her self-criticisms, in every version, in the paragraph before her confession of her 'squalid connection with a European colonial so-called teacher in Hong Kong.'

She waited for sleep.

If she'd been a scholar, she could have written a study about the use of 'so-called' in communist rhetoric.

The night watchman coughed and muttered outside on his rounds.

She wondered if they'd have to move. The house had too many stairs for a wheelchair. She'd be helpless, confined to a couple of rooms. Yes, they'd have to move to a flat eventually. Perhaps it would be a flat in England, if China took back Hong Kong.

She imagined a wheelchair in some gloomy English flat, all shiny chrome and thick rubber wheels. She imagined herself in it, being pushed along. If only she could see who was pushing . . . .

She woke up suddenly, in her dream again, her heart thudding, a strangled scream in her throat.

'Nothing, nothing,' she murmured to Dimitri. 'I just dreamt I was falling.' She'd never told him the truth about her nightmare. She always used to tell him it was only a falling dream. 'Could you rub my back a bit?' she asked.

He massaged it sleepily a few times, then lay still, his hand on her hip. His steady tranquil breathing fanned her neck. She thought again of Peter's obscenely, gloriously supple rubber spine, and listened to the watchman's endless fluctuating soliloquy outside.

She wondered how she would tell Dimitri about her back. Or when. Or if.

12

Thickening with sleep

'Nonsense, it was a positively delightful lunch,' Patrick assured Rachel, leaning back in his deck-chair. 'I almost wish I'd brought Chung Yan along now.'

She was glad he hadn't. She glanced over the stepped roofs of Cheung Chau, down to the black and white Hong Kong ferry, just then sliding past the typhoon-wall. Even in December the sun was fierce, dazzling off the sea and the ferry's windows. She'd got a headache from it; she shouldn't have had them eat up there on the roof — or was it just that single glass of wine? 'But everyone left so early,' she said glumly.

'Mila has a performance to supervise tonight, and you know what children ballet dancers are — not Mila of course.' He raised a languid hand. 'Quite the reverse. But the rest of them. And the fact that Michael and Grace came at all is, if I may say so, a sign of special grace, never mind how long they stayed.'

She tried to visualize Michael and Grace queuing for tickets on that crowded, dirty, noisy barn of a pier with the pungent smells drifting out of the primitive toilets. The yammer, the jostling through the turnstiles, the rush up the gangway to grab seats. 'I thought they'd come on their launch,' she said. 'They seem much too grand to travel with the common people.'

'They're not really grand at all,' he murmured, closing his eyes. 'They just have quite a lot of money, half of which Grace gives unobtrusively away. Which proves that wealth isn't always wasted on the wealthy. I'll help you clear up in a minute.'

She said no, it was OK. He wouldn't know where everything went anyway.

'Don't you know how good queers are at domestic chores, dear girl?'

'I wish you wouldn't say "queers." Why don't you say "gays"?'

'I've never really understood this moral preference for one synonym over another. A poof by any other name, dear girl.'

'I wish you wouldn't say "poof," either. Or "dear girl".'

The clack of mah-jong tiles sounded from the neighbouring roof. From the apartment below, pop music wafted up, a woman crooning Cantonese words to some Western tune, which Rachel couldn't quite recognize. Weekends were always crowded with layer on layer of pop tunes, rising from one floor to the next all day long. Not that she minded; she wasn't particular about music.

She shifted her chair back till she could rest her head against the wall, in the shade of the bougainvillaea growing in one of Alison's discarded pots. She, too, closed her eyes.

Whatever Patrick might say, she still felt the lunch had been a flop. Michael had had nothing to tell about his trip to China — 'Just a bit of business and tourism. Nothing spectacular.' And nothing much to say about anything else, either. And Grace had just smiled and toyed with her food, spending most of the time gazing out at the sea. Wishing she was back in her garden, most likely. Dimitri had scarcely bothered to make more than a couple of his dried-up British wisecracks, and Mila . . . well, something was bothering her all right; maybe it was just the ballet. Thank God for Patrick. It would have been just a throat-clearing concert but for him. Lucky he didn't bring Chung Yan along, though. Everyone else would have buttoned up still more, and Patrick would have just buzzed round him like an infatuated bee.

She heard the mah-jong tiles being shuffled on the next-door roof; round and round and round, a great scraping, rattling, clattering noise, and the players shouting, laughing, complaining. That meant a game was over — she'd come to know the signs. When the rapid single clacks begun and nobody talked, that meant they'd started another game.

'Michael seemed stiffer than usual today,' she said. 'Not in the least bit like his half-sister.'

'Who?'

'Jenny. My stepmother.'

'Oh, her. Yes, I met her when she was here, years and years ago. She seemed to have the vulgar appetites of a Mae West, but none of the more redeeming attributes. I hope I'm not treading on your toes. Not at all like Michael, no. If life were a Rugby game, Michael would be a second-row forward. An allusion, which I'm afraid, may be lost on those fortunate enough to have avoided the rigours of an English public-school education. Did I tell you that I won the diving competition for my house once? It was my sole athletic distinction.'

She let her eyes open for a moment. Patrick's were still closed, the long dark lashes perfectly still. 'What does the allusion mean?' she asked. 'Though I think I get the idea roughly.'

'Unlike Dimitri and myself, Michael does not suffer from the lightness of being. His complaint, if it is one, is the reverse. He suffers from the weight of being. His mass is dense, like a second-row forward's.'

'Very clever. You must tell me what that means now.' Her eyes had closed again. She listened to the renewed mah-jong game clack, scrape, clack, in a taut voiceless silence. And the sun was burning her shins, but she was too lazy to move. Her mind was slowly thickening with sleep. 'It comes from that Hungarian writer, doesn't it?'

'Czechoslovak, actually. Surely you've sometimes felt that we're all just walking on air like those little men in cartoons, and we'd fall for ever if only we once looked down?'

'Well, I do have this fear of flying,' Rachel said.

Patrick sighed. 'Well, imagine yourself flying, then, and suddenly realizing the beastly aeroplane's not there any more.'

'Oh, is that all?'

'Yes. Only at the moral-existential level.'

'Oh, it's kind of precious, is it?'

She felt herself getting drowsier, her breathing growing heavier and heavier. She knew obscurely she was falling asleep, and wouldn't resist it; in half a minute she'd be gone. What on earth did Patrick see in that moody affected Chung Yan, always sulking and flouncing like a spoilt girl? Why didn't he find someone as intelligent as himself, who could share the same interests? If she kept on thinking to herself like this, she might just avoid slipping off into sleep, though she knew she was hovering right on the edge. It was as if an intelligent educated man spent all his time with a bar-girl. They couldn't stay in bed all day after all, could they? She didn't see what kept them *there* for more than twenty minutes anyway. When she saw that stuff on the screen, which occasionally by accident she did in the States, it stirred nothing in her but perplexed embarrassment. It wasn't all that different from the wrestling matches that plugged the gaps between commercials on weekend television. Could there really be any joy in those grotesque contortions, or did each person, as she suspected, fake pleasure before the distorting mirror of the other? Like in that little ditty scratched on the cupboard in her room in Bangkok, back in the summer. *Smile when you're making it . . . even if you're faking it.* Scratched, Bangkok, summer, faking, Bangkok, summer, summer . . . .

This was different

She felt cold when she woke. The sun had weakened as it sank, and she was wholly in the shadow of the wall now. The sea, no longer dazzling, was turning a chill bluish-grey, which the cooling sky reflected like a distant curving mirror.

The mah-jong tiles were silent. Windows had been closed on the radio music. It was almost dusk. Patrick's chair was empty, but a discreet chinking and scraping of dishes sounded up the stairway.

'Patrick, you shouldn't.'

'Why not?' He'd put her apron and rubber gloves on, and was cleaning and washing deftly, not forgetting to rinse the detergent off. Rachel would never have thought Patrick's hands were the same size as hers, but the glistening yellow gloves fitted perfectly.

He nodded at the tea-cloth. 'Could you make some room on the draining-board? It's getting dangerously overcrowded.'

She watched him peeling the gloves off afterwards, rinsing them, draping them over the rack to dry, untying the apron and hanging it from its hook on the door. He did everything neatly, efficiently, with an air of satisfaction at a job well done, and also with slight fastidiousness, as though her kitchen wasn't quite clean enough for him.

'Is it difficult for you in Hong Kong?' she asked abruptly. 'Being gay, I mean, with the law and all that?'

He took the salad-bowl out of her hands. 'Let me put this away before you drop it. In here?' He closed all the cupboards, tightened the dripping faucet, spread the tea-cloth out more tidily on its rail.

'One has to watch one's step,' he answered at last. 'One has to keep one's beady little eyes darting this way and that like a bird on a twig, for fear of being caught in the net. There are righteous citizens and outraged custodians of the law who would desperately like to catch one at it, as it were. But one doesn't exactly walk in fear and trembling. Do you think we could have some tea? I notice you have some Earl Grey up there. One merely avoids buggering young boys in public places.'

'There you go again.'

'Chung Yan was eighteen when I met him, by the way. In case you were wondering. Eighteen and a half. By Chinese reckoning, that is, which makes you one year old when you're born.' He walked into the living-room, plumped the bean-bag Rachel used as a sofa and sank into it. 'My dear, how simply decadently voluptuous! That's why I don't let him live with me incidentally, for fear of getting caught in the act. One of the reasons. The other is he's inclined to borrow things that take his fancy — he has absolutely no respect for private property. At least, as far as other people's is concerned. In that one respect I suppose he might be suited for life under a communist regime.'

Rachel wished he'd wipe that sickening, fond, indulgent smirk off his face when he talked about Chung Yan. She returned to the kitchen and slid the cupboard door open with a little slam.

'But I must admit it gets a trifle wearing sometimes,' Patrick went on, lolling on the bean-bag. 'Always being careful, always jerking one's head about like some damned sparrow on the lookout for the cat.'

Clattering the cups and saucers while the kettle hissed behind her, she asked him if it was like that, too, at school. 'Or weren't you . . . ?'

'Queer then?'

'Gay.'

'No, strangely enough I didn't know what I was then. Though I *was* what I was of course. But, being three-quarters Chink and all that, I expect I developed more slowly. Afraid to flower in that uncongenial soil, as it were. Not that any overt expression of my latent perversity would have been out of place there, I may add. Half of them were at it in the showers every day. But they were the randy louts with hairy chests, merely practising for girls.'

When she brought in the tea, he was ruminatively twisting a lock of his hair, looking out at the last fading glow of the sunset. 'No,' he said musingly as she placed the cup beside him with a little clink, 'I was first brought to realize my true deviant nature by a Chinese boy in Kuala Lumpur. That was an altogether different story, as you will no doubt appreciate when I tell you he was a prostitute. Though I don't suppose you want to hear — '

'Not particularly.'

'And why I'm telling you all this in the first place I simply cannot imagine.'

'Because I'm transcendent?'

'Ah, yes, of course. Because you're transcendent.'

He'd had to stop in Kuala Lumpur overnight and fly on to Hong Kong the next morning. It was the summer between leaving school and going up to Cambridge — perhaps the sense of liberation and expectancy he felt about that had affected him, made him look for adventure. He always remembered the coconut fronds, still against the windless mauve sky, the casual unhurried voices from the kampong outside the airport, and the bumpy, narrow, crowded road, strewn with petrol fumes, leading into the city. In the scruffy hotel, with its memories of departed rubber-planters lingering like the musty smell amongst its tatty colonial pillars, a slim young boy in the corner of the bar had smiled and asked if he was Chinese, too.

When he lay with him on the bed, Patrick became two people, one watching, one acting, the watcher helpless as a shadow. He hadn't known till then, he hadn't let himself know, why girls didn't attract or actually repelled him. But the boy knew, had known at once, and known he was a virgin. Sometimes Patrick wondered how things might have turned out if he'd never met him, never gone to that hotel or walked into that seedy bar or sat at that table in that corner beside that potted palm with those dusty leaves. Perhaps he'd never have become the uneasy double-agent of the half-world that he was, a nervous comedian who parodied himself in order not to be despised. But at other times he felt the prostitute had merely been the instrument of fate. If not him, then someone else. Somebody had to initiate him into the life he was destined to lead, a life marked out for him as definitely as a painter's or a physicist's is marked out for someone else.

The boy knew what he had to do, and he did it matter-of-factly, indifferently, but quite amiably. Afterwards they'd gone out together to view the domes and pillars of the railway station, and to eat a meal in Chinatown, where they found they had nothing more to say to each other and parted gratefully.

Rachel sipped her tea. She didn't really like Earl Grey — it was like drinking scented water — but Grace had pressed it on her when she first moved in. 'How long have you known Chung Yan?' she asked.

'Just over two years. The longest I've known anyone, in that way. I fully realize how vain and childish he can be sometimes incidentally.' His voice had a faint defensive edge on it now, as if he'd read her thoughts and didn't want to hear them. 'But there are compensations you don't see. Oh God, what a dreadful, pathetic, sentimental old queen you must think I am.'

Rachel put down her cup. 'Not all of those,' she said, checking them one by one in her head. 'Or any, for that matter.'

She walked with him down to the last ferry, and was glad he'd made her take a sweater. Once the sun was gone, the chill came in like a returning tide, and a cutting wind blew across the island.

'The iceman cometh,' Patrick said. 'All the way from Siberia.'

The ferry was waiting. The mooring-ropes creaked and groaned, straining against the tug of the choppy sea.

'I was wrong about Michael,' he said as they waited for the crowd to force its way through the turnstiles. 'Not a second-row forward. A full back. Solid, dependable, the last line of defence. Gravity incarnate.'

A gust of wind slapped the ferry's halyards against the mast, and they saw the gangway lurch as the swell lifted the ship. 'Oh God, how positively queasy-making,' Patrick sighed. 'Just wait till we're out in the nauseating open sea. I wish I didn't have to go.'

'You can stay the night if you like. I've got room.'

'After what has passed between us, I suppose I can take it that was not an invitation to amorous dalliance.'

Rachel blushed. 'You can sleep on the bean-bag,' she said brusquely.

'Most kind, but Chung Yan would simply rave with jealousy. You can't imagine how possessive he is. However, thank you for the offer, and for everything.' He hesitated, then took her hand. 'You did so well today.'

Suddenly she was blushing again. Nobody had spoken as warmly as that to her since her father, when he remarried — he'd said those very words, 'You did so well', at the wedding reception, as if he knew after all how much she resented Jenny.

'One does feel rather alone sometimes,' Patrick added wistfully. 'Not quite Chinese, definitely not English, positively not normal. But you did so well.' He smiled gratefully and left.

It was worse than blushing now. She felt an ache in her throat, too, and tears behind her eyes as she watched him go. Just like with her father. But this was different; this was —

Oh no! she thought, walking slowly back along the waterfront. *Oh no!* climbing the steep narrow path up the hill. Was that what it was?

'Nie ha?' she greeted Mr. Chan absently in Mandarin when she met him by the door watering his plants.

'Have party?' Mr. Chan said. 'Very goo'. People come, talky-talky, very goo.'

Why Patrick of all people? she asked herself, gazing at her dim reflection in the speckled spirit-mirror she'd found in Chung Yan's village and fixed over her own door. *Why a gay?*

When she opened her diary later, and sat with it on her knees in bed, she couldn't write a single word.

On the shadowed land

It was late afternoon, and Elena had skipped lunch. She bought a box of chocolates and ate half of them in the taxi to the airport, giving the rest with a two-dollar tip to the perplexed driver.

'Going to meet my lover,' she explained to him as she climbed out. 'I haven't seen him for weeks.'

She was an hour early, but she didn't mind. In fact she'd planned it. She went up the stairs to the open-air observation-deck, passed through the high clanking fifty-cent turnstile, and walked to the corner nearest the runway, a few feet from the telescope.

There she stood watching the planes, silent and absorbed, as she used to stand years and years ago.

Soon after her mother killed herself, she'd started going to the airport secretly when afternoon school was finished, standing always in that same corner near the telescope that hardly ever worked, watching the planes arrive and depart. There was a picture in her history-book (*British ships carried goods to the world*) of a Victorian sailor's shawl-wrapped wife standing on some headland, watching the ships put out to sea; and Elena sometimes imagined herself as that woman, absorbed and solitary on the lonely cliff. But the Victorian sailor's wife was straining anxiously for the last sight of her husband, while there was no one Elena was watching for, or no one she knew of. Certainly she never thought of her just-dead mother or saw the planes as bearers, let alone symbols, of departing souls. What her mother's taking flight from life might have had to do with it — if anything — Elena never knew and never considered. It was only the massive power of the great machines she was aware of, the power that hoisted them effortlessly into the air and eased them smoothly down again; the power, and the complex perfection of the machinery she imagined working inside their rigid gleaming bodies.

Or so she thought when she was older.

She would stay there mesmerized for a couple of hours or more, leaving her place only to go and buy a still orange (she hated fizzy drinks) from the man inside the turnstile, who passed the bottle to her over the top so that she wouldn't have to go in and pay to come out again. They became quite friendly.

When a plane, manoeuvring from the terminal, sent furnace-hot blasts of shimmering fumy air over her, she would never turn away, as other spectators did, squealing and covering their ears. She loved the heat that flattened her school tunic against her body and tore her hair like a fraying flag. She would turn her face towards it with a little thrilled closed-eyes smile of submissive pleasure.

People would come and go, usually whole Chinese families of three or four generations, staying only to wave goodbye, or greet, and fiddle with the telescope. But she would remain. Sometimes they glanced at her curiously and discussed her amongst themselves. Once two policewomen asked her, in uncertain English, what she was doing.

'Watching the planes,' she answered levelly in Cantonese.

'Where's your mother?'

'Dead.'

Even as a child she could stare anyone down with her pale blue eyes. Uncomfortably, they let her be.

Often, when at last she left, she would walk along the road beside the perimeter fence until she stood at the very beginning of the straight solemn runway that seemed to stretch out endlessly to the remote hazy horizon. There she would wait, fingers looped in the chain-link fence, until a plane came sailing gigantically down over the Kowloon hills, over the dense rooftops of the Walled City, then floated majestically overhead, drowning the grind and whine of the traffic, to sink down on the runway with a spurt of smoke from its wheels.

When Ah Wong questioned her anxiously on her return, she'd say she'd been playing at San San's house.

Today Elena stood in her old place till after Tom had landed, watching the planes' immense procession with the same intent fascination as when she was a child. The sun had set when she turned to go; the planes loomed black against the dimming sky, and on the shadowed land a million lights glittered in fading rooms.

Tom was just wheeling his luggage-trolley through the sliding doors when she appeared at the arrival-hall barrier, waving hallo with the slow sideways gesture of her hand that he called her royal wave. When they met she snuggled close to him, her head on his chest. 'Can you tell I'm on you?' she murmured.

He put his arms round her and hugged her till it hurt. 'The Brits are caving in,' he said. 'They've accepted all the Chinese demands.'

Off his rice

He didn't feel like going out any more. Sometimes he stayed in all day long, just staring at the wall and smoking. Couldn't hardly be bothered to count the protection money when Ah Keung brought the takings in and laid them out like decks of cards on the plastic table amongst all the fag ends. Only did count them because he thought Ah Keung might be holding back on him on account of hearing how they'd treated him about the missing dope and making him eat those cakes and all that stuff. Not that he'd breathed a word himself to Ah Keung, but someone always talked, things always got out somehow.

You'd think they'd have apologized after he came through that cakes test, but not a word. Except from that bitch Lai Ying, phoning up a week later to ask if he was still alive in her smart sharp voice, and laughing with someone else when he swore at her. And still he didn't know whether they were having him on or not, whether those cakes really would've killed him if he'd been double-crossing them. Suppose they'd been having him on, making a fool of him, laughing up their sleeves all the time. They wouldn't've dared in the old days, when Pockmark Chen was still around, he was somebody then.

Ah Keung didn't come in so often now — that was another thing; and, when he did, like as not all he'd do would be switch the television on without a word. And when Yin Hong told him to turn that crap down, it got on his nerves, Ah Keung would give him a queer look. No respect, no face at all. Was that what he'd come down to? Who was Ah Keung anyway? Just a look-see boy.

If he went out at all, it was at night, to Wong Tai Sin temple, or the fortune-tellers on Temple Street. They told him to expect a change, but what? He'd moved his bed, too, when the fung-shui man told him it was facing the wrong way, but nothing seemed to help, he still felt bad, as if those cakes were going to poison him after all in the end. That stuff from the herbalist's hadn't helped, either. And it all cost; they didn't give it to you for free.

Truth was he'd never felt right in his belly since they made him eat those cakes. For a few days he really thought they'd poisoned him and he was going to die, especially when Lai Ying said it could take a week to work, the fucking bitch. Even now he still felt sick at the thought of food, and he had these little pains in his gut all the time as if they really were poisoned and it was just starting to work and in an hour or so he'd be screaming in agony. And his heart, too — he could feel that all the time. Whenever he wasn't doing something, which was almost always now, he could feel it tapping away like a clock inside him, a clock with a wonky spring that was always racing or slowing. No wonder he was off his rice.

He kept lighting joss-sticks by the little altar till the place reeked like a temple. Ah Keung always wrinkled his nose when he came in. Well, let him. What was it to do with him? But it hadn't helped so far. Nothing had.

Americans call a headhunter

The phone rang late in the evening. The second he answered, a voice started straight off in Shanghainese. 'Hear you've been having a spot of bother with some of your brothers?' the voice said, all friendly and concerned. 'Perhaps we could meet and have a little chat?' Yin Hong just listened, didn't say a word; he was too flabbergasted. 'Just think about it, eh?' the voice went on, all smooth and cheerful. 'No need to rush things. We've got a little proposal for you. No commitment, eh? Just a friendly chat. I'll ring the same time tomorrow, see how you feel about it, all right?'

And he just sat there like a dummy, looking at the dead phone in his hand. Hadn't answered a single word. What was he going to do?

He didn't know, not when at last he fell asleep, nor when he woke up early thinking about it, with the sour light creeping through his grim bleary window. He didn't know, either, when he went down to place his bets on the Sha Tin races. And when he came back early still he didn't know. But after they'd watched the races on the box he told Ah Keung to collect the winnings by himself and go off with his girl. Didn't want him around if the bloke really did phone again. Which he probably wouldn't, but still. And, if he did, what would he say? Still he didn't know, except he'd got to be a bit cagey in case it was a set-up. He wouldn't put it past Lai Ying, fuck her.

From nine o'clock onwards he just sat near the phone, skimming the pages of Ah Keung's comics. At least, his eyes slid over the cartoons, but he wasn't really taking anything in, he was listening for the phone all the time. He couldn't've said what the simplest one of them was about, except they were all about tits and bums in the end. He kept thinking of that cheery Shanghainese voice, running the words through his head again and again. 'We've got a little proposal for you. No commitment.' He didn't know whether he wanted the phone to ring or not. In fact he was scared. Proposal? What was it, then?

But it rang on the dot anyway, as he'd somehow known it would, the same cheerful friendly voice. He imagined a well-fed smiling face on the other end of the line, the face of someone who had money and liked to enjoy himself.

'Thought about it?' the voice asked straight off. 'What we talked about last night?'

'I didn't talk. You did.'

The voice roared with laughter. Like he was falling off his chair he was so pleased. 'That's right. You didn't say a word, did you? Quite right, too. Who the hell am I, eh? Well, let's meet and I'll tell you.'

'No commitment?' Yin Hong said in his grittiest voice, trying to sound like he didn't give a shit.

'Course not. Just a little chat. After all, we're both from Shanghai, aren't we? My name's Wang by the way. What about some dim-sum tomorrow? It's about the only good food these Cantonese have, eh?'

'Tomorrow? Well, I suppose we could.' Again he tried to make it sound like he wasn't really all that interested but he'd give it a go as he'd got nothing better to do. 'Just for a chat.' When he put the phone down and leant back, he could feel his heart going faster again. But this time it wasn't because he was scared. Maybe this was the change the fortune-tellers had told him about.

Wang was fat and well dressed, just like Yin Hong thought he'd be. And he gave Yin Hong face, right from the start. They went to the Luk Yu teahouse, just the two of them, and ate lotus rice in one of the little private alcoves where they could talk quietly. Yin Hong hadn't been there for years now, not since they moved the place from the other side of Queen's Road. But the furniture was just the same, the dark old wood and brass, the

marble tabletops; it reminded him of Shanghai. How many years was it
since he'd eaten that meal with Pockmark Chen in the old Luk Yu, all of
them round one large table, and he'd sat next to Pockmark . . . well, nearly
next to him? How many of that lot were left now? While Wang ordered the
food, he started ticking their names off in his head, going round the table
starting with Pockmark. And there wasn't one of them that he knew was
still alive except himself. That made him think all right. No, things hadn't
been the same since Pockmark died, and no mistake; his luck had turned
against him since then. And now that business with the dope — to suspect
him of all people, the bastards.

But Wang knew about all that. 'Never mind how.' And he understood
how Yin Hong felt, shaking his head sympathetically, his eyes all warm and
friendly. Who wouldn't feel bad being treated like that? And he knew a bit
about the old days in Shanghai, too, though of course he couldn't know as
much as an old hand like Yin Hong, he said respectfully. He was only a kid
when they'd had to take off to Taiwan because of the Reds. But there were a
lot of people in the Yellow Bamboo who knew of Yin Hong and how close
he'd been to Pockmark Chen (What a man!) and that was why he'd been
sent to look him up. Specially when they heard he wasn't being treated
right. A man deserved some respect from his brothers, that's what *he*
thought anyway! And he slapped his thick strong hand on the table, making
the bowls rattle, looking like he'd kill the first man to say no.

Now that they were getting close to business, he leant across the table
all-confidential and offered Yin Hong a cigarette from a gold case. And a
gold ring on his finger, too, with a great chunk of jade in it. Yin Hong eyed
his suit and tie once more as he took the cigarette and tapped it on the
table. Yes, Wang could go anywhere, no doubt about that, he certainly
wouldn't be put in the shade by Lai Ying and that lot.

All they wanted was a little information, Wang said, flicking his lighter
for Yin Hong.

'Is that gold, that lighter?' Yin Hong couldn't resist asking.

'Solid,' Wang said like it didn't mean a thing to him. 'Feel it. Go on,
feel it. Heavy, eh? Thought you'd know a good piece when you saw one.'

It was solid all right, solid as a rock. And Wang edged back his sleeve to
show his gold Rolex, too. 'No fakes for me,' he said. 'I can afford the real
stuff.' He glanced at Yin Hong's frayed buttonholes as he spoke, but never
said a word. Now, that was respect for you, you couldn't deny it.

Anyway, Wang said, all they wanted was a bit of information now and
then. Because they were thinking of moving into Hong Kong, and naturally
some people weren't going to like the competition. So if they had a bit of

advance notice now and then about what was going on — he leant back, closing his lids in his fat friendly face, just like he was winking with both eyes — it might help them to smooth their way in a bit. And of course they'd pay for anything they heard. Pay pretty well, in fact. Not that they wanted anyone to break their oath or anything like that, even if they had been treated badly. No, nothing like that. Just the odd bit of news a few days in advance — you know, before everybody heard about it anyway.

'Of course' — he laughed, a rumbling full belly-laugh, before lowering his voice again — 'if you are thinking about a change — nobody could blame you if you were, either, could they? — but if you are thinking of a change . . . well, just give us the nod, know what I mean?'

Yin Hong drew on his cigarette and listened. He let Wang know he was interested, but wasn't coming out with anything yet. And Wang understood. He didn't press him at all, he knew he'd have to think about it.

'I'm sort of what Americans call a headhunter,' Wang said, leaving a couple of tens as a tip. 'We don't go looking for just anyone, you know. We pick and choose.'

'We Shanghainese should stick together,' he added, out on the street. 'These Cantonese are just too slippery. Heard you're in the snakeboat business as well, by the way.'

'I bring a few across,' Yin Hong said modestly. 'Someone important next year as a matter of fact. Soon as the weather warms up a bit.'

Wang let out a real happy respectful sort of laugh, deep and rolling. 'What did I say? Just the sort of man we're looking for!' He flagged a taxi down and shut the door courteously after Yin Hong, nodding and waving as friendly as could be from the kerbside.

Leaning back contentedly in the corner, probing his broken tooth with the tip of his tongue, Yin Hong realized that for the first time in weeks he'd eaten with a real appetite.

The martial god

The winter sun shone on the big character signs along Wellington Street, on the printers and lamp-makers, the picture-framers and curtain-shops. Below the signs, the street being so narrow, it was shadowed and cold, and people walked with their hands in their pockets, their padded tunics done up at the collar. But in the taxi it was warm. Yin Hong stretched out with satisfaction, his head lolling on the back of the seat, recalling Wang's comforting Shanghai tones, his deep thick voice. Maybe this really was the change the fortune-tellers had been on about, sitting in their little booths.

As the taxi swung round towards Hollywood Road, he leant forward suddenly. 'Stop at the Man Mo temple,' he told the driver. Might as well see what the fortune-sticks had to tell him, now he was near there anyway. 'I want to try the sticks.'

'Fortune-sticks?' the driver repeated. 'I'll come in, too.'

'Who's a good fortune-teller in this place?' Yin Hong asked, going up the worn stone steps. Hadn't been there, either, for years; it was like he didn't know it any more, like he'd been living in another country almost.

'I'll show you the one I go to.'

'Good, ah?'

'Number one. Went to him before I got married. Number one.'

Past the great red-gold doors, into the old main hall, with their cobwebbed fluorescent lights. The great brown hanging incense-coils were smouldering away with scented smoke so thick you could hardly see the carved roof-beams.

'You throw for me,' Yin Hong said on an impulse. That way he couldn't cheat himself by sliding out a number he fancied. It would all be up to fate.

'Which god, then?'

He hesitated before the two dark figures in their embroidered robes, enthroned side-by-side, stern and black-bearded, at the main altar. Emperor Man, the civil god, or Emperor Kwan, the martial god?

'Emperor Kwan.'

'Thought so,' the driver grunted as he knelt down.

Yin Hong watched him rhythmically shaking the dark round box, the long thin spills rattling like rice inside. 'Two will be enough,' he muttered, thinking what he'd have to pay the fortune-teller, and a tip for the driver, too.

The driver nodded, shaking away, both hands clasped round the box.

Let it be good, let it be good, Yin Hong prayed silently.

A spill slowly worked its way up above the rest of them, and at last fell out onto the floor.

'Number nine,' the driver said. 'That's good.' He began again, closing his eyes while he shook, as if it was his own fortune that was being told and he, too, was praying for a good one. Yin Hong glanced up at the fierce red eyes of Emperor Kwan.

'Thirty-one. You're in luck all right today.'

They got the texts that matched the numbers on the spills and took them to the fortune-teller, a thin-faced old man with bristly grey hair and rimless glasses on the end of his nose. And Yin Hong could sense already it was going to turn out all right. He just had that feeling.

' "The first emperor of the Sung dynasty was crowned at Chan Kiu," ' the old man read in a high trembly voice, spreading the texts out on his narrow table. And: ' "So Hing delivered a message." ' He nodded and studied Yin Hong for a few seconds over the rims of his lenses, then frowned down at the texts again. Yin Hong waited, counting the row of biros in the fortune-teller's tunic pocket. Why would he want five biros, all neatly clipped in like that? Must do a lot of writing.

'In general favourable prospect,' the man said thoughtfully, while the driver listened and nodded *What did I tell you?* to Yin Hong. 'Wealth and position should come soon. Maybe not at once. So Hing isn't as positive about that as the Sung emperor, but it looks prosperous. Have you been ill lately? A gradual recovery is likely. Expecting anyone from a long way off? They both suggest travellers will arrive.'

'Is it a good time for a change?'

The old man rubbed his chin. 'What kind of change? A new business venture? Yes, prosperity and happiness are possible,' he said slowly. His voice was so high it could have been a woman's, and his skin was as white as paper, like he'd spent his whole life in the temple and never been out in the sun. The books he had on his table! Almanacs, horoscopes, palmistry charts — Yin Hong had never seen so many! And behind him on the wall, pictures of his father and his father's father, each one thin and scholarly, their faces pale from living with all those books, passing all that learning down from one generation to the next. You could tell they knew their business all right, just by looking at them.

'What did I tell you?' the taxi-driver said afterwards, folding the note Yin Hong gave him. 'He told me the month to get married in, and ten months later I'd got a son.' He opened his door at the traffic-lights, leant out and let a wad of spittle splat on to the road like a massive raindrop.

13

Treacherous warm flood

'It's not a party exactly,' Dimitri said when Rachel asked if he was going to Michael's New Year party. 'It's just a staid old dinner. He invites all the people he owes something to, and at midnight they go out into the garden and listen to the ships' sirens hooting in the new year. Then everyone goes home, or on to something wilder if they feel like it. What did you do for Christmas, by the way? We pretend it doesn't exist now the children are grown up. Before, we pretended it did. I hope you didn't sit at home feeling bloody?'

'No need to apologize for not inviting me,' she said crisply. 'I had plenty to do.' It was the only thing she was touchy about, people feeling sorry for her because she was alone, and guilty for not inviting her.

'Nothing was further from my mind, I'm ashamed to say. We never invite anyone at Christmas. Much to Ah Wong's disapproval. She insists on giving us all presents, which means we have to give her presents in return. And of course she has to cook a turkey and all that stuff. So the whole ghastly thing just carries on under its own momentum, just because the lower orders want it. Like the Royal Family.'

'I went to Michael and Grace's for dinner, but they didn't have turkey. San San's back from the States.'

'So I gathered from Alex's preoccupied appearance. Yes, we are going on New Year's Eve as a matter of fact. I haven't seen Michael for weeks. He's been in Taiwan, hasn't he? Since going to China?'

'Yes. He is hard to talk to, isn't he?'

'Not for me, but I know what you mean.' They were walking down the grey stone steps of the university main building. At the bottom, poinsettias were blooming, blood-red petals spreading over the green leaves. Ah Wong insisted they should have one of them every Christmas, too. 'Christmassy flower,' she called them. Well, better than a bloody fir-tree at least, in that climate. 'Michael always says what he means and always means what he says,' he went on. 'I suppose that's the trouble. It doesn't make for light witty conversation, I agree. Such as I'm making now, for instance. In case you hadn't noticed.'

'You do seem to be in a good humour today. Not at all monosyllabic, either.'

'Well, Christmas is over and the new term hasn't begun yet. I get thankful for smaller mercies as I grow older. Can I give you a lift somewhere? No? But it's only whistling in the dark really. I've just remembered I retire in 1997, when Hong Kong will presumably revert to China, if they don't take us over before then. Where I'll revert to isn't so clear. But nearly everyone I know is planning to get out. How's your thesis going, by the way? Are you keeping Patrick busy?'

Rachel knew she was blushing again when she answered, and the knowledge made her blush all the more. She could feel a treacherous warm flood spreading over the freckled milky skin of her cheeks and forehead. 'I don't think I'm overworking him,' she muttered, looking away.

A mite glum

There were so many people at the Dentons' on New Year's Eve that they had to have three large round tables, each laid for ten. Grace placed Rachel next to San San on the middle table — 'To talk about America,' she said vaguely. But Alex Johnston was on San San's other side, so Rachel was able to watch and listen to Patrick — who was sitting opposite her — almost uninterruptedly. In any case his ringing voice dominated the table as usual. 'When the British government sells Hong Kong down the river,' he declaimed to Stella and John in particular, 'as sell it in the end they presumably will, will anyone stand up in Parliament to point out that it will be the first time in history that a non-communist people twice as numerous as Denmark have been handed over to the very communist regime that half of them escaped from a few years before? And all without so much as a by-your-leave? Just for the sake of some squalid commercial deals, a sordid nuclear reactor or two! Did you see that pretty lord from the Foreign Office on the box the other night, positively smirking just because China had said something moderately friendly at last? My dear! What a tatty way to end an empire. Not with a bang, but a simper!'

The man in government, on Michael's table, looked up, gave a sheepish smile, then looked away in relief when Stella spoke.

'You make it sound like a disaster,' Stella said in her fluent icy voice, as if reading from a prepared text. 'Whereas it may only be a Change of Flag. In Beijing we met some of the Top Officials, and they assured us they meant to apply the One Country Two Systems Policy. They really Want it to Work. I don't see why we should worry, provided — '

'My dear Stella, it may be necessary to shine one's future patrons' shoes in order to continue making a living here, but one doesn't have to polish their kneecaps as well. Really, how far are you prepared to go? All the way up? One's mind positively boggles!'

But it wasn't what he said that Rachel noticed so much as the tones, the inflections of his voice, the changing, laughing expressions in his eyes, his high-spirited gestures, his rising exhilaration as the evening went on. She'd never observed anyone before with that kind of interest, with that sense of warmth and, yes, pride. She could almost imagine he was performing for her, especially when his eye caught hers. Some hope! Oh God, it would have to be him of all people! She'd never expected to feel like this in the whole of her life, and now she felt it for a gay. How ridiculous could you get? How absurd?

She was glad she hadn't put any of it in her diary yet. It would have committed her too clearly if she'd written it all down, stamped her too definitely as a pathetic natural spinster who'd simply lost her head. So long as she didn't form the words, it wasn't acknowledged yet, it wasn't quite real. So she hadn't opened her diary for weeks — longer than she'd ever left it before.

Paul, sitting as a treat beside Patrick, choked on some soup he was slurping up and knocked Patrick's glass over as he coughed and spluttered. Patrick led him serenely away without a trace of embarrassment or annoyance, while Ah Mui clucked apologetically beside him.

How was she going to bring him the stuff she'd written, and sit there next week, listening to his comments as if nothing had happened, as if everything was just the same as before? How was she going to write it, for that matter? *You schoolgirl dolt*, she scolded herself. As if he'd care. He wouldn't even notice. And, if he did, he'd only laugh. Heartlessly, too.

Promptly at quarter to midnight their glasses were filled with champagne, and they filed out through the french windows on to the lawn. The cold winds from northern China had died down a few days before, and the air was mild, as though the old year wanted a mellow ending. The sky was clear, the stars glistened moistly, the ships in the harbour were lit up from bow to stern, and all their lights had misty haloes round them. 'See, there's not a single ship in the harbour approaches,' someone said. 'They all want to stay in port tonight.' And it was true: the sea was empty, dark except for the desolate flashing of buoys and the lighthouse on the Lamma rocks. Rachel moved to the edge of the lawn, and saw below her that bluish necklace of lights she'd noticed on her first night in Hong Kong.

A minute or two before midnight they all stopped talking, one after another, the last voice — querulous Alison's — fading in mid-sentence. The man in government started counting the seconds off self-importantly on his watch. When he stopped there was a moment of stillness, as though the whole city were holding its breath. Then the sirens started hooting in the harbour — a wild chorus of blasting, whooping, shrieking and screaming from the hundreds of lonely anchored ships. To Rachel it sounded more like a dirge for the old year than a welcome to the new.

'Happy New Year,' Michael said gravely, raising his glass. 'A prosperous 1984.'

'At least not an Orwellian one,' Dimitri murmured.

They drank self-consciously.

'I always feel sad on New Year's Eve,' Rachel said, approaching Patrick despite herself. 'I can't see why everyone else is happy.'

'Who wouldn't be sad, dear girl, listening to that simply monstrous cacophony of ships' hooters? It sounds like an orchestra of out-of-tune French horns conducted by a raving anarchist.'

Elena's friend Tom said he guessed Hong Kong's fate would be settled by the next new year. 'It'll be a Chinese colony from then on, instead of a British one.'

'Oh, hold on tight,' the man in government protested mildly. 'Might be all right in the end.'

'Hong Kong as we know it is finished,' Tom declared in a level certain voice. 'Even if you don't.'

The ships' sirens were giving up now, frayed and tired, as if they knew it, too.

'I spent New Year's Eve on a boat once,' Dimitri said, looking down at the harbour. 'Years and years ago, when people travelled by P & O. It was at Port Swettenham, in Malaysia, and an English rubber-planter came on board just at midnight. He was retiring, going back to England. The thing was, he'd spent thirty years there, it was his whole life he was saying goodbye to, drinking toasts with his friends at the bottom of the gangway. He'd been through the Japanese occupation and the communist rebellion, and everything, just living out there in his jungle bungalow with its verandas and sundowners and parties at the Club on Saturday evenings.'

'It sounds insufferably tedious,' Patrick said. 'I trust there was the consolation of seducing the other planters' wives at least, in authentic Maugham fashion?'

'Or the other planters,' Elena suggested brightly.

'I don't know. But the thing I noticed was that the last person he said goodbye to, while they were all cheering and bawling out "Auld Lang Syne" and throwing those paper streamer things across to the boat, the last person was a Malay girl — well, woman — who'd been standing on the edge of the group all the time in the shadows. And just from the way he turned to her last and the way he took her hands, both of them in his, I thought: That's the one he's going to miss; that's the one that'll give him a wrench when he goes up the gangway — '

'Dimitri dear boy — '

'And I was right, too. You know what Port Swettenham's like, going down the coast at midnight with the silhouettes of palm trees against the sky? Well, he watched her and she watched him without a word or even a wave, till long after they must have been out of sight. I don't know if she was his servant or his mistress or what, but it had meant something to both of them, whatever she was.'

'Dimitri dear boy, I never realized you were a romantic at heart.'

'Only when I'm drunk.' He glanced down at his glass. It was empty, but he raised it to his lips anyway, as though drinking a silent toast to that distant man or that distant year. 'A whole life,' he said. 'Thirty years. And now they fly in for two or three, and stay in identical rooms in identical flats, and work in identical offices on identical contracts with identical brief-cases and identical suits, trying to make the place identical to all the identical places they came from. And never really live here at all.'

'Mila dear girl, he's positively inspired! Did you know he had such depths in him? He should be drunk all the time.'

'Oh, yes,' Mila said, eyeing Dimitri as if there was more she could say if she chose, 'I've always known. He isn't really what he seems at all.'

'I spent New Year's Eve in Mandalay once,' Michael said abruptly.

'Who's next?' Tom asked in his dazed deadly monotone. 'I spent it in Vietnam once, having my ass shot at.'

There was a cripple outside the hotel, Michael nearly said, but didn't. *A young boy who didn't have any legs at all; he just dragged himself along on his hands. He used to whistle birdsongs for a living. He could go on and on for half an hour and never do the same one twice. I used to throw him money, he wouldn't come nearer, he was afraid you'd hit him — sometimes children used to chase him or chuck stones at him for fun. I often used to think: That's Asia; that's what I'm afraid of.*

The words went through his mind, but all he said was 'It was hot and sticky.'

'What on earth were you doing in Mandalay on New Year's Eve?' Elena asked.

'Trying to buy some teak. Nothing romantic, I'm afraid.'

'I think you're holding out on us,' Elena said. 'Something terribly exciting happened, and you're not telling us.'

But Michael was moving away, hunching his shoulders as if somehow dimly ashamed.

'I'm beginning to feel a trifle dullish,' Patrick murmured. 'I think I'll get another drink.'

'So you were in Vietnam?' Mr. Ma from Taiwan said to Tom, holding his glass in both hands as though about to drink another toast. 'A pity the wrong side won.'

'Did it?'

Mr. Ma blinked uneasily behind his thick lenses, as if Tom had told a joke in questionable taste. 'You were reporting the war?' he asked cautiously.

'I didn't know enough about it. I was only fighting it.'

'Ah, on active service,' Mr. Ma said, seeking the restoration of harmony with a polite respectful laugh. His lips didn't quite cover his teeth when the laugh was over. He raised his glass again in salute.

'I was just glad to get my ass out in one piece. More or less.'

'He's got some lovely scars,' Elena assured Mr. Ma. 'You ought to see.'

Mr. Ma laughed again, backing off with a little bow. He touched Michael's arm and went indoors with him, nearly colliding with Alison, who was just coming out, holding a brim-full glass, with intense concentration, in both hands.

'You'd think they'd know better than to drown your gin in tonic,' she said to nobody in particular. 'After all these years. Can't stand champagne; it makes me depressed.' She raised the glass very deliberately towards her lips as though not at all confident she could actually get it there. 'Anyone seen Peter?'

'Not recently,' Elena said. 'Has he slipped his lead again?'

Alison's eyes slewed slowly round towards her, and were followed more slowly still by her head and body. 'Why? You on heat again?'

She walked off with careful swaying steps, then suddenly slumped down on the bench beneath the bauhinia tree and started blubbering silently, her mouth slack and wet.

'Oh Jesus,' Elena said. Rachel had never seen her put down before, and never expected to, either, but now two pink spots had appeared on her cheeks and her lower lip quivered slightly. Was it shame, humiliation, or anger?

'I think Peter's over there,' she said, going across to Alison. Alison nodded, sniffed, drank and lurched off with an old woman's sigh. Rachel sat where Alison had sat and watched the groups dispersing on the lawn, couple by couple, going indoors together to say goodbye, even Alison and Peter. Car doors slammed, engines growled, voices called out, headlights slipped like bright shadows over the trees. Soon she would be the only one left. She felt she could have cried like Alison.

Then Patrick drifted across the lawn towards her, Paul trustfully clutching his wrist. 'The dear child's been showing me his paintings,' he said. 'And unless I'm mistaken Alison has made a scene.'

'I guess she was provoked. But she was witty, too.'

'Oh?' He cocked his head, asking for more.

But Rachel wouldn't give. 'Paul's paintings are good, aren't they?' she said. Paul was gazing at her with those disturbingly attentive yet absent eyes of his. Sometimes she thought maybe he understood everything people said, but just discarded most of it like so much junk at the door of his mind. And wouldn't he have been right?

'Wasn't the grey-haired man sitting next to Michael at dinner the head of that communist publishing company?' she asked when Patrick didn't answer.

'Yes. Most of the authors he publishes have spent so many years on pig-farms during the Cultural Revolution you'd think they'd all write pastoral poetry now. Or pig-breeding manuals. The man on his other side was a luminary of the Taiwan government, by the way. The one with a laugh like English gravy, thick and greasy.'

'Yes, I met him. How does Michael manage to get on with both of them?'

'In Hong Kong one learns to keep all one's options open, dear girl. Particularly in the present dismal situation. Besides, they've probably all known each other half their lives anyway. They're all from Shanghai. You never know which one you might need help from next. Or sometimes you do know.'

Ah Mui came shuffling across the lawn, calling Paul by his Chinese name.

'Beddy-byes,' Patrick said, disengaging Paul's hand. 'Where are you staying the night, dear girl? Here, I suppose. It's beginning to look just the teeniest bit drear and doom-laden, don't you think? Like Hong Kong. I suppose the oldies have gone to bed, and the youngsters are off about their erotic pursuits. Come and have a drink in town; you look a mite glum. I'll show you how some people see the new year in. Oh, you'll be back in an hour or so, I assure you. Chung Yan's working late, but not that late.'

Haven't seen the floor-show

They took a taxi down the Peak, and Rachel thought: *I've never been in a taxi with him before.*

'Where are we going?' she asked, looking out at the forlorn neon Christmas lights in empty Central. 'Nowhere too fancy, I hope,' she added, as they passed the Hong Kong Club, where furred and jewelled women stood with men in evening clothes, waiting to be handed into their long sleek limousines.

'Depends what you mean by "fancy," dear girl.'

She let the 'dear girl' pass. 'Only, I'm not exactly wearing an evening gown.'

Patrick said something to the driver, then leant back. 'Evening gowns are not required, or even usual,' he said with a suggestive little smile. 'It's just a place where birds of a feather flock together.'

She felt a little qualm at that, but she *was* sitting beside him, and he *was* talking to her.

They drove into Wanchai, along a road full of Chinese nightclubs and dance-halls, and stopped round a corner in a wanly lit side street. Patrick led her up a dark staircase in a dingy passage-way between the locked grilles of two nondescript stores with overflowing garbage cans standing outside them. 'I see what you meant about evening gowns,' she said.

Patrick didn't answer. He had rung the bell beside a blank door at the top of the stairs, and was gazing at the spy-hole, while a bright light came on above their heads. 'It's a kind of club,' he said. 'Members only. Hope I can get you in.'

The door opened onto a dim curtained lobby. Two Chinese waiters smiled at Patrick, then stared at Rachel. There was a quick murmured discussion, with dubious glances at Rachel, then Patrick passed a hundred dollars to the elder man (though he couldn't have been more than twenty-five, Rachel thought), who grudgingly pulled aside the curtain and let them both in.

It seemed at first glance what Rachel thought an ordinary nightclub would look like: a small dance-floor with taped music, a bar at one end, and discreet alcoves round the walls, the lights so low that the waiter had to guide them with a torch. But then, as her eyes grew used to the dark, she realized that all the couples on the dance-floor were men or, rather, men and boys. And so were all the people sitting at the bar, or sitting, some with their arms round each other, at the little tables. She was the only woman there, and she sensed from the long cold looks she attracted that they didn't like it.

The waiter put them in the furthest corner. Patrick ordered two gin and tonics before Rachel could protest. 'I don't feel very welcome here,' she said flatly. 'And I don't like gin.' Didn't he know how she must feel, or was that the whole idea? She glanced silently round the tables, thinking that now she understood what it was like to belong to the wrong race or have the wrong colour. It was like finding yourself in Harlem suddenly. Only, here it was the wrong sex; race wasn't the bar — there were Chinese with Chinese, Europeans with Europeans, Chinese with Europeans. And a few darker faces, Malayan, Indian, Filipino . . . .

'Oh, it's just like any other Wanchai establishment, dear girl,' Patrick said affectedly. 'Except of course that everything's perverse.'

'I wouldn't say perverse,' she said levelly. 'Just a bit one-sided.'

'Wait till you see the floor-show.'

Rachel promised herself she'd walk out before that, no matter what it cost her.

'For instance we have money-boys here,' Patrick went on, nodding at the youths lounging by the bar. 'They perform roughly the same services that bar-girls do in the hetero estaminets round the corner.'

'I can't drink that gin.'

'I'll drink both of them, then. Would you like something else?'

'No, thanks.'

'Whisky? Brandy?'

'No, *thanks!*'

He shrugged and drank.

'Is this where you're meeting Chung Yan?'

'Not tonight. He's going straight to my place when he's finished.' He glanced at his watch. 'Shall I teach you the argot, dear girl?'

'Do I have a choice?'

'See that young Chinese boy dancing with that suave though portly European? He's a potato queen. When it's the other way round' — he nodded at the next table, where a European youth was accepting a cigarette from an older Chinese man — 'they're called rice queens. I suppose I needn't tell you what a bog queen is?'

'Is this meant to shock me?' She pushed her gin towards him across the table. 'Because it doesn't.'

'You haven't seen the floor-show yet,' he said in the acid tone he'd used on Stella, earlier in the evening.

'It's your motive that shocks me if anything does, not the place. Why did you have to bring me here? What's the idea?'

'But my motive is the purest,' Patrick said without the acid now, holding her eyes a moment with his.

'Meaning what?' But she felt she was blushing again, and felt she knew very well what. He meant he'd noticed what had happened to her and was warning her off.

Yet all he said was: 'I thought you'd like to see how the other half lives.'

'Pretty much the same as the *other* other half, isn't it?'

'Wait till you've seen the floor-show.'

'I don't want to see the floor-show.'

'Oh, but you must. Dear girl.'

Her lips pressed tight together in helpless humiliation. When she got back to the Dentons', she thought, she'd pull the blanket over her head and scream. But not then, not there. She looked away at the wall behind her, her eyes smarting. It had blown-up photos of boys and gay-looking men on it.

Nothing special, just unbuttoned shirts and pretty faces, like hairdressers' models. Or hairdressers, she guessed. She imagined how innocent it would look if the police raided it — just a men's club with people drinking. She supposed the floorshow could be made to disappear pretty quickly, too, whatever it was — and she certainly didn't mean to find out.

'Can we go when you've finished that drink?' she said coldly, turning back. 'I think I've seen all I need.'

'So have I,' Patrick said.

'Oh?' Then she saw he was staring across the room, and his face seemed suddenly to have collapsed, almost as Alison's had earlier.

She followed his gaze, and saw Chung Yan. Chung Yan, just being ushered to a table. Chung Yan, with a smooth silver-haired European. Chung Yan, glancing across at them, meeting Patrick's hurt eyes without even a flicker of recognition.

Patrick looked at her, drank, glanced across at Chung Yan, drank again. His lip quivered slightly. 'Well, he's a free agent after all,' he said unevenly, forcing a twitchy smile. 'All the same, I think you're right, now. I wish I hadn't brought you. I wish I hadn't brought myself.'

'Let's go, Patrick.' Her voice softened. 'Let's go.'

As they walked out, she saw Patrick's eyes sliding round to where Chung Yan sat with the elderly soft-skinned European. The man had loose hooded lids, and his gaze never left Chung Yan's face.

Patrick stopped a taxi and opened the door for her, telling the driver in Cantonese where to go. He looked as if someone had just sucked the life out of him.

'Aren't you coming, Patrick?'

He gave a crooked shrug, a cracked smile.

'Aren't you coming?'

'See how much better transcendence is?' he said with a little choke in his voice as he closed the door.

The driver pulled down the flag. When she looked back Patrick was gone already.

In her room at the Dentons', she didn't scream beneath the blanket after all. She lay awake staring bleakly at the ceiling, thinking of Patrick's face crumpling like Alison's. And all for that little faggot Chung Yan!

Heavy and trusting

'And there's a girl from the mainland there, too,' San San said. 'On a scholarship. She's terribly good technically. Isn't this Turtle Cove?'

'Mm.' Walking beside her down the long night-shadowed tree-shadowed path to the beach, Alex felt her hand swinging temptingly close to his. 'How d'you get on with her?'

'All right. We were a bit wary of each other at first. You know, like dogs from different packs.' If she'd been Elena, she'd have said 'bitches.' If she'd been Elena, she'd have let him take her hand by now. Or more.

There were uneven steps cut in the earth path as it sloped down more steeply. She tripped on one of them, and he caught her arm to steady her. At first he let go, but then he took her hand as if just to guide her, and there she was letting it stay there while they each remembered the summer, and knew that each remembered. When he experimentally loosened his fingers slightly, she didn't withdraw her hand, but left it there passive, as if she'd forgotten it. Or was that a promise?

'I don't think I've ever been here before,' she said. 'Not in the middle of the night anyway.' A twig cracked under her shoe, and somewhere in the branches above them a bird flew off with a cry of alarm, its wings whirring. 'Doesn't the dark scare you?'

'No, it's comforting.'

'Comforting?'

'Mm. That's why I sleep with a pillow over my head. To make it as dark as I can.'

The overlacing leaves grew thinner. Soon the sky appeared, and then suddenly the path ran out on to the sand, gleaming smooth and pale beneath the starlight. Far out between the two tree-covered headlands that enclosed the beach like embracing arms, the dim yellowish light of a fishing-junk swung rhythmically up and down. The sea was running strongly into the narrow bay. The waves came in like small rolling hills, their foaming crests toppling over the smooth dark valleys beneath to break with a thud on the beach.

They walked down to the surf, and then along it, the sand shifting beneath their feet with a fine grinding sound. They each remembered the summer again, and the beach and the cave and the sandy sprawling figures. *I could never do that*, she thought. *Never*.

'I need a new violin,' she said aloud, speaking as if she wasn't really in her voice, as people speak in the theatre before the play starts, with one eye on the stage.

'I suppose that'll cost thousands?'

'A good one, yes. About fifty thousand US. At least.'

Alex didn't answer. Fifty or five hundred thousand, it was all the same to him. Besides, he was thinking of Elena's hissed words as he left the Dentons' with San San. 'For God's sake, swyve her! Prick her! She's begging you, can't you see?' One of Elena's lovers had been a lecturer on Chaucer at London University, and as Alex taught English she thought he'd appreciate some earthy Chaucerian language. He'd turned away angry and embarrassed, but the words kept coming at him like the waves on the beach, and why else were they there after all? He stopped and faced San San suddenly.

'Let's swim,' he gulped.

'What?'

'Let's swim. A New Year dip.' He was breathless, and amazed at himself in some detached corner of his mind, and wondering if he really meant it.

'It's too cold! Besides, what in?'

'No, the water's quite warm really.'

'But we haven't got swimsuits!'

He was still holding her hand, and she was still not taking it away. He saw his inward picture of her naked back all those years ago in their summer cave. He swallowed. 'There's no one here to see.'

'Well, *you* are, aren't you?' But still she hadn't taken her hand away.

'Besides, it's dark.' And still he didn't know if he meant it.

'Dark! Comforting, I suppose?'

And yet she looked round as if to check they really were alone. And when he pressed her hand encouragingly she seemed to give an absent answering squeeze, as if to say *Don't give up*. And when he looked at her she looked back a second or two before she glanced away.

'Look, I'll undress behind that tree over there,' he coaxed her, 'and you go behind that one over there, and we'll be practically invisible.' He felt a quivering certainty in his limbs now — he was serious, he would go through with it. If she would. 'All right?'

'No!' Yet she hesitated, floating an image of Elena scandalously topless across her mind. And still she hadn't taken her hand away. 'Well, promise you won't look till I say so.'

He nodded. He could sense her giving in; it made him still more breathless.

'Say it. No cheating!'

'I promise.'

Still she hesitated, floating that thrilling scandalous picture of Elena over her mind once more. Then she turned and walked towards the tree. 'Turn round,' she said. 'You go to your tree.' She could feel her heart thudding lightly.

He listened to her shoes crunching the sand, then he marched off, too. Tugging at his shirt buttons, he was suddenly afraid she might just go on walking back to the path, back to the road, and quietly take a taxi home while he hung about on the beach like an abandoned puppy. But when he glanced furtively round he glimpsed the same long pale back he'd seen as a schoolboy, and his body grew light and reckless with excitement. He was still pulling at his socks when he heard her bare feet scudding over the sand, scattering the water, then the splash as she dived in. *My God*, he thought. *My God!*

'Hurry!' she shouted. 'It's freezing!'

And as he ran down the beach he saw her head, round and black as a seal's, bobbing out through the waves.

How fresh the sand felt on his bare soles! How free his body in the air!

He dashed in after her, watching a mental film of himself dashing as he dashed. Into the surf, plunge, and then the sudden quiet coldness closing over him. He gasped as his head slid up into the air again a few clean seconds later.

His skin felt numb with the cold of it, as if the blood had all shrunk away deep inside him. He struck out towards her, quick violent strokes, beating at the waves that were throwing him about, the white crests that were splashing into his face. He caught her foot and saw a phosphorescent shadow of her leg, but she slipped away, kicking spray at him. They swam out past the breakers to where the wave-hills swept in more sedately, swimming round and round each other, he chasing, she eluding. Whenever he came near to grasping her, she wriggled free, kicking water into his face. And they never said a word, they only looked and spluttered and laughed.

'I'm going out,' she panted after a while. 'My fingers have gone dead.' She tossed the slick black scarf of her hair away from her face and swam back towards the beach. Following more slowly, he watched her head, her shoulders, her streaming hair emerge, and then her pale back as she suddenly stood up and ran towards her clothes.

'Don't look!' she called out, shivering or laughing. 'Stay in till I tell you!'

But the mental film was playing in his head again, and it had jumped forward half a reel. Already he could see himself following her deep footprints, finding her by the tree, feeling her wet skin against his.

San San was astonished at herself, elated, scandalized. She'd never meant to do it, not right up to the last moment; it was like vertigo, the way she'd just suddenly launched herself into it. Never mind the underclothes, just pull the dress on quickly. But the air was warmer than the water, it wasn't so cold now, she could take her time. 'No, you've got to wait!' she shouted as she saw Alex leaving the water. Yet she knew she didn't really mean it, and she did nothing to get the dress over her head as she heard his feet in the sand behind her; she only turned and held it up in front of her, and said, 'Your tree's over there,' in a low unsteady voice, and didn't mean that, either. And when he touched her, wet and slippery, and she felt his lips on hers, somehow her lips responded and she dropped the dress on the sand as if she'd known all along they'd sink onto it, as they did.

How did her body know already what he wanted, and what she wanted, too? His lips moist on her eyes and cheeks and mouth, and the salty taste of his skin? Why did she shiver when he nuzzled her throat? Why did she want to clutch his head and press him down when he kissed her breasts? But she did, she did, and she was soft and warm and loose, and when she felt him entering her she wanted that, too, and her body opened as she'd never imagined it could and it hardly hurt at all and she was as taut and eager as he was when he shuddered and shuddered inside her.

And then she held his head still on her breast and smelt his hair and looked up at the stars through the leaves and thought how quiet and peaceful it was to fall asleep like that with him lying so heavy and trusting on top of her.

And she didn't worry at all about the mess her dress was in, not even when they felt cold and got up and he ran off to get his clothes and she watched him running while she slowly knelt and gathered up her own clothes piece by piece.

Natural gift

'Why Turtle Cove?' she asked as he drove her back in his third hand Subaru estate. It was she now who took his hand. 'You planned it all along, didn't you?'

'Not planned. Hoped. There's a towel on the back seat.'

'A towel, and you didn't plan it!'

She dried her hair, watching the headlights glide across the trees and surge into the sky at the brow of every hill. 'Why Turtle Cove?'

'Well, I could hardly expect to get you over to Lamma and our cave, could I? And Turtle Cove seemed the most like that.' Then he told her how he'd seen her when she was fifteen, and had her in his mind ever since.

She wrapped the towel round her head like a turban while she listened. 'You had to wait a long time, though, didn't you?' she smiled. 'How many surrogates have you had up till now? You can't have any more, you know.'

He pursed his lips, shrugged, shook his head.

'Well?'

'Can't you tell?'

'How would I tell? I'm only a beginner.'

His mouth opened and then closed, and he frowned ahead at the road. 'Believe it or not,' he said at last, 'so am I.'

'What? I don't believe it!'

'Well, I am.'

'Men aren't like that!'

'This one is.'

She was silent for so long then, listening to the engine reverberating off the narrow stone walls of the road, that he asked her sheepishly if she was disappointed.

She shook her head with a sly little smile. 'I was just thinking, in that case you must have read a lot of books.'

'Books?' He'd never seen her smile like that before. It was almost salacious. It *was* salacious.

'Manuals.'

'Oh.' He felt as if she'd pinned a medal on him. 'Elena thinks I'm retarded in that direction.'

'Oh, well, compared with Elena . . . . '

'As a matter of fact, I didn't read any.'

She laid her hand on his knee. 'You must have a natural gift.'

And then for some reason he told her what he'd never told anyone in his life before — and perhaps that *was* the reason, he realized as he was telling her — that his mother had come and looked at him in bed the night she killed herself. He'd faked sleep, intending to shock her by suddenly opening his eyes wide when she came closer. But she didn't come closer; she stayed just inside the door, with the light from the hall slanting on her face, and through his just-parted lashes he'd seen she was in her red party-dress and her eyes were . . . were far away.

'Sad?' San San suggested.

He shook his head definitely. 'Far away.' He knew how she looked when she was sad, and that was different. Her eyes looked far away. As if she'd left already.

Something better

Yin Hong turned left at the bottom of the stairs, and took the long slow way through the maze of dark cramped alleys of the walled city, almost as dark by day as by night. He wasn't in a hurry to meet Snakeboat Wong, he wanted to think things out a bit on the way. He couldn't help noticing again what a hole he was living in. Scummy water running down the open drains, greasy muck under your shoes, the slimy walls, the smell of dirt and poverty — yes, he ought to have done better for himself at his age, ought to have something better to live in, ought to be able to take things a bit easy by now, instead of just getting along, hand to mouth, from one day to the next. Or one month anyway. And getting older. Wang was right, he deserved something better.

He nodded to the Lee widow on the stairwell next to the coolies' brothel. There she sat with her two sons, making plastic flowers under a dim light-bulb, like she'd been sitting every day since he'd been in the Walled City. And how long was that? If he wasn't careful, he'd end up like her, with no way out. The kids had their school uniforms on. Why weren't they in school, then?

'No school today?' he asked.

'Afternoon session. They don't go in the mornings this year.'

'Afternoon session, ah?'

She'd told him before, he remembered now. Where would she be if it wasn't for the handouts from the brothers? Inside the brothel instead of next door to it. Lucky for her, her old man had been a Red Pole, a real fighter in his time. Still, was that how he was going to end up himself, rotting away in some windowless room, surviving on handouts from the brothers? Assuming they'd give him any after that business over the dope. He'd never forgive them that. He kicked out at a plump brown rat with shiny button eyes that was snuffling round a pile of garbage spilling out across the path. Only the rats got fat in the Walled City. No, he'd got to do something, get some real money before it was too late. That thing with Lily Denton, he'd got to pull that off, squeeze a better price out of Michael for a start, *he* could afford it. And hand Wang a bit of news, too, now and then, see what happened there. Risky, that, if anyone found out. But after what the fortune-tellers had said he was sure no one would. His luck must be turning; ever since he'd met Wang he'd felt better again. Yes, squeeze Michael Denton a bit more; he'd pay up, bound to, his own sister, what a turn-up, coming across her again. Lily Denton after all these years, he could remember the old place on the Bund like yesterday — Lily and Michael, too. Yes, just like yesterday, doing his homework there in his mother's old whitewashed room with the blue biscuit-tin she kept her money in, he'd had his hand in there a few times as well without her knowing.

Going up the steps out on to the road, he saw Limpy Ng standing by the red lamps of the butcher's, waving his arms about and talking to someone inside. First time Yin Hong had met him since they settled that little matter. Limpy had been keeping out of the way, and so he'd better, too, slimy runt. As Limpy turned round, smiling his greasy smile, Yin Hong saw who he was talking to. Ah Keung. When Limpy saw him his eyes just stiffened a second and then he grinned like they'd always been the best of friends. But Ah Keung just looked.

'No hard feelings, brother?' Limpy said, raising his hand like he didn't know whether to shake hands or only wave.

'No one threw oil over me,' Yin Hong said.

Limpy laughed like it was a good joke. 'Just talking to Ah Keung,' he said.

'I noticed.' Yin Hong looked at Ah Keung. Ah Keung looked back. 'Another tip for the races, was it?'

Yin Hong was still looking at Ah Keung when he asked that, ignoring Limpy, but it was Limpy who answered. 'Thought of cutting him in on a little job.'

'Any job Ah Keung does, he asks me first.' Yin Hong was still looking at Ah Keung, and Ah Keung was still looking back saying nothing. 'He knows the rules.'

'Does he?' Limpy said with his greasy smile, like he knew some thing Yin Hong didn't.

But Ah Keung said, 'Forget it Limpy,' and Limpy shrugged. But the way Ah Keung told him to forget it, it was like he was sorry about passing it up, almost as if he wished he was working for Limpy and not for him. Limpy Ng!

'I'm going to see about *our* little job,' Yin Hong said to Ah Keung, putting his hand out for a taxi. He could have walked, and he was short of cash, too, but he wasn't going to let Limpy see he was hard up. 'Coming along?'

'Girl's day off,' Ah Keung said.

'All right, then, give her one for me.'

Limpy gave a snigger, but Ah Keung just looked like stone. And when Yin Hong glanced back out of the taxi Limpy was talking away to Ah Keung again, limping along beside him across the road and down into the Walled City. And Ah Keung was listening as if he liked what he heard.

Yin Hong kept thinking about that, all the way to the teahouse. Perhaps that was why he started straight off when he saw Snakeboat Wong and two of his sons, almost as soon as he'd sat down with them, instead of waiting and drinking tea a bit first, doing things properly.

'We can squeeze Denton for a bit more,' he said, leaning across the table. 'I'll tell him things have got tighter in China, we've got to get her out a different way and pay off more people.'

Old Wong looked at his sons, then down at his cup, turning it slowly round and round. Yin Hong could see he didn't like it. Or was it just the way he'd started straight off like that? Those Macao people were old-fashioned. As he was himself usually — it was seeing Ah Keung with Limpy that had put him off.

Wong drank and put his cup down, tightening his lips a bit, as if it hadn't tasted good. 'But we've got everything ready,' he said thoughtfully in his light voice, glancing round at his two sons again.

'I'll get you another load. If we play him along a bit, we can push him up twenty per cent at least.'

'So long as we don't lose him. We're charging him a lot already, ah.'

'We won't lose him. I've known him all my life. I know what he's good for.'

Yin Hong leant back as the foki brought his tea, and for some reason the picture of Ah Keung walking along beside Limpy slipped back into his mind like a bad dream.

But Snakeboat Wong nodded at last, after glancing at his sons. 'All right,' he said.

14

Spacious mansion on the Peak

Sometimes Grace would sit with Paul in his room for half an hour or more at a time, without saying a word or moving a muscle. The two of them would just be there like statues, gazing out of the window or at the fireplace or at the wall, in apparent vacancy; and a stranger might well have wondered which of the two was supposed to be the brain-damaged one. Or which was not.

But Grace was not vacant at those times. She was walking the gallery of her memories, from one room to the other. For years now she'd been collecting memories as others collected rare books or scrolls or antique furniture. Some she lost — they slipped out of her consciousness; but she was always gaining others — they came to her unsought during her meditative gardening or painting, or in her long still reveries with Paul, when her mind seemed as empty as his was, if it was. Who knew what jumbled pictures might be drifting through the darkness in his head? And when the memories came she paused and contemplated them; she repossessed her past.

Proust had not been on the reading-lists of the literature courses she took at Wellesley just before Pearl Harbor, and she'd never read him since — she would never have managed twelve volumes of such mannered prose — but when she heard people talking about him she felt she knew already.

Even as a young girl she'd withdrawn from the friction and the fracas of the world into the convent of her inward contemplation. Her teachers always said she was too quiet or, more perceptively, that they couldn't tell what she was thinking. She'd never quarrelled with anyone, not even with her two sisters and one brother, now living in America, to whom she never wrote (and they never wrote to her). And no one really succeeded in quarrelling with her — she never answered back, she merely looked at you with those mild liquid brown eyes that seemed to say 'Oh, well, have it your way if you feel so strongly about it.'

'Too quiet.' It had started in her childhood, perhaps in response to the overbearing noisy dominance of her father. It had developed in her youth. After Paul's illness it had taken her over completely.

And of course she could afford to let it take her over. She'd never had to work for a living, except during those first few years after the war, when she arrived in Hong Kong as a refugee and taught English to first-year students at the university. She looked too fragile and remote even then, even for that, as though she were still half-listening to the shot through the back of the head that killed her father. Michael had tracked her down eventually and courted her with a determination as stolid as the determination he'd brought to running his newly founded business; but with an underlying passion as well, which he never brought to business. She'd never had to lift a finger since, except for her children; and even there of course there were always amahs.

She was uneasy at first about her gradual withdrawal from what others thought was life; it was the time of the famine in China, when thousands struggled starving across the border every week — she saw them day after day, gaunt and tattered, begging in the streets. Surely she should be doing something about all that? Well, she did. She bought her quietude with extravagant anonymous gifts to charities, and had gone on giving to them ever since. The glittery givers like Belinda Lai, who aspired to eat at the governor's table and call his lady by her first name, never gave as much as Grace did to avoid it. And they left their name-cards on their gifts as well, which Grace never did.

She had only a few clothes (though they were costly), she wore no jewellery or perfume (but had expensive toilet water). No furs, pearls or gold. It was easy to give so much money away. What would she spend it on? Besides, she knew that too many riches were a liability; all that her father's massive Shanghai wealth had brought him in the end was a bullet in the brain.

If she'd lived a century or two earlier, Grace said once, she might have become a nun, in one of the contemplative orders.

'But then you couldn't have had us,' San San protested, thirteen at the time. ('Oh, couldn't she!' said Elena.)

Perhaps it was that prodigal giving of Grace's that made Michael a little tight. He never left more than the normal ten per cent as a tip, sometimes even taking the spare cents with him rather than leave them on the plate. But, then, money for him was the costly premium he paid to insure them all against the inevitable hazards of life. He knew someone had to do that, as his mother had known before him.

Rachel never thought him stingy — he'd been generous enough to her after all — but she often wondered if he had any notion of life in the concrete deserts of the resettlement estates and factory towers of North Point, Mongkok, Tuen Mun. Those great bleak blocks with their endless dark corridors giving onto crowded rabbit-warren rooms (she'd seen them in San Po Kong and Wong Tai Sin), where the barred windows looked out on to the grim backs of other concrete blocks, those shared bathrooms and kitchens (one to a floor), that fume-laden roar of traffic night and day — did Michael in his spacious mansion on the Peak have even an inkling of knowledge, let alone concern, about that other teeming world which he could just see if only he bothered to look from his airy windows? She was suspicious of that strange aloof man, always folded in on himself, yet with a cautious eye alertly watching, whose only interest seemed to be the curious irrelevant details of Hong Kong's early history. What about today?

But he knew about all that better than she did. He'd known about it all his life. He knew how most of the people in those Hong Kong tenements had lived in refugee squatter-huts ten years before; and, ten years before that, how they'd starved in the dull misery of rural China. A few years before that, he knew how they were being killed in the civil war or by the Japanese (he knew exactly how they were being killed — he'd seen with his own eyes). He knew they were poor, ill-housed, overworked. But he also knew they were each year a little better off than the year before, and knew what a chancy thing it was to make each year bring something more, how easily things could go wrong, how fine the line was between enough rice in their bowls today and not enough tomorrow. So long as each year brought the rice and something more, they were winning. And when he saw the lengthening lines outside the foreign consulates each day, the patient queues of people trying to get out before China took back Hong Kong, he remembered the last years of Shanghai; and wondered how much longer they would go on winning. And wondered if he, too, should not be getting out.

So Michael thought in the study of his spacious mansion. And would have told Rachel if she'd asked him, but she never did.

Exposed and vulnerable

'You haven't been practising so much recently,' he said, drawing a line of crosses down the edge of his blotter.

'It's not how much that matters, but how well,' San San said sententiously, leaning over the back of his chair. 'Like with your writing.'

But she wasn't practising so well, either. He heard her let things go now which in the summer she'd worked at time and again to get just right. Now they weren't. He started another row of crosses. She was reading what he'd written, and he wished she'd stop.

'Besides, I really do need a new violin,' she said absently, plucking a string as if to prove it. 'This is your thing on Caldwell, isn't it? Is it nearly finished?'

'Getting there.'

' "Apparently an excellent, or at least a competent linguist," ' she read out, ' "Caldwell was one of the few colonial officials trusted by the Chinese population in the early years of Hong Kong . . . . " '

How it embarrassed him to hear his own words read aloud like that. His neck prickled as she went on, he felt so exposed and vulnerable. He frowned down at his pencil point, thickening the crosses with quick heavy strokes.

' "Yet having a Chinese wife who had been a demimondaine and who was connected with known criminals — though herself probably guiltless — and preserving himself from bankruptcy by dubious financial activities, he was never fully accepted by the Europeans." '

'Too long,' he said at once disparagingly, laying his hand on the page so that she couldn't turn it. 'Much too long.'

'You hate me reading your stuff, don't you?'

'In my presence and before it's finished, yes.'

'Is it because you're insecure, you want people to have a high opinion of you, and you're afraid they won't?'

'Perhaps.'

She plucked another string. 'It's what Alex says.'

'About me?'

'About me.'

'Oh.' There'd been a sort of lightness about her recently, a jumpiness, an exhilarated excitement. And she was always out with Alex. No wonder she didn't practise so much, or so well.

'Lucky you don't believe in ghosts, isn't it? Considering how like your father old Caldwell was, and living in this house and everything.'

'Yes, I suppose it is.'

Now that he was himself connected with known criminals, though, Michael had begun to think Caldwell was more like himself than like his father. And there was that suggestion that Caldwell was a Eurasian, too. Sometimes, when he tried to picture the man, he caught himself giving him his own face, his own build, in his own home, amongst his own things. Only the clothes were different. Sometimes he imagined himself coming face to face with Caldwell in the old cellar, and it was like meeting himself in an earlier time. Yes, lucky he didn't believe in ghosts.

The phone rang, and San San hurried to take it. He heard her eager 'Hallo?' and then the disappointed switch to Cantonese. 'Hwei? Tang yat tang.'

'For you,' she said.

'Hwei?'

Yin Hong's scrappy rapid voice grated against his ear.

Grace was walking round the garden in the pale afternoon sun with Paul, though she'd forgotten Paul now — he was muttering at the bauhinia behind her, staring balefully at a long sword-shaped brown pod hanging down from the lowest branch. She'd forgotten Paul, forgotten the garden and the day, but she was remembering another winter afternoon, a cold clear afternoon at Wellesley when she went ice-skating on the lake. It had slipped suddenly into her mind as fresh as yesterday, only it was over forty years ago. She could smell the wood-smoke from a fire on the lakeside, she could see the flames, she could feel her cheeks tingling in the wind and the sun, feel her body glowing all through and her steaming breath warm on the red woollen scarf covering her mouth. Yes, she thought, yes, sensing now the grind of the steel blades under her feet, the taut springy bend of the wide black ice-sheet.

She stood still, oblivious that she stood still, oblivious of the phone ringing indoors, oblivious of Paul's savage muttering, oblivious of the blurred edge of the hill's long shadow inching towards her over the lawn. She was skating at Wellesley, and the leafless branches of the trees were black and stark against the pale cold American winter sky.

'That was Yin Hong,' Michael said quietly in Shanghainese behind her. 'Apparently there's going to be some delay. Some people got caught in China; they'll have to change the route. Of course, he says it'll cost more, too. For another lot of bribes.'

Grace reluctantly let Wellesley go. 'Lily won't like that,' she said slowly.

'She'll have to lump it,' he answered in English, watching Paul clumsily slashing at the bean-pod with his open hand, emitting fierce little grunts as he tried to knock it off its stem. 'Lump it or leave it.'

If only she'd leave it. Well, at least she'd have time to think again, to change her mind. Even — the guilty thought crawled into his head — even to get ill and die. She was of an age for that after all, and she hadn't looked all that well when he'd seen her in Shanghai. He swept the thought out and closed the door, but he knew it was flattening itself outside like a cockroach, trying to creep back in under the ledge. How much he dreaded her coming, dreaded the danger of ruin and disgrace her coming might bring! All his life he'd been raising ramparts against that, all his life making himself secure, and now Lily was coming, sooner or later, to trample all the ramparts carelessly down. And he must let her.

For some reason he remembered the cripple in Mandalay.

And she could have stayed quite legally years and years ago, before they changed the immigration laws. But when she'd come for their mother's funeral, and he'd offered her the chance then, telling himself she was his sister, she was Patrick's mother, after all, blood was thicker than water — she'd only given him a scornful self-righteous smile. 'What would I do here?' she'd asked disdainfully.

Fumbling like Chu

With every winter now the cold seemed colder and longer-lasting. Lily wedged newspaper in the crevices of the loosened window-frames and under the doors; she wore her old quilted coat inside the house and spread it over the bed when, still wearing her woollen jacket, she went to sleep. She even kept her worn cracked leather gloves on unless she was writing or cooking, but still the chill seeped through like damp in a cellar. For two or three hours around noon, if it was a clear day, the sun shone in through the window, and then her feet and hands grew warm and almost supple. She would shift her chair across the floor in time with the sun, keeping its warmth on her face, but the minute it was gone the drained room became cold and sombre again. And shabby.

Then there would be nothing for it but to go out and find the sun in the park. And whenever she did she saw others looking for it, too, especially the old, creeping along the street like stiff-legged crabs, bundled up in their shapeless clothes, sometimes clinging to the arm of a patient bored grand-daughter. They were always on the sunny side of the street; the cold shaded side was for the young, who still walked with a bit of energy and springy hope.

Well, she wouldn't have to face another winter; that was the main thing. When Yin Hong had told her of the delay, she'd felt a great sullen despair at first, like a dark heavy cloud behind her eyes. *I'll never get out*, she thought hopelessly for a time. But then she told herself roughly: *May or June — you can wait till then.* She'd waited long enough already after all, she should be used to it by now.

And now the sunlight in her room was slipping slowly off her face like a fire going out. She watched it moving gradually, a bright warm bar, across the last few inches of wall, until it was gone. At once the room was cold and grey. Yes, like a fire going out. She remembered how the room was when it was her parents' bedroom and it wasn't partitioned and the paint was fresh and the ceiling didn't sag and the gleaming windows fitted their frames — how warm and bright it always seemed then!

Collecting her notes together, she put them behind the medical texts on her bookshelf. Of course, they'd find them there if they looked, but she'd nowhere better to hide them and, besides, she felt a gambler's recklessness now. Her luck must hold this one time at least, just for these last few months. Surely life owed her that. Like the bulging ceiling with its ominous widening crack — she knew it wouldn't come down until she'd gone. Life owed her that, too.

She walked down to the old Public Gardens, now Huang Pu Park. It wasn't far; she could stay in the sun most of the way. And she marched past the shuffling wispy-haired old pensioners as if she were only fifty, no matter how much it made her pant for breath. It was Tuesday afternoon, only three o'clock; but, besides the old people, the usual aimless tribe of the disaffected were wandering in the park as well. Too old to be students, too young to be retired, she knew them for the flotsam of the Cultural Revolution — Red Guards in their teens, packed off to the countryside in their twenties, drifting back now in their thirties, scrounging a living without ration coupons, residence permits or jobs. Like Chu's two sons — she knew she would run into them again one of these days if she stayed long enough. But it was their father she was looking for today.

Chu was sitting on their usual bench, overlooking the river. He was wearing a cap with unbuttoned ear-flaps, and over his blue padded jacket the American college scarf he'd somehow managed to preserve, as he had his equanimity, through all the lost years since his return to China in the fifties.

'How's the Fourth World today?' he asked in his hooty voice, which, as he tried to quieten it, made him sound like a genial laryngitic owl.

'Only notes so far,' she sat down beside him, breathing heavily. 'Outlines, sketches, plans. The actual writing will have to wait till later.'

He showed with a twitch of his lips that he knew what 'later' meant. She watched him fiddling with his glasses, trying to fix the cracked frame with a grubby piece of medical tape that kept sticking to his hairy woollen gloves. 'It's amazing how much you forget until you start writing it all down,' she went on. 'Like that doctor in Shaanxi' — she'd forgotten about him till yesterday, 'who cut condemned prisoners' vocal chords.'

'I guess because we don't want to remember.'

'We should want to. We must.'

'Should a patient want to remember his operation?'

'Patients have anaesthetics. We didn't.'

She was uneasy about her sketches and notes, though. When she read them through, they seemed so heavy and clumsy. Her reading since she left school had been medical textbooks, political pamphlets and an occasional uplifting socialist-realist novel. A starchy diet that had made her own thoughts dull and lumpy. Try as she would, she kept writing prefabricated slabs of jargon instead of plain and simple words that anyone could understand. When she read it through the next day, everything she'd written sounded awkward and obscure. She was fumbling, like Chu with his glasses.

'Why don't you give them to me?' she said impatiently, pulling off her gloves. 'For a former surgeon you have the clumsiest hands I've ever seen.'

Chu watched her ungloved fingers, no more deft than his gloved ones were, wrestling with the tape. When he raised his face gratefully to the last warmth of the slanting sun, he could study her profile, the concentrated frown on her forehead, the screwed-up focusing eyes — she needed glasses, too — the flushed cheeks and still-panting breath. *You are old, you clearly have high blood-pressure, you will be disillusioned in the West, too, he thought. You should make your peace as I have.* Aloud he said: 'I've brought that book back.'

'Did you read it?'

'Some.' He'd found it too grim, remorselessly grim. And he didn't want to be reminded of things like that. And China wasn't Russia. Besides, Wai-chung had made a scene when she saw it lying on the table. 'Haven't we had enough trouble from being mixed up with foreign things already? Do you have to go looking for trouble now, bringing books like this into the house? Suppose one of my students saw it. Pui-yee — her father's a party member. She only has to tell her parents, and then where will we be?'

Useless to argue; she wouldn't listen. She just tightened her lips in a thin bitter line. She'd never believe the Red Guards were really finished. For her, now was just a truce, a lull. They could come back any day to ransack the house again and smash her violin, the pictures, even the Western toilet. Perhaps her fingers, too — it was only luck they didn't last time. Even though they'd been rehabilitated and given that flat, still she was distrustful, half-expecting every morning to wake up and read that the line had changed, or simply hear the battering on the door. She kept the place bare and tidy, like a prisoner in her cell, ready for inspection whenever the wardens came, or the executioners.

So he'd wrapped *The Gulag Archipelago* back in its brown paper and brought it to the park under his arm. 'Things have changed now,' he hooted reproachfully to Lily, as perversely obstinate in her own way as Wai-chung was in hers. 'Why do you have to keep going over it again and again? Why not forget it, give it a rest?'

She handed him his glasses, took the book and placed it carefully on the bench beside her, as if it were a fragile vase. Then she put on her gloves. 'Tell me,' she said unpleasantly, working her fingers deep into the holes. 'Why is it that thirty-three years after the revolution — a whole generation — we still have forced-labour camps, we still have no legal system to speak of, and people who ask for more freedom get put in prison for counter-revolutionary activities?'

'Thirty-four,' Chu said. 'Thirty-four years. Not thirty-three.'

'Is that supposed to make it any better?' And she laid her gloved hand on the book beside her with an air of finality and triumph. As she might have done when she argued the opposite view as a student at St. John's.

Chu fiddled a long time with his glasses, fitting the ear-pieces under his flaps, testing the tape she'd bound them with, shifting the bridge higher and lower on his nose. A sparse growth of glinting white stubble was sprouting on his chin. He could grow a beard if he wanted to, a straggly white one like old men used to wear in the old days. Especially scholars and fortune-tellers, Lily remembered.

'Perhaps freedom is not so important,' he said hesitantly at last. 'What people want first is enough to eat, something to keep them warm, a roof over their heads. And rough justice. Freedom can wait.' His voice had grown hoarser. For a moment it gave out altogether and he sounded like a leaky bellows. 'Rough justice,' he repeated satisfiedly when his voice returned, as though that really hit the nail bang on the head. 'That's what people want. Rough justice.'

Her lips tightened just like Wai-chung's, and her lids drooped witheringly. 'Rough justice?' she repeated with careful precision, as if the words were so unfamiliar she wasn't sure how to say them. 'Is that what I had? Is that what you had? Is that fifteen years for suggesting we might have a bit more democracy? Is that what you mean by rough justice?'

He sighed exasperatedly as if she was perversely refusing to see the point, and they sat for some minutes in hostile silence. Lily watched the ferries crossing the grey wind-chapped river and a black rust-scarred freighter swinging slowly round on the tide to head downstream towards the sea. She wondered how many more times she would see that in her life, and the thought made her unaccountably sad. Would she be sorry, after all, to leave all that behind? 'Have you heard from your sons?' she asked Chu abruptly, but in a tone that offered peace.

'Not for some time.' And he began talking thankfully of his not-quite-abandoned hopes for their future. Perhaps somehow they'd still be able to get into a university or technical institute somewhere, despite being too old and unqualified. There were a few back doors he could still try knocking on.

When the sun went, he accompanied her back to the house. 'If you write to your brother again, would you mind reminding him about those English books?' he asked, contented again. 'And the music?'

The house warden, wheeling her bicycle out, met them at the gate. They all smiled guarded smiles, and the woman glanced interestedly from Lily to Chu. She'd always been friendly to Lily, and even helped her with her case and bags when she moved in. 'Too friendly,' Lily muttered as the woman pedalled off. 'She listens to every phone call I make.'

'Aw, she's just a gossipy old woman.'

'And who does she gossip to?'

They watched her pedal on to Zhongshan Road, her iron-grey hair, sheared at the nape, flying stiff in the wind off the river.

'There may be a reunion,' Chu said absently. 'Class of 'forty-three.'

'Reunion? Reunion of what?'

'Class of 'forty-three. There were twenty-two of us at Boston. Twenty-two Chinese. Most of them stayed of course. I got a letter from one of them. They want me to arrange a reunion, here in Shanghai. They're coming on a tour. With their wives and everything.'

'I suppose the Public Security Bureau read the letter before you did, so why don't you ask them to arrange it?'

'Forty years,' Chu mused in a nostalgic hoot. 'I guess quite a few of them must have died. Three I know of for sure.'

She looked at him with sudden intentness. 'Don't you regret it now, coming back in nineteen fifty instead of staying on in America like the rest of them? After all you've been through, you and Wai-chung?' The question sounded urgent, as though she wanted to wring a confession out of him at last. Or confirmation for herself perhaps.

He didn't move, except to raise his eyebrows, gazing down at the evening flood of traffic washing through the dusk on Zhongshan Road. It was as though he hadn't heard her, too deep in his contemplation of the class of 'forty-three. But then, as she started to repeat her question, he cut her off with a shrug. 'Regrets are pointless,' he said blankly.

Glittering gaily

'There ought to be a special cadegory of award for wriders like Solzhenidsyn,' Professor Branlee declared, holding his glass elegantly, little finger off the stem in an artful curl. 'For condribudions to moral awareness I mean, or something like thad. But nod a lirerary award.' On the three days of the conference on Female Sexuality in Popular Chinese Literature, he'd worn successively Princeton, Oxford and Yale ties, and his transatlantic accent was correspondingly only two-thirds American. Dimitri scarcely noticed it at all, except in the frequent deification of his tees. 'I mean, what has Solzhenidsyn condribuded to *liderary* culture?'

'I'm sure nothing like as much as your paper did yesterday,' Patrick said expressionlessly, but with a pleasant smile.

'Oh, it was just a bagadelle,' Professor Branlee said carelessly, glancing round the room for someone more important to talk to.

'I thought it captured the whole tone of the conference admirably.'

'Oh really? Did you like it that much?'

'I thought it captured the whole tone of the conference admirably,' Patrick repeated in the same deadpan tone.

Professor Branlee's eyes became like those of a man who suddenly senses a ladder being nudged away beneath him. He moved off with an uneasy smile.

'What was his paper about?' Dimitri asked. 'I thought he was supposed to be the star of the show?'

'He was, dear boy, but one couldn't possibly say what his paper was about, since it was the current fashionable twaddle that isn't about anything at all. *Invagination* was the buzz word.' He wrinkled his nose in disgust. 'Apparently lirerary works don't have meaning any more. They are *invaginaded* instead, which I gather means, if one is allowed to use that word, that they are little folds of emptiness which some of us seek to penetrate — not me, I need hardly tell you; I am temperamentally as well as intellectually averse. No association of thought, dear boy, but where is Mila? Couldn't you persuade her to come? I thought she enjoyed watching these academic jamborees?'

'She does as a rule, but her back was playing up. As far as persuasion's concerned, the difficulty was to get myself to come.'

'A conference that should never have taken place, dear boy, is surely one the conclusion of which you should join in celebrating?'

Mila had meant to come. She found academic prima donnas more amusing than the terpsichorean variety, and Patrick's caricatures afterwards were always more piquant if you'd seen the originals. But when Dimitri went home to fetch her she was lying in bed, a hot-water bottle under her back. 'You go,' she said. 'I've twisted something again.' Her face was pale and drawn. Driving unenthusiastically back up the road, he remembered Elena asking Mila some weeks before why she never went to class any more, and Mila not answering, or, as he now thought, answering evasively. A little germ of anxiety was sprouting in his mind.

Robert Smith passed in a suit that smelt of mothballs, bearing two sherry-glasses like a sacred offering before him. 'Local voice was a bit muted in this conference, wasn't it?' he said. 'Apart from my own of course. Pity neither of you could give a paper.' His brittle smile suggested ability was the main problem, not motivation.

'One has standards to preserve, dear boy,' Patrick observed neutrally.

Smith bore his offering away reverentially towards the soignée French critic whom Patrick dubbed 'the salon *marxisté* suffering from a touch of the Sorbonne.' She'd read her paper, ornate with modish jargon, in a weary condescending manner, as if it was too much to hope such remote provincials could possibly understand it, and wherever she went she trailed an invisible scarf of exquisite perfume behind her. Smith approached her devotedly.

'Do my eyes deceive me?' Dimitri asked, frowning across the room at Smith's ankles. 'It looks as though he isn't wearing any socks.'

'I expect he finds it hard to get his boots on, dear boy, now that he's getting too big for them.'

Mila, Dimitri thought. He must get her to go to a specialist. After the Chinese New Year holidays. No point in going before, all they'd be thinking about now would be buying their peach blossom and their tangerine trees, and visiting their relatives for the ritual celebrations. Another week couldn't do any harm.

'I suppose more people die in hospitals over Chinese New Year than at any other time?' he said to Patrick. 'Simply because there's hardly anyone left to treat them.'

'Or possibly more survive, dear boy, for the same reason. What has put that idea into your head, by the way? This conference has reminded me of asylums rather than hospitals.'

'Just the lightness of being.'

'Ah, the irremediable lightness of being.'

They drank steadily, Patrick with exuberant gaiety, Dimitri because there seemed nothing better to do. He watched Patrick with grudging admiration as he quipped his way round the room. Nobody had the right to sparkle quite as brightly as that. It made everyone else feel too dull and stupid. He drank on, growing more and more morose.

Some time later, he realized Rachel was standing beside him, asking Faustus Yu about his anthology of world poetry, and Faustus was telling her he'd only got five more years to go, he'd reached the end of the Qs.

'Who's the publisher?'

'Too soon to think of that,' Faustus said modestly. 'Besides, who'll want to publish twenty volumes anyway?'

'You're a true scholar, Faustus,' Dimitri said, and was detachedly surprised to notice the words came out slurred, as though his lips were numb. 'You're a true scholar.'

Faustus disappeared, and then Patrick was back again. Rachel asked him if it was OK with Chung Yan now, and Patrick said: 'Believe it or not, dear girl, the foolish boy was jealous of you; that's all it was.'

'Whatever for?' Dimitri asked. 'What's Rachel got that Chung Yan hasn't? Apart from unmentionables.'

'Nothing,' Rachel said.

'There you are, then. What's he jealous about?' His voice seemed to be getting still more blurred, still more alien. 'She leaving already? What's got into her?'

'Oh, have another drink, you crude insensitive hetero,' Patrick said sharply. 'I don't want to be bitchy, but really you can he positively crass sometimes.'

But a minute or two later he was glittering gaily again at the other side of the room.

Dimitri had another drink. And, though he couldn't speak distinctly or focus on what people said, inside his head everything seemed bleakly clear. The germ of his anxiety about Mila had sent out little shoots that had quickened others into life, shoots he'd been trying to suppress for months. China would take back Hong Kong, that was certain — either a sudden grab, or else, as the British came to heel, gift-wrapped from London with toothy smiles all round. There was nothing anyone here could do about it; no one was going to give *them* a voice in their own future, so either you stayed put and hoped for the best or you got out. If you could. And Mila at least had no reason to hope for the best. She'd escaped from China once already; she wouldn't want to risk it again. Everyone seemed to be leaving or getting ready to leave anyway. They were all like tenants who'd heard that the landlord they trusted, even if they didn't like him, was selling out to a landlord they didn't trust at all. Clearly the sensible thing was to go while the going was good. But where to? England for him was a land of leaden skies and patient leaden people, who queued long-sufferingly in a perpetual drizzle for buses that were always late and often never came at all. How could Mila stand that, if he couldn't himself? He could still recall the faint sense of nausea that used to seep through his body whenever he landed in England to return to his dreary boarding school after the summer holidays in Hong Kong. The greyness of the light, the coldness of the air, the sad seedy streets of the London suburbs, the impoverished Victorian terraces backing shabbily on to the railway lines — they all seemed to form a chill wet mist that settled in him like rheumatism until he left again. How could Mila stand it, then, she who'd never left the open skies of China? Politics, history, remote indifferent bureaucrats negotiating in Beijing — they were all plotting to make exiles of them, just for the sake of a paltry flag, a tawdry bit of bunting. Exiles from their land, their life, but exiles where? Where would they go? Where would they settle?

He took yet another drink. *I'm very drunk*, he thought distinctly.

Patrick was drunk, too, but exuberantly. His cheeks were flushed, his eyes shone, his voice pealed outrageously. His normally foppish handkerchief hung down six limp inches from his breast pocket. 'Japanese poetry?' he declared, breaking into the breathless circle round the transatlantic Branlee and the perfumed *marxisté*. 'Flower arrangement with words, I assure you. Nothing but verbal ikebana. And as for the Noh theatre . . . well, there they've actually raised tedium to the status of art. Positively uninvaginable, I assure you.'

When Dimitri made unsteadily for the door, feeling his stride was enormous and the room was lurching, Patrick had penned a shrinking Indian lady against the drinks-table and was regaling her with a resounding parody of the paper by a Swiss professor, standing stonily affronted a few feet behind him, on the Psychoanalytic Interpretation of Folk Literature.

'Red Riding-Hood, for instance, dear lady. Isn't it crystal-clear? The little girl in danger of being eaten by a wolf in her grand mamma's clothes? A wholly phallocentrie story, don't you agree? Manifestly the wolf represents the sexually rampant male in search of a little invagination who nevertheless adopts a sexually innocent guise — the grandmamma figure, archetypal symbol of security and protection — in order to lull the suspicions of the young female already no doubt concerned about the onset of puberty — *Red* Riding-Hood, dear lady, compare the *red* snows by which the Chinese refer to menstruation. And as for *eating* her . . . .' He raised his hands, palms up, and rolled his eyes. 'Need I say more?'

'Don't think I've ever seen you so gay,' Dimitri muttered thickly as he swung the door open.

'Dear boy, what a simply *cruel* thing to say!'

Harmonious pair

But it was true; he'd never felt so gay. Admittedly, Chung Yan was subdued and nervy — he'd had trouble with the headwaiter at work — but never mind, Patrick had enough buoyancy for both of them. And they had the whole holiday to look forward to — three days together. He could afford to wait and be patient; they wouldn't be pressed. Already from the balcony he could hear silence drifting over the roads like rain as the traffic dwindled. Tomorrow the city would be flooded by that silence, except for the distant diesel knocking of an occasional taxi and the distant crackling of an occasional firecracker.

Yes, they had the whole holiday in front of them,

He gazed down over the balcony railing at the apron of the visitors' carpark, shaped like a floodlit swimming-pool (he could imagine diving into it), across which two people, a man and a woman, were carrying some peach blossoms. How strange it was to look down on their heads like little black balls and their legs moving beneath them, with almost nothing visible of their foreshortened bodies. Like creatures in cartoons, or from an alien world. He called Chung Yan to come and see, but Chung Yan was scared of heights; he'd never once been out on the balcony. At a party once, Patrick had seen the host climb over the railings of his twentieth-floor balcony and walk round the outside while the women screamed and the men held their breath. It was his party trick; he would do it anywhere. Now Patrick felt a dangerous elation, as if at any moment he might do the same. But the thought of Chung Yen's blanched face and appalled eyes held him back. He went inside and closed the doors.

Chung Yan was sitting by the tangerine tree, glumly fingering the heavy orange fruits that hung down among the deep green leaves.

'I was the life and soul of the party tonight,' Patrick said in English. 'You should have seen me.' He rearranged the long dark stems of the delicate peach blossom in the vase on the table, and gazed contentedly round the room. Everything looked right now: the scrolls, the furniture, the vases, the statues gazing serenely back at him from their shelves and corners. It was worth it after all, spending all that money on them. He'd got it right at last. It wasn't just the euphoria of all the wine he'd drunk; his judgement wasn't at all blurred; he *knew* he'd really got it right. The place was perfect, and not even Chung Yan's glooms could spoil it.

'What about my passport?' Chung Yan said tonelessly. 'You say you get by new year? Why you keep say I should see you at party if you not take me? I think that American girl is there.'

'Is that it?' Patrick smiled. 'Yes, she was if you must know, and I scarcely said a word to her. I'm glad you're jealous, though. It shows you're not indifferent.'

Chung Yan shrugged and pouted. 'And why you haven't get me passport yet?'

Patrick stood back from the peach blossom to admire it. 'Perhaps Nip poetry isn't so bad,' he murmured. 'Flower arrangement with words — it's quite a good idea.'

'What?' Chung Yan sounded suspicious now. Not understanding made him feel talked down to.

'The passport was supposed to be *in* the new year, not *by* it. It takes time, you know. It'll come in the end, though, don't worry.' Would it? Tonight anything seemed possible.

But Chung Yan didn't believe him, and his dissatisfaction disturbed Patrick like a rumple in a carpet. Well, then, smooth it out.

'Look in the bedroom,' he said casually in Cantonese. 'There's something for you, on the bed.'

What eyes he had. How they could change from discontent to doubt, to child-like anticipation. Patrick thought of them both wearing their new gowns tomorrow, walking into this Chinese room like a painting, and being part of the painting. Not even their clothes would jar.

Chung Yan must have moved the pi-pa. Patrick stood it upright again, stroking his fingertips across the strings. The notes tinkled waveringly. The exuberance of the party was beginning to ebb now, like the chime fading behind him. But he wasn't getting low — more like an actor taking off his grease-paint. He wanted to enjoy the quiet now, the release. And Chung Yan.

Chung Yan was gazing down at the two silk gowns, one blue, one brown, that lay outspread on his side of the bed. On Patrick's side was a fine new grey one, six inches longer. Chung Yan's eyes glistened as he picked his two gowns up and handled them one after the other. He held them against himself in front of the full-length mirror, stroking them over his body, striking poses, turning his head this way and that to admire himself. His sulks had evaporated.

Patrick held his own gown up, too, gazing at their smiling reflections. What a harmonious pair they made.

Last Chinese New Year, Chung Yan had wanted to go out to eat expensively — as a waiter he enjoyed being waited on — and then they'd gone to the flower-market in Victoria Park. He loved the crowds, the excitement, and of course being seen. But when Patrick suggested it now (half-heartedly — he was aching to touch him) Chung Yan shook his head. 'No, let's stay in,' he said decidedly. He flopped on to the bed, hugging the gowns across his chest. Then when Patrick lay down beside him he jumped up again, pulling off his clothes. 'I want to try them on, I can't wait till tomorrow.'

The gold chain gleamed on his neck as he turned to reach his arm into the silk.

'Do you realize everything you're wearing now is something I've given you?'

'Not my pants,' Chung Yan said, pulling them off.

'Well, now everything is.'

Chung Yan was too absorbed to answer, strutting and swaying before the mirror, posturing first in one gown then in the other — the flash of his pale skin as he slipped between them! — hands in pockets, hands out, one hand on hip, arms folded, arms akimbo, head coquettishly on one side, hip provocatively stuck out.

'Aren't you going to try yours on?' he asked suddenly, nonchalantly shrugging the blue gown off. It gathered round his hips, but with a little wriggle he freed it. It slithered to his feet, and he paused, glancing down wickedly at his naked body then up at Patrick with raised eyebrows. 'Well?'

Patrick got up slowly, and undressed slowly. Chung Yan waited motionless, eyeing him all the while. Then Patrick embraced him, alternately swallowing him down in great gulps and lapping his lips like a cat. As Chung Yan trailed his fingers down his back, 'What time is it?' he murmured.

'Twenty past ten. Why?'

He shook his head against Patrick's chest. 'You're so kind to me,' he said, pulling him down on top of him on the bed.

When Patrick lowered his head to kiss him again, he saw his own face in Chung Yan's eyes, faintly bulbous and shiny. Chung Yan was watching him gravely, detachedly. Usually he closed his eyes when he was kissed, and it would be the long curving black lashes, faintly quivering, that Patrick saw in the last moments before his own eyes closed. But this time it was Chung Yan who was watching Patrick's face and Patrick's closing lids.

On the bed the broken bottle

He never fully remembered what happened, although he was to recall fragments of it time and time and time again. While it was going on his mind was too shocked to grasp it all, so there were only desultory intense flashes of memory afterwards, like recollections of a nightmare.

His neck bristling with panic a split-second before he consciously heard the door-handle turning.

Chung Yan's startled terrified eyes.

The door flung open. Figures. Faces. Voices. Knives.

Pressing back against the headboard, absurdly clutching his gown over his nakedness. The frantic leaping, pounding of his heart, like an animal trying to escape.

Chung Yan lying still, still except for his hand gripping the blue gown and slowly drawing it up towards his open twisted mouth.

There were only four of them. It seemed like a dozen at first. One of them had a limp, and it was he who did most of the talking, in a greasy voice that had a tone of menacing familiarity about it.

'Lie down on him. Go on. We want to see how you do it.'

'Want us to shove a bottle up instead?' one of the others said.

The crack of glass breaking, the red wine poured over the bed, over their new gowns, like blood.

The jagged green neck of the bottle. When they just touched Chung Yan with it, he screamed. Valmargue 77, with a gold label. Patrick had split a case with Dimitri in some distant careless age a year ago.

Chung Yan's legs spread on the bed, the wine-blood spattered over him. Patrick had never seen anything so obscene or terrifying. Yet he was meekly grateful they weren't going to kill them. Anything, he'd do anything, not to be killed.

Every flash and click of the camera was like a shot. But he knew it meant only blackmail, not death, and he was grateful.

'Do it some other way, come on. Turn him over.'

The one with the limp had brought the pi-pa in and was casually plucking the strings. Patrick was grateful for that, too. Surely he wouldn't be doing something as relaxed as that if he was going to kill them.

'Come on, you're not trying! Make it like the real thing. Do the real thing if you like — might as well enjoy yourself. Go on, have a good meal, ah?'

Chung Yan was as stiff and cold as ice, and he was whimpering all the time. Patrick shunned his eyes. It's not him, he kept telling himself. It's not him I'm doing this to, it's a wax doll. A wax doll that quivered and sobbed.

When they told Chung Yan to get dressed outside, Patrick spoke for the first time. 'Don't hurt him, please,' he pleaded. His voice croaked and trembled.

'Nobody gets hurt if they do what they're told.'

The one with the limp tossed the pi-pa on to the bed, and the strings jangled plaintively. He'd picked up Patrick's hairbrush now and was slapping the back of it against his cupped hand, making a thick plopping sound that he listened to attentively, with enjoyment, occasionally glancing at Patrick still rigid on the bed. 'We'll send you the snaps,' he said, as if doing him a favour. 'See how you like 'em. Then we can talk about you buying the negatives, OK? Wouldn't tell the police, brother, if I were you, in case you were thinking of that. Because then the papers'll get the prints. And your boyfriend might have an accident as well. So might you.'

'Like get splashed with acid,' one of the others said, one with dragons tattooed on his arms. 'Wouldn't like that, would you, pretty boys like you?'

'See these scars?' the one with the limp said genially, opening his shirt. It was like a vast strawberry birthmark all over his chest. 'That's what Ah Keung means. Wouldn't look good on your boyfriend's face, would it, ah? Or yours.' He got up, dropping the brush with a clatter on the dressing-table. 'Quarter to twelve now,' he said matter-of-factly. 'We'd better be going. Don't move till it's twelve, all right? Otherwise Pansy gets it. Your phone's not working, by the way. Better have it mended soon. I'll be calling you after the holiday.'

How long did he lie there shuddering? Long after twelve. Then at last he wrapped his wine-wet gown round him and stepped fearfully out of the bedroom. His heart was still thumping, his legs trembled. Wine dripped down from the gown onto the carpet.

'Chung Yan?' he whispered. 'Chung Yan?'

Nobody. Nothing.

They hadn't forced the door; they must have had a key — but hadn't he put the chain on when he came in?

He looked tremulously in every room, in case Chung Yan was hurt or hiding. But Chung Yan was gone. And his gowns were gone with him. And the clothes he was wearing before. All gone.

And on the bed the broken bottle, with its vicious jagged neck.

15

First moon of the Chinese year

Elena's cat disappeared, on the first day of the Chinese New Year. Usually she slept in Elena's room, on the bed if Elena was there. But now that Tom had persuaded her to move into his mid-levels flat the cat had grown restless, prowling from one room to another, settling nowhere, as if she sensed she'd been finally abandoned. Mila, like most ex-prisoners a light sleeper, would sometimes hear her mewing on the stairs, near where Ah Wong said the ghost walked.

Then, in the first light of the first day of the year of the rat, after the one night in three hundred and sixty-five which was unbroken by the trundling of the midnight road-sweeping truck, undisturbed by the watchman's mad soliloquies, untroubled by the grinding early-morning market-lorries or the squealing of the old scrap-merchant's barrow as he picked through the garbage before the urban council's refuse-lorry came — in the first light of that first day of the year of the rat, when she was for once sleeping undisturbed, Mila was awoken early by the sound of Ah Wong tramping up the back stairs in the half-light. Dressed in her best black tunic and trousers, she was setting out for China, carrying two enormous cloth bundles almost as big as herself, full of toys and clothes for her brother's and sister's children, who would all line up to greet her and thank her, and silently, invidiously, compare the value of their presents. Mila saw Ah Wong gesturing to the cat, telling her to go back inside. Then, half an hour or so later, there was a brief flurry and growling by the porch, and the scamper of clawed paws. When Mila got up a couple of hours later, the cat was gone. Later still, Dimitri found a few dark stains of what might have been blood on the path outside the door.

'Wild dogs,' he said. They came foraging every night from their lair in the hillside behind the house. Often, when he came home late, he would see them by the garage or by the rubbish-bins, shadowy skulking shapes that followed him warily along the path, loping silently, one after the other, a few yards behind him. The pack leader was a half-breed Doberman that gave a warning guttural growl and laid back his ears if ever Dimitri went too close.

When Ah Wong returned, exhausted, after the holiday, the cat was still missing. The crazy night watchman came back the next evening, and she asked him to look out for it. He was followed by a little black and white mongrel dog now, which trotted at his heels as he went his rounds, and lay at the door of his hut afterwards, ears pricked, listening to the man's endless jabbering. The watchman stared at her with his blank bloodshot eyes when Ah Wong asked him, and only shook his head. 'I don't know, I don't know,' he muttered; then, a few seconds later, ignoring her as she patiently asked him all over again, he started off on his jabber once more, in Mandarin, English and Cantonese. Ah Wong could make no sense of it. And still his sad hanging face reminded her of someone, someone from years ago. If only she could remember who, she thought, she could make him listen for once.

Elena accepted the cat's disappearance with her usual composure. 'As long as she didn't suffer much,' she said. It was Ah Wong who missed her most — Ah Wong, who'd fought that grim protracted battle with Dimitri years ago over the placing of the litter-box, and who'd never once picked the cat up or stroked her. For more than a week she went out into the courtyard every evening at the cat's feeding-time, calling her home as she always had, banging her enamel plate with a spoon. And at least once every day she walked round the whole neighbourhood, calling and banging, accosting passers-by, total strangers, to ask them if they'd seen her. Dimitri remembered Helen's funeral; it was Ah Wong who cried openly then, not he or the children — and it was the Chinese who were supposed to be impassive! — Ah Wong, who'd never yielded an inch to Helen right from the start, who'd had her implacable way with her from the moment she walked in with the two plastic bags of her possessions and her dour cantankerous loyalty.

'It must have been the dogs,' Mila agreed. 'But it was all so quiet. You would think she would have made some noise or screamed. There was only a little growling and scuffling, and that hardly lasted a few seconds.'

Dimitri had seen the dogs tearing a stray cat apart on the hillside once. 'They probably broke its neck at the first go,' he said, though what he'd seen there was very different. Necks, backs. 'Why don't you go to class any more, by the way?'

It was late at night. They were lying in bed, gazing up at the swaying branches of the trees outside the window. A silver-bladed sickle moon, the first moon of the Chinese year, glittered fitfully through the branches, and the leaves rustled like rushing water.

'Since I do not perform any more,' she said slowly, 'there is no need.'

'You stopped dancing over a year ago, but you still went to class.'

She didn't answer.

'I wondered if it was your back. It seems to be getting worse.'

'My back is all right.'

'It seems to have been hurting a lot recently, though.'

'No,' she said, too quickly, too lightly.

'Perhaps you should see a specialist.' He turned to look at her.

'I have,' she said, still gazing up at the leaves fluttering like torn flags. Her eyes glistened in the moonlight. 'I saw Peter Denton.'

'When? You didn't tell me.'

'I do not tell you everything I do, Dimitri.'

He couldn't quite see if she was smiling or not, and of course her level tones gave him no clue. 'Well, what did he say? Or is that one of the things you don't tell me?'

'Nothing much. I just have to avoid jarring it, that is all.' She turned on to her side and closed her eyes. 'So I decided to stop going to class.'

After a couple of weeks, Dimitri carried the cat's litter-box out and put it with the rubbish.

'Lose cat, bad luck,' Ah Wong said, watching him carry the box up the back stairs. 'Worse on New Year's Day. Better keep that box.' As if somehow not throwing it away might bring the cat back. But really she'd given up, too. She'd stopped calling and banging, and only sighed occasionally. 'Cats have ghosts,' she said. 'Dogs die, never mind. Cats die, have ghosts.' She pointed to a space above his shoulder, as if the ghost were there already. 'You see them watching you.'

That evening she took out a photo that Elena had given her years before, when the cat was only a kitten, and leant it against the spice-jars; on the middle shelf in the kitchen. Before long the print began to curl, so Dimitri bought a little plastic frame and put the photo in that.

'Spend money,' Ah Wong muttered disapprovingly. But all the same she was pleased, and sometimes talked to it while she cooked.

The far dead wire

The call came at last. It was about midnight, and Patrick knew at once who it was. He answered helplessly, like a man unwillingly assisting at his own execution. Yet it was a relief as well that the waiting was over, that gut-wringing uncertainty which felt by now as though it had been part of him all his life.

'How d'you like the pictures?' the voice asked familiarly, as if they knew each other too well to bother with preliminaries. It was the one who'd done most of the talking before, the one with the limp. He sounded friendly, smarmy, patronizing. Patrick remembered him strumming the pi-pa, smacking the hairbrush against his cupped hand.

He couldn't answer. He felt his mouth open, but his voice wasn't there. Only that curl of panic in the stomach, that juddering of the heart.

'You can have the negatives for two million,' the voice went on calmly, as if offering a favour. 'Two million. Think about it. I'll ring back in a day or two.'

Patrick gazed numbly at the silent black phone, and at his hand holding it like any other hand might hold any other phone. 'Two million?' he whispered. 'Two *million*?' His body sagged on the chair.

The prints had come a few days before, in a plain white envelope posted in Kowloon. He'd had that same sense of participating in his own destruction as just then on the phone, when at last he'd made himself slide the paper-knife under the flap. Then, after the first, shocked, humiliated glance, he'd locked them away in his desk. Later he thought of burning them. But he might need them as evidence. Evidence for what? Would he go to the police? How could he? That would destroy him, too. And yet he might. In the evening, after pretending to be a normal person doing a normal day's work and returning to his normal flat, he unlocked the drawer and looked at the photos more carefully. And he realized that, however gross and crude, they were the only record he had of Chung Yan's face, of Chung Yan's body. He went through them all one by one, all thirty-six of them. looking at Chung Yan alone, with a furtive guilty fascination, like a prurient old man. But it wasn't prurience; it was love. After all, if it weren't for the blackmail, he wouldn't have minded some of them. He put them on one side. A stranger looking at them would never guess the palpitating terror behind those smooth, still, glossy shapes. Chung Yan's wide-gazing eyes, for instance, and his slender arm wound Patrick's bare shoulder, as if they were lying there in a dreamy careless embrace, not —

He went through them again, and again. And again. It was true, you could see beauty there, even in those hard harsh colours. That one, for instance, of Chung Yan's face, eyes closed, lips parted, hair drifting over his lightly frowning forehead — if only you cut off the grotesque tangle of limbs beneath it. Or that one of what appeared a serene gaze beyond the camera, uncorrupted by the contrived contorted bodies, out of focus and crude in the foreground. If those heads and shoulders were cut out and enlarged, who would guess the horror they came from? He imagined them hanging in a gallery, and people strolling round, looking and approving with aesthetic detachment. He'd read somewhere — or had he seen it in some film or exhibition? — that even in the documents of Nazi concentration-camps there were sometimes scenes of awful beauty, some startling look or gesture preserved by the ignorant brutal lens. And weren't there pictures, too, of Khmer Rouge victims who were somehow hauntingly beautiful even on their way to death, as some glance or expression pierced the indifference of the camera?

He locked the prints away again, but each night took them out to gaze at with an aching, longing horror. They sickened him with terror, they sickened him with beauty, they sickened him with pain, they sickened him with desire.

He'd phoned Chung Yan's home from the university the morning after it happened — his own phone wasn't mended for a week. A surprised woman's voice said he wasn't there, and wished him, as he'd politely wished her, a prosperous year. He phoned the restaurant. Chung Yan was on holiday. Of course, Patrick apologized, he'd forgotten. It amazed him, each time he phoned, how normal he sounded, how calmly habit carried him along, disguising the anxiety, ironing out the tremble in his voice. Yet before and afterwards his hand was quivering. After the holiday, he phoned the hairdresser where Chung Yan's sister worked. Patrick used to leave messages for him there, but now the girl said coolly that she hadn't seen him for weeks.

All he had left was the pictures. And the tortured waiting for the phone call, writhing on the hook. He took sleeping pills every night, washed down with half a tumbler of whisky. He slept in the other bedroom — he felt he'd never sleep in that double bed again. He'd put the hairbrush in a drawer, laid the pi-pa out of sight on top of the wardrobe, taken his gown to the cleaner's, and had the locks changed on the doors. And waited with a churning stomach.

Two million dollars. He placed the receiver back on its cradle and stared at it while the words fell through him like lead. *Two million.* If it had been a quarter of a million, or even half . . . but two million! *You're finished, then,* he thought blankly, his stomach cold and still now with the weight of it. *You're done for.* And he could visualize the pictures, smudged but easily recognizable, on the cheap pages of the smutty press, next to the advertisements for sexy masseuses and international escort girls called Ecstasy, Joy or Venus.

But they were going to phone again. Perhaps he could bargain.

He wondered intermittently how it was possible for him ever to forget it. Yet he could, he did. He could give his lectures and teach almost as if nothing had happened, only recalling the reality in sudden gaps between his words, like a man slipping back into the vortex of the nightmare he was struggling to escape from. Those were the moments when his voice faltered in mid-sentence and his eyes emptied. But then, somehow, he would recover and haul himself floundering back into the suspended phrase. Until the lecture was over. Then, when he had no part to play, no audience to act for, the nightmare sucked him down again, down and down. Only, it wasn't a nightmare; it was real.

Was this like knowing you were dying? A sickening, gnawing awareness that was slowly eating you away — and yet there were moments when you forgot it and everything seemed hallucinatorily normal once more?

When he phoned Chung Yan's restaurant again, they said he'd left, he didn't work there any longer, and no, they didn't know where he'd gone. He tried his home and the hairdresser's again. Not there, not there. There was noise, music, talking in the background, and their voices said they didn't care.

It was three days already since the man's phone call, and he'd thought of no answer except to plead with him, to beg him to lower the price. But whenever he tried to rehearse what he'd say his mind was paralysed.

The second call came in the university, where like a fool he'd imagined he'd be immune. It was just after his lecture (did they know that?), and he picked up the receiver unthinkingly.

'Thought about our offer, have you?' the voice asked at once in the same friendly, faintly hectoring manner. 'Don't mind me phoning you at work, do you? Only nobody answered at home.'

Patrick's voice failed him again. He felt panic thrashing the air inside his head. Yet at the same time he had the presence of mind to shut the door carefully with his foot, imagining people passing in the corridor, pausing to listen.

'Well? D'you want to buy them or not?'

'I . . . I can't make it two. I can't make it so much,' Patrick got out at last, hearing a broken frightened man borrowing his voice. 'I mean, I'm only a teacher. I can't get that sort of money.' His words came out in a nervous torrent; so quiet, though, that he wondered if they carried.

There was a silence in his ear. Not an empty silence, but one heavy and solid as an enormous boulder, with a weight that was slowly crushing him.

'I can't possibly get that amount,' he added pleadingly.

The silence grew heavier.

'So you don't want to buy?' the voice concluded, with a tinge of detached reproach — like a salesman whose below-cost offer, made only for the sake of friendship, has been rudely declined.

'No, I do, really. But — '

'Know who'll get them if you don't, don't you?'

'No, I do want to buy them. It's just . . . it's just the price is too high.'

'Well, maybe we can come to an agreement, then,' the voice said, suddenly large and generous. 'If you really want them, I mean. Maybe we can make an arrangement?'

'Yes, yes, I do want them.'

'Well, then.' He sounded relieved himself, as though he wouldn't like any unpleasantness to come between them. 'I'll talk to my partners for you, if you've got a reasonable offer to make.'

If the secretary was listening in, she'd think they were discussing some antique scrolls. Patrick felt abjectly grateful for that. 'Thank you,' he said humbly. 'Yes.'

'Don't mention it. So what is it?'

'What?'

'Your offer. What is it?'

'Oh, well . . . . What about' — he closed his eyes — 'half a million?'

Silence. Blacker, denser, more menacing than ever.

'Hwei?' he asked timidly after a few seconds. 'Hwei?'

'I said a reasonable offer,' the voice said, cold and injured. 'My partners would kill me if I went to them with that, they'd kill me. I'm not so sure you really want these pictures.'

'No, I do, I do, really.' Patrick heard the grovelling stranger who was still borrowing his voice. 'Couldn't you lower the price, though? Please?'

'I said I would, didn't I?'

'How much, then? I really can't pay that much.'

'Well,' the voice said consideringly, 'we'll go down a quarter of a million if it's that hard for you. One and three-quarter million, last price.'

'But I just can't raise anything like that.'

'You sure? Got a lot of paintings and things, haven't you? Worth something, aren't they? And what about your friends? You could touch them for a loan, too. Why don't you ask your uncle? He'd help you out, wouldn't he? If you explained the situation, told him how things stood. I mean, he wouldn't like you to let the pictures pass into someone else's hands, would he? He wouldn't like that at all. Might like to buy them for himself, kind of thing, rather than let that happen, ah?' It was back to the bluff friendly dealer now, trying to do his best for an old friend. 'Why don't you approach him?'

How much did they know about him? How much didn't they? He felt as though they'd put someone right inside his head. His voice quivered. 'You think I should ask my uncle?' he asked meekly.

'Definitely I do. If I was you, I'd've asked him already. Look, I'd like to help you out a bit, but it's my partners, you see; they're getting impatient. I'm having a job holding them back. I'll give you a week, all right? Can't make it any longer, they just won't wait. After that we'll just have to dispose of the stuff somewhere else, know what I mean? And you wouldn't want that to happen, would you? One and three-quarter million and one week, all right? We'll tell you how to pay later. Just tell me yes or no next week. Last offer, all right?'

'I'll try, I'll try,' Patrick promised obsequiously down the far dead wire.

The far dead wire. The far dead wire.

When Rachel knocked and walked in, she saw Patrick sitting at the desk with his face in his hands.

'Oh God,' he said, looking up at her.

'You forgot again,' she accused him.

'No, no, it's just that I feel so awful. I think I'm getting flu. I'm sorry, we'll have to postpone it, I really can't today.'

Flu be damned. That minx Chung Yan again, more likely. She'd pulled *herself* together to come and see him despite her feelings. Surely he could pull himself together, too, whatever Chung Yan had said or done. 'Well, when can we meet?' she said sharply. 'You know I can't get on till we've discussed this.'

He started fumbling through the pages of his diary while she irritably watched. Then suddenly the beaten look in his eyes touched her.

'Are you OK?' she asked, relenting.

'Yes, yes, dear girl. Well, no, actually, I mean. But I hope I will be, in the end.'

His voice was brittle, and he kept turning the pages backwards and forwards as though he didn't even know which week they were in.

Mauve with cold

Ling Kwan leant her head against the rattling window and closed her eyes. But as soon as the bus jolted forward again she in turn was jerked awake. It was cold, too. The raw morning wind, slicing through the cracks, made her shiver. She had only a cheap jumper over the blouse she wore in summer, and her feet were bare in her blue plastic sandals. The girl next to her was nodding, swaying against her. Ling Kwan herself could still taste the fur of sleep in her mouth; she'd had nothing to eat or drink since she stumbled out of bed, splashed her face and hurried down the muddy track to the bus-stop.

Up there on the top deck of the bus, people were standing everywhere in their damp clothes, staring dully out of the windows or smoking. Nobody talked, nobody nodded or greeted anyone, yet they all recognised each other, they all travelled on the same bus every day and got off at the same stop to hurry to their factories or workshops. She thought how strange it was that they still avoided each other's eyes like that and never spoke, and she of course was just the same, she never said a word. She was beginning to feel sick again, what with the swaying and jerking and the smell of cigarette-smoke. She folded her arms and leant her head against the window once more. Two more stops. Her lids smarted when she closed her eyes. What should she tell Ah Keung? She didn't know. She just wanted to curl up deep inside her body and be warm and asleep.

Down the stairs at the bus-stop, out into the damp cold February air, stepping round scummy puddles streaked with blue-green glistening films of oil. She walked past the lorries backed up on the pavement, past the crates waiting to be loaded, past the dinning metal works on the corner, where the workmen just starting their shift grinned and nudged each other as the women passed.

Now what?

The girls were all gathered on the pavement outside the factory, spilling onto the road. 'What's up?' she asked. Then she saw: the doors were still shut and the metal grilles still padlocked across them.

'They've closed down.'

'What d'you mean, "closed down"?'

'Closed down!'

She pushed her way slowly through to the gates. A roughly written notice hung askew on the doors: *This business has ceased operating.* Ling Kwan read the characters twice to make sure.

'What about our money?' an older woman asked behind her.

Nobody answered. People nudged their way to the front, read the notice, turned away to mutter in little groups with their friends.

Ling Kwan huddled against the wall, out of the wind, waiting for something to happen. Only the day before, when some girls had asked about their money, the boss had promised to pay them by the end of the week. Something about the bank clearing a cheque. He'd seemed so large and confident in his suit and his shiny car that they'd believed every word he'd said, and even apologized for bothering him. 'Can't talk now. On my way to a big client,' he'd said. 'Don't you worry about the money, that'll be all right.' And now this. And after lending Ah Keung another thousand as well. She'd only got seventy dollars to last out the month.

The woman who'd asked about the money said they ought to go to the Labour Department. Someone else said the police. But nobody did anything; they just stood about waiting like Ling Kwan, pulling their collars up and turning their backs to the wind.

Ling Kwan watched a crane on the top of the unfinished block opposite hauling up a load of slowly swinging iron girders.

The girl who worked on the next bench to her, who'd come across from Hai Feng County, too, came and stood beside her. 'I bet the boss has gone to Taiwan,' she said, pulling down her lips. 'They're all clearing out because of 1997. Won't be any work for anyone at all before long.'

But she was always full of crap like that, she was just a know-all. Ling Kwan only shrugged and glanced away.

It started to rain. Not very hard, just a few big cold drops that splashed on her hair and jumper. But the sky was getting darker and heavier with it. Ling Kwan huddled closer to the wall. Some of the young girls, just out of school, drifted away to find some shelter. They didn't seem to care; some of them were laughing. It didn't matter much to them, they'd got families to look after them, to find them other jobs.

Then a woman said they were taking people on in a factory in Kwun Tong. But when someone asked where she said she didn't know the name. Everyone's eyes went dull again. The woman who'd first asked about their money said she was going off to phone the Labour Department. She took out a plastic rain-hood and tied it under her chin before she marched off with a real grim look on her face, as much as to say no one was going to do *her* down anyway. The others just watched.

Every so often one of them went up and rattled the grilles or banged on the metal doors, as if she thought the boss might be hiding inside all the time. And the others watched, to see if something would happen, then turned slowly away again when it didn't, their eyes still duller than before.

Some more girls drifted off. Always the younger ones — the older women all stayed, arms folded, faces worried, muttering to each other quietly, like at a funeral. Ling Kwan counted how many were left. About thirty. Must have been fifty to start with. For the first time since Ah Keung had brought her to Hong Kong on Uncle Siu Kong's snakeboat she thought of her home village with a bit of longing. Well, too late now. If only she hadn't lent Ah Keung so much. But when she thought of him on top of her she knew she'd do it all over again. Even if it had the same result. And how was she going to tell him about that, too?

'Let's get out,' the girl from Hai Feng said. 'If the Labour Department cadres come, the first thing they'll do is ask everyone for their ID cards. Then we've had it.'

Cadres! As if they were still in China.

'Think I'll stay on a bit,' Ling Kwan muttered. She didn't want to walk along with her and get her ear filled with all her crap, even if she was right about the Labour Department.

'Suit yourself.' She went off with her nose in the air.

Ling Kwan's feet felt numb. Her toe-nails, under their ragged scarlet varnish, were turning mauve with cold. Now the crane opposite was winching up some timber. What would happen if it fell? She glanced at the men with yellow helmets underneath, imagining the stuff all tumbling down on them and cracking them open like nuts, or like cockroaches when you stamped on them.

Then the woman who'd gone to phone came back. She said someone from the Labour Department was coming, and the police as well. She sounded pleased with herself and looked round at them all proudly, like saying *See what I've done for you?*, but nobody said anything. They all just looked at her and then looked down again or went on muttering amongst themselves. Then an older woman asked, 'When are they coming, then?' and the woman said: 'Right away, they said.'

Ling Kwan decided to go after all. That girl from Hai Feng was probably right. If they came asking for ID cards, she'd had it. And if the police really did come they probably would ask.

So she walked away from the factory, knowing she was walking away from the money they owed her, too. Someone whistled at her from the workshop on the corner, but she scarcely noticed.

There was a shop opposite the bus-stop; she phoned Ah Keung from there.

'Ah Keung?'

'Eh, Ling Kwan!'

'Listen. I've got to see you. Please.'

'I've got to see you, too.'

Make a lot of money

Every few months, Ah Wong took an afternoon off and went to the Housing Authority in Kowloon, to see how her application was doing. As she couldn't read, she often got on the wrong bus once she'd crossed the harbour by the Star Ferry. Then, when she got off and asked people to direct her, they always mentioned street-names she should look out for, but how was she to know which street was which? Was she to tell everyone she couldn't read? And, for some reason, in Kowloon she never could remember the way. She'd been there often enough, but every time was different somehow, what with the building and road-works that always changed the look of things. It was all like a foreign country to her.

This time once again she'd missed her way, and when she eventually found the office, bewildered and over-awed as always by the different desks and counters with signs she couldn't read, a clerk told her she was too late.

'It was only about my number on the waiting-list,' she pleaded. 'I've come all the way from Hong Kong, and they told me the wrong bus . . . .'

The clerk sighed, laid down a sheaf of papers, touched his glasses impatiently and looked across at the pale blue card she was deferentially holding out with both hands. He frowned, took it, turned it the right way round, then dropped it back on the counter. 'At least another year,' he said. 'Your number's got a long way to go yet.'

She thanked him with tittering smiles and nods, and slid the card back into her old black handbag. 'Only a year? That's not so bad,' she said.

'At least a year,' the clerk repeated, thumbing through his papers.

A few years ago, she'd heard on the radio that you could get a room in a government house after you were sixty, but you had to apply two years before because there were so many people. She thought she was nearly sixty then, but she didn't know her age for sure. Nor did her mother. She could only guess to within five years or so; she'd never kept count. All Ah Wong knew for certain was that when she came to Hong Kong as a young girl after the Japanese war they said she had to have an ID card with her date of birth on it, and she'd told them she was five years younger than she thought she really was then, so she'd be able to work longer when she was old. And that became her official age. According to that, she was only fifty-four when she heard about getting a room from the Government.

But she'd asked Dimitri to get the application form anyway, and he'd filled it in for her — she put a cross in the space for her signature. And she'd asked him to write a letter to the Government as well — obviously he'd be able to get her name higher on the list.

'I lost face,' Dimitri told Mila, after he'd had to read Ah Wong the bland official reply that her application could not be accepted until she reached the age of fifty-eight 'in accordance with the age stated on her identity card or other acceptable document.' 'She thinks because I'm a foreign-devil I ought to have some influence with Government.'

'You probably would have if you went about things in the right way,' Mila said calmly. She believed it as well, in the same practical unresentful way that Ah Wong did. It was as much a part of life as typhoons and summer rain, to be accepted and made use of if possible.

'You mean in the Chinese way? Going through the back door?'

'Aren't back doors meant for going in and out of, too?' she asked equably.

So Ah Wong had had to wait until she was officially fifty-eight before Dimitri could make another application for her. This time she was sent a blue card with a number on it, and she guarded it like a lottery ticket, keeping it inside her Hongkong Bank pass-book. Every month, when he gave her her money, she took out her card and asked Dimitri how much longer before she got her room in a government house. He phoned the enquiry number regularly for her, and always got the same reply: one or two years. 'It's like Kafka,' he told Mila. 'They'll keep her waiting till she's dead.' But Ah Wong thought his influence must be working, periodically making her laborious journeys to the office to see for herself how far it had nudged her number up the list.

The traffic, the confusion, the illegible signs and wrong directions, the strain of approaching the superior officials, and the long waiting for crowded buses, trams and ferries — they all wore her out each time she went. She came back tired, pale and irritable; and often weighed down by heavy bags of shopping in each hand — she couldn't resist a market if she saw one, no matter how weary she was.

This time, besides cabbage, spinach, mushrooms, bean-sprouts and peppers, she'd bought some live crabs as well, which were moving about uneasily in a large pink plastic bag, their pincers waving sorrowfully — like people saying goodbye, she thought with a grim inward smile. Her curled fingers were numb with the cold and the weight of her dangling loads.

When she reached the house, she saw Ling Kwan sitting on the gate-post, swinging her feet. A large red-and-blue-striped nylon bag, the kind that people used in China, stood on the pavement beside her.

'Lost the job,' Ling Kwan said in her throaty voice. 'They closed down. Owe us three weeks' money, too.' But she was smiling as if it didn't mean a thing to her.

Ah Wong tipped the crabs into a pail of water and left them in the yard beside the washroom. 'Better come in, then,' she said, rubbing her numbed fingers. She took the key from beneath the flowerpot by the steps and unlocked the kitchen door. Ling Kwan carried her bag down into the basement and shoved it under the trestle bed.

'I'll ask if you can stay here,' Ah Wong said, still rubbing her fingers. 'They won't mind.'

'Won't be for long anyway. Ah Keung's going to find us a place.'

'Ah Keung? Who's Ah Keung? Find who a place?'

Ling Kwan stretched herself out lazily on the bed, smiling a little secretive smile.

Ah Wong stared at her accusingly. 'Who's Ah Keung, you crazy girl? What've you been up to?'

Ling Kwan touched her belly complacently. 'I've got his kid,' she said. 'In here. And we're going to keep it.'

Ah Wong's eyes flared as she suddenly recalled her New Year prophecy. 'I knew it!' she said. 'The day that cat went, there was bound to be bad luck! I knew it!'

'Not bad luck at all,' Ling Kwan said easily, still feeling her belly. 'He's got a big deal on, going to make a lot of money in a few weeks.'

'*Who's* going to — ?'

'Ah Keung!' Ling Kwan said. 'Ah Keung! Then I'm moving in with him. We're going to work together.'

16

Thirty-second consultations

Stella's eyes were pebbly behind her glasses, her face still and rigid. 'What can I do for you?' she asked Patrick. Even on the phone she'd sounded stony, but in person she was granite all through. No wonder, after the way he'd always ridiculed her. But he had to see her first, before going to Michael.

'Nice place you've got here,' he said without conviction, making a show of glancing appreciatively round the cool unwelcoming room.

'What can I do for you?' she repeated from behind the desk.

'Well, er, it's about a friend of mine . . . ' he begun, gazing past her out of the window.

'Yes?'

'Well, it seems he's being, er . . . well, blackmailed about something actually, and he wanted to know . . . I mean, I said I'd find out for him . . . what would happen if, er, if he went to the police about it.'

'Happen?' Stella said after a pause. 'D'you mean the Legal Position?'

'Yes, the legal position.' He felt her eyes interrogating him coldly as he stared doggedly out of the window. Across the road the new Hong Kong and Shanghai Bank Building was slowly rising, a skeleton of massive grey tubes and funnels. When he'd first seen it going up, he'd said it looked as though Meccano had mated with Lego. But that was in another life.

'I mean, should he go to the police?' he said lamely. If he so much as glanced at her he'd cringe, so he just stared at those absurd great tubes like upended plastic sewage-pipes outside the window.

'Clearly, since blackmail is a crime, your *friend* — she paused — 'should Go to the Police.'

'But suppose what he's being blackmailed about is itself a . . . is regarded as a crime.'

'*Regarded* as a crime?'

'Well, technically it is a crime, but it shouldn't be one really.'

'Either it is a crime or it isn't,' Stella said in a voice like sleet on glass. 'So now it appears there are two crimes? Your *friend* — again that little ironic pause — 'should still Go to the Police. That is the Legal Position.'

'Yes, I see, but what I wanted . . . what *we* wanted to know was would the police, er . . . would they be, you know, able to keep his name out of the papers and media and so on?' He did look at her now, pleading.

'No.' She glanced down at her blotter and aligned it fastidiously with the edge of the desk. 'The Court might So Order, but not the police,' she said precisely. 'But in fact it usually gets out by one means or another, whatever the court says. Your friend would be well advised to Consult a Lawyer.'

'I *am* consulting a lawyer.'

'I said your *friend*,' she said, raising her thin plucked eyebrows. 'But I'm afraid we don't handle that kind of case.'

'I see.'

Stella's phone bleeped. 'Yes?' She glanced at Patrick. 'Yes, I'll see him now.' Putting the phone down, she said: 'I think that's all I can do for you on this matter.'

'Thank you,' He got up. 'I'll tell my friend.' He wanted to be dignified, or even mordant, but his voice weakened and he felt his eyes were dark and empty.

Stella watched him through the glass walls of her lenses. 'Why didn't your . . . *friend* come himself?'

'Would your advice be any different if he had?'

'No.'

'Well, then.'

Outside, in the open-plan office, typists were tapping diligently, sipping glasses of tea, one girl leaning back to chat casually with another. What would he give now to be one of them, to lead a normal life, no matter how dull? Normal and safe, sheltered.

'Would you like to pay the bill now?' Stella's secretary asked. 'Or shall I send it?'

What else should he have expected? Why shouldn't Stella charge? And why should she jeopardize her ambitions by representing a blackmailed queer just because he was her husband's cousin — and a queer she disliked at that? No wonder she'd fended him off. No wonder she wanted him to pay.

'Shall I send it?' the girl repeated, arched eyebrow unconcernedly raised. Another girl was leading a well-dressed Chinese into Stella's office. Patrick glimpsed Stella through the door-gap, rising, smiling, coming round the desk to greet him respectfully. He was squat as a beetle, with grey cropped hair, and wore a silk suit.

'Yes, would you send it, please?' Patrick said. 'How much do thirty-second consultations cost?' His voice quivered faintly.

Going down in the lift with ordinary silent men in ordinary dark suits carrying ordinary black brief-cases, he tried to tell himself he'd learnt *something* at least from Stella. His name would get out in the end if he went to the police, even if they didn't prosecute him. So his only hope was Michael. But when he tried to imagine himself speaking to Michael he failed. How could he go to his remote and lofty uncle and tell him he'd been forced at knife-point to bugger a boy on camera because they knew he buggered him off it? As the lift-doors rolled apart and the suited businessmen stepped out, he thought that, although he'd been brought up in Michael's house, and treated like his son, and had even taken his name, Michael had never once said an open unguarded word to him. There was an invisible barrier between them, like magnetic repulsion. It wasn't dislike — he knew that in some ways Michael preferred him to his own sons. It was that inability of his to come close, no matter how hard you pressed. No one ever did except Grace. And, even then, how close? So how was *he* to speak to Michael? And about *this*?

If only he could stop that soft relentless churning of his stomach. If only he could discover it was all merely a nightmare. If only he could go to sleep and wake to find it gone.

He tried to rehearse approaches to Michael as he'd rehearsed them for Stella. But it was no use. Stella was smaller, if harder, and what he'd had to ask her had been smaller. But Michael — all his beginning sentences withered at the thought of what he'd have to say.

Two days had passed. He felt the others pressing on him. He imagined opening the paper and seeing those pictures all over it, with the captions underneath. But how could he tell Michael? Whenever he thought of it, he shrivelled. Perhaps he could speak to Grace first?

And all the time that pulpy churning in his stomach.

Still wheedling receiver

He chose a time when Michael would probably be out reading in the Public Records Office or the University library.

Rags of grey mist hung dripping from the trees and the rooftop when he arrived. The dogs barked and bounded round the taxi; and Paul, seeing him from the garden, came at once to lay his soft welcoming hand on Patrick's wrist and lead him gently into the hall, where Grace was just answering the phone. Was it imagination, or did Paul's eyes really regard him with a mild mute sympathy? And usually Paul would merely follow him about, or else take him to his room to show him his pictures. Why today did he lead him straight to Grace? Waiting where Paul had watchfully placed him, Patrick gazed through his own grey mist at the pale hand still clasping his arm.

'We wondered if we could interview you, Mrs. Denton?' an unctuous voice was asking Grace. 'For the *Social Clime*?'

'Oh, no. Thank you very much, but — '

'We know you have such a beautiful house, and you give such a lot of money to charities,' the voice flowed smoothly on. 'Anonymous gifts, we hear?' A faintly incredulous pause offered her a chance to deny it. 'Our readers would be so interested to read about you. We're very strong on the human angle . . . . '

Grace pictured a grey-haired over-made-up woman decked out with artificial jewellery, a superior assistant in one of the expensive department stores, coaxing rich unhappy women to buy expensive dresses they looked ridiculous in.

'It's very kind of you, but really I'd rather not.' She'd never opened the *Social Clime* in her life, never even seen it except in the hands of people like Belinda Lai.

'It's the portraits page,' the voice oozed on into her ear. 'We do a full-length portrait in your home, it wouldn't take more than an hour all told because I'm sure you must be a busy person with all those welfare activities and so on. We'd just come and talk to you and take a few photos. Would some time next week be convenient? We can arrange it to suit you of course, any time. How about Monday morning?'

Looking helplessly round for some escape from the insistent sugary stream, Grace met Patrick's lustreless eyes and haggard cheeks.

'I believe you have a handicapped child, Mrs. Denton?' the voice enquired, oily with sympathy now. 'It must be a great trial for you. I'm sure our readers would want to hear how you cope. As I said, we do stress the human angle.'

'No, I'm sorry, I can't possibly.' She plonked the still wheedling receiver on its cradle and switched unthinkingly to the Shanghainese of Patrick's boyhood. 'What's the matter, Pak Kay? What's happened?'

Cut the cable

'What are you going to do?' Grace asked Michael that night after Patrick had left.

Sitting at his desk, Michael had steepled his fingers and was tapping the tips meditatively together. 'Bargain and pay, I suppose,' he said, raising his eyebrows. His eyes were staring at the bookcase opposite the desk, but what he saw was inside him. He saw his father bargaining and paying in Shanghai nearly sixty years ago, paying the ransom for his kidnapped son. Was it as simple a decision for him then as it was now for Michael himself? Not if his mother was right about it. He let himself feel the stumpy little finger of his left hand tapping the first joint of its brother on the right. 'He'd be finished if those pictures get out.'

'Into the papers?'

'Anywhere.'

Since she'd left them together in the afternoon, Grace had let the whole business slide out of her mind. She'd assumed from the start it was only a matter of money, and now it was settled she let it recede further, like some disfiguring scar on a jungle river-bank that she'd now floated smoothly past. She often dreamt she was drifting down a wide brown tropical river towards a distant ocean, and the river was gradually widening as it neared the sea. She couldn't make out the trees distinctly any longer, or the people in their stilted huts — only the occasional wisps of smoke from their unseen cooking-fires. Soon all she could see would be the faint dark smudge of the retreating banks on the glittering horizon. And she knew that when they, too, sank away at last she'd have gone too far ever to get back.

In this dream she was always alone, and the slow-flowing water was very tranquil.

'Have you ever read that Maupassant story?' Michael interrupted her over his steepled hands, still thinking of his father. 'About the fisherman whose brother's arm gets caught in the cable as they're pulling in the nets?'

'I did read Maupassant once,' Grace said as if confessing to some youthful folly. 'But I don't remember that one.'

'Well, the only way to save his arm is to cut the cable and lose the catch. And the man hesitates just long enough, thinking of all those fish in the net, so that when he does grab the axe it's too late. So they lose the catch and they lose his arm as well.'

'But you said you are going to pay,' Grace said, only half-following.

'Yes, *I* am.' He leant back, placing his palms flat on the desk to observe his mutilated little finger. 'I was thinking about my father, when I was kidnapped.'

Now she understood. 'But your father didn't hesitate,' she said. 'He cut the cable, he lost the fish and saved the arm.'

'All except the little finger, yes. Perhaps he hesitated just for a second or two. Too long, I mean. Well,' he sighed, 'it *would* have to happen just now, wouldn't it?' He meant: *with Lily coming soon*, but he went on: 'We'll have to sell off some shares, and now's hardly a good time to do that. Or for Patrick to sell off his pots and things. I told him not to.'

'Did he say he would?'

Michael nodded. 'If he had to sell them all in a hurry, though, he'd get next to nothing for them.' He gave one of his rare, rueful, ironic smiles. 'He said he'd pay us back of course eventually. What an idiot he is. Why couldn't he be more careful?' But it was more resignation than anger in his voice. Wasn't it for troubles like this that he'd gathered all his money? That was why, the minute Patrick had started his halting story, his eyes staring at the log burning in the grate, Michael had known he'd find the cash.

He thought of Patrick's fallen face and fallen voice.

'I suppose you'll have to see the pictures?' Patrick had asked, glancing at Michael with his pleading hangdog eyes at last.

Michael had shaken his head. 'Why? It's bad enough that they exist,' he'd said.

Grace left to go to bed. 'Will you tell Lily?' she asked from the door.

He shrugged. 'That's up to him. I can't see why he should, though; it can't mean much to either of them that she's his mother after all. I suppose that has one advantage for her: she won't have to worry whether he became a homosexual because she smothered and spoiled him.' He couldn't bring himself to say 'gay.' It sounded too modish. 'Not that she would have worried, I suppose, anyway.'

'Is that why people become homosexuals?' Grace asked.

Provider, protector

The next morning, soon after dawn, Michael was sitting at his desk again, his hands steepled as before, only now the finger-tips were still, and his chin was resting on them, like a boulder propped to stop it falling. His paper on Caldwell lay in the green cardboard file before him; but, though he'd got up early out of habit to work on it, he wasn't thinking of Caldwell now, and hadn't been thinking of him at all since he woke. Gazing out at the shivering light filtering through the shifting black lattice of the leaves, he was brooding on his sister Lily and her son Patrick, each threatening in their own way to mire him in their troubles. He still remembered the peasant farmyards he used to see as a boy when his father drove him out into the countryside round Shanghai; the dirt, the dung, the grim struggle for life. Now the whole world seemed just another farmyard in which the struggle continued on a vaster scale. He'd scrambled and clawed his way amongst the other animals, out of the muck, up to some precarious niche in the clean air and the sun. But now Lily and Patrick were clinging round his feet, threatening to pull him down again. Why did he feel it was inevitable? Why couldn't he shake them off? Why couldn't he tell them to leave him alone?

Listening to Ah Choi's muttering outside, and to the eager whining snuffling of the dogs, he suddenly understood why. Everyone he knew was first and foremost *someone he had to look after*. Servants, children, wife, friends — whatever else they were to him, his main role was always provider, protector, sustainer. He'd been made — by whom? his mother? — to be a provider. That was his primary relation to other beings. There were few, except Grace, on whom his happiness depended, but many whose happiness depended on him. Those whom he didn't provide for he scarcely knew — unless, like Caldwell, they were dead.

The log from last night had burnt through in the grate. An insubstantial form of grey flaky ash lay in its place around a still faintly glowing core.

From the Yellow Bamboo

How long was it since he'd seen a Shanghai opera, and from the best seats, too? It took you back all right, back to the old Ta Wu Tai in Shanghai, where the manager had orders to throw people out of whichever seats Pockmark Chen happened to want for the night. Yin Hong reckoned he'd hardly seen an opera since those days. What'd he been doing with himself, letting himself go like that?

'Takes you back, this does,' he said appreciatively to Wang, nodding at the stage.

Wang laughed his rolling belly-laugh, stretching his thick legs out into the aisle. Good suit all right, Yin Hong had noticed straight off. Another good suit. Wouldn't mind one like that himself.

'I love this next scene, don't you?' Wang said. 'Remember it, eh?' And he started humming the tune out loud, a second before the actor sung it himself. You got the feeling he could have sung it just as well, too, if not better.

The gorgeous costumes, the singing and the acting, the music Yin Hong drank them all down like he'd drunk the wine down at the restaurant before the show. And what a restaurant that was, too, with all those lights and golden dragons on the walls, and the waiters queuing up to serve you and the view over the harbour, not to mention the best Shanghai food he'd eaten for years, and Wang treating him like an older brother all through the evening, putting the nicest bits in his bowl, asking which wine he liked best and keeping his tea-cup filled. How it must have cost him, he was in the money all right.

How come he hadn't known there was a Shanghai opera in town? Yin Hong wondered, feeling his broken tooth with the edge of his tongue, while the orchestra played an interlude. Living in that dump in the Walled City, he'd really cut himself off. What did he expect? He should've stayed with the Shanghainese in North Point, even if it was more expensive; but that's what it was, money, money, always money, that's what kept you down. Yes, he should've stayed with his own people in North Point instead of letting those slippery Cantonese take advantage of him, and letting himself go, too, just drifting along from day to day. Well, not any more. Especially now they'd gone behind his back with Limpy and Ah Keung.

All through the meal Wang had nodded and laughed and poured the wine as if he knew exactly how Yin Hong felt. And a real fine eater, as well, when he spat the bones out on to his plate he did it behind his napkin, and when Yin Hong noticed that, he did too, remembering his manners after all those years of living alone. Those waiters as well, they knew their job all right, lighting his fag almost before he'd got it in his mouth. Why shouldn't he live like that if Wang could? Wasn't he as good as Wang?

Why not indeed? Wang seemed to be saying in everything he did. *You've only got to make your move. We know what you're worth, even if other people don't.*

The last scene ended in a crashing of gongs and clappers. Wang shouted and stood up to applaud, beaming all over his sleek full face. 'Probably not as good as it used to be, though?' he asked Yin Hong respectfully as they left their seats. 'I expect you've seen better, eh?'

'Well, I did see Mei Lan-fan once,' Yin Hong said modestly. 'You couldn't beat him.'

'Beat Mei Lan-fan? I should think not!' Wang laughed. 'They don't make 'em like him any more.' And he started singing snatches from Mei's roles, in a loud, unselfconscious voice that made people turn and smile admiringly. Yin Hong felt he was included in their respect.

'You could've been a singer yourself,' he told Wang politely.

'Studied it for a time,' Wang acknowledged. 'Got too fat, though,' he laughed, patting his paunch. 'Still love it all the same. What about a nightcap?' He said 'nightcap' in English, but Yin Hong knew what he meant.

Wang took him to another plush place, all red and gold and low lights, and the way he only had to lift his finger you could tell he was known there all right. The waiter offered them a couple of girls, but Wang said: 'Business first, then we'll see, ah?' And he ordered two large brandies. He leant forward when he drank, so that the lower half of his face was lit by the tasselled red silk table-lamp, while the top half stayed shaded as if he was wearing a mask. 'Now, what about this little blackmail job?' he asked quietly, stroking his chin. 'You sure it's the 14K? Someone you know as well, you said?'

And that, too, was something Yin Hong approved of. Wang didn't just rush into business, he took his time about it and waited for the right moment, just like the first time they met. Like Yin Hong did himself, except for that time when he met Snakeboat Wong, and who could blame him then?

But this time he was ready to talk all right, there was no holding back now. It was the 14K handling it for sure, he told Wang. His own brothers, and they'd cut him out, they'd given the job to Limpy and Ah Keung, as if they still didn't trust him, or thought he was too old or something. And he could tell Wang how much loot they were getting and how they were going to collect it, too.

Wang kept stroking his chin all the time Yin Hong talked, leaning halfway across the table. Now and then his eyes gleamed in the shadow, while beneath it his lips smiled, like someone playing mah-jong who sees it's all going his way. And when they'd finished he slid an envelope across the table under his fleshy ringed hand. 'Just a mark of appreciation,' he said. 'From the Yellow Bamboo. Feel like a girl? They've got one or two from Shanghai here, believe it or not.' The cheery laugh rolled up out of his belly like a jolly belch as he placed Yin Hong's hand over the envelope. 'And you'll get some change out of this, too.'

How startlingly heavy and powerful his hand felt as he pressed Yin Hong's down for an instant on the envelope. Like a great bear's paw.

Then, while Yin Hong slipped the envelope into his pocket, feeling how thick it was between his finger and thumb, Wang beckoned one of the hostesses over, a girl in a dark blue cheong-sam slit up to the thigh. 'Lai Wa,' Wang said familiarly in Shanghainese, 'this is my friend, comes from Shanghai, too. You be nice to him all right? He's a big shot.'

'You from Shanghai?' the girl asked, sitting down obediently beside him. 'Which part?'

It made him feel the good times really could come back. Why shouldn't he have a girl again? And why should he still be loyal to the brothers if they weren't loyal to him?

Look what they've done to us

'Well, how was the reunion?' Lily asked when Wai-chung poured the tea. 'Did they all come from America?'

'Most of them, yes,' Wai-chung said. She sat down with them this time, perching on the edge of her chair with hunched shoulders, like a bird too tired to fly any more. *Oh well*, Lily thought, *she'll have a pupil soon.*

'How did it go?' she asked, when nobody else spoke.

'Go?' Wai-chung gave a smile, more like a wince. 'The American Chinese were rich and fat and loud, and the Chinese Chinese were thin and poor and quiet.'

'Except me,' hooted Chu. 'Quiet, I mean.'

'And bitter,' Wai-chung said, hooding her lids.

'Except me,' hooted Chu.

Wai-chung's lips pressed tight, puckering her cheeks. She gave her husband a long cold stare.

'Strange, meeting all those people you haven't seen for thirty-five years or so,' Chu said quickly, avoiding her eyes. 'I thought I wouldn't recognize them, but really their faces were just the same. Only older of course . . . . '

Lily watched Wai-chung's hands, clasping and unclasping in her lap while Chu talked. As if she was only half-listening to her husband while a deeper and darker voice was speaking inside her head.

'You could tell they all felt sorry for us,' Chu went on in his bellowed whisper. 'They thought we'd all made the wrong choice, and had a bad time of it ever since. Of course, they had all the money, there's no denying. They paid all the bills — well, how could we have afforded a banquet in a Foreign Friends hotel? But in the end I thought some of them begun to look a bit uncomfortable, as though they thought maybe *they* were the ones who'd made the wrong choice after all.' He chuckled hoarsely, sipped his tea and sighed, ruefully amused by the irony of it all. 'Conscience, you see?' he said.

Wai-chung couldn't keep her hands still. She kept rubbing the fingers of one against the palm of the other, as if they were burning with chilblains and she was trying to scratch them. But it wasn't so cold now; soon it would be spring.

Spring, and in summer Lily would be off. 'I suppose they're all important people now?' she asked.

'Retired important people,' Chu laughed. 'With nothing to do all day. While we have to give English lessons or violin lessons. It keeps us active, at least.'

He was looking at Lily, but she realized he was really talking to Wai-chung, trying to calm her, to make her believe after all it wasn't so bad, the life they'd had in China. But even as — because? — she realized it Lily was already declaring: 'When I was a girl, people used to give English lessons, too, to students who were going to America, and now they're doing it all over again, fifty years later. Has anything changed? What's it all been for? We'll be having the missionaries back next.'

Wai-chung stood up suddenly with a little gulp in her throat and hurried out of the room. She hadn't even touched her tea.

Chu half-rose, too, as if to follow her, then sat back again with a heavy helpless shrug. His eyes blinked sadly behind his glasses — the frame was still bandaged with that strip of surgical tape.

Lily gazed down at her cup, uncomfortable and almost chastened. She should have kept quiet, she thought. But then she thought why should she? She drank, and gazed down at her cup again. It was one of those blue and white rice-pattern ones, the kind that used to be everywhere, but now you had to ask foreigners or overseas relatives to buy them for you with foreign-exchange certificates in the Friendship Stores. Normally, when Wai-chung left them alone like this, they both relaxed and warmed up, as if a frost had thawed. But this afternoon the chill remained.

'The books came,' Chu said in a loud forced voice.

'What?'

'The books your brother said he'd send.'

'Oh. I suppose the Customs had opened them.'

'I must write and thank him,' Chu said dully, his voice suddenly dropping as if he couldn't be bothered to pretend any more. He stared abstractedly down at the floor between his feet. Then, switching to English, the language of their private talks, 'That reunion really upset her,' he said slowly. 'Yes, she was real upset. I never realized she'd take it like that. Her cousin was there, you see, the one from Colorado. I thought she'd be glad to see him, but he . . . he had his son with him, just finished his doctorate at Harvard. Whereas ours . . . . ' He shrugged. 'That's what upset her; she just couldn't take that. When we got back, she just went to bed and cried. Kept saying "Look what they've done to us, look what they've done to us." Not saying — moaning. Like she had a headache or something. I've never seen her quite like that before, not even in the worst years.'

'Well, what *have* they done to us?' Lily asked sharply. 'If that's what Wai-chung thinks, she's right, and you know it. Or you ought to, at least. Remember how we used to see condemned prisoners being driven through the streets by the KMT, with placards round their necks? Weren't we supposed to put a stop to all that? Well, it's still going on, isn't it? I saw some last week. Only it's *our* police now, not the KMT. And public executions, too. I suppose that's your idea of rough justice, though.'

'Bad elements.' Chu waved them away with his hand. 'Murderers, rapists, crooks. They deserve to be shot.'

'Bad elements? The police were just filling up their quotas! And what sort of trial did they get, may I ask? Don't you realize it could be our turn again next?'

Chu shook his head, frowning and grimacing as if he'd just tasted something sour. But he didn't answer.

Next door a beginner's unsteady bow started an awkward scale, faltered, started again, and faltered yet again, like an old man clambering stiffly up an unfamiliar stairway.

They listened silently for half a minute or more. Lily thought of the prisoners in the police trucks, their heads bowed, hands tied behind their backs, the white rectangular placards which announced their crimes covering their chests. And later a red line drawn through their names on the notice outside the court. Each line meaning a bullet in the back of the neck, in front of thousands of spectators in the public stadium.

'Were they what you wanted?' she asked coolly. 'The books my brother sent?'

'Sure, they were great. I'll write and thank him. But how would I know if the Customs opened them? They were just wrapped up in paper and string. No glue or anything. How would I know?'

'Like that,' Lily said. 'They don't let anything in unless they can unwrap it, do they?'

Everything was different

Whenever she had to phone, Ah Wong brought a much-creased scrap of paper up from her room, smoothed it out and placed it carefully on the directory. Large quavery numerals were written on it in her clumsy childish hand, and she would examine them anxiously as she matched them with the numerals on the disc, frowning near-sightedly as she gingerly dialled. Then she would straighten up and listen, holding the receiver carefully in both hands like a child with a sea shell, her eyes alertly unfocused, waiting for the faraway voice miraculous as the sound of the sea.

And when it came she would give a little start of pleased recognition, and shout down the wire, to make sure her words travelled all the miles between them. She always began standing up, and ended squatting on the floor, cradling the receiver protectively all the time in both her hands — it cost nothing to make a call, but she was always apologetic, as though she were handling someone's precious vase which really she had no right to touch. Her phone calls were rare, so they were long. And they were public. She would keep her voice up, sending it on its way, whoever might be passing near the phone. Besides, she usually chose to phone at meal-times, knowing that no one else would want to then; and since the phone was just outside the dining-room it was hard to ignore what she was saying, especially as she usually gave a commentary on it when she interrupted her shouting to remove plates or bring food in from the kitchen, so that they often heard it all twice over. Down the years Dimitri had come to have an intimate, if piecemeal, knowledge of her brother, sister, cousins, nephews and nieces, most of whom he'd never set eyes on, although he recognized their voices — a knowledge acquired at the cost of food that was often burnt or cold.

With Ling Kwan, everything was different. She received many calls, and made many. She talked only briefly, she never apologized and she was always secretive. She tried to phone when no one was near. And if anybody passed she would lower her voice. And it always seemed to be the same man she was phoning. Already on the day she came the phone rang about midnight, and a strange man's voice, raised above the noise of Cantonese pop music and blurred raucous talking, asked curtly for Ling Kwan. It happened often afterwards, always late at night. Each time the man brusquely uttered her name, without so much as a please or thank-you, and each time he seemed to be speaking from a room full of people clamouring above a blaring continuo of Cantonese pop. The first night Ling Kwan climbed up slowly from the basement, sulky with sleep, but on the following nights she seemed to have been waiting, and ran up the cement steps eagerly.

Otherwise she kept to her aunt's room, listening to the radio or eating the food Ah Wong cooked her. Occasionally she would wash up or peel the vegetables, but it was always lethargically, in a faintly sullen manner, and it was always she who was sitting on the old white wooden chair, which Ah Wong used only as a ladder to the upper shelves, while her aunt was bustling about on her feet. She barely acknowledged Dimitri or Mila when they came in, giving them only a droop of her lids, often followed if it was Dimitri with a slow sidelong glance. If she'd been talking with her aunt, they both stopped until they were alone again. Ah Wong, as if embarrassed by her niece's manners, would smile and titter on her behalf.

'She is a slut,' Mila said, classifying rather than censuring.

Elena, on one of her infrequent visits, said Ling Kwan was giving Dimitri the eye. 'You'd better watch out, Dimitri, you're at a dangerous age. I know one job she'd get quite easily anyway. In a Wanchai bar.'

'How would *you* know?' Dimitri asked.

In fact the two girls regarded each other frankly whenever they met, and smiled with friendly curiosity, as though they recognized some kinship under the skin. But they hardly spoke.

Rite of Spring

Then winter suddenly passed, from one day to the next. On the evening before, the skies were still cold and grey, monotonous as a celestial steppe. The next morning Dimitri and Mila woke sweating under their quilts. Warm southerly winds had shredded the clouds till they lay on the hills and the sea in thick fleecy bundles of mist, waiting for the sun to burn them away. Foghorns bellowed day and night in the harbour approaches as forlornly as lost whales, while inside the house the walls sweated drops of humidity, and the wooden floors grew dark and wet. Their shoes bloomed with whitish flowers of mildew overnight.

Ah Wong closed all the windows to keep the moisture out, Dimitri opened them to avoid suffocation. Then Ah Wong closed them all again. It was the same every year. 'Is it the Rite of Spring?' Mila asked resignedly. She never took sides between them — to Ah Wong she was only the second wife, and Ah Wong had been there first.

The days became gradually longer and warmer. Soon the sun was setting at half-past six. Before long it would be hot enough for the air-conditioners.

Coming home at dusk, when the light was still just glowing on the clouds that draped themselves indolently over the Lantau hills, Dimitri saw

Ling Kwan leaning against the tree-shadowed wall, in the arms of a man. She was nestling her face against his chest, her back to Dimitri. The man, young and muscular, with tattooed arms, glanced at him indifferently over her head, then bent to whisper something in her ear. Dimitri heard her chuckling as he walked on, passing the singing watchman with his mongrel dog. The watchman ignored them all — Dimitri, Ling Kwan, the man — shuffling past them with his wild dazed eyes and ceaseless mutter as if they were only bushes or stones.

'So she has a lover,' Mila said in bed that night. 'Perhaps he will take her off our backs?'

'I'm sure he'll have her on hers anyway. Speaking of which, how is yours these days?' He drew her closer, kissing her throat.

'Lover? Or back?'

'Both.'

'You can find out if you like.'

He wanted to be careful, but she moved so freely he forgot about her back, and for a time about everything else as well.

'Not bad, all things considered,' he sighed afterwards. 'What do you think?'

'I think my back has got much better since I have been having acupuncture. My lover is about the same.'

'You didn't tell me you were having acupuncture?'

'You would only have scoffed.'

'No.'

'Of course you would.' She thought of the elderly man in Happy Valley with his old-fashioned glasses and old-fashioned manners. And the old dusty charts on the wall. 'You think a doctor has to have a white coat and a certificate.'

'I'm a very open-minded person. The only things I scoff at are the *I Ching* and Yin and Yang, and what sane person wouldn't scoff at them?'

She smiled silently, her eyes loosely closed. The bedside lamp made shadow-pools beneath her eyes and beneath her high cheekbones. He trailed his finger slowly across the pools, then down her neck, her breast, her side. On her thigh a tiny frozen drop lay, silvery as frost. He touched it lightly. 'Remember my poem?'

She smiled again, sighed and stretched. 'Switch off the light.'

'Remember my poem?'

Her face vanished as he pressed the switch, then slowly reappeared, paler and more shadowy. 'Yes. But you are better at this. You always were.'

'It must be the spring. Or seeing those two outside tonight.' He propped himself on his elbow to look down at her. He could never tell how to take what she said unless he watched her face. It was with her smile that she expressed irony or mockery or whatever, not with her voice. In English, at least, she was an inscrutable oriental. 'It's been a long time.'

'Since your poem?'

He touched her thigh. 'Since this.'

'Oh, that.' Her smile widened.

'You never thought I'd get it published, did you? My poem?'

'I would not say that,' she murmured drowsily. 'The letters column of the *South China Morning Post*, for instance. I expect I thought you could get it published there.' Then she pulled his head down on to her shoulder. 'Sleep,' she said.

But it had been in one of the literary magazines in England; that was what had pleased him, and still did. Not one of those pseud ones whose editors wore dark sunglasses in winter, beards, beads and chains, the whole phoney lot, but a real one that published real poets like Philip Larkin.

Was it the foghorns' lugubrious lowing that brought that back to him now? But it wasn't that time of year when he wrote it; it was autumn and winter, the bleak season of his life as well, when Helen had killed herself and Mila had returned to China — for good, he'd thought, and so had she. He couldn't recapture now what it felt like then to wake up in the small of every night to his heart's lonely thudding, and to broken images, words and rhythms tumbling through his head like falling stones. He would be awake for hours as the lines slowly formed themselves, until at last they let him sleep again. He didn't write them down at the time. There was no need. He was serving a sentence in solitary confinement, not composing poetry, and the words were the words of his sentence, being branded on his mind. They went in deep; they were always there in the morning when he woke exhausted, the first thoughts that came into his head. Weeks later they were still there, scars in his mind, and then he wrote them down — it seemed they wouldn't leave him till he'd done so.

He'd gone on for five or six months like that. Sometimes he thought the nightly torment was driving him mad, sometimes he thought it was what kept him sane. They were the only poems he'd ever written since adolescence, and he'd never written another one since. If it was catharsis, it was cruel but complete.

Years later, after Mila had come back, he'd shown them to her. 'I do not understand them very well,' she smiled, speaking her deliberate inexpressive English. 'But are they not rough diamonds?' As usual, he couldn't tell whether she was gently mocking or praising them — or both. Was it 'rough' or 'diamonds' she meant to emphasize? The nuns who'd taught her

English had taken such pains to efface her vivid Cantonese tones that they'd taken out expression altogether.

Anyway, he took the most promising diamond and cut and polished it — he wanted to make those stark months, even so much later, yield something of value. He sent it off under a pseudonym, and to his incredulous amazement the magazine accepted it; they even asked for more. Mila smiled when he showed her the letter. 'I will have to leave you again,' she said. 'For the sake of your literary career.'

But he'd never even wanted to write another poem — if that was the price, it was too high. That one was something he could hold on to, though. It was a smooth solid pebble he could close his hand round, instead of the desiccated sands of academe that normally slipped between his fingers, leaving them empty and dry.

'It makes me feel less of a parasite feeding on the corpus of literature,' he'd told Patrick, the only other person who knew.

'Corpse, dear boy, not corpus,' Patrick had corrected him languidly. 'By the time our department's finished with it.'

The next evening Ling Kwan had gone.

'To live with a friend,' Ah Wong said tersely when Dimitri asked about her. 'Has she got a job?'

Ah Wong, busy at the oven, seemed not to hear.

'Has she got a job, Ah Wong?'

'Uh? Yes, soon, soon,' Ah Wong replied peevishly, without turning round.

Despite all his years in Hong Kong, Mila murmured to him in the hall, he was still a clumsy foreign-devil. 'Didn't you see she did not want to answer? She had drawn the curtain.'

'Well, I suppose it takes a Chink to see through a chink,' he answered tartly, stung as always by her we-Chinese-you-barbarian number.

But she was right of course. For all the knowledge he'd acquired of Ah Wong's world, he knew there was an exclusion zone he was forbidden to enter. She was the centre of an intricately spun web connecting her to people and places and things he'd never learn or even dream of. He saw the beginnings of the delicate threads, and a little where they led, but not at all where they ended. In a traditional Chinese house you were invited only as far as the guest-hall.

Near and bleeding

It was the kind of place Patrick would never normally set foot in; but, then, this was hardly a normal occasion. It was garish, noisy and crowded. Cooking smells billowed out through the thumping, swishing swing-doors to the kitchen, and the clatter of pans and dishes, the shouting of cooks and waiters billowed interruptedly out with the smells. The customers, judging by the look of them, were all from the nearby housing estates, large family groups vociferously exhilarated after the week's work. It was the kind of place where the food was cooked at seven and warmed up at eight. The kind of place you had to shout to be heard in. The kind of place Chung Yan would have wrinkled his nose at disgustedly and refused to enter.

Chung Yan. Not a word or a sign. If only he could see him just once. Just once.

A plump greasy-skinned girl in an over-tight vulgar red cheong-sam, was stationed by the door, beside a long bubbling tank full of sentenced fish mournfully exercising like convicts on Death Row. She'd asked him how many people when he came in.

'I've reserved a table for five. For nine o'clock.'

She led him with waddling hips to a corner by the window. He sat facing the door so that he could see them arrive, gripping the brief-case tightly on his lap. He'd never realized so much money could be packed into so little space, and weigh so little, too. One small envelope held a hundred thousand without the slightest difficulty. It seemed to trivialize the whole affair. He was carrying as much as the restaurant was worth, and it weighed no more than a library book. Blackmail ought to be more solemn, more ponderous.

Strange how calm he felt now, though, his heart beating only a little more quickly, his muscles only a little more taut. Ever since they'd settled on the price, he'd dared to hope a little, like a man who learns his illness may not after all be fatal. It was Michael's own monumental calmness that had done it of course — his advice, his listening-in to the phone calls, his nod or shake of the head as Patrick answered them. Yet not once had Michael asked him how it had happened, or about Chung Yan or about anything at all, except what was necessary to deal with them. Like an aloof consultant who stopped gravely by a sick man's bed, listened to his symptoms and prescribed the cure without even examining him, let alone asking who he was or where he came from. He still didn't want to see the prints — they might not exist for all he knew — and whenever Patrick promised he'd slowly pay the money back, Michael merely smiled and shrugged as if he didn't want to hear about it. No word of blame, nor of sympathy for that matter. No further mention of it once it was settled — no further interest apparently, as if he'd merely been dealing in stocks and shares. You'd think he couldn't have cared less, except that he'd immediately done so much. And it was that practical matter-of-factness that had calmed Patrick. Well, now, in an hour or so at most, it should all be over. He'd be free again.

Free. He just wanted to be free of it all at last, free. Free of this constant nagging fear.

At the next table a sour-looking grandmother was keeping stern watch through her silver-rimmed glasses on her daughters-in-law and their noisy children, while her sons ate their rice with dour silent gusto.

It was twenty to nine. Would they be late? There was a constant tingling in his body, as close to excitement as to fear. Would they come at all? He knew they would, as a prisoner knows he's due at last for discharge.

A waiter brought a pot of tea and filled his cup. The way he stood as he poured — leaning slightly back from the hips, casually graceful — reminded Patrick faintly of Chung Yan. Patrick said he'd order later. He sipped the tea; it wasn't too bad. Chung Yan, Chung Yan.

He checked the time once again — quarter to nine now — and wound his watch unnecessarily. Turning the curled knob between his finger and thumb, he wondered whether they'd be wearing digital watches. Of course they would; they'd go in for everything new and flashy. And then he wondered of all things if he'd feel shy with them — after all, the last time they'd seen him he'd been in *flagrante delicto*. How strange to wonder about that! But he knew he wouldn't feel shy; they like Michael had turned it into an impersonal business transaction, so that in the end you couldn't feel anything — not embarrassment, not anger or hate. The man he'd dealt with on the phone was invariably like a friendly salesman, keeping the menace in the background of his voice. Of course, the little maggots of fear still wriggled inside Patrick, nibbling gently at his stomach, but if — *when* — they handed the films over he'd feel only an enormous lightness and relief as the maggots died. Not hate or anger, let alone embarrassment.

He poured some more tea. Ten to nine. Thank God it would all be over before his mother came. He couldn't have handled them both together. He wondered sometimes if somewhere in his being he resented his mother for abandoning him as a baby when she went off with the Red Army. But it would be irrational to resent it really — he might have become a Red Guard if she'd taken him with her — or a Red Guard victim — and who could resent missing that? No, he just didn't care about her one way or the other, that was all.

How his mind wandered while all the time he held the brief-case tight in his hand. Yet all the time, too, there was that faint tremor of anxiety and anticipation running underneath his thoughts, as there used to be when he climbed up to dive from the top board at school, and odd stray thoughts dropped into his mind, inconsequential yet sharp and vivid, like bits of blue sky and white cloud from some vast mental jig-saw puzzle he would never complete.

By ten past nine, though, there were no more thoughts, only that light, nervous, tingling current of apprehension, growing slowly stronger and stronger. He sipped the cooling tea again and again, watching the entrance while his other hand drummed anxiously on the handle of the brief-case. The girl in the tight red cheong-sam stood chatting with a waiter when things were slack. Her boyfriend probably. He tried to imagine them leaving work together, travelling on the same bus, spending their days off together, normal people. But the flow of anxiety was too strong. Everything else paled and faltered. Perhaps they weren't coming after all.

He didn't see them till they were almost at the table. They must have been in different corners of the room; they must have been watching him all the time, making sure he was alone. He might not have recognized them if he'd seen them — except the leader, and then only by the way he limped, swaying from side to side. And perhaps not even him, if he hadn't nodded and raised his hand. But Patrick knew the voice at once.

'Shake hands,' the man said in a quick low voice. 'Shake hands with all of us, that's right. And change places. I don't like sitting with my back to the door.'

Patrick obediently shook their hands, and their hands were just like ordinary hands. He smiled wanly at them, and their answering smiles were just like ordinary smiles.

'Now pour us some tea. Good, that's the way. Take it easy. Don't spill.'

And each one in turn tapped the table politely with his middle finger as Patrick unsteadily poured, just like ordinary people.

'I thought there were four of you?' Patrick asked, in a voice that was almost ordinary, too. Only a little high, only a little wobbly.

'There are. Ah Keung's keeping an eye on things outside, just in case.'

The other two had left the seat next to Patrick empty, as if it was they after all who felt shy, not he. Now they started talking quietly to each other, occasionally looking over their shoulders. The stern bespectacled grandmother, slipping an incurious glance over them all, had begun picking her teeth, watching her grandchildren play the finger-guessing game with a kind of disapproving benevolence. *I'll remember her for the rest of my life*, Patrick thought.

'Here's how we'll do it,' the man with the limp said, holding the menu close as if to study it. 'You put your case on the empty chair. Fat Boy and Woodchopper take it to the toilet and check it. If it's OK, they take off with it. Then I go, too. The films are in this bag on my lap. I'll leave it on my chair. What're you having to eat? Want me to order?'

'How do I know the films are all there?' Patrick's voice quavered only mildly. He was listening to himself like a self-conscious actor. So it's really happening, he thought fleetingly. Life doesn't imitate art; it imitates B movies.

'Talk about trust! You can look at them while these two are checking the money. Then your troubles are over. What're you having?'

Despite the apparent assurance in his voice he was speaking very fast. And the menu was trembling faintly in his hand. So he was acting, too. Patrick thought of the silver hairbrush in the man's hand, slapping against his palm. And the pi-pa. He'd started using the brush again after all. There seemed no point in getting another one. He'd washed it and used it. But he hadn't played the pi-pa; that was different. You had to be in the mood for that.

When the man had ordered, he laid the menu down. 'All right, then?' he asked Fat Boy.

Patrick wondered in that same disconnected way if he would ever know what the man with the limp's name was. Did he have a nickname, too? And, while he wondered, he heard himself say: 'Could you tell me . . . do you know what's happened to . . . to, you know, the boy who was with me?'

'Gone missing, has he?' The man looked at the others, and the others looked back at him, fractionally shaking their heads and shrugging.

It came too pat, Patrick realized. They were holding back. But he was grateful they didn't snigger. So they knew where Chung Yan was, and that meant Chung Yan —

'They do that, you know,' the man said knowingly. 'Fickle. Like women.'

'Because I wanted to give him something,' Patrick said, pleading in spite of himself. 'I mean, I'd known him quite a long time.' He hadn't even said goodbye.

'Fickle,' the man said with a thick little giggle. 'They're like that, aren't they?'

Fat Boy swallowed some tea, pushed back his chair and stood up, taking Patrick's brief-case. 'Bit light, isn't it?' he grinned, and by his grin Patrick remembered it was he who'd taken the pictures and ordered him how to pose. 'Sure it's not empty?'

Patrick smiled weakly and turned back. 'Can I see the films now, then?'

'Why not?'

As Patrick bent over the man's bag, fiddling with the clasp, some waiters approached the table. *Ready-cooked food*, he thought detachedly. *Just warmed up*. His fingers, normally quite agile, fumbled nervously with the catch. Fat Boy and Woodchopper were leaving. Fat Boy muttered 'Fuck!' as if he'd dropped the brief-case, but when Patrick glanced up he saw that the waiters weren't waiters at all, and it was knives they were carrying, not food.

A sudden grunting flurry of stabbing and slashing. Fat Boy screaming, the two others wildly ducking and dodging, then seeming to give up and stand horribly still, hissing and groaning, before collapsing like burst sacks on the floor. The furious slashing and stabbing continuing for some seconds on their inert bodies. Then it was finished, the attackers were gone, Michael's brief-case with them. No one had said a word.

Patrick's eyes saw a scene his mind could not believe they saw. They saw the man with the limp, whose name he'd never learnt, labouring to get up, gasping blood, eyes glazed, pulling the tablecloth off as he clutched it. They saw Fat Boy lying still, blood spurting in slower and slower gushes from his throat, a digital watch, with the strap severed, lying spattered with blood on the floor beside him. They saw Woodchopper lying in the foetal position, moaning, clasping his belly with both hands, blood leaking steadily out between his fingers.

Digital, Patrick thought numbly, still holding the bag up defensively in front of him. *I knew it.* There was blood on the bag, on the table-cloth, on his jacket and trousers.

Oh God, let it not be true.

The next table had collapsed in the fight. The grandmother, pinned against the wall, was bellowing monstrously, wordlessly, in a wild low voice, like a cow at the slaughterhouse, her silver-framed glasses dangling from one ear. The three grandchildren were cowering against the upturned table, eyes stained with silent terror. One of them had his fist in his mouth.

Oh God, let it not be true.

Then at last Patrick started shaking. His whole body quivered and jerked as if he were being electrocuted with jolts of ten thousand volts. He saw there were people shouting and screaming all round him now; he saw that everyone in the restaurant was rushing across to gape in greedy horror, but it was as if they were behind a glass wall, eternally remote. All that was real was near and bleeding, or, like his own body, shuddering to the marrow of its being. *So I'm not free after all*, he kept thinking while he shuddered.

17

Small shadow of Patrick

The phone rang and rang and rang through Dimitri's sleep, so that as he slowly dragged himself awake he dreamt for a few moments that there was a great bell sounding from the depths of a calm clear sea, dreamt the bell was lying on its side on the ridged white sand, rocking slowly in the currents and gently chiming all the shimmering way up to the surface.

Then, shedding the last warm sheltering layers of sleep, he raised his head and reached for the phone.

'Mr. Johnston?' a man's voice asked.

'Yes?'

'Mr. Dimitri Johnston?'

Elena! he thought, *Alex!* knowing at once it was the police. The grave slow tone, the particularity of address, making sure they'd got exactly the right person — he remembered them instantly all the way from fifteen years ago. It might even have been the same voice. 'Yes?' he said tautly, visualizing a smashed and twisted car.

'Sorry to disturb you, Mr. Johnston,' the voice went on at its disciplined, measured pace. Following the prescribed drill presumably, breaking the news slowly, making allowances for sleepiness, ensuring each word sank into the confused, alarmed mind. 'Western Police Station here. Detective Superintendent Holmes.'

'Yes. What's happened?'

'Nothing to worry about Mr. Johnston,' the voice assured him smoothly. 'Only we've got a Mr. Patrick Denton here, says he knows you.'

'Oh.' His whole body sighed relief through his voice. It wasn't Elena. It wasn't Alex. Only Patrick.

'You do know him?'

'Yes, I know him.' Dimitri visualized a caricature of a village policeman to match the cautious plodding voice, a man licking his pencil and holding his notebook out at arm's length, frowning with effort as he read.

'Well, he's been in a spot of bother, and he gave us your name. He's perfectly free to go home now, but he's in a bit of a state. Shock, I mean. I don't know if you could possibly come and pick him up, Mr. Johnston, or . . . ?'

'Er, yes, I suppose so. Was there an accident or something?' But 'a spot of bother' didn't sound like an accident. Or like being arrested for buggery, either, for that matter.

'Well, not exactly an accident. A spot of bother,' the voice said enigmatically. 'I could explain a bit more when you come.'

Dimitri erased the village bobby and drew a sage discreet man in tweeds, fiftyish, with a pipe and significantly hooded lids.

'Would it be possible for you to come now, or . . . ? '

'Well, I could get there in half an hour, about. Would that do?'

'Yes, that'd be fine, Much obliged, Mr. Denton.'

'Johnston, actually.'

'Mr. Johnston, I mean. Forget my own name next. Which is Holmes, by the way.'

'As in Sherlock? How appropriate.'

'Not quite. Eh Cho eh, Emmy 'ess.'

' 'ess?' Dimitri repeated confusedly, wondering wildly if Hess had a daughter. 'Sorry, don't think I got that?'

'My name, Mr. Johnston. It's spelt H-O-A-M-E-S.'

'Ah.'

'Not H-O-L-M-E-S.'

'H-O-A-M-E-S, right.'

'Just ask for me when you get here. I'll tell them to look out for you.'

Mila had propped herself up on the bed, interrogating him with raised eyebrows.

'Patrick,' he said. 'At Western Police Station, in a state of shock.'

'Patrick? Why?'

He shrugged. 'Been in a spot of bother, whatever that means. He was rather cagey. Wouldn't say any more.'

'Patrick said he'd been in — ?'

'No, that was a detective I was talking to. He said it.'

'Oh.' She lay back. 'They want you to pick him up?'

'Perhaps someone beat him up for making a pass at him.' He started dressing. 'What time is it?'

'Nearly four.'

She gazed up at the ceiling, he down at the little brown travel alarm he kept by the bed. They were both remembering.

'Haven't been in Western Police Station since our case,' he said slowly. 'Fifteen years ago.'

'Shall I come, too?'

He shook his head. 'Haven't been in one at all, for that matter.'

'I have,' she said in her thoughtful detached voice. 'But not in a British one.'

He took the harbour road to the police station, driving past the empty markets and the sleeping barges. Occasionally his headlights slipped over watchmen dozing on charpoys, or over street-sleepers lying with their parcelled belongings in shop-fronts. At the tram depot, some maintenance workers were drinking tea beside an unlit tram. With its pole swinging out away from the overhead wires, the tram looked helpless and vulnerable, like a dismasted yacht. At the next corner, as his wheels juddered over the gleaming tram-lines, a pack of memories leapt out at him. *Our case. This is where our case started.* Fifteen years ago he'd been stopped just there in the old blue Mini with Mila, hearing the metal-voiced police loud-hailers rising over the ragged shouting of the mob, hearing the scrape of studded police boots on the road. Hearing the nearby police van's door slamming and that surly English voice shouting 'Put the boot in!' in such bad Cantonese. Hearing the screams. Yes, their case started on that corner, and Helen might still have been alive if it hadn't. And, if she'd still been alive, what would have happened to Mila and him?

He gave it up. The history of the whole world might have been different.

The policeman at the gate peered at his face, then waved him in. As he parked and climbed the steps that he hadn't climbed for fifteen years, *It's not Alex or Elena*, he thought again. And was only faintly ashamed of his relief that it was Patrick, not them; of the buoyancy of his step; of his sense of excitement, even.

'Mr. Johnston? Thought so.' The man shaking his hand wasn't in uniform, just a sports-jacket and old-fashioned club cravat. 'Remember me? I was on that case you were a PW for sixteen years ago. You and that, er, that young lady.'

'PW?'

'Prosecution Witness. Remember?'

'Vividly. The case, I mean.' He glanced at the trim grey moustache and the set lined face, recalling now a young smooth ancestor of it, which at the time he'd thought was like a commercial traveller's. 'Your moustache was fair then, wasn't it? I thought it was *fifteen* years.'

'Sixteen,' he said confidently, stroking the moustache with just the gesture Dimitri remembered, finger and thumb spreading out from the middle.' I just looked it up. Pure coincidence, meeting like this again, I assure you. Nothing sinister; we haven't been keeping tabs on you or anything like that. Got better things to do, if you take my meaning — though I did notice you married the young lady eventually,' he added slily.

'What *is* this case exactly?' Dimitri had no wish to reopen the old one with him. The commercial traveller seemed to have matured into a sales manager now, a man who sat in his office looking at graphs and figures, sending younger men out on the road.

Detective Superintendent Hoames didn't answer at first, leading the way along a dingy school-like corridor painted a grubby cream, then up a stairway with a brown-varnished hand-rail, and along another corridor. The paint looked grubby there, too, just like a school corridor's, grubby with fear and crime. Dimitri had forgotten that. 'Another murder case, I'm afraid,' Hoames said at last, pausing outside a door with a frosted-glass window.

'Murder?!'

'Oh, not your friend; he hasn't killed anyone. Triad fight by the look of it. Your friend was a witness. To say the least.' He glanced assessingly at Dimitri, stroking his moustache again.

'To say the least?'

'Any idea he might have been being blackmailed, had you, Mr. Johnston?'

'Blackmailed? Not the faintest suspicion.'

'But you *do* know him pretty well, I take it?'

'Pretty well, yes.' Dimitri had the uneasy sense that he, too, was being obliquely investigated. Perhaps detectives couldn't drop the habit, even when they talked about the weather. Perhaps it was just a mannerism, like their short hair. He remembered now that when he was a prosecution witness all those fifteen or sixteen or whatever it was years ago, even then they'd somehow contrived to make him feel on trial himself. But perhaps he was, then.

'Expect you can guess why he was being blackmailed, in that case.' He gave Dimitri another look, a sales manager's look, that was neither wink nor leer, yet said more than a wink or leer would ever have said.

'I expect I can,' Dimitri said blankly.

'He'd brought the money, you see, and one triad must have muscled in on the other. Happens quite a lot. I imagine you've read about the kind of thing in the papers and so on. Rather a nasty mess, this one. They went to town. He was pretty upset.'

'Someone got killed?'

'You could say that again. And again, to be exact.' He turned the handle, pushed the door open, then pulled it shut. 'Wouldn't leave him alone too much at first if I was you.'

'I'll take him home with me.'

He nodded approvingly. 'I'll let you out by the other entrance. Avoid the gentlemen of the press. So you'd no idea he was being blackmailed, Mr. Johnston? Weren't you in his confidence?'

'Apparently not to that extent anyway.'

'Yet he gave us your name? Funny, that, isn't it? He's got relatives after all, hasn't he? Uncle's pretty rich, too. You'd think he'd call on him, wouldn't you?'

Dimitri glanced away from the wily enquiring gaze. 'Perhaps it was shame,' he said.

'Shame, eh? Shame?' The idea seemed to appeal to him. He cocked his head, turning the possibility over and over. 'Yes, I suppose it could be that. It could very well be, couldn't it? Loss of face, you mean, eh? Well . . . . ' And he opened the door wide.

Patrick was sitting huddled at the end of a dark-varnished brown bench, gazing somewhere down at his feet. He didn't look up. He seemed to have become smaller, child-like and defenceless, to have withdrawn into a diminished form of himself. He didn't even move when a constable sitting in the other corner — watching him presumably — jumped noisily to attention.

'We offered him some tea, but he wouldn't drink it,' Hoames said, as if he were a doctor discussing an uncooperative patient with a relative. 'Perhaps it was the atmosphere. Can be a bit off-putting, as I expect you may recall yourself. However, something warm should help, when you get him back — all right, Mr. Denton, your friend's here now, come to take you home.'

A small shadow of Patrick turned at last to Dimitri. A small shadow of him gave a crushed feeble smile. And a small shadow of him said precariously: 'Awfully good of you to come like this, dear boy.' The sound of his voice seemed to surprise him, and he glanced away again, down at his feet.

He looked as though he would never have moved if Dimitri hadn't touched his shoulder and said: 'Let's go, Patrick, shall we?'

Still and airless

On April mornings fleecy grey-white clouds still gathered on the sea, huddled along the island shores, and nuzzled up the folded valleys like flocks of grazing sheep. Travelling each day from Cheung Chau to Hong Kong, Rachel would sit at the stern of the ferry, enclosed in a thick cocoon of misty silence, watching the clouds and the lake-still sea, and the slow wake spreading behind her. The ferry moved cautiously at half-speed, and foghorns moaned continually all round, until the rising sun at last broke through and scattered the mist.

Today she was listening on her Walkman to the local announcements which punctuated the morning chat-show on Radio Hong Kong. The Ladies' Ikebana Club meeting had been postponed, but not the YWCA lecture on the Family and the Breast-Fed Baby. There would he special traffic arrangements for the Ching Ming festival . . . Rachel listened impatiently, gazing with anxious eyes through the saloon doors, where sailors were playing cards, students sleeping, heads on arms, and farmers sitting stolidly beside their baskets of spinach and cabbages. A sprinkling of foreign-devils like herself were reading newspapers or drinking coffee from those soft polystyrene cups which she was sure could give you cancer. There'd only been a couple of inches in the English press, but the Chinese papers had grisly photos and a quarter-page spread.

And now with the time at seven twenty-nine, here are the news headlines. Three men were killed in a gang attack at a restaurant in Western District last night. The next round of talks on Hong Kong's future will start next week . . . . The indifferent voice went smoothly on and on.

Why didn't he tell me? she kept thinking. *Why didn't he say something?* The placid mist enveloped her with its bland and unrevealing silence. Then the hesitant engines cut to dead slow, and the silky sea lay smooth and still around them. The ferry would be late again.

Someone phoned the chat-show host to ask when the police would change into their khaki summer uniforms, because they really looked so hot in that thick blue serge at midday. The host promised to ask Police Public Relations.

Then a newcomer to Hong Kong wanted to know what the difference was between the Chung Yeung and Ching Ming festivals, and was told, in a faintly weary voice, that it was the difference between autumn and spring.

She saw the spy-hole darken, then heard the locks turn. Patrick opened the door. Expecting him to look beaten and haggard, she was at first surprised at his appearance. He was wearing the light silk Chinese gown he wore when she called last year and met Chung Yan for the first time. His face wasn't really all that drawn, and at first glance he seemed as dapper and elegant as ever. It was only at the second, longer glance that she saw his skin was very pale, his eyes shadowed and lustreless. He held the door half-open — or, rather, half-shut.

'Dear girl, I know I've missed a lot of our appointments,' he began with tired jauntiness, as though he'd forgotten he'd long since stopped posing before her, but in any case lacked the will to pose properly now. 'The fact is I've been a teeny bit off colour. And I've had a bit of a shock — '

'Grace has just told me about it,' she said firmly. 'Can I come in?'

She made him some jasmine tea. He sat in his chair in the middle of the room, abstractedly gazing at the opposite wall. When she brought the tea in and set it beside him, he hardly stirred. 'I warned you transcendence was better, didn't I?' he said, still gazing at the wall. And then he told her everything, in a low detached voice, frowning faintly as though even now he found it hard to believe. He didn't look at her and didn't drink his tea, only occasionally touching the handle of the cup and stroking it lightly, as if it were a pet bird's head. 'I keep seeing them lying on the floor,' he ended. 'I see them all the time, just lying there with the blood spurting out of them.'

Rachel listened to his leaden voice, and listened to the silence when he'd finished.

The room was still and airless, not a window open. She noticed the typhoon-bars had been fastened across the balcony doors, too. Like a fortress. He'd barricaded himself in.

She looked out at the harbour and the Kowloon Hills, gradually appearing through the dissipating clouds. 'Let's get some air in here,' she said briskly at last. 'Look, the sun's breaking through.'

'No, don't open!' he called out sharply, before she'd got anywhere near the balcony doors. 'Don't touch them!'

Stitched-up slash

'Look, ring me tomorrow, will you?' Wang's voice boomed, cheerily impatient, in his ear. 'I'm just going out. Don't bother me now.'

'Don't bother me now'? Yin Hong felt a gap opening up inside his chest. *'Don't bother me now'?* Where was all the respect gone, then? Where was it? *'Don't bother me now'?* 'But listen!' he said cupping his hand round the mouthpiece and glancing over his shoulder. 'No, wait a minute, listen! I never knew you were going to do that! I was just giving you a tip, wasn't I? Ah Keung got carved up as well, and I'm like his elder brother! If he'd been inside, he'd've been killed, too, wouldn't he?'

'Can't hear you,' Wang shouted. 'What? A tip? Right. That's why we paid you, Ah Hong.'

Ah Hong! The pulse started throbbing in Yin Hong's ears. So that was it! *Ah* Hong again. Like that bitch Lai Ying!

'Why should you worry?' Wang bellowed. 'Who's going to talk? I'm not. And I'll bet you're not, either, eh? Besides, I thought you didn't like this Limpy fellow cutting you out. What did you do with the money, by the way? Spend it on that girl?' The hearty laugh rolled up from his belly. Yin

Hong pictured his sleek podgy face and unexpectedly strong, beringed hand. 'Give you a good time, did she? Man your age, wouldn't've thought you had it in you!'

'Now, listen, I've got to see you!' Yin Hong forgot the resentment, the loss of face, the sense of betrayal. He was scared, plain scared now, that was all. He let the rest go. 'We've got to talk.'

'Well, ring tomorrow, OK?'

'Tomorrow? What time? What time?' But the line was cold and empty; he was talking to himself.

He placed the phone back on its cradle, and the cold empty silence went slowly deeper and deeper into his head. So that was it. Wang hadn't ever really given him face, it was all a trick so they could use him, and he'd gone and let himself be used, and now Limpy and two of the brothers were dead and it was only luck Ah Keung wasn't, too. Not that he cared about Limpy, good riddance to him, but Woodchopper and Fat Boy, they were real brothers. And, if anyone found out, he was as good as dead himself.

He felt like he was hollow inside, and all the time a jumpy throbbing in his veins. *Give you a good time, did she?* Bastard probably knew she didn't, she probably told him he couldn't get it up. Bastard.

He pushed himself off the chair with a long tired sigh and, reaching for his jacket, saw Ah Keung standing by the door. Ah Keung! Just looking at him with his arms all bandaged and that stitched-up slash along his cheek like someone had tried to slice him open.

'Ah Keung! Fuck you! How long have you been there?'

'Just walked in. Why?' He held the key up, dangling on a bit of string.

'Gave me a shock. Thought I'd bolted the door.' He had to breathe deeply to smooth the wobbles out of his voice. 'Where've you been, then? I was looking for you yesterday.'

He didn't like the way Ah Keung shrugged instead of answering. He didn't like the look Ah Keung gave him, either, it was too long and cool.

'Speaking to one of your Shanghai friends, were you?' Ah Keung asked casually.

'Not a friend. Just a . . . just a restaurant I go to sometimes.'

'Ah.'

'Over in North Point.'

'Ah. Thought it might be a friend.'

'No.' Yin Hong tried to recall what he'd been saying, sending the words back in little bursts through his mind. 'How would you know? You don't understand a word of Shanghainese, do you?'

'I get the drift sometimes,' Ah Keung said. 'Thought it was one of your friends.'

'Well, you were wrong, then, weren't you?'

Ah Keung shrugged, sat down and switched the television on. 'I was counting on the money from that job with Limpy,' he said slowly. 'To pay the rent. For the girl and me.'

'Well, what's that to do with me?'

Ah Keung just shrugged again. Yin Hong felt he had to keep talking. He mustn't let Ah Keung's silences or his shrugs get to him; he must just keep on going with words and words and words. 'Why don't you put her on the game, then, ah? What's her name again? Ling Kwan, that's it. Put her on the game now you've put your seal on her, now you've stamped her. Let *her* earn the rent for you, ah?'

'Just shut up about the game, will you!' Ah Keung suddenly hissed furiously, glaring at Yin Hong. 'Shut up! Shut up!' His face was all twisted from the slash. It looked like the wound might pop open at any moment.

'OK, OK, OK,' Yin Hong protested hastily, backing off as if he'd only been joking. 'Take it easy. Do what you like with her. I don't care! Just giving you a bit of advice, that's all.'

'I've told you before, she'd not going on the game!'

'All right, then, she's not going on the game!'

'And I don't want your fucking advice!'

'All right you don't want my advice!'

He jingled the coins in his pockets as if he hadn't noticed Ah Keung's lack of respect, as if he was thinking about something more important. But he felt himself growing smaller from second to second, smaller, older, more alone, more afraid. And his pulse racing all the time!

And what if Ah Keung had caught on to what he'd been saying to Wang? His belly sickened.

After a while Ah Keung took out his knife and started carefully, sullenly paring his nails, slicing thin little curls off them as cleanly as if they were paper. 'She'll take Woodchopper's place on the boat, all right? And get his share of the money, too.'

'*Use a woman?*' Yin Hong wanted to protest. But somehow, looking at Ah Keung, he didn't dare say a thing.

Ah Keung glanced up at him over the point of his knife. 'We can trust *her*,' he said, as if there was someone else they couldn't trust. 'Snakeboat Wong's her uncle, and her old man's in on it, too, at the other end.' He looked down again. 'That's what we'll do.'

For the time being

Dimitri thought irony was the one advantage life had given him over Michael. Not that he'd always had it; it was a quality he acquired only with disillusionment, and he hadn't always been disillusioned. But by now he'd become an ironist of life; he could turn any — well, almost any — misfortune aside, his own or others' with a wry joke. Not so Michael. For him everything was serious. If he had a sense of irony — and Dimitri had never seen it — it was always submerged beneath the grey level sea of his sobriety. So fortune's arrows must hurt him more. As he couldn't deflect their points, they would go straight in, and go in deep. And then, Dimitri guessed, he would bleed long and secretly, an emotional haemophiliac.

On the other hand, the greatest advantage Michael had over Dimitri was his unvarying satisfaction, his completedness, in his inveterate passion for history. Nothing was so weird, so noble or so vile but that some obscure and ordinary person had done it, even on that barren rock of Hong Kong, and Michael had to find out how and why.

He never asked himself *'Why bother? Does it really matter?'* as Dimitri did and thereby paralysed himself. Unravelling a man's life was as significant as uncovering the secrets of the universe — it *was* uncovering one of the secrets. And he would never tire of it; it would never go stale. He had no irony, he couldn't be flippant, but what he had he had completely. It left no gaps.

He'd been tracking Caldwell steadily for months now, coming closer and closer to him day by day. And not just Caldwell, but his wife from the brothel, too, and her shady brother, and the ambiguous supercilious British officials, the self-effacing Chinese merchants, the wily Indian traders. Michael knew them all now, and their wives and mistresses and concubines, their daughters and sons. He knew their veranda'd mansions, their narrow shops and their dim humid godowns smelling of rope and rat-droppings. He could have found each one of them blindfold, if only they were still standing. He was walking daily closer and closer, treading in Caldwell's footsteps; he could almost hear his voice and think his thoughts, here in this house, built where he'd lived. He could feel his breathing down in the cellar where the bricks were bricks that Caldwell had seen and touched. And Caldwell wasn't only Caldwell, wasn't only the long-dead enigmatic man in his sticky web of dubious dealings. He was also an emblem of Hong Kong and Shanghai and Singapore and Penang and a dozen other colonial cities, of the uneasy antagonistic embrace of East and West from which he, and no less Michael himself, had uneasily sprung.

Behind the security of his money-walls he pursued his singular passion for history. But would the walls hold up?

First there was Lily.

And now there was Patrick.

So he laid his work on Caldwell aside for the time being, the last section unfinished. 'Patrick had better come and stay with us,' he said to Grace. 'And we'll have to find somewhere for him to go afterwards.'

'After what?'

'After the trial. He won't be able to live in Hong Kong, I'm afraid; he's finished here. We'll have to help him set up somewhere else.'

Grace didn't answer at first. She was remembering the smudged photos in the *Wah Kiu Yat Po* of bloodstained table-cloths, inert covered bodies, prurient onlookers and indifferently officious policemen. When the communists executed her father in 1949, did they cover his body afterwards, too? She'd never wondered before, but now she'd like to know, even though she realized it didn't really matter at all in the end whether they did or didn't.

'He won't want to stay with us,' she said at last.

'Why not?'

'Too ashamed.'

In China the executioner always stood behind you, so that you couldn't see his face and come back to haunt him. You mustn't know who killed you. She thought of her father being shot from behind. It seemed worse somehow. But the people in the *Wah Kiu Yat Po*, they'd seen their killers, they'd recognized them as they died. And Patrick had seen them, too. 'We'd better make sure someone's always with him,' she said, imagining all the stabbings and slashings being gouged into Patrick's mind. 'He shouldn't ever be alone.' In emergencies, without ever forgoing her detached solitude, she was instantly practical. It was she who'd known by some immediate intuition that Rachel was the one who'd save him if anyone could. She'd phoned Rachel only half an hour after Dimitri had told them about it, on the morning after it happened.

'Well, he's being taken care of tomorrow,' Michael said. 'The Johnstons are doing something with him.'

Clubs and clubs

Dimitri drove past the stadium after picking up Rachel and Patrick. 'I thought this would be a short cut,' he apologized, when they had to dawdle down a road clogged with noisy boisterous young Europeans. 'I forgot it's the Rugby Competition today. Or should I say Thugby?' He viewed the crowd distastefully, as a Chinese might — rowdy, uncouth, arrogant, violent and unpredictable. Most of them were middle-class louts from the local European schools. 'Colonial kids usually turn out badly,' he said wryly.

'Retribution, no doubt,' Patrick murmured faintly from the back seat, like a record of himself with the volume turned down.

A torrent of young rowdies surged across the street, ignoring a Chinese constable's raised hand. The constable's face set hard and flushed as they poured heedlessly past him, then he dropped his arm and moved sheepishly away. Was he invisible to them because he was Chinese?

'Well, I suppose at least that won't happen after 1997,' Dimitri said.

'Is that necessarily a good thing?' Mila asked in those precise and uninflected tones which sounded to Rachel like pieces of delicate porcelain chinking regularly together. Mila was recalling how they handcuffed offenders in the labour-camp, one hand over behind the neck, the other yanked up the back to meet it. After a night of that you did what you were told, even by an ordinary constable on the beat. 'I quite like to see people who feel they can ignore policemen,' she said.

'Easier said than done in my case,' Patrick's muted record said.

Glancing in the driving-mirror, Dimitri glimpsed the trace of a self-mocking smile at the corners of Patrick's faded eyes. 'You're perking up,' he said encouragingly.

'Gallows humour, I assure you.'

But there was a sense of loosening and easing in the car now, as though they'd all stretched and settled back, instead of perching tensely on the edges of their seats.

The highways funnelled them through the harbour tunnel, filtered them along stilted flyovers and decanted them finally on the Sai Kung road. *This is the way we went with Chung Yan last November,* Rachel thought apprehensively as the car climbed over the Kowloon Hills. But Patrick gazed out with impassive eyes as if he scarcely noticed where they were. There wasn't even a flicker as the road reached the crest, and the valley they'd walked through then, which had once filled the emperor's rice-bowl, unrolled beneath them, spreading serenely down to the sea.

She hadn't opened her diary once since moving into his flat. He let her do everything — cook, clean, wash (the part-time amah had left, 'warned by the bamboo telegraph,' Dimitri had said) — while he lay listlessly in bed or, dressed in his long Chinese gown, lolled in his chair and stared vacantly across the room, occasionally adjusting one of his statues with resigned, habitual, absent-minded care. For a long time he didn't speak except to answer her, and even then not always. He almost reminded her of Paul, he'd become so unreachable. He woke early in the morning, often before dawn, and when she heard him moving in his room she would herself get up and make some tea. But then he would frequently go back to bed and just lie there, staring at the ceiling. Once a week he went to a psychiatrist, and came back with pills which he sometimes took and sometimes didn't. An unmarked police car was always in the car-park, a white Ford with an AM licence-plate — they didn't want to lose their star witness. Sometimes Detective Superintendent Hoames would come round, 'to get something straight,' observing Rachel when he met her with a speculative fish-like stare while he caressed his moustache.

Then one morning last week, while she was making some notes for her thesis, the books laid out over the dining-table, Patrick took his pi-pa down from the wardrobe and tried a few notes on it. She looked round with her myopic friendly smile, and he said: 'I've got to come up some time haven't I? But I'm so far down, you see. It takes a long time, floating up.'

He hadn't said so much since the day she moved in.

'You're coming up all right,' she said.

He raised his eyebrows as if to say 'Perhaps, perhaps,' and stood gazing down at her books wonderingly, like someone recognizing a language he knew once but had now forgotten. Then he nodded and turned away. Once or twice since then he'd stroked the pi-pa's strings, coaxing a fragment of some melody out of it before laying it down. And now, today, she felt he was coming up further, the air was not so far above his head. Only a little longer and he'd break the surface and suck life in again.

It was the first day of real summer. The cloudless sky was incandescent with sunlight, the black road shimmered like water at every hollow, and the trees along the verges seemed to be breathing out the moisture of their leaves like panting dogs. Near Jade Bay, Chinese families had parked their polished cars on the grass and were lighting barbecue fires along the tree-shaded shore.

'Here we are,' Dimitri said, turning down a little track. 'The only club I've ever belonged to in my life.'

The car bumped along worn wheel-ruts towards a long low bungalow surrounded by trees and azaleas. In a clearing beside it two or three cars stood, nudged beneath the shade of the overhanging branches. A number of dogs were barking wildly, and some Chinese children were playing badminton across an overgrown hedge. Rachel thought it could have been a rubber-planter's home in Somerset Maugham country.

'Mildly dilapidated, I'm afraid,' Dimitri said, nosing the car under the green spreading leaves of a flame of the forest. 'As befits the oldest club in Hong Kong.'

'It kind of fits you, too,' Rachel said.

'In dilapidation, you mean?'

'No. Well, not exactly.' She wasn't sure what she meant. 'I just couldn't imagine you in something very glitzy.'

'Well, there are clubs and clubs in Hong Kong,' Dimitri was saying. 'Clubs for Europeans, clubs for Chinese, clubs for Indians, clubs for businessmen, clubs for sportsmen, clubs for the *nouveaux riches*, clubs for snobs, clubs for yobs. Mila and I didn't really fit neatly into any of those categories, so we joined this one. It's a club for nondescripts.'

Patrick had walked away from the car and was gazing round like someone waking from a long hibernation. 'I think I would quite like to swim,' he said.

The clubhouse was almost deserted. A few hypnotic ceiling-fans paddled their long wooden blades through the heavy air. Low bamboo chairs and tables stood beside large open windows on a shiny red-tiled floor. Outside the windows were trees, creepers and steps leading down to the sea. It was as though the place had been waiting for them. A lean and smiling steward greeted Dimitri and Mila in Cantonese. Rachel gathered the man had been ill but was better now. His wife appeared behind the bar, and the children who'd been playing badminton peered round the kitchen door with eyes that were darkly bright. *Why, this is normal, human, ordinary,* Rachel thought. *This is what Patrick needs.*

Patrick had gone downstairs to change.

When Dimitri entered the changing-room, a man with freckles, pink skin, and thinning sandy hair was standing in the middle of it, towelling himself energetically.

'Showers are playing up again,' he sang out in a high penetrating voice. 'Roof needs mending, too.'

'Ah,' Dimitri said, glancing up, 'I see.'

'Really think they should do something to smarten the place up a bit, don't you?' He scrubbed his chest briskly. 'Not that I'd like a bunch of liveried flunkeys standing around, mark you, but things really are getting a bit too tatty, wouldn't you say?'

'Well, I must admit I find this, er, this casualness is one of its charms,' Dimitri said blandly.

'Can have a bit too much charm, though, can't you?' he sniffed, towelling vigorously between his legs now. 'Dash of efficiency now and then wouldn't come amiss.'

A woman called hesitantly from behind the half-open door. 'Are you ready, Jeremy?'

'Nearly!'

'Meet you by the car, then?'

'Righty-ho! Yes, I feel it could be smartened up a bit,' Jeremy said decisively, reaching for his capacious white underpants.

'Well, I suppose it takes all sorts,' Dimitri replied evasively. 'What was the water like?'

'Super! Super!'

'Ah.'

Patrick had gone into a cubicle — or hidden in it, Dimitri thought — to change. He emerged now in a bathrobe and walked silently past them, out towards the sea.

'Extraordinarily shy, these Chinese, sometimes,' Jeremy remarked. 'Think he'd say how d'ye do, at least, wouldn't you?'

Do this for a living

They lay in the shade of the trees, on grass that straggled sparsely through the sandy earth. The sea-water left little crusts of salt on their bodies as it dried. It was hot and windless. Rachel, propped on her elbow, gazed out at the viscous sun-glistening sea and the hazed mauve mounds of distant islands. The sea washed so smoothly up the shallow beach you could hardly hear a whisper as it ran along the sand. How thin Patrick looked, how hairy Dimitri, how slim and fine-boned Mila. And she herself? A pale, knobbly, freckled spinster in her shapeless black one-piece. She'd never minded before, but now, lying next to Patrick — she could touch him if she dared — she wanted a different body. Only, what good would that do her with him?

His eyes were closed, but there was a light frown on his forehead, as if even at rest he was worrying, remembering. Well, no wonder. His long black hair was wet, drops of water trickled slowly down his cheeks like tears. She imagined her finger-tip tracing the jerky track of one of those tears, following it all the way down his cheek, under his chin, down his neck into the shadowy hollow of his collarbone . . . . Why him? Why him of all people? And yet she was glad.

'What are you looking for?' Patrick murmured, not opening his eyes. 'The mark of Cain?'

'No, I was just . . . . ' She lay down to give herself time. 'I didn't know you were watching me.'

'I'm always watching,' he said; not proudly, just stating a fact.

The grass pricked her back. She wiggled against it, then gathered some sand and let it sift slowly through her fingers.

'The mark of Cain?' Patrick insisted. 'Or the beast of Sodom?'

'I was just thinking . . . . ' She felt herself mentally pedalling the air. 'Thinking Dimitri was a witness in a murder trial, too, once. Weren't you, Dimitri?' Well, it *was* something she'd thought from time to time. Frank Browning had mentioned it recently, in a boozy aside in the common room.

'And Mila,' Dimitri said after a longish moment. 'Mila was, too.'

'Not quite the same sort of witness, though,' Patrick said, '*They* weren't being blackmailed.'

Dimitri sat up. 'I'm going in again. Anyone coming?'

Mila followed wordlessly.

'Meaning I shouldn't be inquisitive?' Rachel asked Patrick, watching them wading out on the level sand.

'I imagine they thought the subject was . . . inappropriate,' Patrick said detachedly, as if it was too far off to concern him.

Somewhere behind them two screechy-voiced English women were chattering loudly as they came down towards the beach.

'What happened, then?'

'I don't know the exact details. They came upon some police beating up a lefty in the riots in 'sixty-seven. The lefty died, and Dimitri made himself unpopular with the loyal constabulary by making statements and so on, I believe. It was before my time; I was still at Cambridge.'

It was a long speech for Patrick, the longest he'd made for weeks, but he still spoke in the lacklustre remote tone of a man whose thoughts weren't where his words were.

'And there was a trial?'

'Yes. It was fudged somehow in the end, I believe, and the police were acquitted. But it was politically rather sensitive at the time. China was going through the Cultural Revolution, and making waves in Hong Kong. Tidal waves. And, as far as the Hong Kong government was concerned, all the lefties were supposed to be villains and all the police were supposed to be heroes. Rather bad for morale if the police turned out to be villains as well. The subject colonial population might have begun to wonder. So Dimitri and Mila came in for a few poison-pen letters and so on, from outraged patriots. As no doubt I will, from outraged moralists. And his wife got one, too, spilling the beans about his affair with Mila.'

'Oh. Is that when she . . . ?' Rachel listened to her voice trailing as she realized what she was asking.

'Yes,' Patrick said. 'Killed herself.'

They both thought about that for a time.

'And Mila rather foolishly went back to China,' Patrick went on at last. 'With the results we all know about.' He laid his forearm over his eyes, as though so much unaccustomed talking had exhausted him.

Rachel let her eyes close. The sun, slipping between the leaves, dappled her lids like water. 'If *they* could get through a trial like that, I'm sure *you* can, too,' she said.

'I thought you might say that. To divert my mind from the first Mrs. Johnston's fate, no doubt. But Dimitri and Mila didn't happen to be sodomites being blackmailed for buggery.'

'All the same. And stop talking like that, will you?'

'As you like.' Patrick shrugged.

They stopped talking altogether. Patrick seemed to be asleep, and soon Rachel, too, dozed. She heard the others coming back, their wet feet slapping on the sand. She saw their vague dripping bodies through the fringe of her lashes. The screechy-voiced women had fallen silent, like parrots in the heat-drugged afternoon of some jungle. On the warm screen of her eyelids Rachel painted vague images of herself with Patrick, dreamy and unattainable — or were they really? Sometimes she let herself wonder. Then she dozed again.

Dimitri lay next to her, picturing words hand-printed, on a plain white sheet of paper, folded twice, Very exactly. DEAR MRS. JOHNSTON, WHAT DANCE DOES YOUR POLICE-HATING HUSBAND PERFORM WITH YOUR DAUGHTERS COMMUNIST-LOVING DANCE TEACHER WHEN YOU ARE NOT LOOKING?

Mila, next to Dimitri, pressing her back gingerly into the miniature sand-dunes beneath her, thought drowsily of the old solemn-eyed acupuncturist who had taken the pain from her spine, at least for now.

Behind his flickering lids, Patrick saw a vision of his glass balcony-doors swinging open, and the gauzy white curtains floating lazily on the breeze.

'Does anyone want a drink?' he asked softly.

Nobody answered.

'Where's Patrick?' Rachel asked later, yawning and stretching.

'No idea,' Dimitri said.

Mila sat up cross-legged, gently arching and hollowing her back, testing it for pain.

'I can't see him,' Rachel said. 'Where is he?'

Dimitri looked out to sea, shading his eyes. 'I can't see him, either,' he said slowly.

'Where is he?' Rachel started up. '*Where is he?*'

'Here he comes,' Mila said quietly.

'Where? Where?' Rachel stared helplessly. 'Where?'

Patrick was walking down the steps from the clubhouse, carrying a tray with four lime-sodas on it, as elegantly as any waiter. As elegantly as Chung Yan.

'I suppose I could always do this for a living,' he said. 'If the worst comes to the worst.'

When they left in the early evening, 'See how far you've come up today?' Rachel said in a low warm voice to Patrick.

Patrick gave her a shrug and a faint wan smile.

Next week, sixth day

Yin Hong was early. When he trudged up the steps from the subway, there was only a newspaper-seller outside, with a striped plastic awning propped on bamboo poles over his stall. The others hadn't come yet, the ones that used to be there, the cigarette-sellers, the fruit-hawkers, the old women with plastic toys and drinks and things.

Years since he'd been there, though — things might've changed. Not the tenements, they were just the same all right, same old concrete walls with big black numbers on them like prison blocks, same old washing hanging out of every window on poles like they were waving flags — no, they hadn't changed, he could find his way anywhere there. Only the people would have changed. They would have made money and moved on.

Why'd he keep getting that bristly feeling at the back of his neck like someone was creeping up behind him? And his pulse thumping away, too? No one had said a thing. What was he worrying about? It was Ah Keung, that's what it was, ever since he'd come in while he was on the phone to Wang. It was Ah Keung looking at him like that all the time and getting above himself, not giving him face, as if he knew something. But what could he know? He didn't understand a fucking word of Shanghainese.

No, it was Wang, not Ah Keung. Who was Ah Keung anyway? That fat bastard Wang, never answering the phone or always handing out some excuse why they couldn't meet and talk. That's what made him jumpy, didn't know where he stood. Wang could pull the plug on him any time, and him a Shanghainese, too, talking about the slippery Cantonese, the great greasy ball of lard. And as for not giving him face — Ah Keung wasn't in it. After all he'd done for Wang as well.

Still, why not try ringing one more time, though? Early Sunday morning like this, bound to be there, wherever 'there' was. North Point number, that's all you could tell, hopeless going looking for him.

Back down the steps, a dollar in the slot, his heart beating faster as he listened to the dialling tone purring calmly in his ear. It only rang three or four times before a woman answered.

'Can I speak to Wang?' he asked in Shanghainese.

There was a pause, then she said hold on. Never been a woman there before, Shanghainese as well, it threw him a bit, that did. Young and juicy by the sound of her, too, familiar kind of voice, like he'd heard it before somewhere. Seemed a long time before Wang came on, the same big genial voice, a bit sleepy, though.

'It's me, Yin Hong. I've been trying to — '

Reach you for days, the unspoken words ran on in his head as the line died.

When he dialled again, he got the engaged sign. He could just imagine them laughing in bed with the phone off the hook. He felt suddenly old and tired, like he could hardly move any more, like someone had poured lead into his legs. *You're on your own, then*, he told himself numbly, climbing up the subway steps again, into the merciless sunlight. *You're on your own.*

And, for all his legs were so heavy, still his heart wouldn't stop thumping till he was almost giddy with it. And then he suddenly thought: *Suppose that girl on the phone was the one he had with Wang's money — or didn't have, rather. Spoke Shanghainese after all.* He felt sick. No wonder her voice sounded familiar.

Across the road was the same old playground, a bit shabbier now, full of kids running about and shrieking. Their parents were watching they didn't get hurt, pushing the swings, catching them at the bottom of the slide. Leaning back in the shade of the newspaper-seller's awning, he watched a father holding his kid by both hands, teaching him how to walk, grinning all over his face with pride. And the kid was squealing and laughing, too, as he tottered along, practically swinging from his dad's hands while the mum crouched down a few yards away to take a snap. Made you feel lonely, that did, too, it came over you like a gulp of fear. That kid would look after them when they were old, he'd see they were buried properly one day, and sweep their graves. Who'd bury *him* if he died tomorrow? Who'd look after *his* spirit?

Who said anything about dying tomorrow? Yin Hong shivered.

Now the kid was almost toddling on his own, his mum holding him just by one hand, in a minute or two he'd be going by himself, and it was the dad's turn to take a snap. They were all smiling, laughing, happy, carefree. And to think this used to be his territory ten years ago, this used to be his turf.

It was eating bitterness all right. At his age, too. All he'd got left now was that thing with Lily Denton.

He turned to the hawker, a man as old as he was probably, smoking a cigarette, the change for the papers in a red tin box in front of him.

'That's the age, isn't it?' Yin Hong said abruptly, nodding across the road at the kid, his parents, the whole yelling playground. At youth, energy, hope. 'Before you get worn down, ah?'

The man hardly gave them a glance. 'Shade's only free if you want to buy a paper,' he muttered.

'What?' Yin Hong glared at him. '*What?* Know who I am, do you?'

'No.' Didn't even look. 'But I've got my friends, so don't try anything, all right?'

'I used to run this place, you know that?' His voice trembled with the insult of it. 'Fuck your mother, I used to run everything here! *Everything!*' He kicked the pole down as he stalked away, but the man only gave a sort of jeering grunt, and when Yin Hong looked back the awning was upright again, the man just sitting there smoking his cigarette like nothing had happened, nothing at all.

What did he have to talk to the old fool like that for, anyway, like some soft-headed grandpa? Nobody knew about Wang, he'd still got the thing with Lily Denton, so why shouldn't everything be all right, eh? Just keep hold of himself, that's all. But he hardly knew himself any more these days, these weak spells coming over him, what was the matter? Like his heart was turning to water or something.

Ever since that bastard Wang had got hold of him. Or since they made him eat those fucking cakes, that was it. Those fucking cakes.

Snakeboat Wong was waiting for him at the temple, burning lucky money. And Ah Keung was there, too, with his girl. They all looked at each other, and Snakeboat Wong gave him some money to burn, too. 'Know my niece, do you? Yes?' he said lightly. 'She'll be useful, she can handle a sampan better than Ah Keung or you, I bet.' Then he lowered his voice a bit. 'Sixth day next week, can you manage it? There won't be any moon.'

'Course I can manage it,' Yin Hong said. 'I can leave for Shanghai tomorrow.' He looked only at Snakeboat Wong, as if Ah Keung and his girl weren't even there. He'd put up with the girl if he had to, but he wasn't going to give her face as well.

18

Used to be only girls

Wrapped in his academic gown, Dimitri watched from an invigilator's table on the stage as the attendants pushed the great wooden doors of the examination-hall open and the candidates poured in, pale, nervous and silent, branching into little rivulets and streams as they flowed down the aisles to their numbered places.

Pens, pencils and erasers were placed methodically on desks, cardigans draped protectively over shoulders against the meat-safe air-conditioning; chairs were tucked neatly in, heads bowed anxiously over the question papers.

Invigilators patrolled the aisles, their long-sleeved black gowns flapping like vultures' wings. Especially Robert Smith's, with his hunched vulture shoulders and beaky vulture nose. Within half a minute the only sounds were the rustle of paper and an occasional stifled cough. Like silent prayer in church, only probably more dedicated.

Ticking the names on the roll-call, Dimitri glanced at Emmelina Wu's empty seat. Behind it, as if the space had purposely been cleared for her, sat a tall clear-skinned girl, Juliet Mok, wearing her good looks like a saint her halo — pretending not to notice, but all the time demurely conscious it was there. If poor Emmelina Wu had been present, she'd have wilted even more. He thought of her peaked pale face and steel-rimmed glasses. Dealt a lousy hand by fate, but still gamely playing it to the last card. While Juliet had all the aces — rich, beautiful, and radiant with health. He sat down, watching Juliet incline her head gracefully over her answer-book. In all that tense hushed hall, she was the only student who was smiling to herself as she wrote, as if she thought that for her the result wouldn't really matter. Which it probably wouldn't.

Smith leant over Dimitri's chair, sliding the *Principles of Theory* paper in front of him. 'Seen my questions?' he asked challengingly. Even his whisper had a nasal edge to it. Like an adenoidal goat.

Dimitri read through them negligently. Yes, all the cult phrases were there, the empty jargon and pretentious catchwords. An examination in piss-artistry. 'Difficult,' he murmured. 'For the thoughtful students, that is.'

'Ha!' Smith muttered, amazed and gratified.

'I mean, they'll have to consider whether the examiner's gone off his head or not, before they start answering the questions, won't they?'

Smith drew himself up with dignity, taking the paper back. 'Might have known you wouldn't understand it,' he sniffed, moving pointedly away to sit at the other table.

Dimitri walked down the steps, past Emmelina Wu's empty desk and Juliet Mok's self-knowing beauty. Down to the end of the hall and back again. Nobody cheating; he'd earned his money.

Frank Browning was sitting in the chair next to his when he returned to the invigilator's table. Well, rather him than Robert Smith.

'One of your lot's missing, isn't he?' Frank nodded at Emmelina Wu's place, his filmy eyes dwelling over-long on Dimitri's, as if vaguely holding him responsible.

'She, actually. Yes, she's sick.'

'If it's a girl, it's hysteria,' Frank whispered loudly. 'Always is.'

Dimitri thought of Emmelina Wu's self-effacing and diffident face. He hadn't taught her much; she'd been more Patrick's pupil. But she'd endeared herself to him when she dropped Smith's course for his.

'No, not hysteria,' he said. 'I believe it's cancer.'

'Oh. That's bad luck.' Frank scratched his beard, wriggling his moist lips as though even he was for once nonplussed. Then he leant closer, giving Dimitri a phantom nudge. 'Someone missing from the *staff* of your department, too, eh?' he muttered.

Detecting alcohol, garlic and cigarette-smoke, for a start, in the stale salad of Frank's breath, Dimitri tried not to turn his head away too obviously. 'If you mean Patrick, he's sick, too.'

'Thought he'd resigned.'

'Not as far as I know.'

'Well, he'll have to, won't he? Shame, really. I don't go much on poofters myself, but I must say the place won't be the same without him. Not that I'll be around to see it then, thank God.'

Dimitri ostentatiously opened the book he'd brought with him. 'Why should the place be without him?' he murmured with studied casualness. 'He's ill, that's all I know. Nobody's said anything about him resigning.'

'Come off it. Corrupting the youth and mixed up with triads? They'll have his guts for garters, he hasn't got a chance. Exciting, though, isn't it? I keep looking in the paper to see whose name'll come up next.'

'And whose will?'

'Wouldn't need to look in the paper if I knew that, would I?'

Frank's argument seemed compelling. Dimitri started reading.

'Tell you one thing, though.' Frank gave him a real nudge this time. 'There's a whole colony of them in the university jumpy as cats on hot bricks. Fact.'

Dimitri laid his book down with a restrained sigh. Only twenty minutes gone, another hundred and sixty left. 'This begins to sound like the revelations the reading public expects to get from you, eventually.'

'Me?'

'Your autobiography.'

'Oh, that.' Frank looked modestly pleased.

'*A Frank Account*, weren't you going to call it?'

'Funny you should mention that. Name and all. What a memory. That's the subtitle actually. The title's *Exotic Nights*.' He was scratching his beard energetically, burrowing into tufts here and there with clawed fingers, and, after each expedition, examining his nails with suspicious intentness. Dimitri began to wonder if he was foraging for some parasite, then he realized Frank's ape-like behaviour was only the expression of an author's insecurity. 'Matter of fact, I've been trying a few chapters on a publisher or two, but they looked down their snotty little noses. S'pose the trouble is I'm only a nuts-and-bolts man, can't really manage to fit the words together so well. Shame really, because the story-line's all right, I can promise you that.' He leant confidentially closer to Dimitri again. Dimitri held his breath. 'Need one of you literary gents to help me out. You know, polish it up a bit. I s'pose you wouldn't . . . ? Spelling's all right and all that, it's just the finishing touches it needs. What about it? I'll let you have a butcher's if you're interested, see what you think. You'll get to read a few eye-openers in it, I can tell you that.'

Frank leant back with the air of a man who'd got something off his chest, and Dimitri was able to breathe again. 'I'm sure I'd be enthralled by it' — he tried not to gasp — 'but I don't think I've got a knack for that kind of thing.'

'Ah,' Frank said, registering disappointment rather than belief.

Dimitri felt guilty. Undeservedly, but there it was. 'Er, why don't you ask Robert Smith?' he suggested with a sense, unusually satisfying, of both reparation and malice. He nodded towards the other table, where Smith was making a display of reading a volume entitled *Post-Modern Post-Structuralism: Deconstructing the Root Metaphors of Our Age*. 'Just the sort of job for him; he's a great stylist, I believe.'

Frank glanced across dubiously. 'D'you really think so? Always thought he was one of those, you know, super-intellectual types.'

'Yes, well . . . . ' Dimitri swallowed down a succession of libellous rejoinders. 'Yes, he is, in a way. But it's worth a try.'

'Think so?'

'Definitely. Might be right up his street. Only thing is, don't say you asked me first. He can be a bit touchy, if you know what I mean.'

'Well,' Frank said hesitantly, 'if you really think he might be interested.'

Dimitri had twenty minutes of undisturbed reading, then Frank was back again. 'Said he'd take a look at it,' he muttered gratefully. 'Said something about the margins of the text, so I s'pose he's even thinking of layout and so on. Seems a very bright young spark.'

'Oh, scintillating,' Dimitri said.

'I didn't mention your name.'

'No, better not.'

'Funny thing. Did you notice? He isn't wearing any socks.'

Dimitri gazed surreptitiously at Smith's white bony ankles, exposed between the bottoms of neat grey trousers and the tops of polished brown shoes. 'So he isn't.'

'Athlete's foot, I shouldn't wonder,' Frank said.

'Unless he's some kind of eccentric flasher.'

'What? Go on!'

'Well, they're like that, you know, these super-intellectuals. He wasn't wearing socks at the Graduates' Reception, either, I remember. Something about special occasions, I expect. You ought to put it in your book.'

'Graduates' Reception? Get away with you!'

'Fact.'

Frank ruminated on this for some time, and Dimitri was able to return thankfully to his reading. But then he sensed a sudden change, almost a convulsion, in Frank's body, as if his voltage had been abruptly stepped up.

'I say! Who's that piece down there? She one of yours?'

'She's one of my *students*, yes.' Where Frank was concerned, and the subject was Juliet Mok, he thought it wisest to be precise.

'What a raving beauty. She brainy as well?'

'She doesn't need to be.'

'No, s'pose not.' Frank took the *Morning Post* out of his brief-case and opened it, folding and refolding the crackling pages noisily. Disturbed heads were raised reprovingly from the nearest desks, without effect. 'As long as she's got enough brains to try and get out of here by 1997. And her looks should certainly help her there.'

After a few minutes of increasingly impatient slappings and smoothings of the pages, he leant across to Dimitri again, stabbing the headline scornfully with his nicotine-stained finger. 'Look at that,' he muttered, reading disparagingly. ' *"Sino-British Agreement Heralds Bright Future for Hong Kong."* Have you ever read such cock? Anyone who can is moving out like greased lightning — businessmen, manufacturers, doctors, lawyers, you name 'em. The whole damn lot of 'em. Fact. Government daren't publish the figures. Anyone with half an eye can see, though. Or half an ear — you've only got to listen to people talking. Even my dentist's nurse is getting out to Canada, never mind the dentist. I mean, you ask any of these kids here today if they're working on getting a foreign passport, you'll be hard put to find one that isn't. Bet you a hundred bucks. "Bright future" indeed. What a con.'

'It's a con all right,' Dimitri said bleakly.

'Why d'you think Faustus Yu's sent his wife to have her baby in the States?' Frank demanded in a whisper that brought the same reproving heads up, with the same nil effect. 'Not for the climate, you can bet your boots on that. Want the kid to be American, don't they? Stands to reason.' He leant back, reading the paper again, shaking his head and grunting incredulously. 'Find me more than ten Chinese lecturers at the university that haven't got their foreign passports, and I'll give you another hundred dollars. How's that?'

'No deal. Mila says the whole thing's like a — '

'And that includes the Cantonese Mafia, the shoe-shine boys, the whole bloody lot.'

'Like a traditional Chinese marriage,' Mila had said. *'The parents decide everything, and arrange the bride-price, and then they tell her it's that or nothing. All the bride can do is hope resignedly for the best. She does not know how the groom will treat her. Will he rape her? Will he beat her? Will he leave her alone? She only knows that on the marriage-day she will be subjected to him for the rest of her life. It used to be only girls you did that to. Now it is a whole people.'*

Frank dropped the paper disgustedly and stood up. 'Better toddle round a bit, I s'pose, see no one's cheating,' he said in a stentorian whisper that would have alerted anyone doing so, even in the remotest corner of the hall. 'Thank God *I'm* getting out of Hong Kong while the going's good. When d'you retire, by the way?'

'Hong Kong and I,' Dimitri said, 'we wind down together.'

Failing light without her

Lily walked slowly down towards the Public Gardens — she never did get used to calling them Huang Pu Park — for the last time. Now it was June, she walked on the shady side of the street, as she always had in summer, as if today were just the same as any other day. But she was looking at the shops, the shabby buildings, the people loitering or hurrying, with a different eye, the eye of a leaver who does not take her leave.

When she waited on the kerb for a bus to pass, a young man's face in one of the windows caught her eye, as hers caught his. He seemed to recognize her, and smiled a faint sheepish smile, but the bus had passed before his dimly familiar expression slotted into its setting. Of course, the half-secret meeting of young dissidents she'd been invited to three or four years ago, soon after she'd been released from the labour-camp.

They were nearly all students, young, solemn and naive. In a narrow room over a shop on Huaihai Road, sitting on an old iron bedstead, on stools, on the floor, they gave her the only chair as the doubly honoured guest — honoured as the widow of an early communist martyr, honoured as a 'formerly persecuted person.' But the moment she sat down she knew she shouldn't have come. They were tender children in a brutal grown-up world. What could she tell them except that when they became troublesome the cells would be waiting for them, or the bullets?

They were encouraged by the new freedom, a girl had said. They hoped that Marxism would be democratized.

Lily only shook her head.

They hoped they could learn from her experience, though, another said when the chill of that had settled into them. As she reluctantly answered their questions, she was searching each one's face in turn, silently asking: *'And when do the Public Security Bureau come for you?'*

They thanked her politely but disappointedly, and gave her a copy of their ill-printed pamphlet. *Problems in Chinese Marxism*, it was called.

A year later people were being put in prison for writing stuff like that. That young man on the tram at least must have stopped in time. No wonder he looked sheepish.

Would it ever change? Would it ever?

Shadows were leaning out from the shrubs and trees in the Public Gardens, and she watched her own long shadow as she walked, thin, black and angular as her thoughts. She sat down on the usual bench overlooking the river. The sun was weakening, but still strong enough to scorch her cheek. She put her hand up to shield it.

A man swayed towards her, holding a bottle of Fan Yang beer. He was wearing blue trousers, a patched shirt and plastic sandals on his bare dirty feet. 'Where you from?' he asked in a thick voice, gazing at her unfocusedly, his cheeks blotchy red.

She stared away over the river, tinted now by the setting sun. The greyish waters looked as though someone had poured a little gold into them.

The man swigged and belched. 'Not from these parts, are you?' He screwed up his eyes to see her better. 'Not from round here?'

'Not any longer, no.'

The man stood frowning at her uncomprehendingly, then abruptly lurched away. She heard him muttering stupidly to himself as his sandals slithered irregularly along the path.

When Chu came hooting his usual greeting, she felt a senseless rush of guilt. As if somehow she'd cheated him. He started telling her eagerly about some concert by an American orchestra — the first since Liberation — that he wanted to take Wai-chung to. Listening to his genial foghorn of a voice, his trusting genial foghorn, why was it that, now that it had come to the point, she felt she couldn't tell him, she simply didn't know how to start? His cousin's son was something in the mayor's office, Chu said, and he could probably get them a couple of tickets, or one at least, in which case Wai-chung would go by herself of course, being a violinist. Lily wasn't musical, but she asked perfunctorily what the programme was. Chu hooted through it piece by piece; he knew it by heart already. They had a precious record of the Beethoven symphony at home which had somehow survived the Red Guards, and Wai-chung knew a teacher in the Conservatory who would let them listen to it there . . . .

When Lily didn't comment, his voice wound slowly down. He gave her a long quizzical look, then took off his glasses and began polishing them on his shirt.

'I shall miss you,' Lily got out at last, gazing fixedly across the river.

'Ah.' It sounded like a sigh. He looked down at his glasses, still bound with the tape she'd used in the winter. 'I must get some new frames,' he said forlornly. Then: 'It's all settled, then?'

She nodded. 'Tomorrow morning.'

Another sigh. He rubbed his eyes, then put his glasses back on, adjusting them carefully on the bridge of his nose, perhaps to give himself more time. 'I would have liked to invite you to dinner before you go' — he, too, gazed out over the river, 'but . . . .'

'Better not,' she agreed. The PSB would ask questions eventually. 'Besides, I've still got some things to do. And . . . . ' And Wai-chung wouldn't like it. Especially if she knew.

Already the river had rinsed the sunset out, and the waters were running lead-grey again.

'Of course, I guess having your son there makes a difference,' Chu said sadly, as if that could justify both her going and his staying. He'd scarcely ever mentioned her son before, and nor had she except in passing, because they both knew it wasn't for his sake she was leaving. But it made it look natural for her to go if they pretended it was for Patrick's sake; and natural for him not to go, since his sons would certainly never get out.

And after that they couldn't talk.

They couldn't even glance at each other. They gazed out across the river in silence, like two strangers in a train, watching the ferries, the junks, the barges move as they'd always moved, and would move tomorrow in the failing light without her.

Chu thought of the empty space beside him on the bench tomorrow. He looked down at the worn weathered wood as if to start getting used to it in advance. Then he leant forward, elbows on knees, and clasped his hands. 'So we won't see each other again,' he said in a low mournful bellow.

She knew she must leave at once now, get up and go, before he said any more. So she stood abruptly and held out her hand with a stiff jerky gesture. 'Say goodbye to Wai-chung for me,' she muttered gruffly, looking at his hand, not his face.

She walked off quickly, without glancing back. She knew she mustn't see him gazing after her. She'd never considered it might be hard to leave; she'd never dreamt she'd feel this strange, deep, unwonted tug of sadness that made her legs weak and her breath unsteady. *Think what it will be like over there,* she told herself, as she used to tell herself to think what it would be like outside prison, or outside the small number, or after the struggle-meeting — anything to make the present bearable.

But she'd no idea what it would be like over there. She'd never been outside China in the whole of her life, except as a child sixty years ago, when she'd been with her mother in Hong Kong. And all she'd retained of that was one faint image of a narrow street of steps leading down to a harbour, and a room with brown shutters looking out onto the street, a room where she sat in a shadowy corner watching her mother painting her face before the mirror, while strange people came and laughed and talked with her. She'd carried that image with her all her life, a postcard from her childhood.

She thought of that.

But still she fell asleep

Every afternoon, after washing her bowl and chopsticks, Ah Wong went down the rough cement basement-steps to do the ironing. But lately the ironing had hardly ever got done. Tablecloths, shirts, handkerchiefs — all vanished for weeks after they'd been washed, and sometimes never reappeared, lying at the bottom of a pile that grew higher month by month.

Going down to retrieve a blouse one day, Mila found Ah Wong sitting by the ironing-board fast asleep, her mouth slackly open, gently grunting and snoring. Her face looked aged and creased, now that all expression except weariness had left it. Her bright young teeth seemed to be grinning sardonically up at her from the jam-jar where she'd put them while she ate. She hadn't even switched the iron on, although she'd plugged it in and set the board up, and still held the water-sprinkler ready on her lap. It was as though sleep had suddenly poured over her like an invisible lava, and set solid. Mila recovered the blouse without waking her, and quietly left the room.

And it was the same nearly every day. Mila started secretly taking clothes to the dry cleaner's.

'She is getting old, that is all,' Mila said. 'What is so surprising about that?'

But Dimitri didn't want to believe it.

'She used to never rest,' he said. 'She was always doing things.'

'You used to never split infinitives. I used to dance.'

'Perhaps it's that damned musical watchman, robbing her of her beauty-sleep at night.'

'Perhaps it is the heat,' she suggested ironically. 'Perhaps none of us ever gets old.'

'I don't mind getting old; it's getting feeble I object to. Well, I don't mind it as *much* as getting feeble.'

'You mind everything really,' Mila said, not in the least ironically now. 'That is why you pretend you do not mind at all.'

But it *was* very hot that summer. The flames of the forest bloomed all at once, as if suddenly ignited by the sun. Whenever he saw their scarlet petals flowering over their dark green leaves, he thought of Helen. They were flowering then, too, when she killed herself. And she was wearing a red dress as well — almost the same brilliant tone, he seemed to remember.

One of the last things she ever said to him was like a whimper. 'How is it possible that two people who used to like each other so much spend all their time now quarrelling?'

'How is it possible they don't?' he'd answered curtly, staring out over the sea to avoid looking at her.

Perhaps if he'd bitten that back — God knew he'd bitten enough back in his time, enough to give him ulcers — she might have been diverted from her death. But at the time of course the thought of her dying never crossed his mind — suicide was for film stars and hysterical girls, not thirty-year-old mothers of two. Still, even if he had diverted her, it would only have been a delay. She would have come back to it sooner or later, like a terminal patient after a brief remission. Better she got it over and done with at once, and didn't prolong the agony.

Why, then, did he feel so callous, thinking such a thought?

He'd never told anyone, not even Mila, that the worst part about it all for him wasn't finding her body, or even the inquest — though they were bad enough — but seeing it all in the papers, seeing Helen and himself described in the third person, in the clapped-out clichés of page-four journalism. Because they fitted, they were true. He knew what Patrick was going through now. Was going to go through, rather.

The funeral hadn't been so bad; by then he was too exhausted to care — as were the children, he imagined. Why else did they go through it all dry-eyed? The only one to cry was Ah Wong. As though she held herself obscurely responsible, as though of course an amah ought to foretell and forestall her tai tai's suicide, as though it was part of the job like picking up the children when they fell down or mopping the kitchen floor. Or perhaps she just felt guilty for the stony will with which she'd won each skirmish in her long kitchen campaign for domestic hegemony. Not very likely, that, he considered.

The children had been in the front pew of the church, between Ah Wong and himself. She'd snuffled and dabbed her eyes throughout the service, but their faces remained pale and set, without a tear — like all the other impassive occidentals. She thought them heartless at first, but he told her it was shock; only later did he come to think it was just fatigue. Certainly he himself had felt merely a weary sense of relief, just pure tiredness, spreading through him; relief that soon it would all be over.

Like everything else about his relationship with Helen, even her funeral arrangements had been problematic. He forgot to take the death certificate along with him to the crematorium when 'confirming her booking'—that was how they described it — the day before. The clerk was about to cancel the reservation — the last slot on a Saturday, he remembered — and give it to a young Chinese waiting impatiently behind him, when the undertaker passed an envelope across the desk, and the place was his. Dimitri never asked how much it cost — he was too distracted at the time — but five hundred dollars for *Sundries* appeared discreetly on the bill.

The first part of the service was held in the church, then there was a short ride to the crematorium at Cape Collinson, where the last words were read, and the coffin descended silently into the furnace-room. No soapy music, he'd insisted on that. The crematorium had two tapes, one for Chinese, one for foreign-devils, and they both sounded like supermarket muzak. Helen a pianist — he wouldn't let them do that to her. He tried not to think of her body down there, charring, melting, popping and crackling.

Afterwards, Ah Wong grew cheerful. She stood with a child hanging on each hand, looking out over the bay ('Good fung shui,' she said approvingly) and telling Frank Browning in pungent pidgin her opinion of the relative merits of English and Chinese funeral customs. 'Englishy do more betta. No loud noisy all nigh', all day. No frien' come housey all the time say hallo hallo. I no likey Chinesey way, Englishy finish one day, more betta.'

What did the children make of that? He never asked them.

Atheist though he was, whenever he recalled that funeral service afterwards — the simple hymns, the hopes of resurrection, the gravely gracious words (he excepted the imbecilic parson's smugly fatuous homily) — it gave him pause. The hopes were all illusions, but still they moved him — a naive human myth to mitigate a cruel inhuman fact. He couldn't scoff at it as others could — Patrick, for instance. Emptied of feeling though he was at the time, he remembered feeling that.

And was Ah Wong growing old now, taking granny naps in the afternoons, herself entering the long tunnel that didn't have light at the end?

Or was it just that damned singing, talking, raving watchman after all, keeping her awake half the night? Or just boredom, now that her sulky niece had gone off and never phoned any more?

Not the watchman, it turned out. A few nights later, about two in the morning, his rambling soliloquies were interrupted by two young Chinese in a van. They got out, flashing their torches, and interrogated him quietly for several minutes. He scarcely answered, gazing at them uncomprehendingly with his sad pouched eyes. Then they led him away.

He went submissively, only giving a forlorn glance back at the little mongrel that had come and gone with him now for several months. The dog followed at first, then hesitated, lay down head-on-paws, and watched resignedly as they put him in the van and drove away.

Ah Wong watched, too, from behind the curtain of her window.

'I didn't say anything,' she said defensively the next morning. 'I didn't mind if he sang all night, it never bothered me.' She was afraid Dimitri or Mila might have passed on her occasional grumblings about him, afraid she might be responsible for breaking his rice-bowl.

And then at last she remembered who he was. 'He's the man who used to pay the amahs every New Year, at the China Provisions Store. Years and years ago.'

'Pay the amahs? Which amahs?'

'All of us,' she said impatiently, as if only a child could fail to know. 'If the tai tai bought a lot from the store, he gave us more. If she only bought a little, he gave us less. All the amahs went there at the New Year, to get their lai see. He was number one there, big desk, two phones, he could write down the orders in English from the phone. Very clever man. Then he started on heroin. Years and years ago.'

Now that she remembered him she was more remorseful still, more apprehensive. But nothing happened. The new watchman went to sleep promptly each evening, as soon as he'd washed his shirt and hung it up to dry on a branch of the bauhinia beside his hut. And he let them sleep undisturbed as well. Only when he woke at first light would there be any noise. Then for ten or fifteen minutes he would sniff, cough, rasp, hawk and spit in an exhaustive evacuation of phlegm from what sounded like the furthest reaches of every respiratory tube in his body. 'If Dickens had lived here,' Dimitri said to Mila, 'he'd have called it *Great Expectorations*.'

Ah Wong forgot about the number one man who used to give her a commission on her missies' orders, and had strayed back into her life again as a poor mad junkie watchman.

But still she fell asleep each afternoon.

Dimitri didn't ask her if she still got her commission.

The mongrel disappeared, not even staying to sniff out the new watchman. Then, a few weeks later, Dimitri saw it on the hillside, with dirty matted fur, lurking round the wild dogs' lair.

That was just before the festival of Tuen Ng, and just before the trial was to open on what the papers called the *Gay Blackmail Murder Case*. Dimitri and Mila had been invited to go with Rachel and Patrick to watch the dragonboat races on the Dentons' boat — a 'freshener', Patrick called it, before his first appearance in court. 'Up and down', Rachel answered when Dimitri phoned to ask her how he was. 'Strangely enough the idea of performing in court seems to have got him on a kind of high.'

'Well, he always did like camping it up a bit. But wait till he reads the papers the next day. That's different, take it from me. We'll pick you up at nine tomorrow, all right?'

But Michael phoned apologetically an hour or two later to call it off. Someone was arriving unexpectedly, he explained in a guarded tone.

'Well, we all know what that means,' Dimitri said when he told Mila.

Not the main thing

'I guess you won't want me around tomorrow when your mother comes?' Rachel asked from the table that she still used as a desk when (which was more seldom now) she was working on her thesis.

'She'll scarcely be in Hong Kong more than an hour or two,' Patrick answered. 'The plan is to meet at some restaurant before she gets smuggled out to Taiwan. Where I'm supposed to visit her later on, after my own little business is over.' He always spoke about himself now in that cool detached manner, as if about some distant acquaintance in whose affairs he himself could hardly be expected to take more than a passing interest. Rachel judged it a sign of improvement that he was speaking at all. 'That is,' he added, 'if they let me into that righteous little island of theirs, after the revelations about my private life which will doubtless soon be titillating the prurient public's eyes and ears.'

'What I really meant was, do you want me to move out for a time? Or for good?' She tapped a sheaf of notes end-on against the table as though she was ready to leave that minute if he said the word. 'Regardless of your mother.' She hadn't really meant that at all; she wouldn't dream of leaving him alone. It had just come into her mind because she wanted some assurance, some word of appreciation. And she hadn't had one yet, not a single one.

'Dear girl, you know I don't want you to move out.' But he spoke in the same remote tone, gazing absently across the room as if he was only half-attending.

Well, she'd have to make do with that, then.

Patrick plucked the pi-pa's strings. Not a melody, just a few stray chords. He'd taken to carrying it about the flat with him now, like a wandering minstrel. He no longer thought of the limping man, now dead, who'd strummed it when they broke in on Chung Yan and himself. It was just something to hold and occupy his hands with. 'Of course, if you feel contaminated by my depravity . . . ?'

'For God's sake, Patrick, you haven't got anything to be ashamed of, just because the archaic laws of this reactionary little British colony — '

'And yet I do feel ashamed all the same.'

He glanced at her for once when he said that, and she thought that, too, was a sign of improvement. Mostly he avoided her eyes, looking past her like someone at a party wishing he could leave. And still, mostly, he spoke only when spoken to, and even then answered as if his mind was only half there. She sometimes blamed it on the pills the psychiatrist gave him.

'Are you . . . nervous about meeting your mother?' she asked a few minutes later. 'Looking forward,' she was going to say, but obviously he couldn't be that. 'After such a long time, I mean?'

'Nervous?' His brows rose consideringly. 'No, not nervous,' he said after a time. 'It's like being stung by a wasp on the way to Calvary. One would prefer not to be, but clearly it's not the main thing.'

'Calvary! I wish you wouldn't be so melodramatic.'

'Not that she knows about my perverse proclivities yet,' he went on in the same dispassionate voice. 'No doubt when she does, being something of a zealot, she'll deplore them. But I don't think either of us interests the other very deeply. What am I to her but the stranger she gave birth to? What is she to me but the stranger who gave me birth?'

'Very pretty,' Rachel said, more sharply than a moment later she wished. 'Like your old self again.'

Patrick gave no sign that he'd heard. 'She's embarking on her last crusade, and I'm embarking on my first crucifixion, that's all we have in common now.' He struck a chord to show the scene was over.

'I don't see why you should call being a witness in a trial a crucifixion.'

'Should I wear something really poofterish?' he asked with a sudden, if slight, display of interest. 'Something that would really show me up in the witness-box? Rings and perfume and so on — give the press a field-day?'

She thought she'd better not take him up on that. 'Oh, I brought your mail from the U,' she said. 'I forgot all about it.'

When she placed the letters beside him on his chair, he laid his hand on them without looking, as someone might on a cat that had just jumped up — out of habit, without any real interest.

'Mind if I turn the air-con up a bit?' She twisted the knob to maximum. It wasn't really powerful enough for the room in that heat, but as he still wouldn't have the windows or balcony doors open to let the breeze in, that was the best she could do. As if anyone could climb up the drainpipe and over the balcony rail to get at him. With that police car below as well. Let alone wanting to.

'What time is she coming?' she asked. 'Your mother?'

'Michael will ring.'

'Only, I thought I might go and watch the dragonboat races while you're gone.'

'Yes. Why not?'

'Aren't you going to look at your mail?'

'Mm? Oh yes. Later.'

Gave her his hand

Lily was sick in the boat. She'd never realized how much those junks would wallow in the short choppy seas and, besides, she hadn't had a breath of fresh air the whole time, cooped up in the dark stuffy hold with the smell of diesel fumes and rotting fish. And before that the long anxious journey to the south, and waiting in that hut by the shore with nothing to eat or drink all day, and the rats scurrying and squeaking round her feet. No wonder she was sick.

She lay retching weakly for several hours while the bilge water slopped beside her and the thumping engine stopped and started, stopped and started.

But it all went smoothly in the end, as somehow she'd been sure it would. The sea grew calmer, then the engine stopped once more and didn't start.

Yin Hong opened the hatch and called her up on deck in a hoarse murmur.

It was just before dawn. He helped her into a sampan, which the pregnant-looking girl and the tattooed young man with the scarred cheek were holding against the junk's side. Then Yin Hong climbed in beside her and handed her her bag. The girl pushed off, rowing with a single oar from the stern, while the young man peered at the shore from the bow. Lily glanced back at the junk, the old man gave her a courteous nod from the wheelhouse, then turned away. His wife waved. Two younger men watched from the deck. Nobody spoke a single word.

She listened to the creak of the oar behind her, and the swish of the water against the sampan's sides. All the time she gripped her bag tight, nursing it on her knees.

The sampan grounded with a little crunching noise on a pebbly beach. The young man held it still, then shoved it off as Yin Hong and Lily clambered out. Yin Hong led them into the bushes that grew thickly down to the edge of the beach, and they waited there, listening to the creak of the oar as the sampan slowly receded.

She had arrived, then. She was out of China. She was free. But what were they waiting for now? She glanced at Yin Hong enquiringly. He nodded towards the invisible sampan.

It was as humid there as in Shanghai. Her skin was slippery with sweat. Her heart was knocking, too. She listened to the cicadas all round them, and to the trickle of a stream nearby. Then she heard the quiet thudding of the junk's engine, slowly fading, and, a few minutes later, the regular plash of someone swimming. Soon the girl's head appeared, then her whole dripping full-bellied body, her shirt and trousers clinging to her like another, wet, skin. The girl wrung out her long hair as if it were a towel, shook herself like a dog, and they set off along a steep narrow path, the young man leading.

'A pregnant girl shouldn't be doing all the work,' Lily whispered severely to Yin Hong. Yin Hong chuckled and muttered something to the girl in Cantonese.

'M'gan yu ah,' the girl muttered back throatily.

'She says never mind,' Yin Hong whispered.

The young man in front half-turned, then went on.

Lily was out of breath when at last they reached a stone hut on the edge of a hill. Yin Hong pulled out a bundle from a corner. 'Change into Hong Kong clothes,' he said. 'Don't worry — Ah Keung and me, we'll go outside.'

The girl helped her, shining a little torch as she picked out a dress and sandals like the ones Lily had seen foreigners wearing in Shanghai. The girl took some loose jeans and a shirt, then switched off the torch. They changed silently. Then the girl wrung out her wet clothes, took Lily's old ones, and put them all away in the same corner. She sat down with her back against the wall, laid her head on her knees and dozed.

Lily sat down, too, but she couldn't rest. With her hand still on her bag, she gazed out of the small glassless window at the paling sky. *I've done it*, she kept thinking, *I've done it*. Her heart was slower now; but she was still sweating, the new clothes stuck to her skin.

Then Yin Hong and Ah Keung came in through the half-open door. 'Ling Kwan here will take you on, about ten o'clock in the morning,' he said. 'It's a Sunday. There'll be a few hikers around; you'll look just like them.' He gave her his hand, which he'd never done before. 'Ah Keung and me have got a bit of business to settle; we're leaving now. Good luck, Lily.' His hand felt moist and cold, and his voice, she thought a moment later, had weakened.

Lily watched them pass one after the other out of the door and, when she turned back, realized the girl wasn't dozing, but watching her quietly through her slitted eyelids.

'I said I'd give Ling Kwan Woodchopper's share,' Yin Hong said uneasily as they walked along the path that Rachel had followed with Patrick and Chung Yan in the autumn. 'So what's the problem?'

They had reached the abandoned schoolhouse where Ah Keung once had had his lessons. 'The Yellow Bamboo,' Ah Keung said softly, reaching into his pocket. 'That's the problem.' The long furrow of his scar twitched as he spoke.

'Yellow Bamboo?' Yin Hong's stomach turned. 'Yellow Bamboo? What d'you mean?' He tried to bluster, but then a couple of figures moved out from the shadows of the schoolhouse, and they, too, had knives in their hands.

Yin Hong gulped, shuddered, started to run, then just stood and waited, closing his eyes.

Where are the British policemen?

Michael pulled the car off the road, opened the boot, and bent down as if examining the tyres. After a few seconds he heard the grass rustle. Lily stood beside him. She put her bag in the car. Michael forced himself to bend over the tyre a few more seconds, then slowly straightened up and closed the boot. 'Get in beside me,' he said, as naturally as his shaky voice would let him. 'No, the other door.'

It was like going back to her childhood — the greenness, the well-made road, the shabby but prosperous villages, the vulgar villas of the rich. The last time she'd been in a Rolls-Royce — it must be forty-five years ago now — was with her father. She remembered driving out from Shanghai into the hills with him one summer day like this. They saw some hunger-marchers trudging towards the city. Was that the time, or was it another time? There were so many after all; there were always hunger-marchers. Yes, it must've been much more than forty-five years ago; she was still a schoolgirl. And now she was driving in Michael's Rolls-Royce, with Michael saying something about Grace's identity-card. And in between lay the years she'd lost her faith in. Most of her life.

'You'll find Grace's identity-card in that handbag,' Michael was saying. 'That little bit of plastic, that's right. You don't look much like her, but they're not likely to stop a Rolls anyway. There's a police check-point about a mile ahead of us. Just put the sunglasses on and behave normally.'

He was scared; she could tell that by how rapidly he spoke, and by the way he kept licking his lips. It made her mildly contemptuous. What risk was *he* running? *He* wasn't going to be sent back to China if she was caught. But she knew she wouldn't be caught now; she couldn't be.

'I'll take you to a place in Tsim Sha Tsui, and the Taiwan people will take you on from there,' he said in the same tense rapid tone. 'There'll just be time to meet Patrick and Grace first.'

Tsim Sha Tsui — where was that? Never mind. She nodded and put on the glasses. The dark lenses muted all the colours. She couldn't remember when she'd last worn sunglasses. 'How is everyone?' she forced herself to ask, and while he answered thought of all the handwritten notes for *The Fourth World*, safe in her old worn bag in the boot of the car.

'Fine, fine.' His tongue passed over his lips again. 'Patrick's not been too well actually, but . . . . ' He nodded. 'That's the check-point at the bottom of the hill.'

'Well, just keep talking,' she said sharply. 'Don't look as if you're afraid.'

'I can't think what to say.' His mouth scarcely moved.

'Well, say that, then. And what are you going through your pockets like that for?'

'I can't find my diary. I must've dropped it when I was bending down by the car.'

'Well, say that, then, too. Just keep talking, that's all.'

The police were checking a green taxi and a small van. A constable waved the Rolls past with scarcely a glance. And that reminded her of her childhood, too — the same khaki uniforms, the same deference to wealth. Only, she was surprised the policemen were all Chinese; no pink-skinned Britons or bearded Sikhs, as there used to be in Shanghai.

'Is that all?' she asked. 'Where are the British policemen?'

Michael felt his body loosening, a hundred taut muscles letting go. He began cautiously wiping each hand in turn as he drove, crumpling his handkerchief against his palms with his fingers. 'They don't man road-blocks,' he said. 'They do other things usually.'

Lazily in the breeze

'Patrick,' Rachel insisted for the umpteenth time, 'you must decide what you're going to do.'

'Must I?' He was sitting in his usual chair, the pi-pa across his knees. The letters she'd brought the day before lay unopened on the floor beside him, like a pack of abandoned playing-cards.

'You know you must,' she said severely. 'How many times have I told you?'

'I don't *do* things any more. Things happen to me. Next Monday, for instance, I shall be crucified in court. On Tuesday I shall be crucified in the papers. After that, the university. I don't have to *do* anything except stretch out my arms, place one foot on the other, and wait for the nails to go in.'

'So there'll be a bit of gossip in the papers and the common room,' she said. 'And then what will you do?'

'Do? What is there to do?'

'I mean, you've got to think about it.'

'Have I?' He plucked a couple of strings and listened to them shimmering slowly away. 'Well, then, I shall probably be dismissed from the university unless I do what is known as "the decent thing," since *doing* is so much on your mind. And I'll end up a pathetic seedy queer in some bedsit in Bloomsbury or Notting Hill.'

Rachel wasn't sure where those places were, but she reckoned she had his drift. 'I just wish you'd cut out that melodramatic self-pitying bullshit,' she was surprised to hear herself blurting out. *Bullshit*, a word she hadn't used for as long as she could remember. 'I mean, am I supposed to weep or something?'

'I shall be terribly, terribly brave, then. And the end result will be the same. Is that better?'

'God, Patrick, don't you see how cheap that is, just trying to make me feel so goddam *sorry* for you all the time?' Another word that felt unfamiliar in her mouth: *goddam*.

'Alas, dear girl. I'm more egocentric than you think. Forgive me, but I never considered *your* feelings for one moment.'

When she cried, she cried silently. The tears filled her eyes and welled over like a pond overflowing. She didn't sniff or blow her nose, so usually people never noticed. But as she turned away to dab her eyes, 'Transcendence, Rachel,' Patrick murmured, in a tone like a rueful apologetic pat on the back. It was the first time since she'd moved in that he'd actually said a kind word to her.

'Damn you, damn you,' she said unsteadily, smiling and swallowing. His voice reminded her of the ferry pier at Cheung Chau six months before, of the charge that had gone through her then and got her into this mess, which she absurdly didn't even want to get out of. 'Damn you.'

'Transcendence.' He said it warningly this time, but still with something like affection. 'Transcendence.'

'Aren't you going to read your mail?' she asked in almost her normal tone again. 'After I specially got it all for you? I don't usually say "damn" or "bullshit," do I? Or "goddam"?'

'No. You don't usually say "damn" or "bullshit," I mean. Or "goddam".'

'Well, then, *read* it. And let me get on with some work.' As if he'd been chattering to her all morning.

Patrick shrugged and obediently opened a few envelopes. But he discarded their typed contents listlessly on the floor after a perfunctory glance, as if to say 'What can this possibly have to do with me now?' Faculty board meetings, senate meetings, syllabuses, examinations . . . . The papers fluttered down. All except one, which he started scanning as casually as the rest, but then read slowly and carefully, with an intent frown. Then he laid it down on his lap, gazing unfocusedly across the room. So she'd died, then, Emmelina Wu.

'Think I'll make some coffee,' Rachel said from the table, still distracted from her work. 'Want a cup?'

Diligent dowdy Miss Wu, with the earnest eyes and the thin tensed shoulders.

'Patrick? Cup of coffee?'

'All right.' Such an unremarkable girl, he would have thought, and indeed had thought for a long time. From one of those shabby housing estates, Sha Tin or Tsuen Wan or somewhere, the whole flat smaller than his own living-room probably, with half a dozen people living in it, brothers, sisters, mother, aunt — who knew how many? He remembered her showing him her application to do a post-graduate degree at some Canadian university, asking him to be a referee. Only a few months ago, before she found out she was ill. *Father deceased, mother sales assistant. Missionary-school kindergarten, church school, youth group* . . . . It was like the story of a nineteenth-century Manchester working-class family — dogged, industrious, honest people, grinding their way resolutely up out of poverty. The sort of people Hong Kong should be handed over to instead of whoever it was exactly that was going to grab it now (he'd stopped reading the papers or watching television, he felt nothing in the future concerned him any more). But instead of inheriting the place, she was applying to study abroad, the first step obviously to a Canadian passport and an escape route for her mother and younger brothers and sisters.

Yes, a worthy mediocre student, until she discovered she had cancer. Then she was transformed. Beneath the dull topsoil of her personality there ran a vein of quiet granite. She willed herself to live until she got her degree and, if willing could do it, she would have succeeded. What good would a degree have done her? He didn't know. He only knew she became determined, rock-like, courageous. He'd no idea she was seriously ill until she calmly asked him one day about the possibility of an aegrotat degree. 'The doctor says I may not be able to finish the examination,' she said in her pale voice that strengthened as she weakened. 'So I would like to know if I can get an aegrotat.' She'd read the regulations carefully and knew them better than he did of course. Then she gave him the medical certificate, which implied in so many words — Hong Kong doctors never broke it to you gently — that she had at most a few months to live. She never showed a quiver of self-pity, and when he tried to say something sympathetic, led him almost impatiently back to the subject of her degree. Why did she want it so much? She wanted her life to have some completion, he supposed. She wanted it to have a headstone. He felt small and hollow beside her then.

Why did he himself feel this shrinking fear of death — he'd been hovering near the edge for weeks now, months — while she apparently did not? She'd entered it as simply as someone moving to another town, packing her things tidily, paying all the bills, methodically putting everything in order, then calmly leaving the familiar for the unfamiliar place.

'Coffee,' Rachel said, placing the cup on the table beside him. 'Deciding your future after all?'

He didn't answer.

The phone rang in the hall. For some reason it startled her like an alarm-clock shrilling in the middle of the night.

'It's for you,' she said. 'Michael. Guess this is it.'

Yes, it was it.

'I'm supposed to meet them in an hour,' he said when he came back. 'In Tsim Sha Tsui.'

'It'll take you half an hour from here,' Rachel said practically. 'I'll go and watch the dragonboat races. We can leave together.' She had a suspicion he might baulk at the last moment, unless she saw him out of the door and on his way. 'What about the police downstairs? Won't they follow you? Or won't it matter since they won't know what's going on?'

'It won't matter,' he said, sitting down again.

It had suddenly become clear to him all at once that he should do it now, today, this minute. Not that he'd only just decided. As far as decisions went, he'd decided weeks ago; he'd even written letters and locked them in his desk. But decisions were only thoughts and words, unstable fleeting things, recallable at will. Now his will itself had firmed, as if someone had taken hold of him and said: 'Go on now, go!' And someone had. Emmelina Wu.

He felt a quiet relief, almost elation, at that, as though a gaoler bearing down for a long time on his shoulders had now suddenly released him. He was buoyant again. So he wouldn't have to face his alien mother, he wouldn't have to face the cameras outside the court, he wouldn't have to face the sneering, wigged and fox-faced counsel, he wouldn't have to read about himself like some degenerate specimen in a glass case, he wouldn't have to listen any more for people sniggering behind his back, he wouldn't have to torture his mind any more about Chung Yan — had Chung Yan set him up or not, and who was he going with now?

He could leave it all behind; he could just leave.

'Think I'll go and watch at Aberdeen,' Rachel was saying. 'If you're not going to drink that coffee, I'll take it away. Shouldn't you be getting ready? You ought to be leaving soon.'

Leaving soon.

He heard her in the kitchen as he stood up. So this was it, then. It was time to go. He unscrewed the typhoon-bars quietly and deliberately, and opened the balcony doors. Only three steps to the edge. He knew he mustn't look over or hesitate when he got there, it was like diving off the top board. And he mustn't glance back at the room he was forsaking, the things he loved. How strange the brass door-handle looked, and the white mosaic tiles on the balcony floor, the black railing glistening in the sun. They'd acquired a new dimension, a new sharpness and clarity, the dimension of things about to be left. How brilliant the sky was, how burning-hot the railing, so hot he could hardly hold it. Well, just for a second. *Head up*, they used to say, *look straight ahead when you're going off the top board.* It wasn't till he closed his eyes and gripped the rail, and felt the steady quickening of his pulse, that he knew for certain this was real and not just a timid rehearsal after all. The best dive he'd ever done at school was a backward somersault with a clean entry, scarcely a ripple, that had been given full marks by two of the three judges.

He leant over, and leant over further, and felt his feet leaving the floor.

The lightness of being, he thought, as his legs swung up and over, his back arched and his hands wrenched free.

Free.

He was doing a backward somersault again, the best of his life. His ignorant heart pounded against his chest as the air rushed past his ears, but he knew he was free at last, he was free.

Rachel, returning from the kitchen, saw the balcony doors swinging open, and gauzy white curtains floating lazily on the breeze into an empty, empty room.

When Michael phoned anxiously an hour later, he thought at first he'd got the wrong number. It was a police constable who answered. Rachel was lying rigid on her bed, being given a second injection.

The constable passed the receiver to Detective Superintendent Hoames.

Lily frowned and shook her head at first, as if Michael were speaking Dutch or Danish to her. But then, when she'd taken it in, her cheeks set and her eyes stiffened. 'No, there's nothing I can do,' she said grimly. 'Take me to the Taiwan people.'

Grace never said a word, except with her wide absented eyes. She stayed behind to pay the bill.

19

Fountains hissed and splashed

'Funny, that,' Hoames said, meeting Dimitri on the steps from the coroner's court. 'Leaving all those notes for everyone, I mean. Must've been planning it for weeks, but just couldn't get himself to do it, I suppose. Or waiting for the right moment perhaps.'

'No idea,' Dimitri shrugged, narrowing his eyes against the glare as they emerged into the street. Hoames seemed to think his answer inadequate, or even evasive, and paused, waiting for him to do better.

Dimitri thought of Helen carefully posting that letter the afternoon before she killed herself, wishing him luck with Mila and enclosing the mispunctuated poison-pen note as well, to show him how she'd found out about them. How often since then he'd imagined her folding the pages, sliding them into the envelope, sealing it, weighing it in her palm perhaps, thinking she'd be dead when it was opened, or perhaps wondering if after all she shouldn't post it, but simply give the whole thing up as a bit of hysterical dramatics and . . . . And what? 'Well, I suppose people must think about it quite a lot,' he said feebly, conscious of Hoames's sceptical gaze. 'Before they actually . . . .'

'Take the plunge, eh?' He winced. 'Sorry about that. Quite unintentional, I assure you. Well, I suppose you ought to know,' he went on in a tone that was nevertheless rather dubious. 'Got more experience of it than I have, haven't you? First-hand experience, I mean. Which way are you going?'

Dimitri nodded towards Statue Square. 'Bit of shopping,' he murmured vaguely.

'Don't mind if I walk along with you, do you? Know people tend to avoid being seen with policemen, but as I'm not in uniform . . . .'

'Oh, no one would take you for the fuzz,' Dimitri assured him gallantly. 'More like a solicitor, or manager of the Bank. If anyone spots us, it'll be your reputation that suffers, not mine.'

'What's that? Oh, I see.' He fell into step with Dimitri, stroking his moustache. 'Pretty generous to his boyfriend, too, wasn't he, considering?'

'Was he? I didn't read the note.'

'No, of course not,' Hoames agreed, appearing to find that at once laudable and irrelevant. 'Pretty generous all the same, considering.'

They halted at the pedestrian-lights. Dimitri was going to wait dutifully for the green, but Hoames stepped off the kerb. 'Come on. Only perk a copper gets these days, crossing against the lights. Don't like that word "fuzz," by the way. Sounds vaguely obscene.'

'Considering what?' Dimitri asked, ignoring the rebuke with some effort, while Hoames nodded fractionally to a constable lurking in a shaded shop-front, presumably hoping to ambush jaywalkers. The constable gave a performance of a man intently observing a microscopic object a hundred yards behind them. 'Considering what?'

'Considering what? Oh, considering he set him up for the blackmail job — he must've guessed that surely. We had him in the other day — the pansy-boy, I mean. "Potato queens," they're known as in the trade, you know. Specialize in Europeans. I suppose your friend was a sort of honorary European.'

'I thought he'd done a bunk?'

'From your departed friend perhaps. Not from us.' Hoames's emphasis suggested a bunk from them was more or less inconceivable. 'He was pretty co-operative. Too much so, really. Can't use 'em in court, those fancy-boys, they just say what they think you want them to say. The defence sniff them out a mile off. So do the jury.'

The fountains hissed and splashed and kissed the scorching paving stones of Statue Square. Ice-cream and drinks were being sold from tricycle-stalls beneath striped umbrellas. The vendors seemed scruffy and dozy; the buyers, mainly schoolchildren in white uniforms, noisy and smart. Tourists and locals alike memorialized themselves with photos taken against the background of the flowerbeds or the Bank, while spruce men in suits with money-seeking eyes stepped nimbly past. The aldermanic bronze statue of a Victorian gentleman who'd always been anonymous to Dimitri surveyed the scene in a manner expressing confidence that here at last there was an empire on which the sun would never set. Where would they dump him in 1997?

The reflected brilliance dazzled their eyes, and they moved by silent agreement towards the shaded colonnade of Prince's Building. 'Feel sorry for these poofter-boys really,' Hoames said. ' "Set him up" is a bit strong, I suppose. He was as much a victim as the late lamented. Triads get on to them, you see; they don't have a chance. It's either do as you're told, or have your face cut up. Or some other part — no prize for guessing. That's why we aren't bothering with him. It's the big boys we're after, isn't it?' He glanced at Dimitri interrogatively, like a magistrate waiting to hear *his* side of the case.

'I sometimes think the triads must employ more people than government does,' Dimitri offered.

Hoames turned and paused, gazing back over the square. 'About the same,' he said judiciously. 'And a good many of 'em working for both at the same time, I wouldn't be surprised.' He rocked reflectively to and fro on his heels, observing the square with a serenity of expression not unlike the bronze alderman's. 'Probably one in ten of all the people you see about you now,' he hazarded cautiously. 'Rough estimate. School kids included.' His head moved an inch. 'Amazing how those trams have lasted, isn't it? Only place in the world, I imagine. Except San Francisco, they tell me. Never been there, myself. Yes, I wonder what made him decide to do it in the end. That American girl kept muttering something about his mother when she was in shock.'

Watching a crowded green tram haul itself clanking, squealing and groaning round the rising bend towards Wanchai, Dimitri felt Hoames's eyes had slewed to inspect his face. He gazed obstinately after the tram. 'As far as I know, his mother's in China,' he said studiedly. 'Don't think she ever saw him after the early sixties.'

'Before the Red Guards, eh?' He nodded and walked on, correctly assuming Dimitri would follow. 'Well, we both know what trouble *they* could cause, don't we? I suppose he's taken that little secret with him, then, what finally made him do it. Wish he'd waited till after the trial, though; he made a real hole in our case and no mistake. Lucky to get a conviction in the end. Didn't she have something to do with the Communist Party in China, his mother?'

'I believe so, yes. I don't really know. He hardly ever mentioned her.'

Hoames let that sink into a pool of doubting silence. Then, after a few paces, musingly jingling coins in his pocket, he glanced at Dimitri again. 'Rather odd, that American girl living with him, don't you think? Was he AC/DC or what?'

'I would suppose she was *staying* with him rather than *living* with him.'

'Not shacking up? Really?'

'I'm sure you must have asked her yourself, or had the sheets analysed or something.'

'No, we didn't actually. Didn't seem much point really. I was just wondering, that's all.'

'Oh. Just wondering?'

'Matter of fact, I was thinking about this new disease all the queers are getting. Heard about it, have you?'

'AIDS, yes.'

'That's right. Might finish 'em all off apparently.' He sounded like a farmer contemplating the eradication of rabbit pests by myxomatosis. 'Someone should warn her.'

'My guess is she's as safe on that score as you or me. Or more so.'

'Is it, now? That's interesting,' he said without conviction. 'Well, I'd better get back to work. Shopping, did you say? What're you getting?'

Dimitri hesitated, as if he'd been warned that what he said might be used as evidence against him. 'Bread,' he said on impulse. 'Mandarin cake shop. Poppy-seed rolls.'

'Ah, yes, good stuff they have there. Bit pricey of course, but still. Well, I'll leave you to it, then. Oh, by the way, been meaning to ask you for a long time. What d'you think he meant in that note he left you, you know, all that stuff about "lightness of being" or something? Couldn't make head or tail of it myself. Could you? What was he on about?'

Dimitri considered his solid, shrewd, confident face, the face of a man without gaps or fissures, an impervious dense mass of a man, which not the faintest lightness of being would ever penetrate.

'Just playing with words, sort of thing, eh?' Hoames suggested.

'Something like that, yes,' Dimitri agreed.

Only a lull

'I hope this typhoon passes over Hong Kong,' San San said. 'I hope it washes all this misery about poor Patrick away, and then we can just lie still and quiet in the eye of the storm.'

'If it passed right over us, the eye would only be a lull,' Alex said exactly, gazing past her head as the wind spattered rain onto the window. She was lying on top of him, and he wanted her never to move. 'And then the storm would start all over again.'

She shifted so that her cheek was touching his. 'You sound quite like a schoolmaster sometimes.'

'Well, I am one.'

'I know you are,' she murmured. He could feel her breath on his shoulder and her fine black hair drifting over his face. He didn't know whether he liked the dry scent of her hair more, or the moist scent of her skin. After a slow quiet time she said: 'I won't be getting that violin after all. Not yet anyway.'

'Won't you? Why not?'

'Bit short of money.' Her cheek moved against his as she spoke, so that her voice sounded almost inside his head. 'Because of that business with Patrick.'

'You don't know the meaning of "short of money".'

'Well, I'm learning, aren't I?' Everything she said was quiet and dreamy, as if she were on the point of sleep.

And then she was asleep. He could tell by the long steady rhythm of her breathing. He was holding her with one arm round her back, and he could feel his arm rising and falling gently as she breathed.

The wind flung another handful of rain against the window, big heavy drops that slid down in crazy paths as they burst. *I've never watched her sleeping*, Alex thought. He began to edge the sheet slowly down, drawing it off her shoulders, then her waist. When he raised his head he could see the curve of her spine and a mole on her side and the swell of her hip.

'What are you doing?' she asked without moving.

'I thought you were asleep.'

'I was.'

'I was watching you. You've got a mole there. Did you know that?'

'I've got two more.'

'Where?'

She twitched the sheet over them again. 'You can look for them one day.' Then she slipped off him and lay on her back. 'One day I'm going to come here and look at everything in your flat. When you're not here, I mean. So that I can have a background to picture you in when I'm back in the States.'

'Why when I'm not here? It won't change.'

'Too distracting. We should look at everything in Hong Kong like that, too. We ought to go round taking photos of it. So we'll remember it later when everything's changed and we haven't seen it for years. It was our home after all.'

Alex thought of her beach and her cave and the picture of her back he'd carried in his memory all those years. What did they need photos for? '*Was* our home?' he asked.

'Well, my father says all the young people ought to leave. You can't trust China, he says. And I'll have to leave anyway — you can't be a real violinist and live in Hong Kong.'

Alex felt as though he'd stepped unsuspectingly into a sudden dark hole, a pit, while she walked blithely on without him. 'I've never seriously thought of leaving at all,' he said heavily. 'Even now that the commies are going to take it over.'

'You would have if you were Chinese. Or three quarters.'

'Is your whole family leaving?'

'Peter is. Going to Australia. Not my parents. My father says they're too old.' She thought an uneasy second about Paul, then let it go. 'John's going to stick it out with Stella for a time. See how it goes.'

'Well, I suppose they've got British passports and all that anyway, haven't they?'

'Of course. We all have. Safety first.'

'If you go, I'll go.' He reached out to her from the pit. 'Wherever you go.'

She smiled at him with her Chinese eyes in her Chinese face and said a Chinese thought in her English voice. 'That's not the way it's supposed to be, is it? I'm supposed to go where you go.' She pulled him down on top of her. 'You can look for those moles now if you like.'

Now Alex felt she'd hauled him out of the pit and was walking hand in hand with him again, without even noticing what she'd done. *I'm supposed to go where you go. Go where you go. Go where you go.*

'Where shall I start looking, then?' he asked.

She wound her arms round him and held him tight, pressing his face against her throat. 'You're quite warm now,' she murmured into his ear.

Getting the hang of it

Mila passed a card across to Dimitri when he stopped at the traffic-lights outside the airport. 'This is where the company's staying,' she said. 'In case you need to get hold of us.'

'What would he want to do that for?' Elena asked from the back. 'We'll only be gone a week. I bet it's a grotty little dump way out in the suburbs.'

'On the contrary, it says central Taipei.' Dimitri held the card up for her to read before slipping it into his shirt pocket. He glanced across at the runway through the misty curtains of rain that swept over the road and the waiting traffic. The tarmac glistened black and empty behind the chain-link fence. 'Did I give you Michael's sister's address, by the way?' he asked Mila.

'Yes.'

Mila didn't sound eager to meet her. Well, hardly surprising. He wondered whether she *would* meet her in the end.

The roar of a plane's engines sounded overhead. They watched the silvery-grey monster float down through the rain like an aerial whale. Water and smoke spurted as the wheels touched, then the plane settled back and slowed.

A lorry honked impatiently behind them.

'The lights are green,' Mila said.

He turned on to the airport drive. The windscreen-wipers clunked and sloshed the rain aside, but the glass blurred instantly with a new film of water. Despite the air-conditioner, turned to its puny fullest, the windows were misting inside, too. He wiped a patch clear in front of him.

'D'you think Michael had a thing about Patrick?' Elena asked, still gazing at the plane through her own patch of cleared window.

Dimitri watched the rain bouncing noisily off the steaming bonnet, flashing like hail. 'What d'you mean, "a thing"?'

Mila was opening her bag beside him, taking out her ticket and passport.

'Well, you know, he seemed so cut up about it all in his inexpressive way.'

'So were they all,' Dimitri said. 'Even Paul. Though how *he* understood, I don't know.'

'He didn't. He was just upset because everyone else was. Like dogs. Well, I was cut up, too, but it just didn't seem like Michael somehow. He's always so sort of closed off, I mean. But you could tell it really hurt, couldn't you? I mean, I don't think he'd honestly have cared so much if it'd been John.'

'Or Peter,' Dimitri muttered, glancing at her in the mirror. 'Nor would I.'

'What *are* you two talking about?' Mila asked, closing her bag.

'Whether Michael had a thing about Patrick,' Elena said patiently. 'A purely latent homosexual thing.'

Mila tilted her chin. 'Elena, you have sex in the mind.'

'On the brain,' Dimitri corrected her. 'Like clots.' He drew up behind a taxi. 'Of course he didn't have a thing about Patrick, as Elena is pleased to call it. It's just that he was probably fonder of him than he was of his own two sons. Not without reason. And, after all, he did bring Patrick up. People don't necessarily like their own children better than other people's.'

'Did *you*?' Elena asked. 'Don't say if you didn't. I'm sure *I* will. I mean, after all the trouble you go to producing them.'

'What an agonizing question,' Mila remarked in her coolest, driest voice. 'Lucky *I* shall never have to answer it.'

'I'll see you at the check-in-counter,' Dimitri said, before they'd even opened their doors. He didn't want them to keep going on that subject. It was the one thing Mila could be tense about, other people's babies. As if she felt guilty for not having one herself. Well, why didn't she have one, then?

He drove round into the gloomy concrete maze of the carpark, and found an empty bay on the third floor, overlooking the runway. Above the parapet the tail of a KLM jet glided slowly past in the rain, like the fin of some giant prowling shark.

Multi-storey carparks, with their empty cold machines in their dim grim towers, always depressed him. And the grey streaming skies didn't help today, either. Nor did the prospect of going to Patrick's lifeless flat later. He took the lift down to the departure hall.

After they'd checked in, they went to the restaurant, sitting at an empty table by the inward-sloping plate-glass window. Just beneath them, two great planes nuzzled the terminal building like whale pups sucking on a vast indifferent mother. The restaurant windows seemed like the glass walls of a giant aquarium, with a Tristar swimming down to the aquarium floor and a helicopter spinning up from it.

Mila turned to look at the crowded concourse. Tourists were leaving planes and boarding them. Escalators carried them up and down. They flowed in and out of the restaurant like a tide, grasping their souvenirs and their cameras, anxious, excited, uncertain, bored.

'What do they do it for?' she asked Dimitri, who was watching, too. 'They come to this place they know nothing about, they wander around a bit, gazing and gaping, and then they fly off somewhere else, without ever understanding a thing.'

'One might well say the same about life,' he said. 'We all come and gape and wander around the world a bit and then bugger off somewhere else without ever really getting the hang of it. Tourism's the emblem of human existence. Perhaps that's why they do it.'

'Very neat.' Mila smiled at him not quite ironically over the rim of her tea-cup. 'Only a bit precious at the end.'

'Yes, it was a bit bullshitty.' Elena swivelled round on her chair. 'But it's true in a way, isn't it, really?'

At the departure-gate Mila clung to him tightly a moment. It meant, he knew, *You never know when they are going to crash.*

'See you next week,' he said. 'I'll pick you up. Phone if they change the flight.'

Elena brushed his cheek with hers. 'D'you think I should have a baby?' she asked as she drew away.

'Anyone's in particular?'

'Well. Tom's actually.'

'Better his than some men's anyway. Dance well, Elena.'

'Oh, I always do.'

He watched them join the smiling child-like dancers, clustering slim and elegant beyond the barrier.

No, you shouldn't have one really, Elena, he thought. *Not yet. Mila should. Only what if it turned out like Paul?*

Memorial service

In Patrick's flat, empty, stale, silent, mouldy from disuse, Dimitri watched the wind hurl gusts of slanted rain against the quivering windows and rattling balcony doors.

It hadn't taken long to find the two books he'd lent Patrick a few months before and now needed himself; they were lying — unread, he was sure — on top of one of the bookshelves, as if put down for a moment and then forgotten. There must be others he didn't remember now, as there must be books of Patrick's on his own shelves. Let them be. Over the years their trade had roughly balanced.

He turned and wandered round the flat as if wandering round Patrick's life, and saying a last goodbye to it, too. It wasn't the books, the spare elegant furniture, the scrolls and statues that were most expressive. He passed them by like museum pieces; which they'd probably become. It was the black digital alarm clock, still pointlessly measuring time beside his stripped bed, the towel still hanging crooked in the bathroom, the pens and pencils still lying untidily where he'd left them on his desk, the blotter still bearing the inverted image of his writing (his last writing?) — they were the things that saddened him. They had been used, and had no other value except that Patrick used them. Now, without him, they would be discarded, thrown away. They looked forlorn, like orphans mutely pleading.

Pleading for what?

For life, he supposed. For movement, touch, noise, use, misuse — anything but that sepulchral stillness.

He walked into the spare room, where Rachel, whatever Hoames might think, had slept. Patrick hadn't bothered with that room. The solid, ugly, varnished teak wardrobe, the chest of drawers and the bed that the university supplied had all just been stuffed in there, no doubt to get them out of sight. There was nothing on the walls, either, except an ordinary clouded spirit-mirror that someone — surely not Patrick — had fixed on the back of the door. A few dresses still hung in the wardrobe. It was a boarding-house room — almost a cell, when you looked at the rusting iron bars across the window.

As he gazed out at the pelting rain, he heard, sharp and clear, the metal click of the lock turning in the front door.

Rachel started when she saw him in the hall. 'You scared me.'

'I came to pick some books up.' He held them out, as though to prove it if she didn't believe him. 'Michael gave me the key.'

'I came to pick some things up myself.' She shrugged off an empty rucksack and put it by the table. Then she peeled her dripping raincoat off and hung it in the kitchen, standing her umbrella in the sink. Her movements, all her gestures, were habitual and economical, the movements of someone who knew her way around the place, knew where everything was. She was sunburnt he noticed. But thinner; her bare arms looked slight enough to snap.

'How was Beijing?' he asked.

'I just got back, last night.'

'How was it?'

'OK, I guess.'

'Have a good flight back?'

'For me any flight that doesn't crash is good.'

He sat down in the living-room, taking Patrick's pi-pa off the chair and laying it across his lap.

'Is this a typhoon?' Rachel asked, nodding at the streaming windows.

'No, just the edge of one. The real thing's about two hundred miles away. Were they celebrating in Beijing?'

'Celebrating?'

'The prodigal's promised return — Hong Kong to the motherland, I mean.'

'Oh.' She started stacking notebooks and papers on the table.

'Promised but reluctant. Unlike the biblical case.'

'I didn't notice.'

'Ah. I suppose they weren't, then. Nor are they here of course.'

He drifted his fingers across the strings a couple of times, setting up a faint tinkly jangle. 'Never cared much for this instrument, I'm afraid. Even in the hands of someone who could play it. What about Chairman Mao?'

'What?'

'Was he getting moth-eaten in his Mao-soleum, as I seem to recall Patrick once declared?'

'I didn't go to see.'

'No . . . well, not exactly one of the deathless treasures of Chinese culture, it must be admitted. What *did* you see?'

'The usual things. I guess I wasn't in the right mood for tourism, though.'

'Funny you should say that. Mila was just saying something similar at the airport this morning. She can't see why people do it. When you consider most tourists spend large sums of money to do things which the inhabitants of the place would gladly spend the same amount to avoid doing, you can see her point.'

'Very clever,' Rachel said with the ghost of a grin. 'What else can you do?'

'That's about it, I'm afraid. She's just gone to the other China by the way — Mila. The company's performing in Taipei.'

'Are they? She's not dancing, is she?'

'Those days are over.'

Rachel began placing her notes and papers carefully in the rucksack, packing them firmly like an expert hiker. 'I'm glad you're here,' she said.

'You disguised it well, if I may say so.'

'I was kind of nervous about coming by myself.'

'Ghosts?'

She paused, her hand in the rucksack. 'I was afraid I might find the balcony doors open.'

He glanced at the typhoon-bars, securely fastened, and then down at his hand resting on Patrick's pi-pa. He imagined what she must have seen when she ran in panic to look over the balcony. He remembered seeing Helen's body all those years ago, drugged beyond revival, washing drunkenly this way and that in the incoming playful tide.

'You don't forget,' he said. 'You just get used to it.'

'Yes, I know. I saw Frank Browning this morning,' she added quickly, as if she were trying to forget it after all. 'He said he's leaving next week. Retiring, I mean. I always thought he was looking forward to it, but he seemed kind of down.'

'Yes, the forever furlough. It doesn't usually turn out how people expected beforehand. Who likes to accept that life is slowly pulling the plug on them, when it actually comes to the point?'

'Can't we be more cheerful?'

'Sorry. More cheerful, yes. What's happening to your thesis?' He meant, *Do you want me to supervise it now? I will if you like.*

She made a little upwards-pointing gesture, pressing her lips together in another ghostly grin. 'More cheerful still?'

'All right,' he shrugged. *No, thanks*, he supposed. 'Can I give you a lift anywhere? Is that better? I've got my car outside.'

'Yes, that's better. Thanks, I've just got some things to get from my room.'

'Don't forget the spirit-mirror.'

He sat there listening to the coat-hangers knocking hollowly against the wardrobe doors, and to the opening and closing of drawers. Frank Browning today. In thirteen years himself. And then what?

Sometimes, when, as was more and more often the case, he was alone in the house, he had a kind of waking nightmare of paralysis and dereliction. He could hear the traffic whining and rattling past, taxis hooting, hawkers calling, amahs chattering loudly on their way to market, schoolchildren shouting, the whole hustle and bustle of life — he could hear it all, but he seemed to be cut off, immured behind a glass wall, unable ever to move again and join them.

It was the seed of a secret hopeless fear that quietly grew inside him, the fear that he might lie eventually, for years and years, a helpless hulk in some nursing-home bed, aware of nothing but life hurrying past far off, a muted rumble in his ears. Too many things in his life had come to him too late: meeting Mila, publishing his book, Mila's return, his ironic harmony precariously achieved at last. He didn't want death to come too late as well.

Rachel's shoes squeeched wetly down the hall towards him.

'Guess that's about all,' she said.

He nodded, but didn't move. 'I know it's awful in Patrick's case,' he said slowly, gazing at the eyes of a seventeenth-century god smuggled in from some desecrated Chinese temple, 'but there's sometimes something good about knowing when to go, isn't there? I mean, we can't do much about our beginnings, but we could at least arrange our endings less haphazardly than Nature does.'

'Could we?' Rachel was bending over her rucksack, pulling the drawstrings tight. 'So when are you going off *your* balcony?'

He thought, then nodded wryly. 'Yes, well, that is a problem,' he admitted in a chastened voice. 'That spirit-mirror *was* yours by the way, wasn't it?'

'Yes.'

'I didn't think it was quite Patrick's style. It should've been outside the window actually.'

'I know.'

'If you wanted to keep the evil spirits out.'

'I know. It sure didn't keep them out where it was anyway.' She sat down abruptly, the rucksack on her knees. 'It came from Chung Yan's village. He said it was from his house. I guess it might have been, too. I was planning to give it to Patrick, but . . . . '

He nodded.

'Funny, that.' She rested her chin on the rucksack.

'What?'

'Oh . . . . ' She shrugged and shook her head. 'Have you ever kept a diary?'

'I'd feel I was taking myself too seriously.'

'I did. Till recently. I kept it for years, every day.'

'Until Patrick?'

'Until I realized I was . . . . ' She hesitated, winding one of the rucksack straps round her finger, up and down, up and down.

'Did you know I kind of — how I felt about Patrick?'

He thought of Hoames, slily wiping his moustache with his finger and thumb. ' "Know" is a strong word. I assumed.'

She nodded, watching the strap winding up and down. 'Of course he — I mean, he wasn't like that about me. Stupid, wasn't it?'

He shrugged. 'Hopeless anyway. Like driving down a cul-de-sac, I suppose. You wouldn't've got very far.'

'Should've known better, shouldn't I?'

'I expect you did really. You just didn't want to turn round and drive away.'

He stroked the pi-pa strings again.

'Would you mind not sitting there any longer?' she asked quietly. 'Only, it's where Patrick sat before . . . . '

'Is it? All right, let's go.' But he sat still and upright, gazing alertly now round the room, from piece to piece. 'If you come and sit here yourself, though,' he said with a slow wonder in his voice. 'you'll notice something rather strange.'

'What?'

'Come over here.'

He offered her the chair, but she shook her head firmly, standing behind it. 'What?'

'Look at all the statues; they're all gazing at this chair. Even the figures in the scrolls. See? Every one of them. Even behind you. He must have arranged that very carefully.'

Rachel gazed slowly round the room, turning in a full circle. 'It was his favourite chair,' she said.

Dimitri sat a moment longer, regarding the serene still faces which were unconcernedly regarding his.

'Well,' he said at last, and got up.

'Where are you going now?' he asked in the lift. 'Where shall I drop you?'

'I was wondering about my thesis,' she said thoughtfully. 'Would you be willing to take over as my adviser?'

'Supervisor, you mean.' He smiled drily, but his voice sounded pleased, surprised, grateful even. 'It would be an honour to complete any work begun by Patrick. Why don't you come and have something to eat? Ah Wong can test your Cantonese and we can talk about it.'

Rachel shifted the weight of her rucksack. 'OK,' she said.

'Of course, my opinions are generally held to be reactionary, passé, naive and ridiculous. But they might be reasonably compatible with Patrick's. And, whatever else is wrong with them, they won't be modishly phoney. That's about all I can promise.'

'OK.' Something like her old frank amiable smile lightened her face, and they both seemed to relax, as if they'd been holding their breath, tip-toeing round each other until then. She peered short-sightedly up at the descending floor-numbers flashing one after the other on the indicator over the doors. 'Like leaving a memorial service, isn't it?' she said.

'Well, it was one really, wasn't it?'

Not without blood

Lily stood in the Lung Shan temple in Taipei, watching a coach-load of orderly Japanese tourists, loaded cameras at the ready, filing through the gateway after their flag-bearing guide. Before them in the halls and courts, casual disorderly Taiwanese worshippers were lighting candles, drawing fortune-spills, burning paper money, bowing, scraping and praying to their garish incense-wreathed idols.

The dutiful Japanese raised their cameras and shot. Lily thought of her mother at the Hung Miao temple in Shanghai, remembered her bowing again and again, hands clasped in front of her, whispering her superstitious mumbo-jumbo with the other actors, before going on to perform in the Ta Wu Tai.

And here they were two generations later, as ignorant and stupid as ever, muttering the same mumbo-jumbo that had duped them for centuries! It was as bad as the old China; it was almost enough to make her hanker for the new.

Almost, but not quite.

Because she was getting on with *The Fourth World* at last, the words were coming, she was getting them down. And already an American publisher had phoned and met her. A grey-haired man in a neat suit with a neat moustache and rimless glasses. More like an insurance salesman than a publisher, she'd thought (but how did she know what Americans were like?) He'd bought her coffee in the Hilton and said he'd like to read her work, and even talked about an advance. Everything he said and did was neat, even the way he licked his moustache after he'd sipped his coffee. She didn't quite trust him; he was too neatly pressed, too packaged and, besides, his eyes were always shifting behind those rimless glasses. But it was a start, it was an offer. And she was writing, getting things down.

Not that it had been easy at first. She'd had to push and push against soggy walls of inertia and suspicion.

As soon as they'd let her move freely about the place, she'd gone straight to the institutes and libraries, looking for documents and information, explaining time and again what she wanted and why she wanted it. But the polite incomprehensions, the bland evasions, the unaccountable delays! It was only because she insisted that she got anywhere at all. And when she travelled about in buses and taxis, the crowded, hustling, strident city had seemed alien and hostile to her for weeks, harsh and raw, a seething heap of blind money-grubbing ants. She'd wanted to walk at first, but she found she couldn't; she got too short of breath and giddy. A touch of blood-pressure, that was all. Nothing serious, but it had slowed her down; she'd had to rest a bit.

And in the dark of her mind, misgivings had started putting out their roots. Was it only *different* in this other world, not better? Had she left China when it was the time to stay? She hadn't dared think it, but the thought had been there, working on her for a time, sapping her will.

But now that was all past; she'd got used to it all. And she was writing.

She'd remembered Mila's face the minute she saw her, though not the name she went by in the camp. But their meeting was a disappointment. There she was, a fellow-victim, someone who should have been her ally, who should have jumped at the chance to help, but when Lily tried to get precise memories and details out of her, the woman just closed up. She'd forgotten, she said. Wanted to forget, more likely, just like Chu. What was she afraid of?

That doctor, for instance, in Shaanxi, who developed a technique for slitting people's vocal chords so they couldn't shout out when they were being taken to execution — everyone had heard rumours about that. Even Chu. But when she asked her, Mila pretended she'd never heard of him, or couldn't remember anyway. 'They used a wooden gag in Empress Wu's time, didn't they?' was all the help she had to give. Over a thousand years ago! What possible use could that be now? He did it without anaesthetic, that doctor; she was sure she'd heard that. Well, of course. It was little details like that she wanted corroborated. Mila *must* have heard. Everyone had. What was wrong with the woman?

When Mila said something sympathetic about Patrick, Lily acknowledged it only with a lowering of her lids. 'Lucky I didn't leave China just to see him,' she said with chilling realism. Then: 'D'you remember the name of that guard who . . . ?'

She hadn't realized Mila had married an Englishman. 'It won't work,' she'd told her severely, thinking of what she herself had suffered, and Michael no doubt, too, through being Eurasian. 'Your children will have a terrible time of it.'

'I cannot have children,' Mila had said in a voice like a chisel. It wasn't only her back that the Red Guards had damaged.

The disciplined Japanese tourists followed their guide back to their waiting air-conditioned coach, reloading their cameras for the next shoot. Lily, moving back a step into the shade, noticed a woman in black, kneeling on a mat in front of a prayer-book. The woman had high cheekbones and fair northern skin. She was old, but poised and striking despite her age. Even Lily could see how graceful and attractive she must have been once, just from the way she held herself now, on her knees. She was absorbed in some ritual, her eyes unfocused, prostrating herself on the mat to pray before turning the pages of her prayer-book one by one.

Lily watched the lips moving silently in the gaunt, fine, entranced face.

'She was a Manchu princess,' a young woman guide told an American couple standing nearby. 'She comes every day.'

'How old is she?' the woman, bleached blonde and sun-wrinkled, asked, while her grey-haired husband sighted his movie-camera.

'About seventy, seventy-five, I guess,' the girl answered in heavily American English. 'She was a well-known woman once. Notorious.' She gave a suggestive little giggle. 'Too old now.'

The camera whirred for a quarter of a minute on the oblivious Manchu princess. 'Past it now, hey?' the man muttered as he finished. He sounded bored.

But she's my age! Lily thought, amazed. *How can I be as old as her? I must get on with it. I must finish my book, while there's still time.* She'd never really believed, before, that she, too, would be past it one day, any more than, once, she'd believed communism would.

Out in the street, waving to a taxi, she thought again of the Manchu princess, remnant of a collapsed dynasty. Would the communist dynasty ever collapse? *Not without blood*, she thought grimly. *Not without blood.*

She only wished she could see Chu again, and tell him what she was doing. That was her only regret.

The shadow of it lying stark

It was for Patrick that Paul's face used to brighten most quickly. It was only at the sound of that loud voice ringing in the hall that he would leave his drawings or his inner solitudes at once and hurry from his room. Usually, when he was calm enough to eat with the family, it was Patrick he would sit beside, placing his hand trustingly on his arm or shoulder. And Patrick, without looking round or interrupting the flow of his talk, would lay his hand on Paul's as if on the paw of an affectionate loyal dog, for whom communication in words was as unnecessary as it was impossible.

So perhaps it wasn't strange after all that Patrick's suicide disturbed him. Nobody told him — how could they? — but his death was in the air like far-off thunder, and Paul sensed it. Besides, there was Patrick's absence — he couldn't fail to notice that. It was as though he went into prolonged and morbid mourning. He began gradually to recede from them, to become absent in his turn. He drew less and less, then not at all. He grew more and more morose. His eyes stayed staring-blank, like glassless windows. Sometimes, for no apparent reason, he would break out from nothing into a wild rage, flailing at the shrubs with a stick, or chasing the dogs, screaming wordless guttural cries. The savaged leaves and twigs fell to the ground as if from a typhoon, and the dogs bolted yelping. Only Ah Mui or Grace with her mute appealing eyes could calm him then.

'Sometimes they become unmanageable,' Dr. Tsui said calmly, increasing the medication and hinting once more at an institution.

San San tried to coax him back, to reconnect him to their world by the tenuous thread of his drawing. But it was no use; he only stared with stubborn wicked blankness as if he'd never seen a crayon or a pencil in his life. He used to approach Rachel almost as trustingly as he did San San, but now when she came (more rarely than before) he ignored her, too.

'It's no use trying,' Michael said resignedly. 'We can't reach him any more.'

Grace looked at him as if he'd slapped her, and he felt guilty, guiltier still because he hadn't told her he was considering where Paul should be sent when he became impossible or when they were dead — one or the other must happen one day soon. He was colluding with Dr. Tsui.

When they were dead. He'd felt time's nudge giving him its quiet firm warning, and he was too practical not to prepare. Paul would have to go then at the latest; the others would be too busy with their own lives to care more than perfunctorily for his. He told himself Paul wouldn't feel what normal people would in an institution, wouldn't notice the drabness, the monotony, the prison bars of routine, the vacancy of his companions, the long loveless passageways of aimless, hopeless years. He told himself, but it was no use. However you disguised it, he'd be an abandoned dog put out to kennels.

It was soon after Patrick's death that he'd felt time's nudge. He'd woken up one morning with his heart racing, unable to get his breath. Panic rioted through him as he lay there gasping, until gradually the precious air returned to his frantic lungs. 'Delayed shock,' the young Harvard doctor said calmly. 'Nothing to worry about.' But he gave Michael a new and stronger set of pills.

Nothing to worry about? Perhaps, but Michael didn't think now that he'd live to see China take back Hong Kong. He must make his preparations for the others, though, for Grace and Paul and San San and the servants. They must have their escape routes planned and provided. He'd arrange it after he'd finished the Caldwell paper. He'd like to leave his life as tidy as his desk, not in an uncompleted mess as his father had. Yes, he'd felt time's nudge.

He'd come back at last to the Caldwell paper, a year — more than a year, fourteen months — after he'd started it. He'd promised it for October; there was still a lot of work to do. He sat at his blackwood desk, head held long-sightedly back, pencil in hand, and read.

Caldwell was one of those men who, through the accident of their birth, could make their way only in the Orient . . . .

Caldwell? His own father. Himself. It was true of all of them.

Try as he would to shut it out, the image of Patrick's body lying smashed and inert as a burst sack on the concrete of the parking lot kept squeezing back into his mind still. Strange since he never actually saw it there — he'd had to go to the mortuary to identify the body. And he'd never seen the inside of Patrick's flat again, either. He refused to go. But he visualized it clearly often enough, especially the living-room with its abandoned treasures, and the balcony doors swinging open, and the balcony rail.

He would put the flat on the market soon, when prices rose again and people had forgotten why it was vacant. But what to do with all that carefully collected furniture, those vases, statues and scrolls? He didn't want them to go under the hammer piece by piece. They ought to stay together somehow; Patrick would have wanted that. He was thinking of a donation to a museum.

San San started practising upstairs — a Bach sonata, he thought. Grace was standing on the lawn, secateurs in hand, watching Paul, who was swinging his arms about, non-violently at present, like a great unrhythmical child playing windmills.

So things were slowly settling down again; he could be grateful for that at least.

Grace dreamt her dream more often now, the dream that she was drifting down a wide slow river in some fragile shell of a boat. But sometimes she seemed to have drifted further, out of the estuary into the open sea. She was never sitting in the boat; she was always lying in it on her back, like a Pre-Raphaelite illustration she'd seen once of Tennyson's Lady of Shalott. And she saw nothing but the flat smooth sea around her and the curved smooth sky above. She was always alone of course, but she didn't mind that; she even welcomed it. Occasionally she seemed to be hungry or thirsty, but it was more a feeling of emptiness than of pain.

She thought she knew well enough what the dream meant up to that point. But sometimes, not very often, it turned strange. There would be a swoosh of water and suddenly a man appeared beside her, head dripping, black hair plastered flat to the skull. The man's hands clutched the side of the boat, and he started to heave himself in, pulling the boat dangerously down to one side. And then quite deliberately, without panic, Grace chopped the man's fingers off with an axe. The heavy blade sliced cleanly through the flesh and bone, and stuck in the wood. She had to work the haft up and down to get it out. There was no blood. The fingers slid into the boat, where they wriggled like little silvery fish. The man plopped back into the sea, face up, with a tired sigh. And when she looked she saw it was Dr. Tsui, with his white coat ballooning round him in the water.

This cruelty never troubled her in the dream. At the end she was always alone and tranquil, gazing up at the sky. And the boat was still, absolutely still.

Michael was growing closer to Caldwell again as he read himself back into his paper. He felt he was getting to know him properly once more. He felt he'd got the measure of his stride again at last; he could walk in step with him once more from room to room in the house they shared. He could see Caldwell sitting, a hundred and thirty years ago, in the dark corner of the room he himself sat in now; he could hear his wife's bound feet shuffling along the hall to the kitchen. He could hear her whispering to her slippery brother; he could see the two men talking quietly, with the wife sitting watchfully beside them. But one thing he still couldn't see. Did Caldwell take the bait or not? Did he, too, slither into crime? His character was too obscure, the evidence still too uncertain. The question Michael had wanted most of all to answer about his life he couldn't answer. He'd walked in Caldwell's footsteps, lived in his house, learnt all that ever would be learnt about him — he even knew now who'd left those recent flowers on his wife's grave — but still the essence of the man had eluded him, as the essence of Michael's own father had eluded him, too, and as he himself would in his turn elude others. All that was left was the outer shape, a limp blank silhouette. Sometimes, now, inklings of doubt disturbed his faith in history. All that you could know was the outside of things, but it was only the inside that you wanted to know.

He pushed the doubts aside, and went on working.

San San had stopped playing.

He heard a car's wheels crunching the gravel of the drive, then the barking of the dogs.

San San was phoning when the doorbell rang. 'You promised you'd tell me why you always sleep with the pillow over your head.' she said quietly into the misted mouthpiece, which she was half-covering with her hand. 'Why you find it so comforting, I mean.'

'*I don't any more*,' Alex's voice sounded in her ear as she idly watched Ah Yee lead two men towards the study, an Englishman, with a grey moustache and a younger Chinese with short hair. They hesitated and half-bowed as they passed her.

Michael rose from his desk, and closed the Caldwell file with a little protective gesture. 'Mr. Hoames?' he said, in a voice that had suddenly dried.

'Morning. I dare say you can guess why we're here, Mr. Denton.'

Michael shook his head, but the drums were throbbing wildly in his veins already.

The two men eyed him for several seconds, as if to give him a chance to change his plea, then Hoames brushed his moustache. 'We are making enquiries about a snakeboat syndicate, and we have reason to believe you have been involved in assisting and abetting illegal immigrants during a period up to and including June of this year.'

Michael felt fleetingly like an amateur actor in a bad play, a play in which they were all stiffly delivering rehearsed lines and making rehearsed gestures. How self-consciously Hoames spoke the jargon, while the other glanced, not too inquisitively, round the room. Michael even had time to wonder whether they'd brought a warrant with them — all this while Hoames was still speaking and the ground of his whole life lurching beneath him.

'I expect you know this offence carries a maximum penalty of life imprisonment or a five-million-dollar fine?'

Michael opened his mouth, said nothing, swallowed, and started massaging his mutilated little finger. *So it's happening*, he thought. *As I always knew it would. As I always knew.*

'This is Chief Inspector Lee,' Hoames said, in a manner that was less official than apologetic, as if he felt he'd been discourteous in not introducing him earlier.

When Michael looked at him, Chief Inspector Lee gave a nod that could have been either respectful or familiar. He wondered, fleetingly again, if they were taught to behave like that at some school for detectives, or whether it just happened. 'I don't think I understand,' he managed in an almost normal tone, but it sounded like another bad line in the script they all had to act. 'Sit down,' he gestured stiffly as he sat down himself. He felt suddenly weak.

They didn't move. Hoames cleared his throat. 'I believe this is your diary, Mr. Denton,' he said, reaching into his pocket. 'It was found in Sai Kung. Your name's inside it, see?'

Michael swallowed again, and nodded.

'It also has the name of a known snakeboat operator from Macao in it. In your handwriting, Mr. Denton. Plus some notes about your sister.'

He looked back before he got into their car. At Grace, the secateurs still trailing from her hand. At Paul, forlornly, fiercely staring. At the puzzled anxious faces of Ah Yee and Ah Choi by the door, whose eyes he couldn't meet. At the brilliant sunlight on the house, and the shadow of it lying stark across the lawn. So he had failed them after all.

Somewhere, in another world, San San was obliviously playing Bach again. *When she stops playing*, he thought, *she'll find out*.

He willed her to go on playing until he'd gone.

The two men sat one each side of him in the back of the car.

About the author

Christopher New was born in England, educated at Oxford and Princeton Universities, and has lived in Asia for many years. Recently head of the Philosophy Department at Hong Kong University, he now writes full-time.

Christopher New has published several novels, mainly set in Asia. *A Change of Flag* is the unifying novel of *Shanghai,* which is an historical novel set in the city in the first fifty years of the twentieth century, and *The Chinese Box,* which deals with Hong Kong at the time of the Chinese Cultural Revolution. Both are scheduled to appear in Asia 2000 editions. The trilogy's theme, reminiscent of Paul Scott's *Raj Quartet,* is the apogee and decline of the British Empire on the China Coast. Another novel, *Goodbye Chairman Mao* presents a fictional account of the Lin Piao 'plot' against Mao. Christopher New has also published numerous articles in philosophical journals and a book, *Philosophy of Literature: An Introduction.*

His books have been translated into German, Portuguese, Japanese and Chinese. *Shanghai* was on the *New York Times* Best Sellers list for eight weeks.

Best-selling fiction and non-fiction about Asia from Asia 2000

Cheung Chau Dog Fanciers' Society   *by Alan B Pierce*
'A rare read indeed. An accurate slice of Hong Kong life — touching on heroin smuggling, money laundering, corruption in the police force as well as in one of Hong Kong's most wealthy and powerful Chinese families — a thriller with a difference.' — *Hongkong Standard*

Temutma   *by Rebecca Bradley and John Stewart Sloan*
An ancient monster is imprisoned beneath Kowloon Walled City in Hong Kong. It escapes . . . . 'Page-turning . . . intelligent writing and suspense, suspense, suspense . . . thrilling' — *South China Morning Post*

Riding a Tiger   *by Robert Abel*
'Fisher is under house arrest and required to write his testimony as the result of the mysterious death of his friend Chen Tai-pan . . . . Characters richly populate Fisher's life. His observations are philosophical and heartfelt. A lively, upbeat and humorous look at Beijing life through the eyes of an unabashed Westerner.' — *South China Morning Post*

Last Seen in Shanghai   *by Howard Turk*
Murder and intrigue in 1920s Shanghai. An American casino owner is embroiled in a plot involving warlords, pirates, revolutionaries and smugglers in a city divided between the British, French and Japanese.

Hong Kong Rose   *by Xu Xi*
From a crumbling perch with a view of the Statue of Liberty, Rose Kho, Hong Kong girl who made it, lost it, and may be about to make it or lose it again, reflects, scotch in hand, on a life that 'like an Indonesian mosquito disrupting my Chinese sleep' has controls of its own

Chinese Walls   *by Xu Xi*
'Although simply written, *Chinese Walls* tells a complex and controversial story of a Chinese family. The author goes boldly where other, perhaps overly-sensitive, Asian authors fear to tread in tackling such subjects as sex, Aids, homosexuality, incest and adultery.' — *Eastern Express*

Daughters of Hui   *by Xu Xi*
'Their menfolk are arrogant, absent Chinese husbands who neglect their wives for even more arrogant parents. Their extended families are xenophobic, diaspora Chinese whose worst nightmare is the horror of their offspring assimilated with the loathsome *gweilo*.' — *South China Morning Post*

Chinese Opera   *by Alex Kuo*
'Kuo gave himself an ambitious task, setting his story of an American-Chinese exploring his cultural roots against one of the most vivid historical backdrops of the century.' — *South China Morning Post*

Best-selling fiction and non-fiction about Asia from Asia 2000

Getting to Lamma   *by Jan Alexander*
A young American woman carves out a place for herself in Hong Kong. To do so she must deal with an old flame, a handsome young Shanghainese, two babies and an elderly Chinese nurse.

Farewell My Colony   *by Todd Crowell*
A journal of the final two years of Hong Kong under British rule.
'An intelligent and illuminating book, the stylish writing is itself a source of pleasure.' — *Asiaweek*

Cantonese Culture   *by Shirley Ingram & Rebecca Ng*
A guide to the etiquette and customs of Hong Kong and other Southeast Asian cities. The rituals of daily life — birth, death, marriage, and the many festivals that make up the Chinese calendar are described and explained.

Hong Kong, Macau and the Muddy Pearl   *by Annabel Jackson*
'A pleasure to read and an inspiration to learn more about a region that has a surprising amount to offer.' — *Asiaweek*

Hong Kong Pathfinder   *by Martin Williams*
Explore Hong Kong's rugged hills, forested valleys, reservoirs and waterfalls, temples and aging villages, long-abandoned forts and near-uninhabited islands, lead by this informative pocket guide.
'Thoughtful and meticulously researched' — *Action Asia Magazine*
'A boon for neophyte ramblers in Hong Kong and a handy reference for old hiking hands.' — *Discovery*

Getting Along With the Chinese for fun and profit   *by Fred Schneiter*
Schneiter delves into the lighter side of Chinese psychology and demystifies one of the toughest markets in the world. He explains when you should and how you can apply pressure, what to do and what not to do when hosting Chinese guests, and much more. 'Facts on China no degree of study can give' — *The Shanghai Star*

Red Chips: the globalisation of China's enterprises   *by de Trenck et al*
'A useful resource for anyone seeking to find out about the structures and operations of China's conglomerates.' — *Finance Asia*

Walking to the Mountain   *by Wendy Teasdill*
'Wendy Teasdill provides a vivid personal account of how she was drawn to Mount Kailash. Inspired by the beauty of the landscape and her admiration for the Tibetan people she met, she reached her goal.' — *The Dalai Lama*

Round   *by Madeleine Slavick & Barbara Baker*
Award-winning photographs and poems forming a meandering circle through Asia, through Hong Kong, Japan, Korea, India, Tibet and other countries.

Books From Asia 2000

Non-fiction

Behind the Brushstrokes Appreciating Chinese Calligraphy	*Khoo & Penrose*
Cantonese Culture	*Shirley Ingram & Rebecca Ng*
Concise World Atlas	*Maps International*
Egg Woman's Daughter	*Mary Chan*
Farewell, My Colony	*Todd Crowell*
Getting Along With the Chinese	*Fred Schneiter*
The Great Red Hope	*Jonathan Eley*
Hong Kong, Macau and the Muddy Pearl	*Annabel Jackson*
Hong Kong Pathfinder	*Martin Williams*
Hyundai	*Donald Kirk*
Macau's Gardens and Landscape Art	*Cabral, Jackson & Leung*
Quaille's Chinese Horoscope	
Quaille's Practical Chinese-English Dictionary	
Red Chips and the Globalisation of China's Enterprises	*Charles de Trenck*
The Rise & Decline of the Asian Century	*Christopher Lingle*
Tokyo: City on the Edge	*Todd Crowell & Stephanie Forman Morimura*
Walking to the Mountain	*Wendy Teasdill*

Fiction

Cheung Chau Dog Fanciers' Society	*Alan B Pierce*
Chinese Opera	*Alex Kuo*
Chinese Walls	*Xu Xi*
Daughters of Hui	*Xu Xi*
Getting to Lamma	*Jan Alexander*
The Ghost Locust	*Heather Stroud*
Hong Kong Rose	*Xu Xi*
Last Seen in Shanghai	*Howard Turk*
Riding a Tiger	*Robert Abel*
Temutma	*Rebecca Bradley & Stewart Sloan*

Poetry

An Amorphous Melody	*Kavita*
The Last Beach	*Mani Rao*
New Ends, Old Beginnings	*Louise Ho*
Round Poems and Photographs of Asia	*Madeleine Slavick & Barbara Baker*
Woman to Woman and other poems	*Agnes Lam*

Order from Asia 2000 Ltd
Fifth Floor Tung Yiu Commercial Building, 31A Wyndham St, Central, Hong Kong
tel (852) 2530-1409; fax (852) 2526-1107
email sales@asia2000.com.hk; http://www.asia2000.com.hk/